From Broadway
to the Bowery

From Broadway to the Bowery

*A History and Filmography of
the Dead End Kids, Little Tough Guys,
East Side Kids and Bowery Boys Films,
with Cast Biographies*

LEONARD GETZ

WITH A FOREWORD BY LEO GORCEY, JR.

McFarland & Company, Inc., Publishers
Jefferson, North Carolina, and London

LIBRARY OF CONGRESS CATALOGUING-IN-PUBLICATION DATA

Getz, Leonard, 1954–
From Broadway to the Bowery : a history and filmography of
the Dead End Kids, Little Tough guys, East Side Kids and Bowery Boys films,
with cast biographies / Leonard Getz ; with a foreword by Leo Gorcey, Jr.
p.   cm.
Includes bibliographical references and index.

ISBN-13: 978-0-7864-2535-8
ISBN-10: 0-7864-2535-0 (illustrated case binding : 50# alkaline paper) ∞

1. Bowery Boys films — History and criticism.
I. Title.
PN1995.9.B68G48   2006   791.43'75 — dc22   2006016736

British Library cataloguing data are available

Cover photograph ©2004 Brand X Pictures

Manufactured in the United States of America

McFarland & Company, Inc., Publishers
Box 611, Jefferson, North Carolina 28640
www.mcfarlandpub.com

With love to my wife, Susan,
who has been by my side
and helped me from the very beginning,
and whose support and encouragement guided me
through this book and through life.

Acknowledgments

Robert Pickell—For his generosity of spirit, and giving me access to his extraordinary collection of Dead End Kids, Little Tough Guy, East Side Kids and Bowery Boys illustrations and memorabilia, and for helping me find Billy Halop's niece and Bobby Jordan's first girlfriend, Edith Fellows.

Leo Gorcey, Jr.—For his support, his knowledge, his book about his dad, Leo Gorcey, and for graciously writing the foreword to this book.

Brandy Jo Ziesemer—For her support, for sharing with me her insights, information and family history, and for writing a tribute to her dad, Leo Gorcey.

Reverend Gary Hall—For sitting and talking with me about his dad, Huntz Hall, for giving me a glimpse of the man behind the character, and for sharing with me his eulogy of his dad.

Robert Jordan, Jr.—For his willingness to share with me his memories about his dad, Bobby Jordan, and family, and his family pictures.

Gabe Dell, Jr.—For our long conversations about his dad, Gabe Dell, allowing me to know him better, and for sharing with me his dad's dreams and his fears.

Brian Punsly—For chatting with me about his dad, Bernard Punsly, and allowing me to get to know his dad a little better.

Bonnie Bowen—For graciously offering her memories and heartfelt tribute to her uncle, Billy Halop.

Julia Thibodeau—For sharing her memories of being Leo Gorcey's girlfriend between wives #4 and #5.

Edith Fellows—For sharing her precious memories of her first boyfriend, Bobby Jordan, for whom there is always a place in her heart.

"Annie Oakley" Michelle Sautner—My new friend and fellow fan who was only too happy to share her memorabilia and personal pictures of Huntz Hall and Stanley Clements, and the stage setting of the *Dead End* revival in Los Angeles.

Lori Parkinson—For her wonderful enthusiasm for the Kids and sharing with me her pictures of Huntz Hall in drag.

Rabbi Matt Futterman—My lifelong friend who helped me research numerous files and microfilm at the Lincoln Center Library of the Performing Arts back in the seventies, and who continued forwarding me new information about the Kids over the next 25 years.

Charles Reintz—Who, over twenty-five years ago, before the age of video, allowed me to use the projector in his basement to view East Side Kids, Little Tough Guys and Bowery Boys films.

Richard Roat—For relating his tales of meeting up with many of the Dead End Kids, East Side Kids and Bowery Boys, and being there for the ailing East Side Kid David Durand.

Professor Morton Leavitt—My English professor at Temple University whose approach to critical analysis of 20th century European novels also works for the films of the Dead End Kids, Little Tough Guys, East Side Kids and the Bowery Boys.

Bernie Bubnis—For providing me with the recordings of Leo Gorcey's and Billy Halop's interview with Richard Lamparski many years ago.

Morris Bartash—An elderly blind man who audiotaped *Jungle Gents* while I was out of town.

Ariella, Philip and Sharona Getz—my dear children for their encouragement and proofreading, and for letting me know about an excerpt of *Kid Dynamite* in the "American Tongues" documentary.

Steven Kaplan (of *Alpha Video*)—who encouraged me to send my manuscript to McFarland.

Contents

Foreword

by Leo Gorcey, Jr.

I'm amazed at how the fans cherish the films of the Dead End Kids, the East Side Kids, and the Bowery Boys. Since my book *Me and the Dead End Kid* was published, numerous fans have e-mailed to tell me that the Bowery Boys actually helped them survive adolescence and that, even now, when life gets rough, they just shove a Bowery Boys movie in the VCR and they're feeling better in no time! "I grew up with those guys!" they say.

As I frequent the various Bowery Boys fan sites, I'm introduced to a universe of Bowery Boys fans who "speak" to each other in sentences peppered with lines of dialogue such as "It's purely a matter of scientific seduction!"

One of my cherished moments was when the Fort Lee Film Commission invited me to attend a screening of *Angels with Dirty Faces* in the spring of 2004. Over 300 people happily purchased tickets to Jersey City's Loew's Theatre and enjoyed Michael Curtiz's classic gangster film. But mostly, they came to savor the shenanigans of the Dead End Kids.

But what amazes me the most is that decades after the first Dead End Kids film hit the streets of New York, these films have never been off the air. You can still catch these black & white flicks on your big-screen plasma TV. Not too many movies are still making the rounds over half a century after they were made (and years before the advent of television)!

I must say that I'm very pleased to see this book being published. Many fans of these films will finally have the opportunity to "peruse duh lay of duh land," as one Terrence Aloyisius Mahoney might have put it.

Happy reading!

Preface

Over seventy years ago, on October 28, 1935, Sidney Kingsley's play *Dead End* opened at the Belasco Theatre in New York City, and its impact on the American culture was immediate, far-reaching and long-lasting. (Its revival at the Ahmanson Theatre in Los Angeles in the summer of 2005, complete with water-filled orchestra pit, attests to its influence.) The play touched a nerve, and the six kids touched audiences' hearts. It caught the attention of First Lady Eleanor Roosevelt and propelled the passing of the Wagner Housing Act, requiring low-income housing to be safe and clean. It caused caring patrons to contribute to boys clubs all over America. It introduced a new term in our lexicon, "dead end kid"—a rowdy, rebellious urchin, innocently born into squalor.

Like other popular plays, *Dead End* became a movie. Like *no* other play, it was also the catalyst for 92 movies spanning a period of 23 years. The themes and the actors shifted only slightly over the years. The kids were always poor yet always prevailed, both on the screen and at the box office.

But after *Dead End*, adults had little use for the films that followed. And after *Angels with Dirty Faces*, likewise the critics. The other 90 belonged to the Saturday matinee crowd. Young audiences kept coming back to watch their tough young heroes out-fight and out-smart their adult adversaries. Paradoxically, the films' popularity came at a price; the original message was lost. Instead of being a motivating force for good, the Dead End Kids encouraged impressionable American youth to be bad. Kids left theaters high-spirited wise guys, disrespecting parents, eager to knock off the first candy store they came across.

What was it about *Dead End* that triggered such a following? What was it about the 91 films that followed that kept attracting audiences long after the subject became repetitive and the plots predictable? Who were these actors who repeated their roles film after film, yet jumped into each with steadfast vigor?

These were not the questions that ran through the minds of my generation, introduced to the kids via East Side Comedy on channels 5 and 11 in New York in the 1960s and 1970s. We just glued ourselves to the box to watch our heroes, Muggs, Danny, Glimpy, Slip, Sach, and Tommy. We looked up to them because they were fearless, defiant, confident, straightforward and forthright. Our generation knew nothing about the original *Dead End* play, we knew nothing about how these series of films began. For us East Side Comedy aficionados, the only question was, which movie that we've seen a hundred times already will it be this week? Will it be a purely comical Bowery Boys flick, a semi-serious East Side Kids film or a tongue-in-cheek Little Tough Guys movie? We knew there was a difference. We just didn't know why.

To find out why, I spent months at the Performing Arts Library at Lincoln Center, rolling through reams of microfilm and rummaging through files buried in the stacks collection. I pulled every film book that made as much as a passing reference to the Dead End Kids; I scanned every biography of every actor that had any connection to any of the kids during his or her career; I read old magazine and newspaper articles about and reviews of the play and every film follow-up; read as many interviews with the kids, both collectively and individually, I could find; visited nostalgia stores in New York. I special-ordered research through the *Encyclopædia Britannica*.

Soon the pieces came together, a chronology was formed, the evolution came into focus. What was missing was a critical analysis.

Defying those who would scoff at the idea that these films warrant more than a cursory comment, I screened every one again for nuance.

I discerned and tracked the various themes that are taken up. Little Tough Guys films are particularly strong on the war and hone in on the subject of spies in America, especially in the three serials. Noteworthy yet often overlooked is Universal's *Newsboys Home*, which focuses on how newspapers contributed to the welfare of homeless boys, and the fierce competition among rival newspapers. In the East Side Kids we find the motifs of friendship, loyalty, patriotism. In the Bowery Boys the comedy lies in the subjects of mistaken identity, hidden powers, mad scientists, search for treasure, satirizing folktales and the armed forces.

One of the trademarks of these films is the peppering of malapropisms, especially the ones delivered by the Bowery Boys' Slip Mahoney. Highlighted are the ones most irreverent.

I took note of plot complexities, plausibility and similarities among the films and compared them with other films. Was any Bowery Boys flick so ridiculous as to render it utterly preposterous? Well, yes, but no, not really.

I also compared characters, their inter-relationships and changes in personality. Did the filmmakers strive for continuity? In the Little Tough Guys, Tommy (Billy Halop) sometimes lives with his mother and sister; sometimes just a sister; sometimes he has a brother. In the East Side Kids, Muggs (Leo Gorcey) sometimes has a mother and/or a sister. Conclusion? Continuity may have mattered at first, but wasn't a concern later. If the situation called for a mother or sister, she was in; if not, she was out, no explanation, none needed.

And then there are the actors themselves. How did early fame, fortune and success prepare them for life after the Dead End Kids? For Leo Gorcey, the Dead End Kids was all there ever was and that was just fine; for Gabe Dell, and eventually Huntz Hall, it wasn't enough, and both found their way back on stage and screen; for Bernard Punsly, it hardly made a blip on the radar screen in his life as a physician; for Billy Halop and Bobby Jordan, whom the press thought had the most promise, it was a painful trick.

Since we can no longer talk to any of the original actors, the next best thing is a personal perspective of them as individuals and as fathers (in the case of Halop, an uncle). Included are interviews with, and written tributes from, their next of kin.

And what of their legacy? Would we ever have had *Happy Days or Welcome Back, Kotter* if not for the Dead End Kids? Would we have had *Cheers* if not for Gabe Dell's *Corner Bar*?

Dead End was not just a play that ran for 684 performances; it was not just a series of movies made from 1937 through 1958; it was not just a TV show on every week in some corner of the world since the early 1960s. If you look closely, the Dead End Kids peek through every corner of our pop culture. (See the cover of the Beatles' *Sgt. Pepper's Lonely Hearts Club Band* album, read Terry Southern's risqué novel *Candy*.) As Gabe Dell, Jr., tells it, "Looking for pop is no dead end."

— Leonard Getz
Summer 2006

The Dead End Kids

On a warm spring afternoon in 1934, young Sidney Kingsley, who had just won the Pulitzer Prize for his play *Men in White*, took a stroll down the quay of New York's East River on 53rd Street and saw several slum children splashing in and out of the water. He stopped to watch their rough play, to listen to their raw street language, noticed their tattered clothes. Then he gazed up at a huge luxury apartment building towering over them.

Nine months later, he had not only completed a graphic, contemporary social drama, but created a group of urchins destined to dominate stage and screen for the next twenty-three years. The drama was *Dead End*.

For two and a half weeks, Kingsley searched amateur theater companies, radio stations, schools and settlement houses before deciding on 14 children whom he believed could handle the genuine East Side dialogue. Among those chosen were Billy Halop (Tommy) Gabriel Dell (T.B.), Huntz Hall (Dippy), Bobby Jordan (Angel), Bernard Punsly (Milty),

From the original play **Dead End** on Broadway. Left to right: Bernard Punsly, Elspeth Eric, Leo Gorcey, Gabe Dell, Bobby Jordan, Billy Halop and Huntz Hall.

The set from the original play *Dead End* (1935). See Gabe Dell, upper right.

Charles Duncan* (Spit), Sidney Lumet (small boy) and Leo and David Gorcey (Second Avenue boys).

Kingsley worked closely with his cast of adolescents. After three and a half weeks of rehearsal, the result was a stunning performance of young unknowns who won the hearts of the public. It was largely due to their appeal that *Dead End* ran for 684 performances (two years) on Broadway before it toured in Boston, Chicago, San Francisco and Los Angeles.

The kids became known as the Dead End Kids. It became a household term, meaning deprived youths growing up in city squalor, one step away from a life of crime. Since the thirties the term has been used descriptively in such periodicals as *The New York Times Book Review Section* and *Commentary Magazine* and the television show *M*A*S*H*. The late actor Walter Matthau discussed the origin of the term on *The Dick Cavett Show*. Many years later, a rock band called itself the Dead End Kids.

When the curtain rose for the first time on October 28, 1935, at the Belasco Theatre in New York, Norman Bel Geddes' setting received a five-minute ovation. The scene clearly conveyed the theme and dramatic tension between the two distinct social classes living side by side. In the background was a wall representing a tall, red, decaying tenement swarming with people of poverty. Stretched from one side of the building to the other were clotheslines

According to Brandy Gorcey, her uncle David Gorcey said that Duncan left for a role in Red Light *before* Dead End *opened and never played the role of Spit. Leo Gorcey opened as Spit.*

draped with wrinkled clothing that appeared to be suspended in the thick air. A mattress riddled with holes looked as if it was about to drop from the clothesline onto the narrow, dirty sidewalk alive with empty milk bottles, newspapers, coal and a steam shovel. The street was paved with slate, and the sidewalk with asphalt, so that the sound of hard heels or a cane could be heard in the back row. Wire lath padded with cinderblocks gave the idea of rotted timber underfoot. The steam shovel and scaffold blocked out most of the back street and all of the sky. The evening scene was created by the rays of a gas light at the end of the street that gave the effect of a real street lamp.

Flush against the collapsing tenement was a high rise apartment, inhabited by the well-to-do who thought it fashionable to live near the East River. The overwhelming power of the posh lifestyle,

The playbill for the Broadway play *Dead End*.

contrasted with the small boys in rags, augmented the hopelessness conveyed in the play's title.

Bel Geddes was not satisfied with artificial sounds that merely suggested the arrival of a ship or the police. Taking great pains to produce as realistic a play as possible, he spent days and nights on the docks of the East River recording the natural sounds of the surroundings. When the audience heard the tooting of a steamboat, it did not come from a prop man behind the stage blowing a flute, but from an RCA amplification of a real steamship docking at the New York pier. Also heard were the sounds of real waves slapping the wooden wharf and the actual sputtering of a speedboat. Bel Geddes inquired if the owner of a yacht anchored off East 52nd Street would mind having a party on his boat if Bel Geddes arranged the invitations. The owner agreed, and the party sounds were recorded and used in the boat party scene. Also recorded were police car sirens and radios. These sounds were used to call the patrons back from intermission.

Although ghettoes existed in the thirties, their impact on society was diminished by the Depression. Crowded tenements of the East Side were not the major concerns of the community. *Dead End* brought to public attention the plight of the poor who had little hope of changing their environment without the support of the community. It put on the stage what

From *Dead End*. Most likely a publicity shot since Charles Duncan (standing, holding a stick) never played the part of Spit, according to David Gorcey. Left to right: Two of the three "small boys" either Billy Winston, Joseph Taibi or Sidney Lumet, Huntz Hall, Duncan, Gabe Dell, Bernard Punsly and Bobby Jordan.

most people only read about in newspapers. Kingsley intended for the people of New York to realize that this was *their* society, that these evils were happening in *their* backyard, and that they should be more involved with the drama.

In the play, a gang of street-wise kids beat up and rob a wealthy boy. When the boy's father tries to stop them, Tommy, the leader of the gang, stabs him.

Gimpty is a lame young man who, after receiving his degree in architecture, continues to live in the tenements. He is in love with his neighbor, Kay. But Kay is now a mistress to a rich man and living in the fashionable apartment that adjoins the tenement.

Meanwhile, fugitive Baby Face Martin has returned to his old tenement neighborhood to visit his mother and old girlfriend. Snubbed by his mother and shocked to find his girl-friend Francie a common streetwalker, Baby Face makes plans to kidnap the wealthy boy.

But Gimpty recognizes Baby Face and informs the FBI. Before Baby Face can escape, the agents shoot him. Gimpty is given reward money but Kay, in spite of her love for the young architect, decides to remain with the rich man. The play concludes with Gimpty offering the reward money to Drina, Tommy's sister, to help prevent her brother from going to reform school and coming out a rough-and-ready criminal like Baby Face Martin.

Reviewed in numerous periodicals when it first opened, *Dead End* was given credit for everything it contributed to the theater. Brooks Atkinson of *The New York Times* wrote: "It takes an observer as thoughtful as Sidney Kingsley to see the whole drama of our social order concentrated in a foul and ugly tenement street that lies at the rear of an aristocratic apartment house.... As thought it is a contribution to public knowledge. As drama it is vivid and bold." *The Nation* said of *Dead End*: "The play owes much more of its effectiveness to the extraordinary convincing realism of the troupe of boys and to the solid and accurate set by Norman Bel Geddes." Edith Isaacs in *Theatre Arts* magazine compared the play to *Street Scene* and *Winterset* in "that its theme is social injustices, form is melodrama and set in NYC ... it is magnificently set and acted, it has boldness and freedom of attack, it is full of excitement and strong currents of resentment and pity." *The Theatre Club Inc.* awarded *Dead End* its annual gold medal for "the most worthy play by an American playwright this season." But the most precious reward for Sidney Kingsley must have been the news that thousands of philanthropists contributed to Boys' Clubs all over America, and active slum clearance projects got underway.

The man responsible for the film version of *Dead End* was Samuel Goldwyn, who, by that time, had 61 movie productions to his credit. On his way to Europe on a family vacation, Goldwyn took his favorite director William Wyler to see *Dead End* at the Belasco Theatre. Turning to Wyler, Goldwyn asked him what he thought of it. Wyler said, "Great." The next day Goldwyn had his lieutenant, Sam Mulney, put a down payment of $25,000 to purchase the film rights to *Dead End*. Upon his return from Europe, Goldwyn became very ill. Immediate payment of the balance was demanded or the rights would be sold to another producer. Sam's wife, Frances Goldwyn, with her husband in bed, made the decision to complete the deal for *Dead End*. The balance of $140,000 was paid. At that time, $165,000 was the highest price ever paid for a hit play. An additional $50,000 would be needed to build the set.

After searching throughout Los Angeles for the right actors and coming up empty-handed, Goldwyn transported to Hollywood Halop, Gorcey, Hall, Dell, Jordan and Punsly and put them under a contract that gave him an option to use the boys for future films. Humphrey Bogart was borrowed from Warner Brothers. Added to the cast were Joel McCrea, Sylvia Sidney, Wendy Barrie, Allen Jenkins, Claire Trevor and Ward Bond. Besides the Dead End Kids, the only other player from the original play was Marjorie Main, who gave a sensational performance as Mrs. Martin, the murderer's mother.

Goldwyn opposed Wyler's idea of doing the film on location, fearing he would lose complete control of its production. Instead, he had Richard Day create the dead end street complex based on Bel Geddes' design. A stickler for beauty and cleanliness, Goldwyn walked on the set one day and shouted, "Why is everything so dirty here?" showing that in spite of his movie successes, he had little understanding of what was necessary to the convey the realism of the script.

The film, released by United Artists on August 27, 1937, was not identical to Kingsley's play. Goldwyn had Lillian Hellman adapt the original script to fit a Hollywood interpretation. Although the storyline remained intact, the characters' personalities were tweaked.

In the play, the anti-hero is Gimpty, a cripple who cringes at the sight of gangster Baby Face Martin. In the movie, he is Dave, a much stronger character, in good health, and unintimidated by Martin. In the play, Gimpty calls the FBI to do the shooting; in the movie, it is Dave who chases Martin to the roof and shoots him dead. Gimpty is also the weaker character in his relationship with Kay, the rich girl who lives in the high-rise apartment with the rich man. Kay must convince him that for her to leave the rich man and be with him would get them nowhere. But in the movie it is Dave who tells Kay to leave and go on the boat trip with her rich companion.

The Dead End Kids arrive in Hollywood (1937). Top, left to right: Leo Gorcey, Gabe Dell and Huntz Hall; bottom, left to right: Bernard Punsly and Bobby Jordan.

In the play, the camaraderie between Baby Face and his partner Hunk is evident. Martin appreciates Hunk's sympathy after his mother slaps him in the face. In the movie, Martin knocks Hunk's drink onto the floor and tells him to go buy another one someplace else.

Regardless of whether or not these changes affected the story, the message was clear. All across the country, audiences, reviewers and critics raved about the film. *The New York Times* said it "deserves a place among the important motion pictures of 1937 for its stout and well

Director William Wyler and camera crew rehearsing a scene in the film *Dead End*.

presented reiteration of the social protest that was the theme of the original Sidney Kingsley stage play." Robbin Coons, Hollywood correspondent for the Associated Press Feature Service, named it Movie of the Month of September 1937 and declared Claire Trevor (Francie) Character of the Month. *The New York Post* wrote, "The best thing that could have been done at the last session of Congress would have been to show the film *Dead End* to the committee which crippled the Wagner Housing Act." Although it was Oscar-nominated for Best Picture, Best Supporting Actress, Best Director and Best Art Director, *Dead End* did not win any Academy Awards. (Because of the kids' antics, according to Gabe Dell, Jr., Goldwyn refused to allow them to attend the Academy Awards.)

As good as the movie was, it (like the play) owed most of its triumph to the Kids, whose ages ranged from 13 to 20. Paul Harrison, a Hollywood movie reviewer, affirmed, "Most realistic touch to the whole thing is given by the kids.... They're always in character, swaggering and scrapping and talking their east side dialect." *Literary Digest* said, "[T]he six New York tenement kids imported for the occasion ... are far and away the most authentic, unabashed notes in the cast.... First acting honors, of course, go to the six kids." *The N.Y. Times* made no bones about where they stood: "The show undoubtedly belongs to the six incomparable urchins imported from the stage production whenever they are in view...."

Scene from *Dead End* with Humphrey Bogart and Allen Jenkins. Jenkins would appear in a few
Bowery Boys pictures.

At the height of all this publicity, including the kids' personal and radio stints, Goldwyn
lifted their options and handed all six to Mervyn Leroy. Leroy had planned to star them in
a film called *Who Asked to Be Born?*, written by Leonardo Bercovici. But Leroy never made
the picture nor any picture with the Dead End Kids. Warner Brothers was quick to jump on
the band wagon and signed them to contracts.

The first film the kids appeared in after *Dead End* was *Crime School* (1938). Crane Wilbur
wrote the screenplay especially for the Dead End Kids. In it, the six kids are guilty of thiev-
ery, and possibly murder. They are sent to reform school where superintendent Mark Braden
(Bogart) does his best to reverse the reputation reform schools have for turning out hardened criminals.

Although *Crime School* did not match *Dead End* in any respect, it did fine-tune the indi-
viduality of the kids that was only partially developed in *Dead End*. Gorcey's character was
especially vicious, merciless and selfish — one who reacts quickly to those who cross him, and
even quicker to save his own skin, even at the expense of his pals.

Jordan's character was a cute but vulnerable little guy who looked to Halop for protection (or, if Halop is not around, to those in authority most sympathetic to his predicament).
Hall's character continued to show contempt for authority through his cynicism and goofy
actions. Punsly's character got away with as much tomfoolery as the kids allowed him before
a sharp eye from Gorcey or a figure of authority put him in his place. Dell's character was a

Dave (Joel McCrea) shooting Baby Face Martin (Bogart).

happy medium; not too rough but never getting directly involved in any real confrontations. Halop's character was still the leader, the smart one, making the decisions and making sure there was no dissension, not even from the tough Gorcey. He was also the most sensitive and the most deeply involved in all the kids' activities.

Warner Brothers, however, was dissatisfied with *Crime School* and withheld its release. When the kids' contracts were dropped temporarily, Universal grabbed the chance to do a film with the kids, *Little Tough Guy*. This film was the first to give the kids top billing. Gorcey and Jordan, however, were not in it. They remained at Warners, playing minor roles in major films.

In addition to Halop, Hall, Dell and Punsly, Universal signed Hally Chester and David Gorcey. Chester had a bit part as one of the reform schoolmates in *Crime School*, and David Gorcey hadn't appeared in anything since taking over the role of Spit on Broadway when his older brother went to Hollywood.

Despite what the executives at Warner Brothers felt about *Crime School*, and what the critics said about Universal's *Little Tough Guy*, audiences raved about the films. Warner Brothers not only re-gathered the original six and Humphrey Bogart, but added James Cagney, Pat O'Brien and Ann Sheridan for one of the best examples of crime drama ever made. *Angels with Dirty Faces* is remembered for being the story about two childhood friends, one who becomes a criminal, the other a priest. It is also known for making good use of its camera by

Los Angeles, California.
August 6   , 1937.

Mr. Mervyn LeRoy,
c/o Warner Bros. Pictures, Inc.,
Burbank, California.

Dear Mr. LeRoy:

We hereby assign and transfer to you all of our
right, title and interest in and to that certain contract of
employment of January 5, 1937 between HUNTZ HALL and ourselves
(said contract of employment having been entered into originally
by said HUNTZ HALL and SAMUEL GOLDWYN, INC., and all of the
right, title and interest of SAMUEL GOLDWYN, INC. in said contract having heretofore been assigned to us) as amended under
date of August 6, 1937. A copy of said contract of employment,
and a copy of the amendment thereof, are attached hereto and
marked Exhibits "A" and "B" respectively. We make this assignment pursuant to the provisions of that certain contract between you and us dated July 29, 1937, and accordingly the
provisions of said contract of July 29, 1937, as to the effective
date of this assignment and transfer, and otherwise, is applicable
hereto.

Very truly yours,

SAMUEL GOLDWYN INC., LTD.,

By _____
                    Secretary

Samuel Goldwyn Inc., Ltd.,
7210 Santa Monica Blvd.,
Los Angeles, California.

Gentlemen:

In consideration of your assignment to me, by an
instrument executed concurrently herewith, of that certain contract of employment between you and HUNTZ HALL, dated January 5,
1937, as amended, I hereby accept said assignment and the terms
on which the same was made. I agree to carry out and be bound
by all of the terms and conditions of said contract of employment with the same effect as though said HUNTZ HALL had originally
entered into said contract with me, rather than with SAMUEL GOLD-
WYN, INC. Referring to that certain agreement between us dated
July 29, 1937, I hereby ratify and confirm the same, and agree
to perform and be bound by all of the terms, agreements and
indemnities assumed and undertaken by me thereunder.

Very truly yours,

(Mervyn LeRoy)

Copy of contract between Samuel Goldwyn and Mervyn LeRoy regarding Huntz Hall. LeRoy never
made a picture with Hall or any other Dead End Kid.

seizing various images of a city that breeds corruption; the basement hideout, the sleazy bar, stashing cash in bedposts, a machine-gun battle between criminal and police.

One view is that *Angels with Dirty Faces* owes its debt to Cagney's performance, Michael Curtiz's direction and the John Wexley–Warren Duff screenplay. Warners was wary of that and, although they were eager to capitalize on the success of *Angels with Dirty Faces*, were not ready to see how the Dead End Kids would fare without the support of a well-known actor. So Jack Warner combined the talents of John Garfield, Claude Rains, Ann Sheridan and director Busby Berkeley for the film, *They Made Me a Criminal*, based on the Bertram Millhauser–Beulah M. Dix story, "The Life of Jimmy Dolan." (Berkeley, who is famous for his choreography, needed to prove to his producers and himself that directing dance was not the only thing he could do. It was the last film he directed for Warner Brothers.)

They Made Me a Criminal comes closest to being a sequel to *Dead End*. Here the boys re-assume the character names Kingsley gave them; in the movie, T.B. tells Bradfield (Garfield), a former boxing champ and fugitive, that a priest arranged their stay at Grandma's date farm in Arizona so that Tommy wouldn't have to go to reform school for stabbing a judge. The film is "quieter" than the other Warners films in that its focus is on relationships between the kids and Bradfield, and Bradfield and Tommy's sister Peg, rather than pitting the kids against society or persons intent on making them good or keeping them bad. In this respect, there is a little bit of Rocky Sullivan and Father Connolly (Cagney and O'Brien in *Angels with Dirty Faces*) in Johnny Bradfield.

Hell's Kitchen was the next feature the Dead End Kids made at Warner Brothers. For the first time Warner Brothers apparently felt confident enough to let the kids ride on their own popularity without a lead star. Written by Crane Wilbur, *Hell's Kitchen* is about a racketeer, Buck Caesar, who gets a suspended sentence, thanks to the sound legal advice of his nephew Jim. Here Warner Brothers follows Universal's *Little Tough Guy* by letting one of the kids, Bobby Jordan (Joey), get killed. His death discharges an untapped passion for cruel revenge. The kids overpower the school guards and prepare to bury alive the despicable school superintendent.

Logic would tell us that in their next film they would be hardened criminals. On the contrary, *Angels Wash Their Faces* puts them in a public school where they are actually expected to relate with their peers. Based on Jonathan Finn's story, "Battle of City Hall," the film finds the Dead End Kids taking advantage of the city's contest to grant the best qualified student the opportunity to sit in the mayoral seat for one week.

Here another Dead End Kid dies, in this case Bernard Punsly (Sleepy), in a fire set by some well-paid arsonist on orders from a crooked politician. But unlike their vicious reaction to the death of Joey in the previous film, the Dead End Kids strive to win the city contest in order to stop the corruption legally, and to free from jail a pal who's accused of starting the fire.

Beyond maintaining Halop as the gang's leader, and Gorcey fighting upstream to become one, the producers apparently gave little or no thought to the continuity of succeeding films. Being dubbed the sequel to *Angels with Dirty Faces* can be misleading as *Angels Wash Their Faces* does a complete turnabout with the kids. They fight a corrupt society not with hooliganism, but with law-abiding methods. This change of attitude on the part of the kids prepared them for the following Warner Brothers feature, *On Dress Parade*, in which the boys patriotically enroll in a military school.

Already nostalgic, one reviewer regretted the loss of the Dead End Kids, particularly Leo Gorcey, from the ranks of the incorrigibles. As a result, this film was Warners' least successful Dead End Kids film.

Regardless of the monetary rewards reaped from all six films, the two years it took for

James Cagney (left) and Leo Gorcey (right). This shot must have been taken before their altercation.

Warner Brothers to make them was enough to destroy the original purpose of the kids' creation. Instead of being a constructive force in society, as Kingsley intended them to be, the
Dead End Kids became a counter-productive influence on impressionable American youth.
Shortly after *Angels with Dirty Faces* was released, cries of outrage came from angry parents,
school organizations and church groups whose children looked up to the Dead End Kids as
role models.

Role model number one is Billy Halop. Halop understands that dukes alone don't make
a leader. In *Crime School* and *Hell's Kitchen* he's straightforward with his adult adversaries
and assumes the brunt of responsibilities for the kids' actions. He takes punishment on their
behalf. In *Angels with Dirty Faces* he is the only kid ever seen outside the company of the other
kids, and that is only when an adult, Cagney, gives *him* money to hide. In *They Made Me a
Criminal* he acts on his own initiative by hopping on the train intended to take John Garfield
back to New York.

Role model number two, at this stage at least, is Leo Gorcey. Gorcey remains the frustrated leader who seems never to forget that Halop threatened to cut his throat in *Dead End*.
In *Hell's Kitchen*, after Halop is overwhelmingly chosen student mayor of the reformatory,
Gorcey warns that if Halop ever tries to discipline him, he (Halop) will find his teeth down
his throat. He is the first kid to handle a gun in *Crime School* and *Hell's Kitchen*, but on both
occasions the gun ends up in the more responsible hands of Billy Halop. *On Dress Parade* is

the only Warners film in which Gorcey, rather than Halop, is the central character. Though Gorcey may not be a better actor than Halop, he is always more fascinating to watch.

Personal hardships are borne most on Bobby Jordan, the smallest and thus the most vulnerable. In *Crime School* it is he who is caught in a boiler room that's about to explode; In *They Made Me a Criminal* it is he who has difficulty keeping his head above water while swimming. His solidarity with Halop, as first established in *Dead End* when he helps Tommy positively identify Spit as the one who betrayed him, is reaffirmed in *Hell's Kitchen* when he opens the door to the freezer where Halop is expected to remain all night. Unfortunately, Halop cannot return the favor when Jordan is put into the freezer and freezes to death. It is one of the few times where Halop does not come through for his friends.

Neither Huntz Hall nor

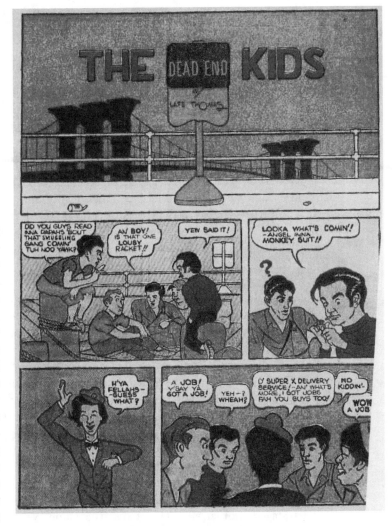

Page from a "Dead End Kids" comic of the 1930s by Lafe Thomas.

Gabriel Dell have formidable parts in the Warner Brothers films. The only times Hall has any outstanding comment are brief instances in *Crime School* and *Angels Wash Their Faces*. In *Crime School* he is the one who comes up with the idea of stuffing food in the mouths of the shackled arsonists since the law says that criminals must be fed.

Dell's only action of any consequence is in *They Made Me a Criminal* where his yen for taking pictures puts stubborn detective Claude Rains on the right track to find fugitive John Garfield.

Bernard Punsly is never fully accepted into the gang and nowhere is this more apparent than in *Angels Wash Their Faces*. As Sleepy, Punsly is killed in a fire that burns a building to the ground. Extending their condolences to Sleepy's family, Tommy tells Sleepy's mother (played by Marjorie Main) that although Sleepy was never made a member of the gang, they would like to bestow this honor upon him posthumously. The fact that Tommy makes this request is another testament to his leadership.

Abroad, the films were received with mixed reviews. In England, audiences abhorred the kids' street language. In Germany, Nazi leader Joseph Goebbels edited the films to fit his propaganda campaign against America. Instead of allowing them to be shown "as is," Goebbels edited them into evidence of American social depravity.

The films alone were not the sole reason for this kind of response. Publicists lost sight of the fact that the kids were not real kids pulled off the docks and pushed on stage, but ordinary in the sense that their curiosity and wild behavior could be found in any normal household. That they happened to be actors did not alter the fact that they were children who enjoyed towel fights, pitching pennies, and hiding costumes from the adults back stage at the Belasco. And when the kids were brought to Hollywood, their behind-the-scenes antics were a continual source of news for gossip columnists. It was publicized that, during class at the studio school, Bobby Jordan nailed the inside covers of a teacher's textbook to the desk; Huntz Hall glued the completed IQ test papers together; Gabe Dell put steel shavings in the blackboard eraser; and all engaged in hearty games of spitball.

It is also true that, given their freedom and power, some of their antics were excessive. When director William Wyler, whom the boys did not like at first, invited them to ride his motorcycle, he had no idea that their racing it all over the set almost caused Sam Goldwyn a heart attack.

With their taste for the road whetted, the kids collectively acquired a used 1930 Ford roadster offered for $125 with a $20 down payment for a three day trial period. Since Huntz Hall was unlicensed, the other kids refused to let him drive. When the others were out shopping, however, Huntz took the car for a spin and returned, *sans* car. He had driven it into a tree. It cost them $35 to have it restored to a condition conducive to continuing their trip to Tijuana, Mexico, Lake Arrowhead and a tour of Los Angeles. On the third day of the trial period, they returned the car to the dealer, telling the dealer that its service did not satisfy them.

In another incident involving a moving vehicle, Huntz Hall sneaked into a huge truck that was idling on the Goldwyn lot. Gorcey and a couple of the other kids jumped on board too, and soon the truck began to roll towards a sound stage and into other adjoining sets. Unable to control the vehicle, the kids bailed out and let the truck crash into the sets, destroying thousands of dollars worth of material. Threatening a sit-down strike, as they did on several occasions when their studios sought to punish them for their destructive behavior, the kids forced Goldwyn to promise that no money would be docked from their pay.

They staged another sit-down strike after using William Wyler's private telephone to call their parents in New York. Each talked for about an hour. When Goldwyn promised not to dock anyone's pay, the boys stood up to work again.

At Warner Brothers, Humphrey Bogart contributed ideas for the kids' pranks. It was his brainchild to set fire to somebody's newspaper while it was being read, and nail an actor's slippers to his dressing room floor so that he would fall on his face as he stepped into them.

But his chumminess with the Dead End Kids did not render Bogart immune from the kids' practical jokes. Exhausted from doing a scene, Bogart was ready for a nap. When he was comfortable, the boys tossed a package of firecrackers through his window. Bogart never schemed with them again.

Gorcey and James Cagney, in their respective autobiography and biography, recalled an incident when they were shooting a basement scene in *Angels with Dirty Faces*. Their views on it are quite dissimilar. Gorcey claims that Cagney straight-armed him because he had the nerve to try to steal a scene from Cagney. Cagney maintains that Gorcey and the kids were up to their old tricks, ad libbing lines that ruined the rhythm of the moment.

The kids' mischievousness was a significant factor in their inevitable release from their contracts with Warner Brothers. The studio would have liked to keep Halop, but refused to honor their contract with him and raise his salary from $1000 to $1200 a week; Halop left

Bogart horsing around with the kids. From bottom up, left to right: Huntz Hall, Gabe Dell, Bernard Punsly, Leo Gorcey, Billy Halop, Humphrey Bogart, Bobby Jordan (on top).

the studio and signed with Universal. Huntz Hall, Gabe Dell and Bernard Punsly joined him and they took up where they left off in *Little Tough Guys*. Jordan joined them later. Gorcey and Halop were never on good terms, Gorcey vying for star billing on and off the screen. Gorcey remained with Warner Brothers a short time and also did some freelance pictures with MGM. Bobby Jordan appeared in several Warner Brothers flicks and several Little Tough Guys films, then teamed up with Gorcey at Monogram Pictures.

This was the end of the Dead End Kids days, and the beginning of the splinter groups soon to be known as the Little Tough Guys, the East Side Kids and the Bowery Boys.

Dead End

October 28, 1935, at the Belasco Theatre (three acts)

CAST

Role	Actor	Role	Actor
Gimpty	Theodore Newton	*Lady with Dog*	Margaret Linden
T.B.	Gabriel Dell	*Three Small Boys*	Billy Winston,
Tommy	Billy Halop		Joseph Taibi,
Dippy	Huntz Hall		Sidney Lumet
Angel	Bobby Jordan	*Second Chauffeur*	Richard Clark
Spit	Charles Duncan	*Second Avenue Boys*	David Gorcey,
Doorman	George Cotton		Leo Gorcey
Old Lady	Marie R. Burke	*Mrs. Martin*	Marjorie Main
Old Gentleman	George N. Price	*Patrolman Mulligan*	Robert Mulligan
First Chauffeur	Charles Benjamin	*Francie*	Sheila Trent
"Baby Face" Martin	Joseph Downing	*G-Men*	Francis de Sales,
Hunk	Martin Gabel		Edward P. Good-
Phillip Griswald	Charles Bellin		now, Dan Duryea
Governess	Sidonie Espero	*Policemen*	Frances G. Cleve-
Milty	Bernard Punsly		land, William
Drina	Elspeth Eric		Toubin
Mr. Griswald	Carroll Ashburn	*Plainclothesman*	Harry Selbyr
Mr. Jones	Louis Lord	*Interne*	Philip Bourneuf
Kay	Margret Mullen	*Medical Examiner*	Lewis Z. Russel
Jack Hilton	Cyril Gordon Weld	*Sailor*	Bernard Zaneville

Inhabitants of East River Terrace, Ambulance Men, etc.: Elizabeth Wragge, Drina Hill, Blossom MacDonald, Ethel Dell, Marc Daniels, Elizabeth Perlowin, Edith Jordan, Marie Dell, Bea Punsly, Bess Winston, Anne Miller, Elizabeth Zabelin, George Bond, Mathew Purcell, Herman Osmond, Rose Taibi, George Buzante, Betty Rheingold, Lizzie Leonard, Catherine Kemp, Mag Davis, Neilie Ransom, Betsy Ross, Charles Harue, Paul Meacham, Tom McIntyre, George Anspecke, Jack Keliert, Elizabeth Zowe, Gene Lowe, Charlotte Salkow, Morris Chertov, Charlotte Julien, Willis Duncan.

Scenery Supervisor, Robert Barnhart; Clothes Supervisor, Frances Waite; Scenery built by MacDonald Construction Co.; Painted by Triangle Scenic Studios; Lighting, Centuries Lighting Co.; Gowns, Helen Johnson.

Dead End

Released August 27, 1937; United Artists; Screenplay: Lillian Hellman; Based on Sidney Kingsley's play; Producer, Samuel Goldwyn; Associate Producer, Merritt Hulburd; Director, William Wyler; Released by United Artists; opened at the Rivoli.

CAST

Drina	Sylvia Sidney		*T.B.*	Gabriel Dell
Dave	Joel McCrea		*Milty*	Bernard Punsly
"Baby Face" Martin	Humphrey Bogart		*Philip*	Charles Peck
Kay	Wendy Barrie		*Mr. Griswald*	Minor Watson
Francie	Claire Trevor		*Mulligan*	James Burke
Hunk	Allen Jenkins		*Doorman*	Ward Bond
Mrs. Martin	Marjorie Main		*Mrs. Connell*	Elisabeth Risdon
Tommy	Billy Halop		*Mrs. Fenner*	Esther Dale
Dippy	Huntz Hall		*Mr. Pascagli*	George Humbert
Angel	Bobby Jordan		*Governess*	Marcelle Corday
Spit	Leo Gorcey			

Counted among the most outstanding films of social consciousness, *Dead End* introduces the kids in a realistic view of slum life in the thirties, and in doing so, depicts the disease of poverty, the sins of ignorance, the failures of correctional institutions, and the virtues of sound family relationships. Not only is possible to tell the story of *Dead End* looking through the telescope of irony, but it is also possible to discern how the characters' social and economic situations bear upon their lives.

Before we meet any one individual, director William Wyler scans an early morning scene conveying discontent among the slum tenants and a sophistic impression that today, like any other day on the dead end street, symptoms of disquietude will be tempered: the cop on the beat tapping his huge club on a city bench to awaken a sleeping lazzarone, a poor old man noisily dragging his garbage can to the street for collection, and a clothesline, heavy with children's clothing, being pulled through the fire escape window. The images are very real and very potent.

The kids, who begin their day taunting the doorman of the luxury high-rise by mimicking a rich old man, eye a new kid on the block, Milty, with suspicion. In the original play, Spit yells, "Aw, it's a Jew-kid." This line is not in the movie. Upon leader Tommy's arrival, Milty is commanded to stand before the kids. To be admitted to the gang, he must come up with a quarter. Where would poor kids get a quarter? Spit knows: "Ya know where ya ma keeps 'er dough, don't ya?"

This might seem to be an alarmingly dishonest move, stealing from one's own parents, but it is consistent with the disrespect for personal property prevalent in these slums. In an earlier, extremely telling scene, Milty is sitting on the curb needlessly rocking his wide-eyed sister in her carriage. A distraught, elderly woman approaches the child, who is nibbling on a cookie. The woman appears to be playing with the little girl, tickling her, but soon her intention is clear. With the cunning of a pickpocket, the woman spirits away the cookie and pops it into her own mouth. Immediately following this scene is a shot of rich kid Philip Griswald pouring his unwanted milk into a nearby flower pot.

This poignant, purely visual contrast between a desperately hungry woman and a child

The janitress (Esther Dale) helps Milty (Bernard Punsly) with his two young charges (Jerry Cooper and Phillip Rabin). She cuddles the baby before copping the cookie.

of doting parents not only conveys sharply the differences between the two social classes, but also the similarities among people when it comes to trickery. We the audience cannot condone the actions of the woman, but we are more appalled by the spilling of the milk than the stealing of the cookie.

Just as the woman seizes the cookie because she has a need, so too does Milty have a need — a need to belong to the tough gang of the neighborhood, if for no other reason than his own survival. He expresses his delight in being accepted by giving Tommy a penknife for which he overpays Angel.

The acquisition of the knife marks the commencement of Tommy's life of crime (and relinquishing it to Dave at the end of the film symbolizes his intention to be good). Goodness, however, is something that will inevitably evade Tommy and every other kid who grows up in the slums, like his adult counterpart, "Baby Face" Martin, who appears just in time to teach him the correct way to hold a knife in attack mode.

To further emphasize the idea that Martin is Tommy grown-up, aspiring architect Dave compares the two. Although he does not point him out, he tells Drina that "Baby Face" Martin grew up here and, like Tommy, had a lot of "good" which would have come out if someone had given him a break. And if Drina cannot take care of Tommy, he too will begin with knives and end up with guns.

Martin does have some sense of decency hidden under his mask of ruthlessness. He and Dave talk like old friends who have not seen each other in years. Martin is genuinely interested in how Dave has fared. He is impressed that Dave is now an architect but laughs when Dave tells him the only work he can get is painting the window sill of his neighbor's restaurant. That only reaffirms for Martin that choosing a life of crime was the sharp thing to do.

But Martin has not found happiness. He's sick of the gangster life, of suspecting everybody. He wants to settle down. He wants a home. So after some cosmetic surgery to conceal his identity, he returns to New York with the idea of seeing his mother and marrying his childhood sweetheart.

His mother, an old, sickly woman (marvelously played by Marjorie Main), glares at her son as if he's the landlord demanding the rent he knows she does not have.

"Stay away," she tells him. "You murderer. Leave us alone, and die."

When Francie, his old girlfriend, comes down to see Martin in an alley, his image of her ten years ago on the roof veils the reality that she has become a common street whore. Repulsed, Martin steps back.

"Why didn't ya get a job?" he cries. "Why didn't ya starve first?"

"Why didn't *you*?" she counters.

Martin fishes in his pockets for a few bucks and hands it to her. Although this might seem like a generous gesture on Martin's part, it is more like dirt shoveled on top of the coffin of the Francie he knew, gone forever. As Francie struts back to her hotel room, his partner Hunk belatedly advises Martin, "Never go back; always move forward."

Moving forward in the footsteps of "Baby Face" Martin, the kids scheme to get rich kid Philip Griswald alone. They lure him into a cellar where they beat him up, tear his clothes and steal his watch. Poetic justice for spilling his milk?

Martin watches it all with a snicker, and comes up with an idea. Frustrated by the two emotional blows delivered from the women he once loved, he makes plans to kidnap Philip Griswald.

"I came here for somethin', I'm going out with something," he tells Hunk. "Even if it's only dough."

And then we witness Martin attempting another murder. The setting is intriguing: It's night. There is a loud party in one of the high-rise apartments. The street lights are lit. Dave looks out his window and sees Martin talking to a stranger. He knows from experience that this type of gathering could only mean trouble. He goes down and warns Martin to leave. When Martin does not move, Dave threatens to tell the police Martin's whereabouts. As Dave turns to leave, Martin throws a knife into Dave's back. The young man falls into the river. The party music gets louder and jazzier, providing the scene's own background music.

As the local policeman makes his rounds, Martin and Hunk stand still and silent, their nervousness hidden in the stillness of their bodies. While the policeman jabbers away about the loud music and the trouble he's having finding the kid who stabbed the judge's brother, Dave pulls himself out of the water. After the policeman leaves, Dave, bleeding from the back, jumps both Martin and Hunk. He knocks out Hunk and takes his gun. Martin runs, pursued by Dave to the fire escape where Martin is shot down.

Meanwhile, Drina, Tommy's hard-working sister, is ready to abandon everything she's lived and worked for to run away with her fugitive brother. All her life she's been striving to keep Tommy out of trouble and has suddenly comes to realize that whatever she does, as long as she lives in the tenements, she cannot win.

Before they leave, though, Tommy is determined to take vengeance on the kid who divulged his identity to the police. A close-up of Tommy's pensive expression, as he over-

Tommy (Billy Halop) eyeing Spit and the others from above. Left to right: Huntz Hall, Bobby Jordan, Gabe Dell, Leo Gorcey, Bernard Punsly, Halop (above).

hears a description of the kid who squealed on him, beautifully conveys the fact that he knows it's Spit. He is about to cut Spit's face with the knife when Dave stops him. Earlier, when Dave had asked him to put down the knife, Tommy threw it at the dock, in defiance of Dave. But killing "Baby Face" Martin has boosted Dave's image among the urchins. Tommy has seen how a criminal's life ends and does not want his to end that way. He hands Dave the knife and decides to turn himself over to the police.

Ignoring Drina's pleas, Mr. Griswald remains adamant about pressing charges. As the police take Tommy away, probably to the same reform school where "Baby Face" Martin learned all about knives, T.B., one of the kids, puts into perspective what it will be like for Tommy, for he has had the honor of attending the same school.

"You tell Tommy to look up a guy named Smokey," he tells Drina. "And you tell Tommy to be real nice to him 'cause this guy Smokey he can get him cigarettes and stuff." Drina breaks down and cries.

The film ends ambiguously. The odds that Dave's reward money will be enough to hire a good lawyer and keep Tommy from going to reform school is uncertain. That Drina will marry Dave is fairly certain. And whether the kids grow up to be a "Baby Face" Martin or a

Dell (second from left), Gorcey (fourth from left) and Jordan (bottom right) with the three small boys (Sidney Kibrick, Larry Harris and Norman Salling) just before Halop pounces on Gorcey.

Dave may be indicated by the song T.B. learned in reform school, which he sings and Angel plays on the kazoo, as darkness falls over the docks of the East River:

> If I had the wings of an angel over these walls I would fly
> Straight to the arms of me mother and there I'd be willing to die.

At the time of *Dead End*'s release, some critics accused the film of soapboxing the plight of the poor. But *Dead End* is more clever than that in that its message is inherent in its art, and the film never succumbs to blatant appeals for the underprivileged. Comments of despair are always in context and reveal aspects of personality. Drina fantasizes about meeting a rich man on the subway who promises to take her away to his country home; Dave dreams about tearing down the ugly tenement walls and erecting newer, brighter apartments.

There is no question that Sidney Kingsley yearned to make viewers more socially aware. And to do this he chose the most common denominator in us all, youth. All children are innocent until they are affected by the world that surrounds them. Thus, the environment, not "Baby Face" Martin, is the "bad guy." "Baby Face" Martin is a product of that environment, as are Tommy, Spit, Angel, T.B., Dippy and Milty. The parallel works brilliantly and evokes an outpouring of sympathy for the kids.

Gorcey (left) and Hall in a publicity shot for *Dead End*.

Nowhere in the history of film was there a team so exploited, beginning with a Broadway play, that became a movie, that later became the basis for 91 other movies. Yet, not one was better than *Dead End*.

Crime School

Released May 28, 1938; 86 minutes; 7793 ft.; Warner Brothers; Director, Lewis Seiler; Associate Producer, Bryan Foy; Screenplay, Crane Wilbur and Vincent Sherman; Original Story, Crane Wilbur; Photography, Arthur Todd; Film Editor, Terry Morse; Music, Max Steiner; Dialogue Director, Vincent Sherman; Assistant Director, Fred Tyler; Art Director, Charles Novi; Gowns, N'Was McKenzie; Sound Recorder, Francis J. Scheid; Orchestrators, Hugo Friedhofer and George Parrish. Opened at the Strand.

CAST

Mark Braden	Humphrey Bogart	Guard	Harry Cording
Sue Warren	Gale Page	Old Doctor	Spencer Charters
Frankie Warren	Billy Halop	New Doctor	Donald Briggs
Squirt	Bobby Jordan	Commissioner	Frank Jaquet
Goofy	Huntz Hall	Mrs. Burke	Helen MacKellar
Spike	Leo Gorcey	Mrs. Hawking	Sibyl Harris
Fats	Bernard Punsly	Nick Papadopolo	Paul Porcasi
Bugs	Gabriel Dell	John Brower	Jack Mower
Red	George Offerman, Jr.	Junkie	Frank Otto
Cooper	Weldon Heyburn	Officer Hogan	Ed Gargan
Morgan	Cy Kendall	Schwartz	James B. Carson
Judge Clinton	Charles Trowbridge	Reporter	John Ridgely
Joe Delaney	Milburn Stone	Boy	Hally Chester

(*Note: For simplicity, the Kids' real names will be used in the Warner Brothers critiques.*)

Crime School picks up with the Kids where *Dead End* left them, on the street, bored with picking on smaller kids and heckling doormen.

Halop is still the leader, towing old tires, bathtubs, telephones and watches for Junkie the pawnbroker. For this, Halop expects at least $20. Junkie offers them five. Halop starts a scuffle and Gorcey ends it by clobbering Junkie over the head with a lead pipe.

Hauled before Judge Clinton, Halop shows signs of nobility by taking full responsibility. (He repeats this bravery in *Hell's Kitchen* but without the support of the Kids.) Gorcey is elated with Halop's false confession, and noticeably angry when the rest of the Kids refuse to let Halop face the punishment alone. So Judge Clinton sends them all to Galeville Settlement House.

Upon their arrival, Superintendent Morgan, a corrupt political hack, refuses them dinner. Halop complains and Morgan has him whipped without treating his gashes. It is the only instance in the series where beating is the punishment.

After being pushed around by almost every adult the Kids have come in contact with (Junkie, Morgan, Judge Clinton and Judge Griswald from *Dead End*), they can hardly be expected to recognize an ally in Deputy Commissioner Mark Braden (Humphrey Bogart). Lying on his stomach, Halop rejects Braden's sympathetic overtures, muttering under his breath, "I'll take care of myself."

Morgan tries to impress Braden by reprimanding Jordan because his pants are constantly falling to his ankles. "Put this boy on a special diet," Morgan tells Cooper, the head guard. Turning to Braden he smiles, "You see, here we make the punishment fit the crime."

Braden grimaces, "Don't you think you ought to make the pants fit the boy?"

Left to right: Humphrey Bogart, Cy Kendall and Bobby Jordan (with his pants down). Looking on are (left to right) Gabe Dell, Huntz Hall, Leo Gorcey, Bernard Punsly and Hally Chester in *Crime School.*

The most dramatic scene in the film leads to an acceptance of Braden. As punishment for something they did not do, the boys are put in the boiler room. At Halop's urging, they overload the boiler. When the boiler is about to explode, the boys drop their shovels and race towards the exit. Jordan is trapped. Braden, risking his own life, saves Jordan seconds before the explosion. All now respect him, except Gorcey. To Gorcey, Braden is still a cop.

Cooper, loyal to Morgan, blackmails Gorcey into convincing Halop that his sister Sue is "paying off" Braden with sexual favors. This is the only time in the Warner Brothers pictures that the subject of sex is an issue. Halop reacts violently. Gorcey gives Halop a gun, compliments of Cooper.

The Kids escape and head for Halop's apartment, where Halop expects to find and kill Braden.

But Braden dislodges the gun from Halop. Gorcey admits that Cooper coaxed him into duping Halop.

Meanwhile Cooper has telephoned Morgan, Judge Clinton, the Commissioner, and the newspapers to tell them how he "discovered" the boys' escape, and blames it on Braden's lax

The kids taking a school lesson break from the painting scene in *Crime School*. Left to right: unidentified teacher, Bobby Jordan, Huntz Hall, Bernard Punsly, Billy Halop, Gabe Dell and Leo Gorcey.

policies. But Braden has the kids in bed before the commissioner arrives, winning the cat-and-mouse game.

So it won't be a total loss for the reporters, Braden has Morgan and Cooper arrested on the spot.

The Kids are rewarded for exposing the crooked guards. Actually, the Kids do nothing to bring the evidence to light, and ridding the school of inept authorities is not their concern. Nor could they care less about the quality of the school or the other schoolmates. They are interested in only one thing: getting out.

Crime School is loaded with shortcomings. Whereas *Dead End* has layers of depth, *Crime School* is single-dimensional. Though it touches on subjects such as corruption, love and family ties, its main concern is the plight of the Kids in the reform school. The love affair between Sue Warren and Mark Braden is superficially developed and does not hold our interest. Its only purpose is to serve as a conduit to conclude a film that seems to be grasping at straws for a way to resolve the Kids' predicament.

Bogart seems bored with his role and should be. He is wasted in it. Any tough-talking actor could have played Mark Braden. Bogart starred with the Kids in three films, and it's a

Bogart (center, in white shirt) refereeing a boxing match between Dell (left) and Gorcey. Dell, Jr., said his dad was the "glue" that held the kids together. Others are (left to right) Bobby Jordan, Billy Halop, Bernard Punsly and Huntz Hall.

pity that his weakest performance is in the one where his character's relationship with the Kids is the closest.

Cy Kendall as the fiendish superintendent is perfect. While his wide, charming smile greets the visiting Braden, his sharp, glaring eyes terrify the Kids. Kendall also plays one of the bad guys in *Angels Wash Their Faces* and has a major part in an East Side Kids film, *Docks of New York*.

The ending of *Crime School* abandons realism, the heart of *Dead End*, for sentimentality. Sybil Harris, who plays Gorcey's mother, is wonderful as a distraught woman whose life-forces have been drained by the demon-like behavior of her son. So it's corny seeing Gorcey blush from his mother's kisses, as if life from now on will be forever rosy.

The marriage of Halop's sister to Mark Braden doesn't work as well as Dave and Drina's coming together at the conclusion of *Dead End*.

Crime School seems to have taught Warner Brothers a lesson. Gifted and experienced actors will not sustain a film with a perfunctory script. *Angels with Dirty Faces* and *They Made Me a Criminal* are the results of a lesson well learned.

Hall (center, in suit) and Halop shake hands at the opening of *Crime School* at the Strand in New York.

Angels with Dirty Faces

Released November 24, 1938: 97 minutes; 8827 ft.; Warner Brothers; Director, Michael Curtiz; Associate Producer, Samuel Bischoff; Screenplay, John Wexley and Warren Duff; Original Story, Rowland Brown; Photography, Sol Polito; Film Editor, Owen Marks; Music, Max Steiner; Dialogue Director, Jo Graham; Assistant Director, Sherry Shourds; Art Director, Robert Haas; Gowns, Orry-Kelly; Sound Recorder, Everett A. Brown; Orchestrator, Hugo Friedhofer; Technical Advisor, Father J.J. Devlin.

CAST

Rocky Sullivan	James Cagney	*Swing*	Bobby Jordan
Jerry Connolly	Pat O'Brien	*Bim*	Leo Gorcey
James Frazier	Humphrey Bogart	*Patsy*	Gabriel Dell
Laury Ferguson	Ann Sheridan	*Crab*	Huntz Hall
Mac Keefer	George Bancroft	*Hunky*	Bernard Punsly
Soapy	Billy Halop	*Steve*	Joseph Dowling

Edwards	Edward Pawley	*Poolroom Boys*	Frank Coghlan, Jr.,
Blackie	Adrian Morris		Dave Durand
Rocky (as a boy)	Frankie Burke	*Older Boy in*	George Offerman,
Jerry (as a boy)	William Tracy	*Poolroom*	Jr.
Laury (as a girl)	Marilyn Knowlden	*Norton J. White*	Charles Trowbridge
Warden	William Worthington	*Managing Editor*	Joe Cunningham
		Record Editor	James Spottswood
Priest	Earl Dwire	*Chronicle Editor*	John Dilson
Guard Kennedy	Oscar O'Shea	*Press City Editor*	Tommy Jackson
Bugs, gunman	William Pawley	*Policemen at*	Ralph Sanford,
Police Captain	John Hamilton	*Call Box*	Galan Galt
Mrs. McGee	Mary Gordon	*Police Officers*	Emory Parnell,
Soapy's Mother	Vera Lewis		Wilfred Lucas,
Railroad Yard			Elliott Sullivan
Watchman	James Farley	*Prison Guards*	Lane Chandler, Ben
Red	Chuck Stubbs		Hendricks
Johnny Maggione	Eddie Syracuse	*Convicts*	Sidney Bracey,
Mrs. Maggione	Belle Mitchell		George Taylor,
Policeman	Robert Homans		Oscar G. Hendrian, Dan
Basketball Captain	Harris Berger		Wolheim, Brian
Woman	Lottie Williams		Burke
Pharmacist	Harry Hayden		
Gangsters	Dick Rich, Steve	*Death Row Guard*	Jack Perrin
	Darrell, Joe	*Girl at Gaming*	
	Devlin	*Table*	Poppy Wilde
Reporters	Donald Kerr, Jack	*Well-Dressed Man*	John Marston
	Goodrich, Al	*Janitor*	Billy McClain
	Lloyd, Jeffrey	*Hanger-on*	Claude Wisberg
	Sayre, Charles	*Whimpering Convict*	William Crowell
	Marsh, Alexander	*Sharpies*	Frank Hagney,
	Lockwood, Earl		Dick Wessel,
	Gunn, Carlye		John Harron
	Moore	*Croupier*	Wilbur Mack
Detectives	Lee Philips, Jack	*Themselves*	Robert B. Mitchell's,
	Mower		St. Brendan Boys
Italian Storekeeper	William Edmunds		Choir
Police Chief Buckley	Charles Wilson		

In *Dead End*, the environment is blamed for the sorry lives of individuals. In *Angels with Dirty Faces* an individual stirs the environment. The present comes face to face with the future when the kids make the mistake of picking the pocket of notorious neighborhood alumnus Rocky Sullivan.

Rocky follows them to their hideout. When he leads the bewildered boys to a basement wall and shows them his carved initials, R.S., the Kids go ballistic.

This admiration for a gangster-hero sets a precedent for one East Side Kids film (*East Side Kids*) and one Little Tough Guys film *Mob Town*. *Dead End* did not set this precedent, for "Baby Face" Martin is too self-absorbed to realize what reverence the Kids would have for him. Martin has no use for casual relationships. He's intolerant of his partner Hunk, and

James Cagney and the Kids getting ready for a take in *Angels with Dirty Faces*.

scorns his own meaningless affairs. ("They don't mean nothin' t' me," he tells Francie, the girl whose been closest to his heart since their childhood nights on the roof.)

Rocky, on the other hand, is emotionally unburdened and appreciates the Kids' admiration. Casual relationships are the only kind he knows or cares to know. And his romance with Laura, who, like Francie, is from the old neighborhood, is not one based on longing through anguished years of separation, but simply a resolution to their lonely lives. Though we might give Laura the benefit of the doubt that love plays a role, we know for sure that love is farthest from Rocky's mind. Before Rocky takes his walk to the electric chair, Father Connolly asks him if he's scared. Rocky says, "Ya gotta have a heart t' be scared. I guess I ain't got a heart."

Rocky returns to the old neighborhood not for retrospection but to collect $100,000 and 50 percent of whatever his former partner, crooked lawyer Jim Frazier (Humphrey Bogart), owns. To collect it he must kidnap Frazier and steal his securities and bankbooks. Rocky forces Frazier to telephone Mac Keefer, co-owner of the El Toro Club, to have him pay Rocky the $100,000 the next day. After doing so, Keefer tells the police that Rocky has kidnapped Frazier and that the ransom has already been paid.

Back at his apartment, Rocky can think of numerous places to hide the money. One option is in the hands of the Dead End Kids.

For the most part, the Kids are portrayed collectively. The only one given any individual recognition is Halop. Rocky brings him to his apartment, shoves the money into his hands and sends him on his way before the police arrive. Though Rocky is using Halop for his own protection, Halop is honored to start his career under the auspices of such a notorious criminal.

As a reward for hiding the money, Rocky gives Halop and the Kids a few hundred dollars. Father Connolly, symbolizing the kids' conscience, finds them in Murphy's poolroom. He tries to encourage them to come to the gym but the Kids tighten their grasp around their cue sticks. "Look, fodder," Halop tells the priest, "we don't fall for that 'pie in the sky' stuff, see?"

In a short time Rocky has a share in the El Toro Club and has enough money to anonymously donate $10,000 to Father Connolly for a new recreation center. Father Connolly tries to return the check.

"Don't give it to me," Rocky tells him, faking bewilderment, "it's not mine."

"I know. That's why I can't take it... You got the city, Rocky. You got my boys too. You showed them the easy way. Do me a favor. Don't give them any more money. Don't encourage them to admire you."

Realizing he cannot shield the Kids from corruption, Father Connolly declares war against corruption itself, his friendship with Rocky Sullivan notwithstanding. The priest procures the support of the *Morning Press*. The newspaper investigates the backgrounds of Keefer, Frazier and Sullivan and prints editorials in favor of Father Connolly's crusade.

Frazier and Keefer panic. Rocky overhears them planning to kill Father Connolly so he kills *them*. Police surround the building. Rocky answers their surrender demand with a barrage of bullets; the police respond with tear gas. Father Connolly enters the building and persuades Rocky to give up. As both come out into the street, Rocky makes one final attempt to flee before he is caught by police.

The newspapers play up Rocky's callousness in the face of death, his contempt for the judge and for the police. The Kids root for him all the way. Father Connolly realizes that Rocky's execution will make him a martyr and that he (Connolly) will again fail in his attempt to turn the Kids away from crime. He cannot compete with his colorful cohort of childhood;

Final scene from *Angels with Dirty Faces*. Left to right: Gabe Dell, Bobby Jordan, Huntz Hall, Leo Gorcey, Bernard Punsly and Billy Halop. Pat O'Brien is on the stairs in the background.

he lacks his friend's charisma. What he lacks in charisma, he makes up for in dedication. With ten minutes remaining before Rocky takes his last breath, Father Connolly pleads for one last favor — to feign cowardice, to go to the chair screaming in fright. "I want you to let them down. I want them to despise your memory."

When the Kids, grieving in their clubhouse, ask him if what the newspapers say is true, that Rocky died a coward, Father Connolly answers, "He died like they said." It is a withholding of truth that is not an act of deceit but of concern for members of his community for whom he feels a deep-rooted kinship.

We don't see Rocky Sullivan being electrocuted, we hear his screams as we see Father Connolly praying for his departing friend. At the time of this movie, realism taken as far as the actual strapping of the condemned man to the chair would be considered poor taste. We can appreciate how our attitudes have changed by comparing this scene with the execution of Louis "Lepke" Buckhalter in *Lepke* (1974). Tony Curtis is seen being shaved, strapped to the seat and blindfolded. The switch is thrown and smoke emanates from the spots where his skin makes contact with the metal. His body twitches in reaction to the electricity.

The only flaw in Michael Curtiz's direction is that whenever the Kids and Cagney are together, they vie for the spotlight, pushing Cagney into the shadows. Thus, they perform against one another, rendering their scenes unbalanced.

Pat O'Brien plays Father Connolly with confidence. He is a priest at ease recollecting his wayward childhood and not averse to laughing about the pranks he once played.

The main theme of *Angels with Dirty Faces* is the same as the prototype: Neglected neighborhoods breed hardened criminals. But here, more attention is given to the mechanics of crime than with the psyche of the criminal. We know how Rocky attains prominence in the gangster world, but in *Dead End* we don't get an inkling of how "Baby Face" Martin began his climb to notoriety.

In *Angels with Dirty Faces* the Kids, at the news of Rocky Sullivan's death, are disappointed, not because he is dead, but because he died a coward. Rocky let them down. This sparked an onslaught of viewer criticism; many felt that giving the Dead End Kids such a cold attitude towards human life set a poor example for the children of America who looked up to the Kids as their idols.* Their next film, *They Made Me a Criminal*, turned this view around.

They Made Me a Criminal

Released January 28, 1939; 92 minutes; Warner Brothers; Director, Busby Berkeley; Producers, Jack L. Warner, Hal B. Wallis; Associate Producer, Benjamin Glazer; Screenplay, Sig Herzig; From the story "The Life of Jimmy Dolan" by Bertram Millhauser and Beulah A. Dix; Photography, James Wong Howe; Film Editor, Jack Killifer; Musical Score, Max Steiner.

CAST

Johnnie	John Garfield		T. B.	Gabriel Dell
Detective Phelan	Claude Rains		Milt	Bernard Punsly
Goldie	Ann Sheridan		Doc Ward	Robert Gleckler
Grandma	May Robson		Magee	John Ridgely
Peggy	Gloria Dickson		Budgie	Barbara Pepper
Tommy	Billy Halop		Ennis	William Davidson
Angel	Bobby Jordan		Lenihan	Ward Bond
Spit	Leo Gorcey		Malven	Robert Strange
Dippy	Huntz Hall			

with Louis Jean Heydt, Frank Riggi, Cliff Clark, Dick Wessel, Raymond Brown, Sam Hayes

What begins with a left hook to save his secret becomes a long trek across America to save his life. The ironic thing about the title is that this film, different from the previous ones, includes no criminal characters of any significance. Instead, it explores themes barely touched in other films: faithfulness, responsibility, dedication.

In contrast with the Kids' restlessness in the prior films (Gorcey flirting with the idea of kidnapping a baby in *Angels with Dirty Faces*, Halop bullying Punsly in *Dead End*), here the Kids are relaxed, away from the overcrowded city, picking fruit instead of stealing it.

Unrest comes when Johnny Bradfield appears, like Moses wandering in the wilderness, to cleanse himself of his past.

The Kids share Bradfield's exile from New York City. Hardened by his joyless journey,

---

Interview with Huntz Hall on The Tom Snyder Show, *1981.*

A game of strip poker in *They Made Me a Criminal*. Left to right: Bernard Punsly, Billy Halop, Leo Gorcey, unidentified actor playing J. Douglass Williamson, Gabe Dell, Bobby Jordan and Huntz Hall.

he dares Halop to steal a pack of cigarettes. Here, Halop is not the uninhibited, raw youth of *Crime School*, cocksure of his capabilities and arrogant in the face of people telling him what to do. In the country, away from the atmosphere of dishonesty, Halop is like a rehabilitated alcoholic tempted with a drink. While his sister looks the other way, Halop succumbs to peer pressure ("Ya gotta take a dare, Tommy") and steals a pack of cigarettes from the farm kiosk.

The difference between copping a pack of cigarettes for Bradfield and hiding $100,000 for Rocky Sullivan in *Angels with Dirty Faces* is trenchant. The act does not symbolize a stepping stone in his criminal career, nor is there any reward awaiting him at the completion of his wayward task. Not only does he get no personal satisfaction from the theft, he suffers the ultimate humiliation by being caught by his sister. And Bradfield doesn't even say thank you.

Ambivalence about stealing is not the only change since the Kids have been brought to the farm to "de-generate" (Hall). ("Regenerate, ya dope"—Halop, the first malapropism.) Unlike the conflicts in the previous films, the emphasis is not on confrontation but cooperation. *They Made Me a Criminal* is the only Dead End Kid movie in which the cause will not result in the fall of a criminal, but the creation of an enterprising operation. The transformation is most apparent in Halop who, concerned about easing Grandma's financial strife, comes up with the idea of opening a gas station on the farm.

John Garfield and Ann Sheridan in *They Made Me a Criminal*.

Bradfield wants to help too and signs up to box Gaspar Rurchek for $500 per round. To show their appreciation, the Kids want to get Bradfield boxing gloves. Halop insists they acquire the gloves honestly. As they search through their empty pockets, their eyes fall upon J. Douglas Williamson, counterpart to *Dead End*'s rich kid Philip Griswald. Williamson owns a camera. The Kids lure the innocent youth into a basement hide away and engage in a game of strip poker. With the shrewd Gorcey on his side Williamson's pair of aces loses to Halop's pair of twos. "Twos are higher," Gorcey explains. (A similar situation would arise in the Bowery Boys' *Hold That Baby!*). Soon Williamson loses his camera.

Bradfield has become selflessly devoted to the Kids, to Peggy, and to the farm. He agrees to drive the Kids to the water tower to swim. The scene is the most visually dramatic of any Dead End Kids flick. Its excellence is attributable to director Busby Berkeley. Unlike the scenes in *Crime School* where Jordan is trapped in the explosive boiler room, or in *Angels Wash Their Faces* where Punsly is helplessly cornered in a burning building, the Kids and Bradfield must be self-reliant to extricate themselves from the water tower. Shots of the boys' fruitless attempts to grab the top ledge, together with numerous dives to the bottom to open the floor drain, brilliantly convey the desperation of their situation. A long shot of the tower, from which an exhausted arm is finally seen hanging over the edge, indicates that the tower

Gloria Dickson and Garfield taking a swim break from *They Made Me a Criminal*. Both died young.

has been emptied and the boys can now stand one on top of another to form a human ladder.

Meanwhile, Dell has taken up photography. Twice he makes Bradfield his subject and both times Bradfield reacts angrily. His warnings go unheeded. While Bradfield, after a long training session, sits under a makeshift outdoor shower (similar to the type of constructions in Our Gang comedies), Dell glowingly displays his amateur award–winning photograph of

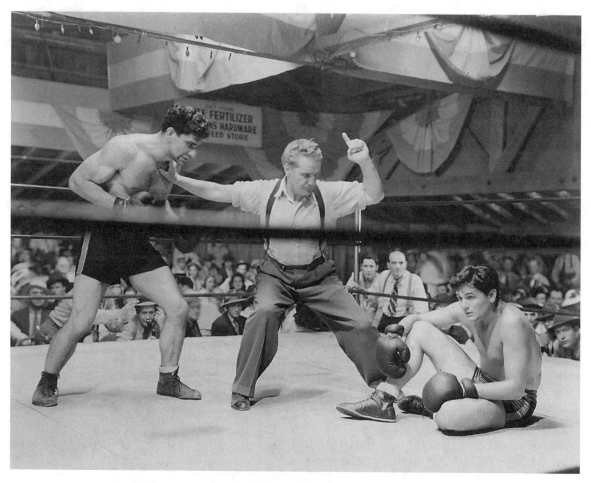

Garfield down for the count in *They Made Me a Criminal*. Left to right: Frank Riggi, unidentified actor, John Garfield.

Bradfield in his boxing stance in a magazine. Bradfield worries that New York detectives might see the picture.

Bradfield's worst fears are realized when he spots New York Detective Phalen buying a ticket to the boxing attraction. It awakens him to the fact that he is still a fugitive who has not yet eluded the authorities.

In New York, Johnny Bradfield was the newly crowned lightweight champion of the world. At the victory celebration, Magee, a reporter, discovers that the image of Johnny Bradfield as a teetotaling mama's-boy is merely a public relations gimmick and threatens to expose him. Bradfield takes a swing at Magee but in his drunkenness misses and passes out. Bradfield's manager, Doc, hits Magee on the head with a bottle and kills him. Frightened, Doc takes the unconscious Bradfield and his girlfriend Goldie (Ann Sheridan) to their training camp. He tells Goldie that it was Bradfield who killed the reporter and that it would be best to leave Bradfield at the camp.

The following morning, when Bradfield awakes, he reads in the newspaper that after killing Magee, *he* was killed in an auto accident with his girlfriend Goldie. The police are unaware that it was Doc who was killed in the accident because Doc had Bradfield's car, money and wristwatch.

Unsure of what to do, he seeks the advice of his lawyer, who takes advantage of Bradfield by stealing his $10,000, leaving the boxer with only $250.

"Stay dead, from now on, ya gotta be afraid," he advises Bradfield. "Jack Dorney, that's who you are from now on. Can you remember that?" The confused boxer takes the money and heads west. The only person who does not believe Bradfield is dead is Detective Phelan (Claude Rains), who bets his retirement on it.

After spotting Phelan, Bradfield returns to the ranch where a party and his gift of boxing gloves await him. Sadly he announces that he has decided not to fight due to health reasons. The Kids know he is lying. For the second time in as many films, the Kids experience disappointment in an adult whom they hold in high esteem.

But Halop's skepticism about Bradfield backing out of the fight persists. Bradfield breaks down and agrees to fight, hoping that a different boxing stance will confuse the hot detective.

The boxing scene, the first in a long line of boxing sequences in East Side Kids and Bowery Boys comedies, is unconvincing because it is based on the ridiculous premise that Bradfield hitting with his right instead of his left will confound an experienced New York detective like Phelan. It does nothing of the kind. Phelan pegs Bradfield the minute he steps into the ring. And when Bradfield uses his new stance, Phelan laughs, while the former champion, trying to win and remain unnoticed at the same time, is pummeled in four and half rounds.

Why Bradfield continues to fight after he has earned enough money is unclear. Perhaps for the unconscious father-to-be (he was knocked out within seconds)? If so, then it is a mistake to have him lose. If he loses the fight on purpose to confuse Phelan, it is pointless since Phelan knows who he is. But if Bradfield really is knocked out, which is what the film seems to want us to believe, then he never should have been the champion in the first place.

Phelan perceives Bradfield's importance to the Kids and to Peggy. He shows compassion by pushing Johnny off the train, saying, "Maybe you're not Johnny Bradfield," and returns to New York alone, sacrificing the rest of his career for the good of the Kids and the lives of Peggy and Johnny Bradfield. Who else jumps off the train? Billy Halop!

They Made Me a Criminal comes closest to being the sequel to *Dead End* for several reasons. First, the Kids assume the character names of the original film. Second, Jordan states that Halop would have gone to reform school for stabbing a judge. Third, Halop's sister Peggy is as completely devoted to him as Drina is in *Dead End*.

They Made Me a Criminal is a rich story composed of remarkable characters sensitively played by John Garfield, Gloria Dickson, Mary Robson and Claude Rains. Although the beginning threatens to be just another movie, the shift to Arizona is a welcomed event and presents a provocative setting for fresh thinking on the part of the Dead End Kids.

Hell's Kitchen

Released July 8, 1939; 82 minutes; Warner Brothers; Directors, Lewis Seiler, E.A. DuPont; Associate Producers, Mark Hellinger, Bryan Foy; Screenplay, Crane Wilbur, Fred Niblo, Jr.; Story, Crane Wilbur; Photography, Charles Rosher; Film Editor, Clarence Kolster; Art Director, Hugh Reticker; Dialogue Director, Hugo Cummings; Gowns, Milo Anderson; Sound Recorder, Dolph Thomas.

CAST

Tony	Billy Halop	*Judge Chandler*	George Irving
Joey	Bobby Jordan	*Bailiff*	Lee Phelps
Gyp	Leo Gorcey	*Maizie*	Ila Rhodes
Ace	Huntz Hall	*Chick*	Don Turner
Bingo	Gabriel Dell	*Nails*	Joe Devlin
Ouch	Bernard Punsly	*Roll Mop*	Jimmie Lucas
Soap	Frankie Burke	*Pants*	Jack Kenny
Beth	Margaret Lindsey	*Sweet Al*	Sol Gorss
Jim	Ronald Reagan	*Guard*	Cliff Saum
Buck Caesar	Stanley Fields	*Announcer*	Reid Kilpatrick
Hiram Krispan	Grant Mitchell	*Usher*	George O'Hanlon
Steve Garvey	Fred Tozere	*Henchmen*	Charles Sullivan,
Jed Krispan	Arthur Loft		Jack Gardner
Sarah Krispan	Vera Lewis	*Guards*	Max Hoffman, Jr.,
Hardy	Robert Homans		Dick Rich,
Flugue	Charles Foy		Tom Wilson
Callahan	Robert Strange	*Mrs. Chandler*	Ruth Robinson
Whitey	Raymond Bailey	*Jury Foreman*	George Offerman
Mr. Quill	Clem Bevans		

Bird's-eye view of (left to right) Halop, Jordan, Hall and Margaret Lindsay in a publicity shot for *Hell's Kitchen*.

Gorcey and Margaret Lindsay share a laugh on the set of *Hell's Kitchen*.

Hell's Kitchen combines the character of Rocky Sullivan of *Angels with Dirty Faces* with Mark Braden of *Crime School* and comes up with Buck Caesar, an upbeat criminal bent on reforming the Hudson Shelter for Boys. It also builds on the evil of superintendent Morgan from *Crime School* and comes up with the more sinister Hiram Krispan.

Hell's Kitchen also risks starring the Dead End Kids without the support of a well-known actor (unless you count Ronald Reagan). What it also does is unwittingly stunt the growth of the Kids' individual professional careers. They were forever perceived (until the epilogue of their careers) as "Kids." The script, though based on a 1933 film (*The Mayor of Hell* [see Bibliography]) released two years before the Kids appeared on Broadway, has the feel of being written exclusively for them.

When we first meet Krispan, he is a timid old gentleman, meekly but conscientiously soliciting the notorious gangster Buck Caesar for a charitable contribution to the Shelter. Not until Krispan punishes Billy Halop for taking the teacher's car for a joy ride do we realize what a tyrant he really is.

Halop gives dimension to his character. His restrained voice conveys both confidence in himself and disgust for his superiors. He says to Krispan, "You want to know whose idea it was? It was mine."

Later, when Krispan is brought to kangaroo court and sentenced to a live burial, Halop points to the coffin and says coolly, "That's for you," turning the tables on him for putting Halop in the freezer earlier.

Halop and Jordan re-ignite their special friendship from *Dead End* when Jordan sneaks out of the dormitory to free a shivering Halop. "I just couldn't let you freeze in dere."

There is a marked difference between Halop after his whipping in *Crime School* and Halop after his release from the freezer in *Hell's Kitchen*. In *Crime School* he rejects Mark Braden's words of support, maintaining that he can take care of himself. But in *Hell's Kitchen* he eagerly seeks the advice of their teacher Miss Avery. It is the only time in the series where any kid asks a woman for such a favor. And who does she introduce him to, of all people? Buck Caesar!

One of the conditions on which the judge grants Buck probation is that he must show definite character improvement. When Krispan comes seeking a donation, Buck's lawyer (and nephew) Jim O'Donahue (Reagan) urges him to make it a sizable one. Like Rocky Sullivan, Buck has an affinity for kids with backgrounds similar to his own. It is interesting to note that James Cagney, who, as Rocky Sullivan, offered a donation to the church, also played the equivalent role in *The Mayor of Hell*.

Like Mark Braden in *Crime School*, Buck uncovers the horrendous conditions at the shelter. Keeping in step with his counterpart, Buck dethrones the corrupt Krispan and takes charge of the school.

As in *Angels with Dirty Faces*, the adult hoodlum is able to interest the boys in sports. Hockey equipment, uniforms and an ice rink are provided. Whether the Kids are doing the actual skating is not determinable from the film.

Similar to the boxing match in *They Made Me a Criminal*, more is at stake here than simply winning or losing. Krispan, like his *Crime School* counterpart, provokes Buck into taking action in violation of his parole. Krispan and Garvey arrange to have semi-pro hockey players make up the Gladstone Orphanage team that plays against the Dead End Kids. Before the game, Garvey, an ex-employee of Buck, bets him $5000 that Gladstone will win. Buck, knowing that all his money has been spent on the Hudson Shelter for Boys, nevertheless accepts the challenge.

When Buck gets wind of the fact that his team is playing against semi-pros, he lets loose a terrific wallop that sends Garvey over the railing, and into a coma.

Up to this point, Buck Caesar (Stanley Fields) keeps the film alive. But when he "takes it on the lam" the film depends solely on the Dead End Kids. In a series of thrilling events, from the saving of a dog to the smoking-out of Hiram Krispan, the Kids succeed in keeping the pace lively.

Halop trying to warm Jordan after a stint in the freezer in *Hell's Kitchen*.

Krispan reassumes command of the shelter. Our hatred for him increases when Jordan is put in the freezer.

In *Crime School* it is Jordan who is too slow in leaving the volcanic boiler room; in *They Made Me a Criminal* it is Jordan who cannot keep his head above water without help. But in *Hell's Kitchen* there is no Mark Braden or Johnny Bradfield to rescue him. The following morning, Jordan's lifeless body is carried out of the freezer.

In the eulogy, under the vengeful stares of the Dead End Kids, Krispan blames the Kids for Jordan's death; if not for their adverse influence on him, Jordan would still be alive.

One of the things that sets this film and *Angels Wash Their Faces* apart from the rest is that the Kids confront their actual enemy, Krispan, a personification of the society that mistreats them. The opportunity stirs in them a behavior that smacks of savagery similar to that of the children in *Lord of the Flies*. Indeed, Warners was criticized by the Youth Authorities and the Production Code, and the British gave *Hell's Kitchen* an "X" rating for violence.*

Their takeover of the school is a raging spectacle, from one close-up to the next, focusing on angry faces of youths who take up a menacing chant, "He killed Joey." When the Kids overpower the guards, it is the first time they are in the forefront of a large crowd scene (many crowd scenes are staged in East Side Kids and Bowery Boys films). The decision to bury Krispan alive is shocking but consistent with Halop's tendency to inflict pain upon unscrupulous people (for example, Spit in *Dead End* and *Crime School*).

*Page 148, *Me and the Dead End Kid* by Leo Gorcey, Jr.

The near lynching of Krispan (Arthur Loft) in *Hell's Kitchen*.

Krispan escapes from the coffin and locks himself into a garage.

Gorcey, in keeping with the character who wouldn't hesitate to hit someone on the head with a lead pipe (*Crime School*), throws a lighted torch into the garage. (Earlier, during a school meeting, even Buck notes Gorcey's antics. "Looks like we got an agitator in the bunch.")

Krispan escapes from the burning garage and into the grip of Buck Caesar before the Kids are able to do more premeditated damage.

With Krispan behind bars for at least 20 years, Buck, like Rocky Sullivan, but more straightforward, attempts to guide the Kids on the right track.

"We gotta get this thing right. I ain't gonna do time because I hit Garvey. I'm gonna do time because I ain't never had nobody tell me what I'm tellin' ya now. It's okay for you to like me, but it ain't okay for you to *be* like me."

One flaw is that we are neither shown nor specifically told why the Kids are in the shelter in the first place. The film avoids this by introducing them already *in* the shelter. And it is not until the takeover that the Kids play a part in shaping the outcome of the film. Until the takeover, all changes of events are initiated or motivated by adults. An example is the high-spirited, enjoyable school meeting during which Buck announces all the changes he plans to implement.

But when their time comes, the Kids act for the good of all the schoolmates, a quality that was first cultivated in *They Made Me a Criminal*. Here, they want to rid the school of

Krispan, not escape from it as in *Crime School*. They want to make the Hudson Shelter for Boys livable.

Like *Crime School*, *Hell's Kitchen* has a straightforward plot, hardly making a distinction between the tale of Buck's period of probation and the plight of the Dead End Kids. What is most disappointing is to see the Kids remain at the shelter without any inkling as to when they might leave it and what they will do once they are out.

They are so much more fun and unpredictable when the reins are let loose and they are free to wander the streets. It wasn't until they arrived at Universal Studios and Monogram Pictures that they were again given that freedom.

Angels Wash Their Faces

Released August 26, 1939; 76 minutes; Warner Brothers; Director, Ray Enright; Associate Producer, Max Siegel; Screenplay, Michael Fessier, Niven Busch, Robert Buckner; From the Story "Battle of City Hall" by Jonathan Finn; Photography, Arthur Todd; Film Editor, James Gibbons.

CAST

Joy Ryan	Ann Sheridan	*Gildersleeve*	Grady Sutton
Pat Remson	Ronald Reagan	*Turnkey*	Aldrich Bowker
Billy Shafter	Billy Halop	*Mrs. Arkelian*	Marjorie Main
Peggy Finnegan	Bonita Granville	*Simpkins*	Robert Strange
Gabe Ryan	Frankie Thomas	*Mr. Smith*	Egon Brecher
Bernie	Bobby Jordan	*Mrs. Smith*	Sibyl Harris
Sleepy Arkelian	Bernard Punsly	*Boy*	Frank Coghlan, Jr.
Lee Finnegan	Leo Gorcey	*Al*	Claude Wisberg
Huntz	Huntz Hall	*Drivers*	Nat Carr, Garry
Luigi	Gabe Dell		Owens
Mr. Remson	Henry O'Neill	*Marsh*	Jack Wagner
Martino	Eduardo Ciannelli	*Assistant Turnkey*	Harry Strang
Mayor Dooley	Berton Churchill	*Reporters*	John Ridgely, John
Maloney	Minor Watson		Harron, Max
Miss Hannaberry	Margaret Hamilton		Hoffman, Jr.
Alfred Goonplatz	Jackie Searl	*Cops*	Jack Clifford,
Kronar	Bernard Nedell		Tom Wilson,
Hynos	Cy Kendall		Eddy Chandler
Shuffle	Dick Rich		

In *Angels Wash Their Faces*, the Dead End Kids are barely recognizable. School books replace knives, collegiate sweaters have been slipped over dirty sweatshirts, and concern for the safety of their community, instead of pickpocketing its residents, is now uppermost in their minds. In sharp contrast to Gorcey's remark during the basketball game in *Angels with Dirty Faces* ("Can't ya even shove a guy in this game?"), here the Kids are law-abiding citizens to the core. Nobody can get away with spitting or even going bowling on Sundays. In previous films, the Dead End Kids constituted an entire third front. Here, even their club name, the Beale Street Termites, reduces the sting of their bite.

What is also a surprise, and perhaps a bit humiliating, is Frankie Thomas playing the lead, and not too convincingly at that, while most of the Dead End Kids are wasted. Thomas is too angelic for a kid fresh out of reform school.

At first the Kids bear a grudge against Gabe (Thomas) yet they initiate him as a Beale Street Termite. The initiation ritual is imaginative, frightening, and yet harmless. Gabe is told to bring lighter fluid to the Beale Street basement. Once there he is blindfolded. What he thinks is happening: The fluid is poured all around him, a match is struck and flames engulf him. Actually, the Dead End Kids pour a bucket of water on the floor, scratch two pieces of sandpaper together and rustle a ball of cellophane. It is the most inventive moment for the Kids since the makeshift shower in *They Made Me a Criminal*.

Joy Ryan, Gabe's sister (as opposed to Halop's sister), appeals to Al Martino, head of the Civic Progressive League, to help parents combat arson in their neighborhood. Unbeknownst to Joy, Martino *is* responsible for the fires. To divert her attention from her organization, and quell any suspicion focusing on him, Martino orders his henchmen, Kronar and Shuffle, to frame a reform school alumnus: Gabe Ryan.

The campaign works unbelievably well. Kronar widely publicizes that Gabe was seen with a can of lighter fluid in the Beale Street basement. That the parents and teachers join together against one boy is a bit hard to swallow, but in the thick of all the gossip-mongering, the building where Punsly resides is set ablaze.

The danger of fire is more fully realized here than in any other picture when Punsly falls to his death. As the building falls, we hear Pat Remson (Ronald Reagan), son of the district attorney, say to Fire Commissioner Hynos (well played by Cy Kendall), "That was one of the buildings you refused to condemn."

Although Pat is on Gabe's side (and has taken a liking to Joy), the circumstantial evidence, coupled with the lies spattered out by city officials at the trial, result in Gabe being found guilty and sentenced to ten years in the state penitentiary. He is taken from the courtroom, screaming in desperation.

We would expect the Dead End Kids, as we know them, to help their pal break out of jail. But in this film, the Kids are strictly legitimate, and it's dull to see them work within the confines of bureaucracy and social acceptability. Whereas in *Hell's Kitchen* the system was real and the kangaroo court fake, in *Angels Wash Their Faces* the Kids compete for a week of make-believe power in a city of real corrupt courts.

Enthusiasm for the competition matches their glee for guarding Rocky Sullivan's money in *Angels with Dirty Faces*. But for Halop to become an American history wiz kid overnight is too much even for these filmmakers. To ease the competition (and for old times' sake), the Kids rough up some of the more studious competitors, rendering them physically incapable of showing up for the contest.

The greatest digression from the traditional realism of Dead End Kids films is Halop's dream about American and local history. As we watch Halop's sleeping face, the Dead End Kids are superimposed, jumping on Halop's nose while randomly throwing history question at him. Halop answers them all in his sleep.

The Kids learn quickly that "Boys Week" is a farce. Halop has no power; he's thrown out of every city office he visits. But Pat collaborates with the Kids in outsmarting the crooked politicians. He gives the Kids the idea of pilfering Fire Commissioner Hynos' expense account book. (This type of support is similar to Father Donovan's advice to Slip in the Bowery Boys' *In Fast Company*. When it seems inevitable that Slip will be engaging in a fistfight, which the priest abhors, he reminds Slip not to lead with his right.)

Once again Jordan has a small but distinct role. He is excused from the mission of appro-

Halop (second from right) and Hall (right) pull a prank on Ann Sheridan, driving her car to the rack during recess in A*ngels Wash Their Faces.*

priating the expense book because his family is having meat for supper. He learns from his father, a warehouse guard, that the warehouse is being prepared for a fire. Jordan informs Pat. Kronar and Shuffle are caught red-handed. Unfortunately, their lawyer Simpkins produces an immediate release signed by the judge.

Resorting to the restrictions established by the neglected but nevertheless existing blue laws, the Dead End Kids and Pat apprehend Kronar and Shuffle in the bowling alley, put them in shackles and take them to the schoolyard. Halop and the Kids, as mayor and staff, are given carte blanche to do with them as they will.

A circle is formed around them and the people shout at them to admit their guilt. Rain falls as Kronar and Shuffle remain silent. It is only when copies of recent passport pictures of their bosses Martino and Simpkins are shown to them, proof that they are skipping the country for South America, do Kronar and Shuffle talk.

The circumstances in this story are too absurd to be plausible. Putting official power in the hands of the Dead End Kids is impossible for any viewer to take seriously; that the film takes itself seriously is one of the reasons for its failure.

Except for Marjorie Main, doing a repeat of her role as a heartbroken mother (this time of Punsly, who dies in the fire), there are no outstanding performances, no good development of characters or relationships, and nothing threatens the kids' future. The Kids are basically financially secure and more at peace with the world than they have ever been.

Although the neighborhood may benefit from their change of disposition, the film does not. It is their toughness that gives them appeal. Here, they are about as tough as My Little Margie.

On Dress Parade

Released November 18, 1939; 62 minutes; Warner Brothers; Director, William Clemens; Associate Producer, Bryan Foy; Screenplay, Tom Reed, Charles Belden; From the Story "Dead End Kids in Military School" by Tom Reed; Photography, Arthur Todd; Film Editor, Doug Gould.

CAST

Cadet Major Rollins	Billy Halop	*Cadet Lt. Murphy*	Frank Thomas
Cadet Ronmy Morgan	Bobby Jordan	*Mrs. Neeley*	Cissie Loftus
Cadet Johnny Cabot	Huntz Hall	*Capt. Evans Dover*	Selmer Jackson
Cadet George Warren	Gabriel Dell	*Father Ryan*	Aldrich Bowker
Slip Duncan	Leo Gorcey	*Hathaway*	Douglas Meins
Dutch	Bernard Punsly	*Dr. Lewis*	William Gould
Col. Michael Reiker	John Litel	*Col. William Duncan*	Don Douglas

The basic theme of this film is getting Slip Duncan (Leo Gorcey) to go to military school and, once there, getting him to like it. Indeed, this film is a showcase for Gorcey, who clearly surpasses Halop as the star. As the *New York Times* reviewer put it in his review, "Spit, as he was known in the original production, was our baby, the littlest, the one most stunned by cigarette smoking, a venomous expectorator for whom the eye of an enemy was like flying quail to a huntsman ... they didn't have to take Spit away from us ... we don't regret the others but in the case of Leo Gorcey we feel like exclaiming sadly, 'Et tu, Spit?'"[*]

What the reviewer means is that, for the first time, four of the Dead End Kids have evolved to full-fledged conformists. It is also the first time the Dead End Kids do not know each other at the beginning of the film (except for Gorcey and Punsly, his pool hall companion). Hall, Dell and Jordan are from well-to–do families and meet upon arrival at the school, eager to excel. Halop is already an upperclassman.

[*]*New York Times* review of *"Dead End Kids On Dress Parade"* November 1939; Leo Gorcey's New York Times *obituary, June 3, 1969.*

Pool hall buddies Punsly (left) and Gorcey in *On Dress Parade*.

Although reviews of this film, from *Variety* in 1939 to the Internet Movie Database in 2006, have unkind things to say, there are several noteworthy features here. The first is the inclusion of actual World War I footage at the very beginning of the film that segues to the heroic scene where Col. William Duncan saves Col. Reiker. This opens the way for Col. Duncan, many years later, as he lies on his death bed, to ask his old buddy Col. Michael Reiker, to take care of his wayward boy, Slip — to enroll him in the Washington Military Academy where he can at least be kept off the streets.

Slip Duncan, whose aunt calls him "hell on wheels," can be found in the poolroom where he has demonstrated uncanny proficiency. Col. Reiker deceives Slip into thinking the police want to send him to reform school. Preferring military academy over reform school (he's had his fill of that in *Crime School* and *Hell's Kitchen*), Slip arrives at the academy and, once there, behaves as if he's above the rules. He doesn't make his bed, gets into fights, and shows disrespect to Nathan Hale.

Shortly thereafter, his pool hall pal Punsly shows up and we are supposed to believe he just hitchhiked 300 miles and waltzed unnoticed through the front gate and up to Gorcey's cubby just to tell him he was tricked into volunteering for military school. A letter would have been simpler.

Cadet Major Rollins (Halop) appeals to Slip to remain. He tries showing the rambunctious rascal the advantages of a military school but Slip will have none of that. So the boys take his luggage and toss it around until Gorcey lunges for it and accidental pushes Halop out the window. Suddenly Slip is transformed to a teary-eyed, remorseful lost soul.

Begging now to be accepted, he is shunned. Nevertheless, he remains at the school and excels in his studies. One day, a plane crashes into an ammunition depot and Cadet Warren (Dell) is trapped inside. Gorcey, like his father, risks his life to save his friend. Both boys end up mummified in bandages. When Gorcey recovers, he returns to his old barracks wearing a cape and is hailed a hero. Dell doesn't return and we are left wondering if he healed or died.

Another item of note is Gorcey's given name in the film, "Shirley," and his nickname, Slip. Clearly it is from *On Dress Parade* that the name Slip was taken and pinned on Gorcey for the Bowery Boys films. And the idea of Gorcey having a female first name, Ethelbert, was repeated several times in the East Side Kids films, after being introduced in *Mr. Wise Guy*.

That Gorcey fumes when the other cadets call him Shirley is no surprise. That he shows them his fist and threatens them with "Iron Mike" if they dare repeat the mistake his parents made leads us to conclude that this term is older than Mike Tyson. An Internet search directs users to a statue titled "The Spirit of the CCC," also known as "Iron Mike," dedicated on October 1, 1935, at the Civilian Conservation Corps in Griffith Park Los Angeles.* A flood a year before this film was made washed it away. Several years later, the East Side Kids made a film called *Pride of the Bowery* that took place at a CCC camp. Coincidence?

The average viewer would be disappointed in *On Dress Parade*. A major weakness is that the Dead End Kids have their confrontations among themselves, thus eliminating the fundamental aspect of their identity and charm —coping with survival amidst a society that would like to see them disappear. That wouldn't happen for about another 20 years and over 90 more films.

―――――――――――――

www.cccalumni.org/ironmike.html.

The Little Tough Guys

The popular response to Universal's *Little Tough Guy* (1938) was unquestionably positive. The critical response was unenthusiastic. *The New York Times* commented, "Poverty is apparently a disease from which motion picture producers and scenarists as well as society suffer."

After this film was released, Universal temporarily lost the services of four *Dead End Kids*. But Universal kept the Little Tough Guys alive by retaining David Gorcey and Hally Chester, and adding William Benedict, Charles Duncan, Harris Berger and Frankie Thomas for the film *Little Tough Guys in Society* (November 1938); Duncan, as previously stated, was cast as the original Spit in the Broadway production of *Dead End*, while Harris Berger was an understudy for the same play. Benedict and Thomas were already veterans of about twenty films apiece. Thomas also played a lead role in *Angels Wash Their Faces* and a smaller role in *On Dress Parade*. Benedict was to remain with the gang through the middle of the Bowery Boys series.

At best, *Little Tough Guys in Society* was amusing (supported by such actors as Mischa Auer, Mary Boland and Edward Everett Horton) but it was overshadowed by *Angels with Dirty Faces*, released five days later. Universal continued to keep pace with Warner Brothers, releasing *Newsboys' Home* two days after Warner Brothers' *They Made Me a Criminal*. It basically consisted of the same kids but in exchange for Frankie Thomas, Elisha Cook, Jr., took over as the leader. Also in this film were Jackie Cooper and Wendy Barrie, who played Kay in Goldwyn's *Dead End*. At this point, the Little Tough Guys were taken for second string Dead Enders and the critics felt it would be "unsporting" of them to add to the verbal abuse inflicted upon the film by the audience.

Unrelentingly, Universal came forth with another Little Tough Guy film in April 1939, *Code of the Streets*. Back was Frankie Thomas but his help wasn't enough to warrant a *New York Times* review.

In November 1939, Universal no longer had to rely on their second-stringers. In fact, Harris Berger appeared only in a couple of cameo spots, Charles Duncan dropped out completely, and Hally Chester joined Monogram Picture for its first two East Side Kids films before dropping out altogether. Benedict and David Gorcey were kept for Universal's next film, *Call a Messenger*, which starred Halop and Hall. They were billed as the combined forces of the Dead End Kids and Little Tough Guys and remained as such even after Benedict and David Gorcey left Universal; Punsly, Dell and Jordan joined them for the rest of the series beginning with *You're Not So Tough* (1940).

These last two pictures, which first opened at the Rialto in New York, were greeted by adolescent cheers—as all the films were—but movie reviewers grabbed every opportunity to poke fun at them. For example, in *Call a Messenger*, Billy Halop had become so tame that the

New York Times reviewer would not have been "surprised if he took up Latin in the next installment." The reviewer of *You're Not So Tough* considered the title a direct challenge to his profession, but turned it down saying, "[T]he Dead End Kids have long since taken the fight out of us."

In 1940, Universal launched a 12-chapter serial with the Dead End Kids and Little Tough Guys called *Junior G-Men*. The popularity of this serial, (and of serials in general) paved the way for two more *Sea Raiders* (1941) and *Junior G-Men of the Air* (1942). The latter one included Benedict and David Gorcey and introduced Frankie Darro into the fold. Although the serials raised their credibility a bit with the media, there was no doubt that the Dead End Kids, as a factor in American films, were becoming less and less important.

Between *Junior G-Men* and *Sea Raiders* they made a feature called *Give Us Wings*. By far this was given the most uncomplimentary treatment by the press. *Give Us Wings* is not a good, or even a passable entertainment; in fact it is so bad that ... we never did quite figure out the story..." (*New York Times*).

After *Sea Raiders*, the boys were seen as sons of a gang of criminals who were wiped out by a rival gang. *Hit the Road* provided another outlet for reviewers to take potshots at the gang of kids whose routines lacked the innovations they once had. What was once a gang of youth were now "big boys and have been exposed to the civilized graces of heaven knows how many films. One might reasonably expect that they would know better than to toss rolls across the table like footballs" (*New York Times*).

Either the producers at Universal never read the reviews or were simply undeterred by them. Their next two films before the serial *Junior G-Men of the Air*, *Mob Town* and *Tough As They Come*, mimicked the same themes as *Hit the Road*, but the methods used to reform the kids were different. *Mob Town* resembled *Little Tough Guy* in that both starred Halop as a boy who had no respect for the law that saw fit to execute his father or brother, and was certain that the only way to survive in this world was to steal.

The film after *Junior G-Men of the Air* was unfortunately Billy Halop's last. *Mug Town* was one of the better Universal productions. It featured Halop, Hall, Dell and Punsly on the road selling magazine subscriptions. The fact that they were out of the city expanded the plot and type of adventure that would befall them. This was a good idea but Universal did not follow up on it. Their last Little Tough Guy film, *Keep 'Em Slugging*, starred Bobby Jordan as the leader in the familiar surroundings of New York.

Except for *Little Tough Guy* where Halop was Johnny, and *Call a Messenger* where Halop was Jimmy, the kids' names in the feature films were always Tommy (Halop), Pig (Hall), String (Dell), Ape (Punsly) and Rap (Jordan). But when Halop and Jordan joined the armed forces in 1943 there was no one who could assume the leadership and muster audience appeal. Thus, the Little Tough Guys came to an end.

Little Tough Guy

Released July 22, 1938; 63 minutes; Universal; Director, Harold Young; Producer, Ken Goldsmith; Screenplay, Gibson Brown, Brenda Weisberg; Story, Brenda Weisberg; Photography, Elwood Bredell; Editor, Philip Cahn; Music, Charles Previn; Art Director, Jack Otterson; Sound, Bernard B. Brown; Sound Engineer, Charles Carroll; Opened at the Rivoli.

CAST

Johnny Boylan	Billy Halop	*Policeman*	Monte Montague
Kay Boylan	Helen Parrish	*Band Leader*	Frank Bishell
Pig	Huntz Hall	*Usher*	Johnny Green
String	Gabriel Dell	*Truant Officer*	Robert Homans
Ape	Bernard Punsly	*Bertis*	James Zahner
Sniper	David Gorcey	*Clerk*	Stanley Hughes
Dopey	Hally Chester	*Secretary*	Raymond Parker
Paul Wilson	Robert Wilcox	*Peddler*	Pat C. Flick
Cyril Gerrard	Jackie Searl	*Mrs. Wanmaker*	Helen MacKellar
Mrs. Boylan	Marjorie Main	*Mr. Gerrard*	Alan Edwards
Rita Belle	Peggy Stewart	*Domino, Cop*	Jack Carr
Jim Boylan	Ed Pawley	*D.A.*	Edwin Stanley
Carl	Edward Oehmen	*Superintendent*	Harry Hayden
Cashier	Eleanor Hanson	*Dot LaFleur*	Janet McLeay
Baxter	Olin Howland	*Secretary*	Victor Adams
Judges	Charles Trowbridge	*Chuck*	Paul Dubov
	Selmer Jackson	*Proprietor*	Paul Weigel
Kids	Buster Phelps	*Police Sergeant*	J. Pat O'Malley
	George Billings	*Truck Driver*	Bert Young
Detectives	William Ruhl	*Detective*	George Sherwood
	Ben Taggart	*Woman*	Georgia O'Dell
Eddie	John Fitzgerald	*Office Boy*	John Estes
Bud	Richard Selzer	*Sales Girl*	Gwen Seager
Mr. Randall	Hooper Atchley	*Policemen*	Mike Pat Donovan
Mrs. Daniels	Clara Macklin Blore		Jack Daley
Supervisor	Jason Robards, Sr.		

Even without star power, *Little Tough Guy* gives Warner Brothers' *Crime School* credible competition. While Warners treats the kids collectively, *Little Tough Guy* centers on Billy Halop's character — Johnny Boylan — and stays with him until he's rehabilitated.

Johnny has reason to distrust a society that saw fit to kill his father, whose guilt was never really proven. The Boylans are forced to move into cheaper digs in a seedy part of the East Side. Kay, Johnny's sister, is fired from her job and resorts to burlesque dancing. She avoids her former fiancé, Paul Wilson, even though he is only too happy to empty his wallet on the Boylan kitchen table.

More is required of Halop than in any other film. At first he's untroublesome, not the type to lead a gang of criminal youths. The change comes when he reads about his dad in the newspaper.

"Here's your headline, fellas," Johnny mumbles to his newsboys pals. "Innocent man goes to chair."

Johnny changes. He becomes a young man charged with the challenge of saving his father's life. But Judge Knox, like Judge Griswald in *Dead End*, refuses to be lenient. Frustrated, Johnny throws a brick through the judge's car window, and thus his life of crime begins.

Huntz Hall does an excellent job in his most important and toughest kid acting role.

Billy Halop and Helen Parrish in *Little Tough Guy*.

His stunning performance as Johnny's partner makes us wonder why Hall was not given higher billing in subsequent films.

We meet Hall (Pig), a long-haired, wild-eyed adolescent, when Johnny claims his newspaper route.

"Jerk out of it and pass across the dough ya took," Pig demands.

Johnny refuses, beats Pig in a fistfight and declares leader of the gang.

Holed up in Guggenhiem's drugstore after a robbery, Johnny turns his gun on Pig, who begs Johnny to let him surrender to the cops waiting outside with guns drawn. Pig's agony and fear is expressed through in his voice and body movements as he slides down against the wall. Johnny lets him go. The cops fire and Pig falls to his death.

While the desperation theme clearly comes through, the impact would have been far greater had Johnny fought it out with the police as does "Baby Face" Martin, and been killed. We care more about Johnny Boylan than we do about Pig.

Little Tough Guy's other message is that environment is not the sole cause of crime; everyone has the ability to distinguish between right and wrong. The character of Cyril Gerrard is an example. Sharply played by Jackie Searl, he meets the kids at the Young Americans Onward and Upward League. He's well-dressed, rich and bored with life. He provides the kids with money, transportation and shelter as they go from robbery to robbery. He asks for

Peggy Stewart gives Halop a lick of an ice-cream cone in *Little Tough Guy*.

Bernard Punsly, Billy Halop, Hally Chester, Jackie Searl, David Gorcey, Gabe Dell and Huntz Hall in *Little Tough Guy*.

nothing in return; he's doing it for the ride. The message: Wealth is meaningless without a close family that cares.

What does *The New York Times* say?

"If there is still a message to be delivered in this package, at least it would be more effective had the boys been kept bitter and forbidding, as they originally were."*

Cyril proves that not every criminal hails from poverty, and Rita Belle, Johnny's girl-friend, proves that not every poverty-stricken youth will end up a criminal. When the judge asks her if Johnny ever gave her anything, meaning money, Rita misunderstands, and says, "Yes, he gave me an ice cream cone once." It's a wonderfully innocent, romantic moment. She sees only good in Johnny Boylan, even with a gun in his hand.

Personal relationships are relatively well-handled and contribute to the development of the characters. Johnny is basically a shy boy who cannot get himself to say the words "I love you" to little Rita Belle. Instead, he whittles the words in a wooden plaque and places it on her lap just before he jumps onto a moving truck taking him to his new home.

On the whole, the picture is well-paced, and uncommonly unpredictable. That *New York Times* review saw it differently:

*New York Times, *August 18, 1938, page 23.*

"[T]he kids are compelled by Universal to confront substantially the same social barriers and get over them in substantially the same as they did for Mr. Goldwyn in *Dead End* and for Warner Brothers in *Crime School*."

Not really.

Little Tough Guys in Society

Released November 1938; 63 minutes; Universal; Director, Erle C. Kenton; Producer, Max H. Gordon; Sreenplay, Edward Eliscu, Mortimer Offner; Opened at the Rivoli.

CAST

Dr. Trenkle	Mischa Auer		*Footman*	David Oliver
Mrs. Berry	Mary Boland		*Danny*	Frankie Thomas
Oliver	Edward Everett Horton		*Sailor*	Harris Berger
			Murphy	Hally Chester
Penny	Helen Parrish		*Monk*	Charles Duncan
Randolph	Jackie Searl		*Yap*	David Gorcey
Jane	Peggy Stewart		*Trouble*	William Benedict
Uncle Buck	Harold Huber			

Little Tough Guys in Society, the first of three Little Tough Guys films without any original Dead End Kids, marked the beginning of splinter gangs and Universal's tenacity to capitalize on the "Kids craze." It's also interweaves comedy and drama, a style more fully realized by the Bowery Boys.

Blessed with a variety of prissy characters and rowdy kids, *Little Tough Guys in Society* is the lightest film to date. Whereas in *Dead End*, the rich would like to see the poor simply disappear, here the rich, namely Mrs. Berry, on the advice of her son's psychiatrist, Dr. Trenkle (and against the advice of her butler, Oliver), invites the wild street urchins to her country estate to breathe life into her melancholy son, Randolph, who refuses to get out of bed.

Jackie Searl, making his final appearance in the series, convincingly portrays an obnoxious spoiled rich kid, determined to make the kids' stay as unpleasant as possible.

The confrontations between the kids and Randolph keep the film alive. Their tit-for-tat gags are amusing, surprising, and handled well by the camera. There are other good moments with some female involvement. The youths are invited onto Penny's sailboat, where her friends bask in the sun.

"What does your old man do?" Sailor asks Jane.

"Oh, my father is in ladies' underwear," she innocently answers.

"Yeah? He must sure look funny."

Edward Everett Horton, as the prudent butler Oliver, teaches them how to dance, and the proper etiquette when asking a lady to dance.

The kids have their own version.

"Hey, babe, ya dancin'?"

"Are you askin'?"

"Yeah, I'm askin'."

Left to right: Frankie Thomas, Hally Chester, Charles Duncan, Edward Everett Horton, Harris Berger, David Gorcey and Billy Benedict in *Little Tough Guys in Society*.

"Then I'm dancin'."

Oliver shows them how to bow and say, "May I please have the honor of this dance?" But at the party, under the watchful eyes of Oliver, Monk approaches a girl in the manner he was taught, and she answers, "Sure, mate, let's hit it!"

Mary Boland is annoying as the fast-talking dowager Mrs. Berry, whose biggest concern in life is fussing over petty affairs such as the timing of the surprise party.

There are some items that would have best been omitted. Too much time is spent on the shower scene in which the kids horde the entire bathroom. There is an over-abundance of horseplay with Danny slapping his pals to keep them in line. This detracts from their authenticity, an important aspect of this series which these filmmakers seem to forget.

While Danny, adequately played by Frankie Thomas, is the leader and has the most to say in the film, Sailor has his moments with Jane on the boat; Monk mixes with the girls at the party; Yap and Murphy do a dance routine for Oliver; and Trouble begins the kids' trip with his terrific telephone impersonation of a butler, and ends it by swiping a roast turkey before the police haul them into the car to take them back to the city.

Nothing really "happens" in *Little Tough Guys in Society* until Uncle Buck visits the kids at the Berry residence. Danny senses that his uncle is planning to raid Randolph's party and tells him to drop the idea. Uncle Buck tells Danny to mind his own business.

Eating, Little Tough Guys style. Left to right, standing: Hally Chester, Frankie Thomas, and Harris Berger. Sitting: David Gorcey, Billy Benedict, and Charles Duncan.

In the end, Randolph is the hero. He sneaks up behind Buck and hits him on the head with a vase.

Unlike the previous film, desperation is not a theme. Rather, by casting such "name" actors as Mischa Auer, Mary Boland and Edward Everett Horton, the producers experiment with comedy, and for this film, it works.

But not for the *New York Times* reviewer, Frank Nugent: "Mischa Auer, Mary Boland and Edward Everett Horton put up with the nonsense with splendid patience. Ours was exhausted in the first five minutes."

Obviously, not a fan.

Publicity Shot for *Little Tough Guys in Society* with Helen Parrish. Top, left to right: Billy Benedict, Charles Duncan. Bottom, left to right: David Gorcey, Harris Berger, Parrish, Frankie Thomas and Hally Chester.

Newsboys' Home

Released January 1939; Universal; Director, Harold Young; Screenplay, Gordon Kahn; From a story written in collaboration with Charles Grayson; Associate Producer, Ken Goldsmith; opened at Central Stage.

CAST

"Rifle" Edwards	Jackie Cooper		Murphy	Hally Chester
Perry Warner	Edmund Lowe		Monk	Charles Duncan
Gwen Dutton	Wendy Barrie		Yap	David Gorcey
Frankie Barber	Edward Norris		Trouble	William Benedict
Howard Price Dutton	Samuel S. Hinds		O'Dowd	Harry Beresford
Tom Davenport	Irving Pichel		Bartsch	Horace MacMahon
Danny	Elisha Cook, Jr.		Hartley	George McKay
Sailor	Harris Berger			

After Nebraska Sherrif Edwards is killed, his son "Rifle" Edwards throws his fate to the winds and ends up at the Newsboys' Home, a charity home for the Little Tough Guys in New York, sponsored by the *Globe* newspaper. When the publisher dies, his daughter Gwen Dutton assumes the job and the paper takes a nose dive. Her far-out ideas about how to run the paper force star reporter Perry Warner to work instead at the *Star Journal*, owned by crafty politician Tom Davenport. Davenport also hires mobster Frankie Barber. Financially wrecked and realizing her mistake, Gwen asks Perry to come back and assume the editorship of the newspaper. Soon the *Globe* is back on top.

Universal's *Newsboys' Home* crosses paths with Warner Brothers' *They Made Me a Criminal*. Both were released in January 1939; both protagonists, played by Jackie Cooper and John Garfield respectively, trek across country, one west to east, the other east to west.

One of the ways Gwen Dutton, played by the lovely Wendy Barrie (*Dead End*'s Kay), changes direction is fleetingly mentioned in pass-

Charles Duncan, who died young during a cross-country trip.

ing by one of the kids: "European problems, who cares?" Local murder sells papers. This film was made in 1938, the time of Hitler and America's isolationist policy. Newspapers were burying news of European atrocities on page 20. Gwen Dutton was putting it on page 1. In retrospect, everyone else had it wrong, Gwen got it right.

Newsboys' Home is a patient film, guiding us through the *Globe*'s demise. Barber's men set fire to truckloads of *Globe* newspapers, smash newsstands and literally pull the *Globe* out of newsboys' hands, replacing them with the *Star Journal*. The *Globe* is forced to stop refunding the boys for unsold papers. Next, the shelter stops serving food. Finally, advertisers pull their ads and the shelter closes. All the boys, except for "Rifle" and Sailor, get jobs with the *Star Journal*.

The film cleverly culminates with "Rifle" coming face to face with Barber, the man who also killed his father. A swarm of kids arrive in the nick of time to save "Rifle" and turn Barber over to the police.

To be sure, there are things about this film that are questionable. For example, how "Rifle"'s father, an experienced sheriff, got himself killed. It was well-known that Barber was dangerous. We have no idea how he's apprehended, but there he is sitting alone with the sheriff, who's removing his handcuffs so Barber can be fingerprinted. The second his hands are free, Barber takes the old sheriff's gun and shoots him. Duh!

When "Rifle" first arrives at the home, he tells everyone he's hungry but the boys won't give him a bite until he fights the toughest guy there. Miraculously, he knocks the guy out on an empty stomach.

Two scenes can be left out entirely, the hospital room scene where the boys are reading Sailor a fairy tale; and the mock trial scene where Sailor's guilt (he told the crooked members of the *Star* about their secret meeting) is pretty much decided before the trial begins.

The Little Tough Guys starred with Jackie Cooper in *Newsboys' Home.* Top, left to right: Hally Chester, Cooper, David Gorcey. Bottom, left to right: Harris Berger, Charles Duncan and Billy Benedict.

There are some corny-cutesy lines such as Warner to Davenport: "I'd rather see a .45 in your hand than a decent newspaper." And Gwen to Perry: "This is between you, me and the linotype."

Jackie Cooper and Elisha Cook, Jr., never do another Kids film but both were stars *before* this picture and became bigger stars *after* this picture, well into the 1980s. In 1971, Cook found himself next to Huntz Hall on the TV show *The Chicago Teddy Bears.*

In retrospect, *Newsboys' Home* is rich in historic content. The first Newsboys' Home was founded in St. Louis in February 1906 by Father Peter J. Dunne: it provided shelter, food, clothing and education to as many as 200 boys at a time through the 1930s. The home was supported in part by the boys themselves through the sale of a weekly *Journal.* Coincidentally, Father Dunne died in 1939, the year *Newsboys' Home* was released.*

Coincidentally, other related events took place at the time of this film's release. The Brace Memorial Newsboys Home in New York boasted of giving 100 homeless boys Christmas dinners. Some of the attendees seemed to have followed similar paths as "Rifle" Edwards, making

www.fatherdunnes.com

Scene from *Newsboys' Home*. Hally Chester is on the left; others unidentified.

their way from other parts of the country such as Louisville, Kentucky, and Georgia to the welcoming arms of New York and financier Thomas W. Lamont, who sponsored the dinner.*

And in Ithaca, Michigan, Judge Kelly Searl (perhaps related to actor Jackie Searl?) ruled that the newspaper *The State Journal* could not terminate its contract with a 13-year-old newsboy because his job did not fall under the purview of the Federal Fair Labor Standards Act of 1938 with regard to age limitation. Parts of the judge's brief seem to apply to the Little Tough Guys. "[The Act] will result in the filling by the coming generations of the reformatory institutions and prisons ... failure of parents to teach children to perform reasonable labor ... is the prime cause of the wave of crime in this country...."†

A far cry from the comedy and the smallness of the previous Little Tough Guy film, this film is serious and socially significant.

The *New York Times* reviewer Bosley Crowther was not so charitable; on January 23, 1939, he reported: *Newsboys' Home* receives so many verbal tomatoes from the audience that it would be unsporting of us to add anything to the barrage."

---

*New York Times, *December 26, 1938, page 3, "100 Homeless Boys Guests of Lamont."*
†New York Times, *January 1, 1939, page 7, "Newsboy Is Ruled Beyond Wage Law."*

Code of the Streets

Released April 1939; 72 minutes; Universal; Director, Harold Young; Associate Producer, Burt Kelly; Original Screenplay, Arthur T. Horman; Art Director, Jack Otterson; Photography, Elwood Bredell.

CAST

Lt. Lewis	Harry Carey	*Lt. Carson*	Monte Montague
Bob Lewis	Frankie Thomas	*Lt. Welles*	William Ruhl
Danny Shay	James McCallion	*Lab Man*	Rex Lipton
Chick Foster	Leon Ames	*Reception Guard*	Wade Boteler
Cynthia	Juanita Quigley	*Joe*	Bert Roach
Thomas Shay	Paul Fix	*Mrs. Flaherty*	Mary Gordon
Halstead	Marc Lawrence	*Visiting Guest*	Pat Flaherty
Mildred	Dorothy Arnold	*Sailor*	Harris Berger
Sticky Winston	El Brendel	*Murph*	Hally Chester
Young Man	Stanley Hughes	*Monk*	Charles Duncan
Second Guard	Eddy Chandler	*Trouble*	William Benedict
Doorman	James Flavin	*Yap*	David Gorcey

Code of the Streets introduces the falsely-accused-big-brother theme (Monogram runs with it in *their* first East Side Kids film, *East Side Kids*, and later in *Mr. Wise Guy*). There's also the reformed-big-brother motif such as in the very next Little Tough Guys film *Call a Messenger* and the second East Side Kids flick, *Boys of the City*.

Big brother Thomas Shay gets picked up for the murder of Lt. Carson after playing poker with some strangers. It was his gun that killed the lieutenant; the other poker players lie about Shay playing poker all night. They say it was Tommy who left earlier, not a guy named Denver Collins.

In the popular method of moving the story along through flashes of newspaper headlines, we learn from the *Press Herald, Daily Globe, Daily Star and Daily Herald* that Tommy is convicted of first degree murder and sentenced to die. (Were there such newspapers in New York City in 1939?)

Tommy's two prison scenes with his younger brother Danny are full of Tommy's rage, regret for the kind of life he lived, and pleads for his brother to leave the squalid neighborhood of Front Street that breeds only hopelessness.

Angry and depressed, Danny returns to Front Street where his gang heroically steals a dime from a harmless kid from Sharp Street.

Cut to the home of Lt. Lewis, the arresting officer, who now believes Tommy is innocent and is demoted to beat cop for raising the issue. His son Bob, a ham radio buff, picks up the investigation where his father left off. He meets up with the Little Tough Guys and their joint investigation leads them to Chick Foster's gambling establishment.

One good thing about this film is that it's solely the kids' detective work that outsmarts the bad guys. Planting an electronic devises in Foster's office, the kids learn that Denver Collins killed Carson. As Foster leaves, the kids pull up with a taxicab and take him to their hideout. Blindfolded, Foster believes he is about to be tortured with boiling water (the kids dump ice in it before the torture begins) and confesses to killing Carson.

Frankie Thomas, who plays Bob Lewis, was on the other end of a fake torture scene a

Publicity shot for *Code of the Streets*. Left to right: Monte Montague, Paul Fix, James McCallion and Harry Carey.

few months later when he joined the Dead End Kids in *Angels Wash Their Faces*. There, the Dead End Kids make the blindfolded youth think they're going to set his body on fire by making him smell kerosene (then dump water on him) and starting a "fire" (rustling their hands in cellophane).

The ham radio as a tool to fight crime is used again in a much later Bowery Boys film, *Triple Trouble*. In that film, Whitey, played by Billy Benedict, is the ham radio operator. Here, Benedict plays Trouble.

Comic relief is in the form of El Brendel, a Philadelphia-born vaudeville comedian who plays a Swedish buffoon. Here he's a street vendor trying to remember the description of Denver Collins that Bob Lewis just gave him. "Let's see, he's ten foot five, 150 pot marks and curled fingernails." He plays the same character in the next film, *Call a Messenger*, and in the following year's *Gallant Sons* with Jackie Cooper and Leo Gorcey.

James McCallion, who we never see again in any Kids film, plays gang leader Danny Shay. In fact, hardly anyone sees him again. He made four pictures in 1939 and then disappeared from the screen. He re-emerges in 1954 in *Vera Cruz*, plays a valet in Alfred Hitchcock's *North by Northwest* and a room clerk in *Coogan's Bluff*. *Code of the Streets* may have been McCallion's finest hour.

The final scene of *Code of the Streets* is full of disturbing contradictions. Tommy Shay is released from prison and arrives back on Front Street. He gives the boys a quick hello and thanks, then heads off to the bar, as if those gut-wrenching speeches he made to his brother were just an act. But it gets worse. Bob Lewis, who is a good kid with a good upbringing, is given permission by his father, the reinstated lieutenant, to hang out with the Little Tough Guys. And what's the first thing these five kids do? Beat up on a kid from another neighborhood. And Bob, who had been the victim of the kids beating earlier in the film, and who should know better, joins in the beating.

Up until now, at the end of each Little Tough Guys film, there is at least some hope that the kids are on the right path. Here, they're back where their started. Worse, because after all they've seen and done, they've learned absolutely nothing.

Call a Messenger

Released November 3, 1939; 65 minutes; Universal; Director, Arthur Lubin; Producer, Ken Goldsmith; Screenplay, Arthur T. Horman; Original story, Sally Sandlin, Michael Kraike; Photography, Elwood Bredell; Editor, Charles Maynard; Music, Hans J. Salter; Art Director, Jack Otterson; Sound, Bernard B. Brown. Opened at the Rialto

CAST

Jimmy Hogan	Billy Halop	*Virginia*	Kay Sutton
Pig	Huntz Hall	*Cop*	James Morton
Kirk Graham	Robert Armstrong	*Sweeney*	Sherwood Bailey
Marge Hogan	Mary Carlisle	*Clerk*	Joe Ray
Frances O'Neil	Anne Nagel	*Miss Clarington*	Ruth Rickaby
Ed Hogan	Victor Jory	*Barber*	Frank Mitchell
Chuck Walsh	Larry "Buster" Crabbe	*Desk Sergeant*	James Farley
Baldy	El Brendel	*Cop*	Frank O'Connor
Bob Prichard	Jimmy Butler	*Clerk*	Lyle Moraine
Big Lip	George Offerman	*Kid*	Payne Johnson
Trouble	William Benedict	*Paymaster*	Jack Gardner
Yap	David Gorcey	*Police Officer*	Kernan Cripps
Al	Jimmy O'Gatty	*Watchman*	Russ Powell
Nail	Joe Gray	*Butler*	Wilson Benge
Gardner	Anthony Hughes	*Black Maid*	Louise Franklin
Sgt. Harrison	Cliff Clark	*Sailor*	Harris Berger
		Murph	Hally Chester

Jimmy Hogan is given the choice of job or jail after he gets caught robbing the Postal Union warehouse. Grudgingly but smugly he agrees to be a messenger boy for Kirk Graham (*King Kong*'s Robert Armstrong), the man he punched out at the warehouse. Subplot #1: Jimmy stops his sister Marge from going out with thug Chuck ("Buster" Crabbe) Walsh by inviting his buttoned-down boss Bob Prichard to dinner; Subplot #2: Jimmy keeps his freshly-released-from-jail older brother Ed from getting mixed up with Chuck and his thugs who are on a roll knocking off Postal Union outlets, no thanks to big mouth Jimmy who boasts about the cash that's put in the vault every night. Conflicted Ed gets shot after tipping off

Halop "convincing" Hall he should be a messenger too, in *Call a Messenger*. Billy Benedict, Hally Chester, David Gorcey and Harris Berger look on.

Little Tough Guy Jimmy about a planned robbery. The kids prevent the robbery, with Jimmy jumping onto the driver side of the getaway car and steering it smack into a storefront window. For a reward, the kids are given motorcycles.

Call a Messenger is the first Universal picture that combines the antics of the Little Tough Guys with the rowdiness of the Dead End Kids. What does that mean?

Brief recap: Universal's first film, *Little Tough Guy*, starred the Dead End Kids (*sans* Leo Gorcey and Bobby Jordan) plus David Gorcey and Hally Chester. The term "Little Tough Guys" was not in the credits. But the next three films featured the "Little Tough Guys" only in the credits, i.e., Hally Chester, Harris Berger, David Gorcey and William (Billy) Benedict. None of the original six Dead End Kids is in these films. Now comes *Call a Messenger* where the credits read "Billy Halop and Huntz Hall of the 'Dead End Kids' and the 'Little Tough Guys' David Gorcey, Hally Chester, William Benedict, Harris Berger."

On November 11, 1939, *The New York Times*' Bosley Crowther prophetically put it this way: "It was probably a forgone conclusion that the Dead End Kids sooner or later would effect a merger with that apochryphal [apocryphal] hoodlum organization known as the Little Tough Guys. But the merger ... comes at a felicitous surprise, nevertheless and this *review may one day achieve a measure of immortality* [italics added] by announcing that the big combination has finally been completed." The day has come.

Tough guy Halop takes it on the chin from sister Mary Carlisle in *Call a Messenger*.

The film is also a loose hybrid sequel to *Little Tough Guy* and *Code of the Streets*. As in *Little Tough Guy*, Halop is the gang leader whose father is dead, and Hall resurrects his role as Pig, but more submissively. As in *Code of the Streets* the kids hang out on Front Street and beat up on two kids from Sharp Street.

No one escapes Jimmy Hogan's wrath. After getting angry at Graham and the police who arrest him, he smacks Pig, the only person waiting for him outside the police station. He pushes, hits and nastily wipes the lipstick off his sister Marge because he doesn't like her going out with Chuck. He challenges his new boss to a fight in the alley because he makes him work; he beats up Pig, then beats up the rest of the gang, forcing them to take messenger jobs; he threatens to shoot his own brother if he tries to rob the Postal Union company. And of course, he gets into a fight with Chuck.

But in the end it's all good. Instead of fighting his boss in the alley, he invites him for dinner to meet his sister Marge, thereby keeping Chuck at bay. Aiming a gun at his brother motivates Ed to turn on Chuck and helps prevent the robbery of the Postal Union company. And the boys, told by Jimmy that the messenger job is just a breeze, are all the better off, even though at the end of the first day, with their feet soaking in hot water, Pig yells at him, "This ain't no breeze, it's a tornado!"

There are some comical moments. When Pig rides his bike into Sailor, Sailor turns to him and says, "Can't you see where you're going, are you blind?'

"I hit you, didn't I?" Pig retorts.

Baldy (El Brendel) has been a messenger boy for 38 years. "What if they fire you?" Dopey asks.

"That's all right. I knew when I got the job it wouldn't be steady."

We also hear our second malapropism. It's a twist on the first one, heard ten months earlier in *They Made Me a Criminal.* In that film, the kids are sent to Arizona to get "debilitated." Here, Halop says the job is supposed to "rebilitate" him.

There's some above-par photography here, especially in the opening scene. It begins with eerie shadows of moving figures on the walls, then segues to each kid as Jimmy shines a flashlight on their faces. Later, there's a superimposed city scene giving the impression that Jimmy and Ed have been walking all through the city.

Wasted in this film is "Buster" (*Tarzan, Flash Gordon*) Crabbe, whose role and performance anyone could match.

For the most part, *Call a Messenger* is structurally sound. It builds the characters, sets the scene, then introduces the next layer of conflict when big brother Ed is released from prison and challenges Jimmy's loyalties.

But there are loose ends. During the robbery, Ed gets shot and we never find out if he dies or survives. Nor do we find out if Bob recovers from an assault during a robbery.

And what happens to the kids? Do they move on or become another Baldy? *The New York Times* made a prediction: "We would not be surprised if [Halop] takes up Latin in the next installment."

You're Not So Tough

Released July 26, 1940; 65 minutes; Universal; Director, Joe May; Associate Producer, Ken Goldsmith; Screenplay, Arthur T. Horman; Based on the Story "Son of Mama Posita" by Maxwell Aley; Additional Writing, Brenda Weisberg; Photography, Elwood Bredell; Film Editor, Frank Gross; Music, Hans J. Salter; Art Director, Jack Otterson; Sound, Bernard B. Brown; Assistant Director, Phil Karlson. Opened at the Rialto.

CAST

Tommy Lincoln	Billy Halop	*Conley*	Don Rowan
Pig (Albert)	Huntz Hall	*Valley Truck Driver*	Ralph
Rap	Bobby Jordan		Dunn
Ape	Bernard Punsly	*Guard*	Kernan Cripps
String	Gabe Dell	*Jorgenson*	Eddie Phillips
Millie	Nan Grey	*Pickers*	Harry Humphreys,
Salvatore	Henry Armetta		Marty Faust,
Mama Posita	Rosina Galli		Ralph LaPere
Griswald	Cliff Clark	*Worker*	Frank Bischell
Collins	Joe King	*Store Proprietor*	Heinie Conklin
Marshall	Arthur Loft	*Truck Driver*	Harry Strang
Lacey	Harry Hayden	*Carstens*	Ed Peil, Sr.
Les	Eddy Waller	*Little Tough Guys*	David Gorcey, Hally
Bianca	Evelyn Selbie		Chester, Harris
Brakeman	Joe Whitehead		Berger

This film is outside the box. Instead of being rooted in New York, with the leader living at home with an older sister, the kids are rootless and homeless in Southern California, panhandling and playing with crooked dice for dough.

How did they get here? We learn very little, except that Tommy (Halop's name for the remaining Little Tough Guys films, except for the serials where it's Billy) grew up in an orphanage in California. We can only assume the same for the others.

After landing in jail for cheating at dice and getting into a fight with the locals, the kids are sent to Mama Posita's Ranch to work, something they loathe to do. Tommy takes advantage of Mama Posita's kindness by deluding her into thinking he might be her long-lost son. Soon he's living in her house, wearing nice clothes and put in charge of the workers. His goal is to steal her stash of cash. But when Mama Posita not only shows him where she hides her money but gives it to him to buy a car, he has a change of heart. He becomes her advocate in her fight against the Calato Valley Growers Association, who are out to destroy her crops before they go to market.

"We don't want foreigners to run a farm that encourages trouble makers and agitators," they tell her. Mama Posita pays her workers higher wages than the other ranch owners do, and they're afraid their workers will want the same. The Association retaliates. They refuse to grant her a loan, and refuse to provide her with trucks to bring her crops to market. When she calls an outside trucking company, the Association surreptitiously destroys the bridge leading to her farm and tie up the back road with idle trucks. If Mama Posita's crops don't get to market soon, they'll rot.

Here's where Tommy makes good on the film's title. Instead of stealing her cash horde, Tommy uses it to buy two of the idle trucks, gets the workers to load the produce, then bulldozes his way through the idle trucks while spraying kerosene on anyone getting in his way.

For the first time Halop is romantically inclined. He's smitten by Millie, the very pretty soup-kitchen girl (Nan Grey from *Dracula's Daughter* [1936] and *The Invisible Man Returns* [1940]. She's understandably unimpressed with his line, "I do things the smart way. I work with my brains, that's how I'll get places." She sees where it's got him so far and gives him the brush-off. But the wind of a speeding train does magic and he manages to sneak in a hug and kiss. Mama Posita does her unsubtle best as well, squeezing them together as they drive to town to face the wrath of the fruit growers' association. In the end, Millie sees that Halop does use his brains in coming to Mama Posita's rescue.

Except for Hall (still Pig, but we learn his real name is Albert), the other Dead End Kids add meager comic moments, nothing more. Some of it is embarrassing, especially when they dance with the male mannequins. And the three Little Tough Guys? Their presence is of absolutely no consequence. They hardly interact. Their names are not even in the credits.

The last scene is not on the kids, as it usually is, but on Mama Posita, telling the sheriff she realizes Tommy is not her son, but watches with pride as he and the kids drive off to the market to sell her stock.

Up until now, the running social theme is that society has suppressed the kids' will to change but, given the chance, they'll do good. Here the social commentary takes a turn. The kids are just not interested in work; they work hard avoiding work. Here, the social theme is prejudice against foreign-born Americans, a timely topic during a period when America's immigration policy was being revisited as a result of the changes in Europe.

As usual, *New York Times* reviewer Bosley Crowther missed that. All he saw was "an obvious little fable about a juvenile hoodlum ... boys can be boisterous just so long and then it's time some one should take a stick to them" (July 9, 1940).

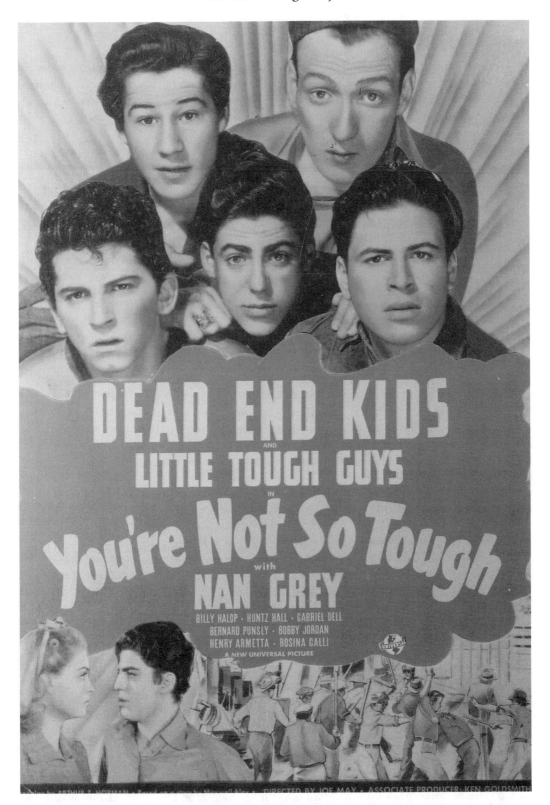

Poster for *You're Not So Tough.*

Junior G-Men

Serial, 12 Chapters; Universal; Directors, Ford Beebe, John Rawlins; Associate Producer, Henry MacRae; Original Screenplay, George H. Plympton, Basil Dickey, Rex Taylor; Photography, Jerome Ash; Editors, Alvin Todd, Loui Sackin, Joseph Glick; Art Director, Ralph DeLacy; August 1940.

CAST

Billy Barton	Billy Halop		*Brand*	Cy Kendall
Gyp	Huntz Hall		*Harry Trent*	Kenneth Howell
Terry	Gabriel Dell		*Severn*	Ben Taggart
Lug	Bernard Punsly		*Corey*	Victor Zimmerman
Jim Bradford	Phillip Terry		*Evans*	Edgar Edwards
Midge	Roger Daniels		*Foster*	Gene Rizzi
Buck	Kenneth Lundy		*Mary*	Florence Halop
Sailor	Harris Berger		*Flaming Torch*	Ralph Peters
Murph	Hally Chester		*Member*	
Col. Barton	Russell Hicks			

CHAPTER 1—"ENEMIES WITHIN"

This serial is about the disappearance of Col. Barton, inventor of a deadly explosive. His son Billy is leader of the Little Tough Guys, who join forces with a group of Junior G-Men for the dual purpose of finding the missing inventor-dad and destroying an anarchist gang called the Order of the Flaming Torch. There you go.

The serial is quick to portray Billy Barton as a gutsy, independent individual. Similar to how Muggs McGinnis in *Pride of the Bowery* (also written by George Plympton) saves Al (Kenneth Howell, who also plays Harry Trent) from being crushed under a falling tree, Billy tackles his pal Terry out of the path of a moving automobile.

The first two minutes of this quarter-hour episode are big on simple camera technique and editing, keeping the action and the story moving as fast as possible. Precision and plausibility are thrown to the wind. This photographic style remains throughout the serial.

When we meet the kids, they are causing as much mischief as the Dead End Kids in *Angels with Dirty Faces*—stealing fruit, throwing ice cream in a man's face, and causing a car accident which triggers a fight between two drivers. Billy gets arrested.

When he's brought to FBI headquarters and told his life may be in danger because his father has been captured by the Order of the Flaming Torch, the organization that's plotting to overthrow our existing social order, Billy retorts, "I can take care of myself."

These are the very words he utters in *Crime School* after being lashed by the vicious superintendent Morgan (also played by Cy Kendall).

The camera presents an unrealistic sense of time. While the kids are at the FBI headquarters, Brand, leader of the Order, learns of Billy's arrest through a newspaper story and plans to kidnap him when he leaves the FBI headquarters.

Too much is learned and too much happens in too short a time. Nevertheless, the kidnapping triggers an action-packed sequence that leaves the audience hanging until the next episode. Brand's men grab Billy and pull him into the elevator. Harry Trent jumps into the elevator car too. The photographic impression is that the elevator has suddenly lost control

Menacing the public in *Junior G-Men*. Left to right: first two actors unidentified, Billy Halop (partially hidden), Gabe Dell (in striped shirt), Huntz Hall (with upturned cap brim), Kenneth Lundy (back row, foreground), Harris Berger (back row, obscured), Bernard Punsly (next to wall, in cap).

and is plummeting to the ground while Billy and Harry are fighting their captors inside the car. (A similar affair takes place in an airplane in Chapter 9.)

CHAPTER 2—"THE BLAST OF DOOM" AND CHAPTER 3—"HUMAN DYNAMITE"

If Billy's survival of the falling elevator is an indication of how the kids overcome the next ten pending disasters, it is doubtful the cliffhanger endings were what brought the loyal Dead End Kids fans back to theaters every week. The elevator lands with little damage and no injuries, Barton and Trent quickly overpower the enemy agent, Trent pushes a few buttons and the elevator is on its way up.

More appealing than the cliffhangers is watching the kids be arrogant and disrespectful to the police ("Listen flatfoot, the government or the cops never did nothin' for me!").

In contrast to the first episode, Chapter 2 is slow-moving with people spending a lot of time waiting. Two Torch agents drive through the East Side neighborhood in a conspicuous car waiting for the kids to turn up so that they might kidnap them. The agents do too many thoughtless things. Instead of one remaining in the car while the other makes a telephone call, both go to make the call, leaving the car vulnerable to Little Tough Guy pranks. Terry

Tasting the "free samples" in *Junior G-Men*. Left to right: Huntz Hall, Billy Halop, Kenneth Lundy, Harris Berger, Bernard Punsly and Gabriel Dell.

rips off the ignition cable. While the agents wait for their mechanic, Billy and Gyp lie in wait. When another truck comes to pick up the agents, Billy and Gyp jump in the back.

It is ironic that while Billy and Gyp are on Flaming Torch territory, they miss being shot at, survive an explosion and sneak a ride out in the same truck, and they are never spotted. Except for Col. Barton's demonstration of his explosive, a highly dramatic moment since Billy and Terry are hiding in the building where the demonstration will take place, the kids are not in any real danger.

Since the filmmakers do not prepare the audience to anticipate the shooting of Gyp, there is no sense of danger, no build-up of excitement. Thus the opportunity to maximize the intensity is missed. The only way we know that Gyp has been hit is that Billy is carrying him. But a moment later Gyp is on his feet, as wild as ever.

CHAPTER 4—"BLAZING DANGER," CHAPTER 5—"TRAPPED BY TRADERS" AND CHAPTER 6—"TRAITORS TREACHERY"

Chapters 4, 5and 6 are chock-full of loose ends and snarls and seem more eager to hasten the friendship between the Little Tough Guys and the Junior G-Men than advancing the

Halop in a literal "cliff hanger" in *Junior G-Men*. Other two actors are unidentified.

plot. Harry invites them to lunch, but like several other events that gets lost in the shuffle, lunch never takes place. Instead, the next scene has Harry and Billy bound to chairs. The FBI show their incompetence, particularly Jim Bradford. He is suckered by Evans, who promises to show him where the blueprints are kept if his handcuffs are removed. Bradford obliges and Evans escapes. This is no surprise to the audience, only to Jim Bradford. Harry and Billy, on the other hand, find the blueprints.

Ineptitude rules when Bradford does not heed Billy's suggestion to go after the "Torchy" who drove the car. ("That's only one of them. We can bag the whole lot of them if you tell us where that hideout is.") Even if Billy and Gyp knew where that hideout was (the truck they were in was windowless), it would still make more sense to get one crook who could tell them a lot more than the kids could do. What renders this segment particularly corny is the confidence Bradford has in his own judgment, displayed by the intonation of his voice. In the end, the FBI not only misses getting the one "Torchy" but all four who return, intent on spiriting away Billy. The kids, hiding behind a huge stone, ward them off by throwing rocks. The FBI do nothing but hide.

FBI incompetence is matched by the absurdity of the Flaming Torch tattoos. They serve only as targets for their enemies. Without them they could blend in as respectable citizens.

After being hit too many times with rocks, the "Torchies" take off. A siren is heard and a police car appears. The police seem to anticipate trouble but how they know there's trouble out on a country road is puzzling. Even Bradford is surprised to see them. Nevertheless he quickly tells the police who he is (without proving it with proper identification) and commands them to chase the fleeing car, which they do. And we never hear from them again.

Back at FBI headquarters, Gyp complains he hurt his leg during a crash. Bradford looks at the leg and strongly recommends that he see a doctor. A close-up of Billy's face shows he's annoyed and does not believe a doctor is necessary. ("He don't have to go to no clinic. I know a vet three blocks away.")

The final scene is similar to the one that left us hanging in Chapter 2: Col. Barton demonstrating his explosive. Once again we are treated to an explanation about its combustibility before the chapter leaves us in the middle of an explosion in close proximity of our heroes. The repetitiveness of these endings shows how little the plot has advanced.

Disaster is the series' strong point and is quickly foreshadowed by a passing reference Brand makes about explosives "in number eight." The reference could easily be overlooked since "number eight" at this point could be anything from a baseball field to a dog house. It hasn't been identified to the audience. When Brand gets wind that "number eight" has been discovered by the FBI and decides to destroy it, he reveals a complex mechanism which detonates the explosives planted in "number eight." The shot of the apparatus is not a good one because Brand (Cy Kendall) is heavyset and stands most of the time between the camera and the machine. But we are treated to a grandiose view of a building imploding. Nevertheless, the kids and Bradford miraculously emerge from it.

Chapter 7—"Flaming Death," Chapter 8—"Hurdled Through Space" and Chapter 9—"The Plunge of Peril"

Absurd and unrealistic describe Chapters 7, 8 and 9. The best that can be said is that the rapid-fire escapades, frequently involving physical confrontations with the "Torchies," maintains the flick's fast pace. It's the unlikeliness of events linking these action-packed moments, and the lack of plot advancement, that try our patience.

In a long sequence where the kids and "Torchies" match wits and wallops, kid ingenuity is combined with script absurdity and unintentional comedy. Before we even have time to ask ourselves what the kids were doing in the building, they drive away. Soon they are caught.

Gyp and Lug storm the apartment. In the course of a brawl that takes Billy onto the fire escape fighting two "Torchies," the fire escape collapses and Billy falls to the ground. He mutters, "I could have beat up those two guys if that balcony didn't fall." Good macho image-boosting line, but something like "I think my leg is broken" would be more in order. Then, to add absurdity on top of absurdity, the kids carry Billy into an 18-wheel truck which happens to be parked right outside, and "commandeer" it. In spite of all the ruckus, Lug has the presence of mind to pickpocket a wallet from one of the "Torchies." From a single piece of paper inside this wallet, the kids acquire an incredible amount of information that demands immediate action. The airplane Prof. Farraday will take to the university is going to be hijacked in one half-hour. Harry and Billy concur that the only way to save the inventor of the "aerial torpedo" is to get on that airplane, beat up the pilot while the plane is in the air, then fly the plane back to the airport. We are not surprised at Billy's recklessness but Harry should have more sense than to pursue such a suicidal endeavor. The scene is poorly directed and poorly acted. While the kids engage the pilot in a lackadaisical fight in the back of the airplane, Prof. Farraday sits quietly in his seat either waiting for the fight to be over or for the plane, plunging nose first towards the ground, to crash.

CHAPTER 10—"THE TOLL OF TREASON," CHAPTER 11—"DESCENDING DOOM" AND CHAPTER 12—"THE POWER OF PATRIOTISM"

Not only is the airplane affair inconsequential but it is grossly obtuse in direction and script. The pilot is captured but no information is sought. This event, like all the rest, brings the kids no closer to locating the Flaming Torch hideout.

While Harry and Billy are fighting the pilot, Prof. Farraday picks up a gun from the floor (apparently it fell from the pilot's pocket) and knocks out the pilot. This is an odd move on the professor's part because from his point of view the pilot has done no wrong. It is the kids who are putting his life in danger. Harry takes control of the plane and the professor reclaims his seat, abnormally unperturbed by the whole affair and only mildly curious as to why it all took place. "Why should they want to make me a prisoner?" he asks himself.

Script inconsistency is obvious when the kids, through their astonishing detective work, discover that the Flaming Torch members hide out in a Chinese imports warehouse. If we recall Chapter 2, the hideout was on an estate in the country. Gyp and Terry spot a "Torchy" on the street and succeed only in getting a shoe. In his laboratory, Harry Trent finds rice embedded in the soles of the shoe. By comparing the rice with all the different brands of rice Merv buys for a nickel a bag, they learn that it is Chinese rice. Thus, it "follows" that the Flaming Torch hideout is in a Chinese imports warehouse.

Somehow Billy and Harry get into the warehouse without being seen and overhear Col. Barton being threatened behind a closed door. Gyp is taken prisoner (how he is caught is not shown). There is a lot of hiding, walking, sneaking, whispering. In addition to freeing Gyp and transmitting a message to the FBI from the Flaming Torch's own radio before more kids show up, the kids get caught, get free and finally engage the Torchies in a fistfight to end all fights, which the Torchies lose.

What is most disappointing is the moment we've been awaiting, that emotional reunion between father and son. It never takes place. The only interaction between them is a telephone call Billy gets from his father during the celebration party, telling him that he will be right over with food. The kids jump for joy over this and the serial is over.

Obvious flaws in direction, plot deficiencies, redundancy and superfluous events notwithstanding, the fast and plentiful action, accompanied by the ever-present quick-beat music contained enough pizzazz to make *Junior G-Men* a big hit with the kids of the 1940s. It cleared the way for two more serials, *Sea Raiders* (1941) and *Junior G-Men of the Air* (1942).

Give Us Wings

Released December 20, 1940; 62 minutes; Universal; Director, Charles Lamont; Associate Producer, Ken Goldsmith; Screenplay, Arthur T. Horman, Robert Lee Johnson; Based on the Story "Crop Dusters" by Eliot Gibbons; Photography, John Doyle; Film Editor, Frank Gross; Music Director, Charles Previn; Art Director, Jack Otterson; Assistant Director, Charles S. Gould; Costumes, Vera West. Opened at the Rialto.

CAST

Tom	Billy Halop		*Ape*	Bernard Punsly
Pig	Huntz Hall		*String*	Gabriel Dell

Rap	Bobby Jordan	*Bud*	Harris Berger
York	Wallace Ford	*Whitey*	James Flavin
Carter	Victor Jory	*Capt. Stern*	Addison Richards
Julie	Anne Gwynne	*Mammy*	Etta McDaniel
Tex	Milburn Stone	*Servant*	Paul White
Buzz	Shemp Howard	*Station Attendant*	Milton Kibbee
Link	William Benedict	*Forman*	Ben Lewis

Realizing their lack of scholastic achievement will prevent them from becoming pilots as long as they remain with the Civic Aeronautics Authority Youth Program, the kids eagerly accept an offer from Arnold Carter, a disreputable businessman, to fly his crop-dusting plane, its mechanical failings notwithstanding.

Carter's main foreman, York, refuses to send the boys up because he knows they're not ready. (The kids, of course, think they were born ready; "I got bird blood in me," declares Halop.) Fearing he may lose his clients, Carter offers Rap (Jordan) a pay raise to crop-dust a dangerous area surrounded by high trees. Rap accepts, crashes and dies.

Tommy (Halop) goes after Carter and engages him in a mixed vehicle chase. First, it's car vs. plane, then plane vs. crop duster. Halop dumps dust on Carter's open-air speeding car

Shemp Howard (second from left) and Paul White carrying Bobby Jordan in *Give Us Wings*. Also shown are Huntz Hall (left), Gabe Dell, Bernard Punsly and Billy Halop.

and blinds him. He's caught, beaten up by all the kids and convicted. York takes over the business and the kids agree to work and play by his rules.

Give Us Wings opens in a patriotic mood with marching band music and a scan of various planes earmarked for the war effort. The camera zooms in on a sign, "Safety First."

But within minutes, concerns for patriotism and safety are shattered as the five Dead End Kids drop tools on each other, spill oil deliberately, and generally smack each other around. They complain of not getting enough "air time" and feel that tooling with engines entitles them to fly. Clearly, they are in it for the thrill, not for love of country.

Halop's character Tommy could benefit from a few sessions in anger management. There is hardly a scene where he is not hitting someone or uttering an unkind word. Not just in this picture, but most of these Little Tough Guys films. (Could this be the reason he found it almost impossible to find acting roles when he returned from the armed service?) Unlike Hall and Jordan, whose characters display different moods and a variety of expressions, Halop's remains indignant. Pig gets so fed up he kicks Tommy off the truck.

Jordan, as Rap, is happy, sad, playful, shocked and annoyed, especially when Hall caresses his face. The third time Hall does this, Jordan proudly punches him out. He also has a death scene, done well enough, but we wonder why he walks into danger with eyes wide open? Early in the film he witnesses a pilot crash and burn to death. He notices the relic airplanes used for these crop-dusting flights, and observes, "This is a suicide club." At this point, one would high-tail it out of there. So why does Rap put himself in the same seat as that pilot he saw burned to death? It just doesn't ring true.

Another example of their poor judgment is thinking York is their enemy because he won't let them fly, and Carter their friend who wants them to fly prematurely. What do you say about a man who sends to the family of an employee killed while on the job, the balance of his paycheck less the cost of the plane he crashed?

The names of the two Little Tough Guys, Harris Berger and William Benedict, are buried in the cast list and they are not even identified as Little Tough Guys. The only thing they do is lick envelopes and stand to attention when York walks in, like he's an officer or a priest. Other than that, nothing.

There's a scene that tries to be funny, where Pig is continually being pushed off the bed when the other two roll over. When he finally finds an opening in the middle, the other two roll towards the center and push him out like toothpaste.

But what wins the award for most irrelevancy is the long-winded fish fry scene. It begins with all the kids groping for Julie (Anne Gwynne) but they lose to York, who steals her away from Rap and takes her to the fish fry. The fish fry starts out clean with music and square dancing, and degenerates to a brawl and food fight. Here the Huntz Hall character establishes himself as the guy who stands on the periphery of the fight, making strategic pinpoint strikes at the enemy. How does all this add to the plot? It doesn't.

The most impressive part of the film are the aerial shots with the kids' hair flying abound (why aren't they wearing helmets like the other pilots?) It gives a sense of the thrill of the flight even with the fake background.

Not surprisingly, *The New York Times* (in a November 21, 1940, review) didn't think much of this film. "[W]e'll wager audiences will find themselves in the embarrassing position of laughing involuntarily at the lunatic doings ... with planes which sound like a death wheeze every time they come into range of the microphone ... *Give Us Wings* [is a] contender for the title of the year's best bad picture."

Agreed. A better title would have been *Give Us a Break*.

Hit the Road

Released June 27, 1941; 61 minutes; Universal; Director, Joe May; Associate Producer, Ken Goldsmith; Screenplay, Robert Lee Johnson, Brenda Weisberg; Original story, Robert Lee Johnson; Photography, Jerome Ash; Film Editor, Bernard Burton; Music Director, Hans J. Salter; Art Director, Jack Otterson; Assistant, Harold H. MacArthur; Costumes, Vera West, Set Decorator, R.A. Gausman; Sound, Bernard B. Brown; Sound Engineer, William Heddock; Opened at the Rialto.

CAST

Molly Ryan	Gladys George	*Spike the Butcher*	Edward Pawley
James T. Ryan	Barton	*Pesky*	Bobs Watson
a.k.a. Valentine	MacLane	*Creeper*	John Harmon
Tom	Billy Halop	*Col. Smith*	Walter Kingsford
Pig	Huntz Hall	*Cathy Crookshank*	Eily Malyon
String	Gabriel Dell	*Rufus*	Jess Lee Brooks
Ape	Bernard Punsly	*Martin*	Charles Moore
Patience Ryan	Evelyn Ankers	*Sullivan, Chauffeur*	Charles Sullivan
Paul Revere Smith	Charles Lang	*Trusty*	Hally Chester
Dingbat	Shemp Howard	*O'Brien, First Guard*	Ernie Stanton

Feeling responsible for the death of the several men murdered by Spike the Butcher, the former head of the defunct Valentine Gang, James T. Ryan (a.k.a Valentine), just released from prison, assumes custody of the dead men's kids. At first the kids are thrilled, then crestfallen when they realize Valentine doesn't seek revenge on Spike as they do. What's worse, they may be forced to attend a trade school.

Unimpressed with Ryan's Green Meadows estate and what it has to offer (horseback riding, gardens, two servants, Ryan's beautiful daughter and a chance for a new lease on life), the kids make plans to escape this paradise so they can find and kill Spike. They get their wish, but not on their terms. Tommy is duped by Spike, and spills all about the $50,000 cash that's been collected for the trade school. Spike steals the money and somehow he and his gang find their way to Tommy's bedroom. Soon everyone's in Tommy bedroom. A brawl erupts in which the women score the most points by smashing furniture on the bad guys' heads. But the last laugh is on the kids. Their heroics saves the money for the trade school — very uncool.

There's a good deal here that makes no sense. For starters, when Tommy runs to tell his pals that Valentine has just been sprung from prison and will be sponsoring their release from the orphanage, he sounds like a little boy who's just been told the circus is coming to town. But in the very next scene we realize that Valentine himself doesn't know anything about this, so how do the kids know?

Then there's the lavish estate with servants and fancy cars and horses. How did Valentine's wife accumulate such wealth? And why does the daughter look at her father as if for the first time? Didn't they have visitation rights in prison?

Why are Spike and his gang lurking in the shadows as soon as Valentine is released from prison? Don't they have a life, albeit a crooked one? Paradoxically, this lurking keeps the film somewhat interesting. It offers another layer of conflict on top of the Valentine going legit vs. the kids going astray friction.

Fight scene in *Hit the Road*. Actors whose faces are shown (left to right): Barton MacLane, Billy Halop, Gabe Dell.

There are some funny and corny lines. When Pig makes an attempt at a malapropism — "I want to show some initiation" — Tommy smacks and corrects him. "Initiative, ya dope. Save that pigeon brain for emergencies."

When Molly Ryan tries to sway Tommy away from the dark side, he responds, "I had so much of that baloney I could eat it with mustard." And we know that's true.

Then there's ten-year-old Bobs Watson, who gets his way either by crying or tough-talking. Either way he's irresistible and steals the show. When he returns from horseback riding (we never actually see any horses), he says "I guess I just ain't got a saddle personality."

But he also has a disturbing line. When he tells the story of how he got rid of his Lord Fauntleroy clothes, he says, "Then this crow came along. I gave him the old one-two and put the clothes on him." The crow is the black servant's young son. But Bobs Watson made amends. He left show business to become a Methodist priest.

Hall, as Pig, does some good facial and arm expressions, changing from excitement to fear when Tommy says they're going after Spike themselves. He fears he's being pursued in the forest and climbs up a tree. When the kids grab him after the limb he's on cracks, and he's about to fall into the abyss, we realize the scene is faked because he *walks* straight into safety, instead of climbing up.

Even though "The Little Tough Guys" follows the "Dead End Kids" and "Barton

Halop is choked by Mr. and Mrs. Huntz Hall as Dell strangles his sister Ethel during the filming of *Hit the Road*.

MacLane" in the credits, only Hally Chester appears in the film and his name is not even listed in the front credits. His only function is to be used as a mop.

Which is more than can be said for Shemp Howard, who plays Spike's patsy and doesn't utter a line until the very end. The line is, "I know, 'shut up.' Beat ya that time."

Once again, the *New York Times* critics regarded this film with scorn. The July 3, 1941, review doesn't even bother with a plot summary, it goes right to advice. "Society, or Universal Pictures might well keep them in off-screen confinement with a copy of Emily Post's treatise. ... [T]heir dour behavior is becoming a chronic boredom."

Obviously, no faith.

Sea Raiders

Serial, 12 chapters, each about 20 minutes; Universal; Directors, Ford Beebe, John Rawlins; Original Screenplay, Clarence Upson Young, Paul Huston; Associate Producer, Henry MacRae; Art Director, Ralph DeLacy; Editor, Saul A. Goodkind; Photography, William Sickner; August 1941.

CAST

Billy Adams	Billy Halop	*Leah Carlton*	Marcia Ralston
Toby Nelson	Huntz Hall	*Carl Tonjes*	Reed Hadley
Bilge	Gabriel Dell	*Capt. Olaf Nelson*	Stanley Blystone
Butch	Bernard Punsly	*Jenkins*	Richard Alexander
Swab	Hally Chester	*Zeke*	Ernie Adams
Lug	Joe Recht	*Anderson*	Jack Clifford
Brack Warren	William Hall	*Krans*	Richard Bond
Tom Adams	John McGuire	*Capt. Lester*	Morgan Wallace
Aggie Nelson	Mary Field	*Capt. Meredith*	Eddie Dunn
Elliott Carlton	Edward Keane		

CHAPTER 1—"THE RAIDER STRIKES"

This serial is about the mysterious sinking of American ships carrying passengers and arms for the Allies' war effort. It is also about a bumbling policeman, Brack Warren, who's more interested in chasing the kids for minor offenses that can't be proven, than in real enemies. Eventually the cop and the kids work together in toppling the sinister sea raiders in 12 chapters, some thrilling, some meandering.

This first chapter shows us exactly how the sinking is accomplished. Two torpedoes fastened together at the tails by a long chain, dropped into the ocean, float to the target ship, wrap themselves around the front hull, and cling to the sides until a timer triggers an explosion that sinks the ship. The destruction of the SS *Dolphin* occurs right in front of the kids as they sail in their makeshift sailboat. The superimposed blast destroys the *Titanic*-size ship but the little boat merely capsizes with the boys hanging on.

More amazing than this is the identity of the people who are doing the sinking: an American sea captain, Elliott Carlton, and a few American henchmen, including Toby's (Huntz Hall) Uncle Olaf Nelson. Carlton has no qualms about killing hundreds of people at a swipe, then sitting down for tea with his daughter Leah and her friend Tom Adams, whose new tor-

Publicity illustration for Sea Raiders.

pedo gunboat Carlton is funding, then planning to steal and sell to foreign agents. (We assume they're German though that's never mentioned.)

Officer Warren wins the award for biggest buffoon cop in the entire string of Dead End Kids–Bowery Boys films. He cringes when his girlfriend Aggie Nelson (Hall's sister) calls him Blubberpuss, and she berates him for chasing the kids.

"I'm a cop. I gotta chase them when they break the law," he pouts.

Chapter 2—"The Flaming Torch"

This chapter, and each subsequent chapter, begins with a scroll-up narrative summary of the previous chapter, with the ocean and ships in the background. As it scrolls up, the beginning of the narrative seems to disappear in the distance.

The only real Little Tough Guy in this serial is Hally Chester, who conspires *against* the kids. He makes a deal with the cops and the Italian vegetable vendor by telling the kids the vendor will give them food for cleaning out his store. The kids spot the cops just in time and escape by hopping on a moving truck. In doing so, they knock down the poor vendor's fruit and vegetable crates. This is supposed to be funny but it's not. When the truck crashes, Officer Warren is again more interested in chasing the kids than arresting the reckless driver.

Afraid that Billy's Uncle Tom will send him to the "desert" (what desert? and why a desert?) for disobedience, he and the kids come up with the idiotic idea of rowing to Mexico. Realizing they will need food, they concoct an equally idiotic plan to break into Aggie's food warehouse. It's not stealing, they reason, because it's Toby's sister. In fact, Toby (Hall) figures he's in line for a commission on the sale, once they get jobs in Mexico. What a plan!

But things don't exactly work out that way. The sea raiders steal blueprints of Tom's torpedo boat and set the warehouse on fire. Toby and Billy are locked inside with Toby unconscious and Billy carrying him on his back, avoiding the falling fiery debris. It's a good, thrilling scene and shows the talents of director Ford Beebe (*Fantasia* and *Flash Gordon* as well as the previous Little Tough Guy serial *Junior G-Men*.)

Chapter 3—"The Tragic Crash"

What could have continued to be a very thrilling scene of the burning warehouse and the kids trying to escape, deflates when the kids enter the room next door and are more interested in copping a box of canned corned beef than in the fire that still rages. Officer Warren and Aggie go after them in the warehouse. Warren actually fires a shot towards them which

Left to right: Punsly, Hall, Halop and Dell in *Sea Raiders*.

hardly fazes Aggie. But when Warren threatens to arrest them for starting the fire, Aggie scolds him for even thinking that, and there's a close-up of her foot stepping on his.

Tom's torpedo boat is stolen and the kids believe Toby's uncle Capt. Nelson is behind it. How they figure this is pure speculation. They are caught searching the uncle's boat and jump into a speedboat to escape. Toby's dear uncle has no qualms about shooting at them.

The kids are chased by the cops who unbelievably jump from one speedboat to the next, as the kids' boat crashes into a dock.

CHAPTER 4 — "THE RAIDER STRIKES AGAIN"

The kids emerge unscathed and drag Toby, who can't swim, out of the water. The sea raiders show up again and throw Billy and Toby into a car, with Billy fighting them all the way. And wins! But once again, they end up in the water.

Caught between the sea raiders who know the kids are on to them, and the cops who blame them for everything, Billy and Toby take their chances and stow away on the SS *Astoria* that's about to ship out.

But somehow the other kids find out the SS *Astoria* is the sea raiders' next target and they speedboat over to it. Shouting up at Billy and Toby from the speedboat, Bilge (Dell) and Butch (Punsly) warn them and the captain. The captain ignores the warning but Billy and Toby jump into the water. Immediately after they jump, the SS *Astoria* blows up. Another *Titanic* disaster. Hundreds dead. Not a peep from the Coast Guard or anyone else.

CHAPTER 5—"FLAMES OF FURY"

This chapter moves the plot a bit further along and culminates in another fiery scene on board Nelson's boat, with the kids trapped on it.

The kids get a message to Tom about whom the sea raiders might be. Tom is having dinner with Carlton, his pretty daughter Leah and Capt. Carl Tonjes. Tom doesn't realize that Carlton, who is bankrolling his torpedo boat, is the master sea raider, along with foreigner Carl Tonjes (ominously played by Reed Hadley), and plans to sell the boat to foreign agents.

Interestingly, Reed Hadley was the narrator for atomic testing films from 1950–58. He was aboard the USS *Estes* and *Rendova* interviewing scientists and describing the operation during the last hour before the detonation. When he died in 1974, his work was still classified.*

CHAPTER 6—"BLASTED FROM THE AIR"

This chapter is pivotal. First, we realize that the end of the last chapter skipped the part where the kids escape the blast by taking off in Tom's torpedo boat along with henchman Anderson, who's unconscious and taken to the hospital. Carlton's deadly underhandedness is not limited to demonic destruction at sea, but land as well, as he sends one of his assassins to the hospital to kill Anderson before he has a chance to talk.

The kids and the police converge on Carlton's boat. Carlton's sailor-hat—wearing henchmen emerge from nowhere and engage the cops in fisticuffs. The kids jump into the water to save Police Capt. Lester and fly over Carlton's ship dropping hand grenades from a hydroplane. In the end, Carlton remains in control of his boat, with Tom and Warren as captors. He and shoots down the hydroplane with Toby and Billy on board.

CHAPTER 7—"VICTIMS OF THE STORM"

Incredible is how this chapter can be described.

First, the lackadaisical attitude of the police rises to a new level. The desk sergeant, without even looking up from his paperwork, let alone looking out the window, dismisses the kids' entreaties to save Tom and Warren from the murderous sea raiders, because of the "fog." Apparently he either doesn't realize or care that the boys just returned from attacking the ship from a hydroplane, fog or no fog. The least he could do is show some interest.

Then there's pretty Leah Carlton. She hears her father's explanation as to why he's committed treason, mass murder and destroyed much-needed weapons for the allied forces in Europe ("It was my chance to make a clean-up") and then makes a request that could only come from a daughter with unconditional love for her father: "I don't question the right or wrong of what you're doing, but couldn't you just let Tom and Warren go?"

He does. And what does he get for it? Shot dead by Capt. Tonjes.

The scene ends with the kids aboard Nelson's ship in the middle of a terrific, wave-

http://www.aracnet.com/~pdxavets

pounding storm. The special effects are first-rate, albeit repeated (the same sail falls three times).

CHAPTER 8—"DRAGGED TO THEIR DOOM"

The next three chapters hardly move the plot. They pit Dead End Kid Billy Halop against a whale, an octopus and a black panther. Not your typical New York street fight.

In this chapter, the kids are picked up by a fishing boat and try to lend a hand harpooning a whale. The rope gets locked around Swab's (Hally Chester) leg and he gets thrown into the water. Halop goes after him. There's some decent superimposed background ocean scenes and a whale jumping in and out of the water.

CHAPTER 9—"BATTLING THE SEA BEAST"

Back on the SS *Pigeon* Capt. Tonjes is holding Leah, Aggie, Tom and Brack Warren. Warren goes after Tonjes while the girls and Tom just watch. Tom is about to help but gets this advice from his girlfriend Leah; "Tom, you can't, it won't do any good." So he doesn't. What a wimp.

But maybe not! A minute later he jumps into the water, suspenders and all, and goes after a German submarine and is attacked by a shark. What a guy!

Back on the fishing boat, Nelson has taken over and Tonjes joins him. The kids bail out and swim to Manachi Island, the sea raiders' headquarters. But as Halop is about to climb onto a slippery rock, he's dragged back into the water by an octopus. To make things even more interesting, who comes along but a shark! The octopus and shark battle it out, with the shark delivering the final lethal bite.

CHAPTER 10—"PERILED BY A PANTHER"

Several noteworthy technical effects occur in this chapter. The first is a repeat of the previous chapter's last scene but from a different camera angle. Nelson wants to shoot the escaping kids, his nephew Toby included, but Tonjes is more pragmatic. "If they get to the island, they'll never get off." Tonjes and Nelson both laugh malevolently.

Then there are interesting sound effects. When the kids get to shore, they are in a cavernous enclave where Swab's voice reverberates like an echo when he calls Billy. Billy is in the water trying to pull himself free from the octopus. New swimmer Toby dives into the water, but before he pulls Billy away from the octopus, checks to make sure the brim of his hat stays upturned in the water. First things first.

But the most frightening effect is the sound and sight of the black panther. First we hear his deadly yelp in the distance. Tonjes informs Leah and Aggie, now captives of Tonjes on the island (everyone's on the island by now), that the sound is coming from his pet leopard who has apparently escaped from his cage and is now running free.

A moment later we are granted a good close-up of his fierce face and teeth. The kids show fear by lifting their shoulders. The next moment the panther pounces on Dead End Kid Billy Halop. They wrestle on the ground before Swab shoots the panther with a rifle they had whisked away from one of Tonjes' men. Since Billy had saved Swab from a whale, now they're even. Swab is quick to remind Billy of this.

Billy Halop, unidentified actor, Huntz Hall, Mary Field, Marcia Ralson and Hally Chester in *Sea Raiders*.

Chapter 11—"Entombed in the Tunnel"

"What's the use?" This phrase is over-used throughout the serial, usually by either Aggie or Leah. Here it's used by Leah, who has resigned herself to the "fact" that she will remain on this island for the rest of her life. Apparently she never heard Edmund Wilson's quote, "All that's necessary for evil to happen is for good men to do nothing." Not Aggie. She hides behind a door waiting for Tonjes to enter so she can break a vase over his head.

Tonjes calls his guard an "idiot" even though it was he who got hit over the head with a vase and allowed the girls to escape.

Meanwhile, Toby and Billy find an arsenal of torpedoes hidden in a tunnel. At that moment, Tonjes gets word that a U.S. Navy boat is approaching, and decides to blow up the arsenal. While Toby and Billy are at the arsenal fighting off the guards, the tunnel explodes.

Chapter 12—"Paying the Penalty"

It's the race of the torpedoes. Somehow the kids, Brack, Tom and the girls make their way to the SS *Pigeon* and punch out all remaining personnel to take control of the sea raiders' vessel. Tonjes and company get on the enemy submarine that's been hovering offshore. There are good close-ups of hands pushing the torpedoes inside the launchers. But the kids send off the sea raiders' torpedoes towards the submarine. Guess which set of torpedoes blows its target out of the water? Yes, the Dead End Kids will be back!

Mob Town

Released October 3, 1941; 60 minutes; Universal; Director, William Nigh; Associate Producer, Ken Goldsmith; Original Story and Screenplay, Brenda Weisberg, Walter Doniger; Photography, Elwood Bredell; Film Editor, Arthur Hilton; Music, Hans J. Salter; Art Director, Jack Otterson; Set Decorator, R.A. Gausman; Costumes, Vera West; Sound, Bernard B. Brown.

CAST

Frank Conroy	Dick Foran	*Pawnbroker*	Will Wright
Marion Barker	Anne Gwynne	*Mrs. Minch*	Eva Puig
Tom Barker	Billy Halop	*Mrs. Flynn*	Dorothy Vaughan
Pig	Huntz Hall	*Nutsy*	Edward Emerson
Ape	Bernard Punsly	*Women*	Rosina Galli, Mary
String	Gabriel Dell		Kelly
Butch (Shrimp)	Darryl Hickman	*Manager*	Dick Rich
Judge Luther Bryson	Samuel S. Hinds	*Police Officer*	Bob Gregory
Uncle Lon Barker	Victor Kilian	*Mrs. Simpson*	Claire Wilson
Cutler, Cop	Truman Bradley	*Henderson*	Terry Frost
Rummel, Auto Junker	John Butler	*Brick*	John Kellogg
Mr. Loomis	John Sheehan	*Woman*	Clara Blore
Boys	Roy Harris, Peter	*Charlie, Paperboy*	Harris Berger
	Sullivan	*Burly Man*	Duke York
Girls	Dorothy Darrell,	*Boys*	Hally Chester, Joe
	Elaine Morey,		Recht
	Beverly Roberts	*Court Clerk*	Eddie Dew
Police Chief	Cliff Clark	*Man*	Pat Costello
Monk Bangor	Paul Fix		

Mob Town is little more than a compilation of segments from *Little Tough Guy*, *Angels with Dirty Faces* and *East Side Kids* (Monogram's first kids film, released a year earlier).

The execution of Tommy's brother Eddie has sparked his anger. But it's in the form of disorderly conduct in a movie theater, not larceny and possession of a deadly weapon (as when Tommy reacted to the execution of his father in *Little Tough Guys*).

The kids' idol is Monk Bangor, Eddie's partner, serving time for robbery (as Danny is the brother of Mileway's convicted brother Knuckles in *East Side Kids*). Although he never personally met Monk, Tommy figures they'll have a great future together as soon as Monk is released from prison. Officer Frank Conroy's warning sounds like a Bob Dylan lyric: "Don't let your future get mixed up with Bangor's past."

Officer Conroy is a carbon copy of Officer O'Day in *East Side Kids* in that both try to steer the kids toward the right path. But Dick Foran (#10 popular western actor in 1938, according to *Motion Picture Herald*) is less of an actor than Leon Ames and that alone accounts for part of the problem with this film. Foran's Officer Conroy is stiff, dull, vacant. While Officer O'Day commands some respect, Tommy calls Officer Conroy "flatfoot" right to his face.

But when Officer Conroy "dares" Tommy to get a job, Tommy and the kids take up the challenge and work as automobile wreckers. When they receive their first paycheck, they are elated.

"We oughta open a bank account," suggest Ape.

"Yeah?" says the one-track-minded Pig. "Where we gonna get the tools?"

With Officer Conroy's temporary victory, the major conflict is eliminated, and there's a lull in the film. It's filled with Officer Conroy's dinner party but neither this, nor showing the boys a model airplane, makes for worthy footage.

Not since lunching with Rocky Sullivan have the kids been so friendly with an adult. But during the party, Tommy happens to glance through a magazine and discovers that Officer Conroy received a citation for the capture of Tommy's brother Eddie.

Tommy turns against Officer Conroy, but String, Pig and Ape side with the policeman. Monk Bangor is released from prison and tempts Tommy with adventure.

Dell and Hall in *Mob Town*.

Monk Bangor (Paul Fix) forcing Tommy (Halop) to drive the getaway car.

Just as Tommy in *Dead End* tells Milty (Punsly), the new kid, to steal from his mom, Monk tells Tommy to swipe his sister's jewelry if he wants to join him on his trip to California.

The kids stage their second mock trial, but here the courtroom drama is nowhere near as intense as the one in *Hell's Kitchen*, where Krispan is charged with murder. Tommy is merely accused of hindering the community's plan for a boys' club. Tommy laughs the whole thing off as he pushes his pals aside and runs to keep his rendezvous with the notorious Monk Bangor.

Like Danny of *East Side Kids*, Tommy finds himself in the front seat of an automobile with his mentor besides him. On the spur of the moment, Monk robs a drugstore and Tommy, with Monk shooting out the window, tries to out-drive Officer Conroy. He crashes. Officer Conroy apprehends Bangor. Tommy, a chastened young man, rejoins his real friends.

The inclusion of nine-year-old Darryl Hickman as Shrimp exemplifies how the Dead End Kids influenced American youth. He looks up to Tommy the way Tommy looks up to Monk. When Officer Conroy offers to drive Marion and Shrimp home, Shrimp says, "Will ya do me a favor? Put the handcuffs on me so nobody will think I'm pal-ling around with a cop."

Unlike other films in which Tommy's family is close and warm, here there's only friction between Tommy and his live-in uncle. But in the last scene, after Tommy rejoins his pals in the boys' club parade, his uncle has a change of heart. Except that Halop is nowhere to be seen. The camera remains on the people who seem to be looking at Tommy and complimenting him on how nice he looks. We can only assume that Halop did not show up for the scene and director William Nigh decided to film it anyway.

Mob Town is not one of the better films, lacking in originality, photographic technique, decent adult acting and tight, compelling scenes. But in the mind of *The New York Times*, this film was no different than the rest: "Every film in the series has an almost identical 'smash finish' but unfortunately the producers never smash nor finish" (November 20, 1941).

It would be another year before the Little Tough Guys would make a good feature-length film, that being *Mug Town*.

Junior G-Men of the Air

Serial, 12 chapters; Universal; Directors, Ray Taylor, Lewis D. Collins; Original Screenplay, Paul Huston, George H. Plympton, Griffen Jay; Additional Dialogue, Brenda Weisberg; June 1942.

CAST

"Ace" Holden	Billy Halop		Dogara	Jay Novello
Eddie Holden	Gene Reynolds		Sergeant	Lynton Brent
The Baron	Lionel Atwill		Conductor	Pat O'Malley
Jerry Markham	Frank Albertson		Soldier	Guy Kingsford
Don Ames	Richard Lane		Man	Joey Ray
"Bolts" Larson	Huntz Hall		Policemen	Bill Moss, Bill
"Stick" Munsey	Gabriel Dell			Hunter, Charles
"Greaseball" Plunket	Bernard Punsly			McAvoy
Jack	Frankie Darro		Patrolman	Dick Thomas
Arka	Turhan Bey		Japanese Clerk	Rico de Montez
Beal	John Bleifer		Uamalka	Edward Colebrook
Monk	Noel Cravat		Customers	Rolland Morris,
Comora	Edward Foster			William Desmond
Augar	John Bagni		Senator	Guy Usher
Dick Parson	Paul Phillips		Scientist	Bert Freeman
Double Face Barker	David Gorcey		Lieutenant	Hugh Prosser
Jed	Eddy Waller		Watchman	Heenan Elliott
Oriental Chemist	Paul Bryar		Corporal	Ben Wright
Colonel	Fred Burton		Instructor	George Sherwood
Flyer	Jack Arnold		Blackie	Billy Benedict
Official	Mel Ruick		Newsboy	Ken Lundy

CHAPTER 1—"WINGS AFLAME"

Less than six months after December 7, 1941, Universal cleverly came up with a Dead End Kids–Little Tough Guys serial that suggests Japanese saboteurs have melded into American society, secretly stealing and destroying vital assets, and coordinating their insurgencies with the bombing of Pearl Harbor. The date is mentioned several times, along with stressing the view that Americans are blind to evil that surrounds them. As State Officer Ames puts it in Chapter 5, "The enemies are gathering all around us. Trouble is, we're too smart to believe them." The unwitting lesson, in the aftermath of 9/11, is that, 60 years later, little has changed. We are like Ace Holden (Billy Halop) who believes until the very end that destroying a federal building (Chapter 6), destroying the *High Gate Dam* (Chapter 9) and the theft of his brother Eddie's invention of an airplane engine muffler (Chapter 3) are the dastardly deeds of common criminals.

Unlike the other two serials, this one does not begin with the kids wandering aimlessly. They work for Ace's dad, who runs a scrap yard for airplane parts. The Billy Halop character is a bit more mature than in the films, refraining from walloping his friends for every wisecrack. But he'll still bang his car into another and lead his gang into a fistfight with the owners of the other car for no reason. And he still hates cops. He refuses to help identify the Japanese thugs (actually American actors made-up to look Japanese) who rob a bank and steal Ace's truck. He refuses to say anything about the medallion he ripped off of one of their well-tailored suits as they were getting away. He repeats the same line for the third time in four years, "I can take care of myself." (We are led to believe that if the police knew about the medallion, capture will be imminent; but when Ace finally does agree to cooperate and turns over the medallion in Chapter 5, it has little value.)

This first chapter adequately establishes the plot but raises a few questions. For example, how can the kids look up and watch a plane with mountains and open fields in the background when they are in New York City? This incongruity lasts throughout the series.

Then there's David Gorcey, or "Double Face." He's the "outsider" who tampers with the airplanes and is ready to rat on his friends for pay. Sort of the same role as Hally Chester in *Sea Raiders* but, unlike Chester, Gorcey never redeems himself. Billy Benedict is the only other original Little Tough Guy in this series, and his appearance is merely a cameo.

And a minor question: Who is the girl who stops Bolts (Huntz Hall) from fighting in Chapter 1 and listens to his tale of heroism in Chapter 7? Her identity is never established.

Chapter 2—"The Plunge of Peril" and Chapter 3—"Hidden Danger"

It's soon apparent that the cliffhangers are not so cliffhangy. The recap of the previous chapter reveals much that was omitted. And unlike the innovative review scrolling up the screen in *Sea Raiders*, here it's basically the same verbal summary at the beginning of every chapter.

There are some humorous lines delivered by Huntz Hall. As the boys are walking near the road, the bad guys almost drive into them. Angry, Hall says, "I'll liquidate them. I'll spit in their eye."

Now that Ace has seen the bad guys twice, "His Excellency," evilly played by horror actor Lionel Atwill, orders Ace killed, and his brother's invention confiscated for good measure. Soon Ace finds himself up in a plane, his hands tied behind his back, and told that he will soon be forced to do "a little cloud-walking." But he manages to free himself and fights his captor in this two-seater while the plane continues to fly. Eventually it does crash right onto railroad tracks, and Ace, unscathed, apologies for "stopping the train on your right of way." The bad guy pilot escapes.

When the kids ask what kept Ace from falling out of the plane, Bolts has the answer: "Fly paper."

What was lost was Eddie's invention.

Scene from *Junior G-Men of the Air.* Top, left to right: Hall, Frank Albertson, Dell. Bottom, left to right: Punsly and Halop.

"No invention is lost," declares the Baron who, unlike the head bad guys in the previous serial, never engages in scuffles, just sits, makes decisions, gives orders, jots down notes, and smokes a pipe. "It's in the mind of the inventor." Thus he orders the kidnapping of Eddie Holden.

If we had any doubt who these spies are, this chapter puts them to rest. When the Baron calls his counterpart in Honolulu, the man who picks up the phone sits behind a sign that reads **Tokio Rome Berlin.** We hear the Baron tell him, "It's important that it arrives before the seventh of December."

CHAPTER 4—"THE TUNNEL OF TERROR" AND
CHAPTER 5—"THE BLACK DRAGON STRIKES"

No matter how hard the photographers try, every plane looks like a toy, especially when they crash. This goes for the plane carrying Eddie.

"We'll never get any junk out of all this hardware," says the enterprising Greaseball Plunket (Punsly).

Hall with the unidentified woman who appears twice in *Junior-G Men of the Air.*

"We ain't looking for junk, we're looking for Eddie," Ace reminds him.

"But it's like looking for a clam in a bowl of chowder," Greaseball persists.

They do find something: Peculiar, sticky brown clay.

"I got eyes, I can see," Ace declares, not to be one upped by Jerry, leader of the Junior G-Men who made this important find.

While this dirt is being worked on in the lab, the kids follow up on their own clues: They find the pilot, lose the pilot, follow the bad guys down through a manhole, survive an underground explosion, and escape a hand-grenade attack from an airplane.

Chapter 6—"Flaming Havoc" and Chapter 7—"The Death Mist"

More chasing, more fighting and more fires. At one point, a spy opens a door to reveal people working in a factory but we never see them again and we never find out what they're working on. Repeating the same set of punches three times extends a fight scene in a burning government building. Greaseball can't take all the fighting and smoke and passes out. Lucky for him that Junior G-Man Jerry is on the scene and knows artificial respiration. But what he doesn't know is that he doesn't have time to explain how it works to the others before administering it to the unconscious Greaseball. When Jerry finally does get around to apply-ing it to Greaseball, it's more like a mild back massage. Nevertheless, Greaseball awakes and feels like "a fighting rooster."

CHAPTER 8—"SATAN FIRES THE FUSE" AND CHAPTER 9—"SATANIC SABOTAGE"

More fire and more chase scenes as we see the spies loading shipments of weapons in preparation for more strikes on the domestic front. The Baron decides to blow up the High Gate Dam which provides power to American weapons factories. The scene is executed well with water rushing out of the exploding dam.

But the scene where Ace is pulled out of the muddy water is an obvious patch job. When Halop first comes out, his hair is matted down around his head like an upside down bowl. But in the next shot his hair is ruffled. Next shot, his hair is again matted, but the very next shot it's ruffled again and he's wrapped in a blanket. Where did the blanket come from? Evi-dently this scene was shot at least twice and parts of each spliced together. A real hatchet job, easily avoidable if *Dick Tracy* director Ray Taylor had been paying attention.

Chalking up more patriotic points, the kids go on a humanitarian mission, airlifting food to those made homeless due to the ruptured dam.

We notice in-fighting among the spies. We are led to believe this will lead to a Japanese spy implosion but it never happens. Instead they bomb electric towers and the kids just miss driving into one.

CHAPTER 10—"TRAPPED IN A BLAZING CHUTE"

The saboteurs go from bombing electric towers to oil wells and both are photographed well. But the kids keep getting in their way so the Baron punts. He tells his cronies, "Your mission is to destroy those boys."

One of them expresses his frustration this way: "Those kids are inhuman. Lucky I brought the sedan." Whatever that means.

What doesn't make sense is when the boys spot the saboteurs loading more weapons onto a truck, and run all the way back to the scrap yard to get their truck to chase them. The sabo-teurs would be long gone by then.

Another thing that seems too random is when they are flying in the two-seaters and only sometimes do they wear their flying gear. When Ace and Eddie are up in the air, only Ace is wearing it. Which matters because the plane catches fire and they have to bail out. Eddie has to hold onto his brother with the parachute. But the parachute catches fire too. It's one of the better cliffhangers in this serial. What happens? See the next chapter.

CHAPTER 11—"UNDECLARED WAR" AND
CHAPTER 12—"CIVILIAN COURAGE CONQUERS"

They fall into a lake, unharmed.

Now things get serious. The State Guard is brought in but the leader is hesitant about attacking a group of Japanese on American soil while our leaders are talking peace with them.

"It wouldn't be the first time the Japanese talk peace and plan war," State Officer Ames tells then lieutenant of the State Guard. In theory, Ames knows his stuff. But practically, throughout the entire serial, he is no help. It's the kids who find all the clues, track down the bad guys, get caught in fires and narrowly escape death. When the kids do call for help, Ames shows up late.

When the lieutenant finally agrees to send out his State troops, it's an all-out frontal attack. Hundreds of State Guardsman converge on the Japanese hideaway on the farm. They send so many, the directors even had to borrow footage from other war films(!).

It's the climax of the serial but unfortunately it's too long and unconvincing. The saboteurs are outnumbered yet they seem to hold off the onslaught. There's an abundance of shooting but few people get shot. It's hard to follow which group is which, since they seem to be dressed alike. One Japanese gunman fires a machine-gun mounted on a tractor. He's finally blown away by an American bazooka. In the middle of all the shooting, the kids drive up to the gate but don't get in because it's locked. Why does that stop them? Why don't they just bust through it like they did previously?

In the end, the Baron is captured, Ace spells subversive "J-a-p" and a representative from the governors' office (not even the governor himself, so how important could this whole matter be?) comes to thank them.

The final scene depicts a fleet of big American planes, obviously to inspire patriotism and morale among the viewers approaching draft age. No final cut to the kids. It leaves us flat.

Tough as They Come

Released June 5, 1942; 61 minutes; Universal; Director, William Nigh; Associate Producer, Ken Goldsmith; Screenplay, Lewis Amster, Brenda Weisberg; Original Story, Lewis Amster, Albert Bein; Photography, Elwood Bredell; Film Editor, Bernard Burton; Music, Hans J. Salter; Art Director, Jack Otterson; Costumes, Vera West; Sound, Bernard B. Brown.

CAST

Tommy Clark	Billy Halop		*Ma*	Giselle Werbiseck
Ann Wilson	Helen Parrish		*Eddie*	Clarence Muse
Ben Stevens	Paul Kelly		*Eddie's Wife*	Theresa Harris
Frankie Taylor	Ann Gillis		*Rogers*	John Eldredge
Pig	Huntz Hall		*Process Server*	James Flavin
Ape	Bernard Punsly		*Dave*	George Offerman
String	Gabriel Dell		*Fruit Vendor*	Antonio Filauri
Mrs. Clark	Virginia Brissac		*Jim Bond*	Dick Hogan
Mike Taylor	John Gallaudet		*Collector*	Frank Faylen
Esther	Mala Powers			

Here Billy Halop's character, Tommy Clark, is close to becoming an adult, while the others remain childish.

As a law student, Tommy has joined the ranks of the go-getters, snubbing a job from the Legal Aid Society to work for the crooked, but much more lucrative, Apex Finance Company. He's seen how they treat his own neighbors, pulling radios out of old ladies' apartments because they missed a single payment. Undeterred, and determined to succeed, he squeezes the last nickel out of a black family before allowing them to keep their piano another month.

Also motivating him is his love for pretty Ann Wilson (Helen Parrish), whose father, Dr. Wilson (who we never see), helped get him the job. But like in *Call a Messenger*, he's embarrassed to bring a person of Ann's stature to his apartment.

Meanwhile, Pig, String and Ape behave like annoying kid brothers, starting a food fight at the dinner table, and embarrassing Tommy in front of Ann. They're also embarrassing to themselves in two other scenes. In the first, String is supposed to be Ape's fighting manager. But Ape can't hit a punching bag without the bag hitting him back and knocking him down. Which isn't as bad as watching Pig imitate Ape and knocking himself down with his own fist. Just too goofy.

The other scene is a mock tightrope act, with String as the announcer and Pig doing a zip line on the clothes line and landing on the ground. Again silly, but it gives Gabe Dell a chance to display his acting talents, which eventually brought him back to Broadway in the 1970s.

There's a semi-sweet, tongue-in-cheek scene with Ann visiting the younger Frankie Taylor (Ann Gillis) who is also in love with Tommy and is now in the hospital after sitting in the rain eavesdropping on Tommy and Ann on the roof.

"We really can't be friends," Frankie tells Ann, who came with flowers. "We both love the same man."

But when Ann explains that Tommy is dating her because she is older and, when she is old, Frankie will still be young, Frankie asks, "Will you give him up then?"

"If he wants to go to you, I'll give him up," Ann relents. And they become friends.

Tommy verbally and physically reveals how committed he is to becoming a success. He says to Ann, "Maybe you have to hurt a few people to get somewhere in this world."

"But not your own people," Ann warns.

He does exactly that. With ease he overcomes the moral dilemma of confiscating Frankie's father's cab, the man's only source of income. Mike Taylor missed a payment because of his daughter's hospital bills.

Defeated, Mike climbs to the roof and threatens to jump off. Tommy tries to talk him out of it by telling him life is more important than a cab. But Mike tells him it's not the cab, it's the realization that life will never get better. Pig distracts him and Tommy pulls him off the ledge.

Back on the street the crowd wants to lynch Tommy for almost sending a man to his death. Pig, String and Ape beat on Tommy for turning on his neighbors, and Tommy, who has beaten up several people in the film, including String when the kids hid the cab from him, allows himself to be beaten up.

Like water, coming face to face with death, and the near-lynching, cleanses him, as he walks into the Legal Aid Society office.

"I see you've had a change of heart," says the lawyer.

"A change of mind," Tommy's friend Ben corrects him. "His heart has always been in the right place."

Tommy decides to go after the Apex Finance Company, but the way in which he does it is, for an aspiring lawyer, a bit backwards. He has seen the company's documents of misrepresentation, which could easily be used as evidence against them. A subpoena would be the legal way of getting them. But what does law student Tommy decide to do? He reverts to his Dead End Kid ways; he and the other kids break and enter the office and steal the records, an act that could very well make the documents inadmissible in court. But being a Dead End Kids film (despite being billed as a Dead End Kids and Little Tough Guy film, when in fact there is no Little Tough Guy in this film), it works.

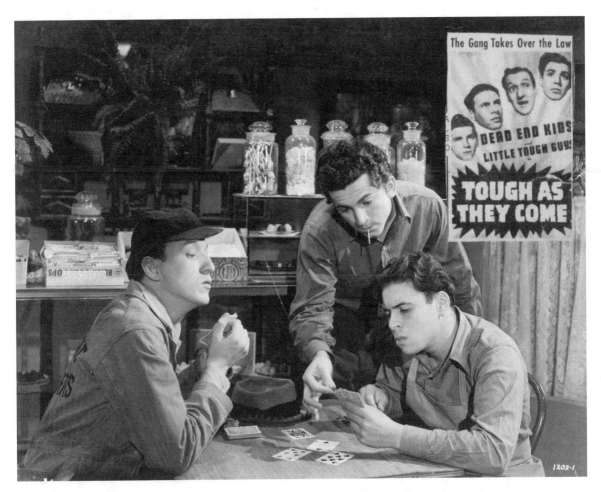

Hall (left), Dell (center) and Punsly all have jobs, yet hardly do them, in *Tough as They Come*.

There's an absorbing camera angle as if the camera is coming out of the wall in the telephone booth where Halop is on the phone, and Dell is outside the booth, seen through the window, eavesdropping. One angle, giving two perspectives on a scene, simple and exact.

Having quashed the evil finance company, Tommy announces he will start a credit union in the community. In fact, between 1939 and 1942, over 200 credit unions were opened in New York.* One cannot ignore the possibility that this film was partially being used as a public service announcement for credit unions.

Mug Town

Released January 22, 1943; 60 minutes; Universal; Director, Ray Taylor; Associate Producer, Ken Goldsmith; Screenplay, Brenda Weisberg, Lewis Amster, Harold Tarshis, Harry Sucher; Original Story, Charles Grayson; Photography, Jack MacKenzie; Film Editor, Ed Curtiss; Art Director, Jack Otterson; Sound Director, Bernard B. Brown; Sound Technician, Paul Neal; Music Director, H. J. Salter; Gowns, Vera West; Set Decorator, R.A. Gausman.

*www.cuna.org

CAST

Tommy	Billy Halop		Thief	Ernie Adams
Noreen Seward	Grace McDonald		Waiters	Paul Dubov, Sid Melton
Pig	Huntz Hall		Matilda	June Bryde (Gittleson)
Ape	Bernard Punsly			
String	Gabriel Dell		D.A.	William Forrest
Clinker	Edward Norris		Man in Flophouse	Danny Beck
Mrs. Bell	Virginia Brissac		Detective #1	William Gould
Mack Stewart	Jed Prouty		Detective #2	John Bagni
Don Bell	Dick Hogan		Manager	John Sheehan
Shorty	Murray Alper		Chef	Dan Seymour
Marco	Paul Fix		Detective	Jack Marvin
Perkle	Lee "Lasses" White		Girls	Jolin Westbrook, Evelyn Cooke, Dorothy Cordray
Steve	Tommy Kelly			
Drunk	Syd Saylor			
Cop	Ralph Dunn			
Singer	Napoleon Simpson		Hatchet Face Woman	Clara Blore
Bouncers	William Hall, Matt Willis		Motorcycle Cop	Eddie Parker
			Crap Shooter	Johnny Walsh

Of the four Little Tough Guys films that take place outside New York, *Mug Town*'s approach is novel. The kids are self-motivated, trekking across country by foot and freight, selling magazine subscriptions to Middle America.

In spite of the intimidating surroundings of a small town flophouse, Tommy has not lost an ounce of nerve. He confronts a derelict stealing money from Steve, a sickly boy.

"Why don't ya wait till he's dead first," Tommy says to him. A fistfight erupts, which ends in a snowstorm of white pillow feathers and the kids, along with Steve, out on the street.

The kids grasp a technique for hopping freight trains and outsmarting railroad conductors. Unfortunately, Steve has not. He gets caught lying on his stomach straddling two cars. The camera focuses on his hands as they slowly let go of the rail, giving the unmistakable impression that he has fallen between the cars. The kids stop running after him and gaze downward to where they expect to see his mutilated body. There is no death more brutal nor as impressionistically photographed as this one in the entire series.

Steve's death gives the kids—and the film—direction. But when they arrive at Steve's mother's house, Tommy gets tongue-tied. Instead of telling the mother about Steve's death, Tommy gives her hope for Steve's return. Grateful, she invites them to stay with her until Steve comes back. The fact that she does not ask why Steve is not with them shows she may know something is amiss.

While Pig, String and Ape continue to pound the pavements selling magazine subscriptions, Tommy is taken under Mrs. Bell's wing. She gets him a job right beside her son Don at Mr. Stuart's garage. The situation is similar to *You're Not So Tough* where Mama Posita invites Tommy to stay in her house and gives him the foreman job.

Pig, String and Ape find out that Klinker and Don plan to steal a shipment of furs and implicate Tommy.

For the second time in the film, the kids play the stooge, trying to cover up Don's involvement for his mother's sake. (Similar to how Slip Mahoney, in the Bowery Boys' *Angels' Alley*, assumes responsibility for Jimmy's theft of the warehouse merchandise.)

Dell (left), Hall (at the wheel) and Punsly in their jalopy in *Mug Town*.

As the boys arrive at the garage in their newly acquired and recently repaired jalopy, they see Klinker and a truck pulling out of the garage with its back door unlatched. Tommy and Pig ride after the truck.

Tommy and Pig jump Klinker and Don. Klinker shoots Don (the reason for this is not clear) before driving away and crashing. Like Steve's terrible death, we cannot see Klinker's crash; the camera is on Tommy and Pig facing in the direction of the crash.

Tommy and Pig put Don in the jalopy and take him to a doctor that Don knows. Why they don't also take Shorty is hazy.

The overlapping problems of the kids' self-imposed exile, and the knowledge that Mrs. Bell is bound to learn about the son's death, insures *Mug Town* from lapsing into mere footage, which it has a tendency to do. That Mrs. Bell does not turn against the kids when she does find out is anticlimactic.

For amusement, Pig, String and Ape present little skits for themselves on how to sell magazine subscriptions to housewives. Pig is wonderfully comical as the uninterested house-wife, while String and Ape play the persistent pushers of periodicals.

The patriotic theme of the film is overtly apparent, for *Mug Town* is the only film in which a real historic event is incorporated. The bombing of Pearl Harbor (announced on a radio news bulletin) changes Tommy's attitude towards his country and affects the outcome of the film when a precautionary civil defense blackout is imposed.

Early in the film, while Tommy is working alone in the garage, Noreen comes in and is invited to share Tommy's skimpy supper.

"Don't you care about this country's future?" Noreen asks Tommy.

"Why should I be? Nobody's interested in mine."

But the final shot of the picture has the Kids dressed in Army uniforms. They march into the Bells' house, turn towards the camera and Tommy declares, "And we're not kiddin.'" Indeed they were not. In the next and last Little Tough Guys film, *Keep 'Em Slugging*, Halop and Punsly are absent, never to return as Dead End Kids or Little Tough Guys or East Side Kids.

Keep 'Em Slugging

Released August 2, 1943; 66 minutes; Universal; Director, Christy Cabanne; Associate Producer, Ben Pivar; Screenplay, Brenda Weisberg; Story, Edward Handler, Robert Gordon; Photography, William Sickner; Film Editor, Ray Snyder; Music, Hans J. Salter; Art Director, John B. Goodman; Sound, Bernard B. Brown.

CAST

Pig	Huntz Hall	*Bingo*	David Durand
Tommy Banning	Bobby Jordan	*Dugan*	Ernie Adams
String	Gabriel Dell	*McGann*	Milton Kibbee
Ape	Norman Abbott	*Lady in Poiple*	Fern Emmett
Sheila	Evelyn Ankers	*Shorty*	Jimmy Dodd
Suzanne	Elyse Knox	*Fat Man*	Harry Holman
Frank	Frank Albertson	*Sammy*	Dick Chandlee
Jerry	Don Porter	*Students*	Budge Patty, Johnny Walsh
Binky	Shemp Howard		
Mr. Carruthers	Sameul S. Hinds	*Jailer*	Lew Kelly
Lola	Joan Marsh	*Sharkey*	Ben Erway
Duke Rodman	Milburn Stone	*Thugs*	Joey Ray, Anthony Warde
Sergeant Detective	Joseph Crehan		
Police Sergeant	Wade Boteler	*Young Lover*	Peter Michael
Mr. Meecham	Paul McVey	*Young Lover's girl*	Harryette Vine
Scott	Joe King	*Second Detective*	Frank O'Connor
Miss Billings	Minerva Urecal	*Languid Customer*	Caroline Cooke
Mr. Quink	Arthur Hoyt	*Personnel Managers*	Rex Lease, Bob Hill, Howard Mitchell
Macklin	Cliff Clark		
Matron	Alice Fleming	*Mike*	Bob Spencer
Mrs. Meegan	Dorothy Vaughan	*Policeman*	Jack C. Smith
Mrs. Banning	Mary Gordon	*Waiter*	Roy Brent
First Detective	William Gould	*Stars in Movie*	Jane Frazee, Robert Paige
Customer	Mira McKinney		
Young Girl	Janet Shaw		

Universal's final entry is one of its best. It has a realistic plot, comedy, and Bobby Jordan as the leader (even though Huntz Hall tops him in the billing). Why Jordan never was the leader before or after could not have anything to do with ability. His character's demeanor is smooth, unlike Halop's who's always angry. Jordan is angry when appropriate. Halop slaps his pals gratuitously and sometimes views them as irritants. Jordan genuinely likes Pig, String and Ape (Bud Abbott's nephew Norman takes over for Punsly).

Determined to stay out of trouble to free up the policemen for the war effort, Tommy (Jordan) convinces the kids to get legitimate summer jobs. But with "no experience, no references and a [police] record," the kids are stuck at Shemp's luncheonette, causing havoc with the soda fountain. Tommy's sister's boyfriend Jerry, whose father owns the National Department Store, gets Tommy a job in the shipping department and Tommy gets the rest of the kids jobs there as well.

Things are fine until sexy Lola lures Tommy to a nightclub, and he realizes his meager job is not going to pay for "champagne and orchids." Nightclub owner Duke Rodman offers to help out but Tommy quickly catches on that Duke is a "high-class fence" and he's been set up. He warns Duke to keep away from the store.

Tommy's supervisor, Frank, is in cahoots with Duke, and plants stolen store jewelry on Tommy. Tommy is jailed, his friends are fired, and his sister quits. Jerry posts bail but nei-

Mary Gordon (who also played Gorcey's mother in the East Side Kids series), Bobby Jordan and Evelyn Ankers in *Keep 'Em Slugging*, the only film in which Jordan played the gang's leader.

ther his sister nor his mother believe he's innocent. Tommy heads back onto the street "where I belong."

Now ready to work for Duke, he goes to the nightclub and catches Frank and Lola together. He follows them to a warehouse and overhears Duke making plans to heist silk from the department store. Tommy gets the kids and with a fire hose captures the whole crooked lot red-handed.

Tommy's character is borne out through subtle facial expressions. When he's first sitting with Duke, lamenting his financial inability to keep up with high-maintenance Lola, his facial expression communicates mediocrity. But as soon as Duke makes an offer, a slight shift of the eyes and mouth suddenly gives him the face of a street-wise kid who knows he's being set up.

At his apartment the camera is on Jordan as his expression changes from serene to incensed, as he listens to his sister tell her boyfriend not to waste time with the Bannings, "they're bad medicine."

Screenwriter Brenda Weisberg is to be commended for funny lines and situations.

When the kids are making an alphabetical list of possible jobs, Pig comes up with "a, a salesman; b, balloon blower upper; c, cheese taster."

Watching a love scene in a movie theater, Pig comments, "That guy must have creeping paralysis of the kisser."

As Pig wipes lint off a woman's coat, and Tommy quietly calls him a dope, the woman retorts, "I'd rather have a polite dope than an uncouth genius." When she leaves, Tommy says, "You're gonna go from a polite dope to a gold-plated moron."

At the police station they poke fun at the desk sergeant. "His face looks like it was thrown together when the quitting whistle blew."

There's also a funny but unnecessary scene when Ape (Abbott) accidentally breaks a mannequin and String (Dell) forces him to dress up like a mannequin so no one will find out. Sheila comes over to fix the dress. She pricks Ape, who shrieks and runs through the store.

This is the second time (after *You're Not So Tough* the kids play with a mannequin and also the second time the Ape character laments, "Why was I born?" (Punsly says it in *Tough As They Come*.)

Abbott and Dell remained friends. It was Abbott who informed Gabe Dell, Jr., about his father's death in 1988.

There's one scene that today would never get past the sexual harassment police. Sheila asks Frank, the shipping manager, if he would hire her brother Tommy. Frank has been trying to date Sheila forever. So what's his answer? "You give me a date and I'll give your brother a job!"

Sheila walks away, her dignity intact.

But a pivotal scene, where Tommy is lured away by Lola, actually makes no sense. Lola is feigning difficulty parallel parking. Tommy offers to help and parks the car. In gratitude she says, "If it wasn't for you I'd be here for hours. Can I give you a lift somewhere?"

Wait, didn't he just park...? Oh, forget it.

The East Side Kids

Gabe Dell summed up best the situation at Monogram. "When you landed there, even the unemployed actors at Schwab's Drug Store wouldn't talk to you."

Monogram Pictures was known to provide employment to the up and coming (Ava Gardner, Sheldon Leonard) or the has-beens (Robert Armstrong, Bela Lugosi, Harry Langdon). But the actors making up the East Side Kids (Leo Gorcey, Huntz Hall, Bobby Jordan and Dell) fit neither description.

Sam Katzman, who produced all the East Side Kids films at Monogram, was highly cost-conscious and, as a result, produced pictures with sparse settings and loose plots. Working with him was William Beaudine, who directed six East Side Kids films (and 25 Bowery Boys films). Like Katzman, Beaudine was by no means considered artistic. He was famous for doing one take, and one take only. "One-Shot Beaudine" he was called. While working late one night on an East Side Kids movie, and being rather exhausted, Beaudine murmured to no one in particular, "You'd think somebody was waiting for this one."

Both producer and director made the East Side Kids do exactly what they wanted them to do—appeal to a specialized audience (adolescent) and earn a lot of fast money with quickly made films. What the films lacked in originality, they made up for with vitality. Usually played with another movie on Saturday afternoons during the six years they were produced, the films of the East Side Kids soared in popularity.

The series began early in 1940 when Katzman corralled the Little Tough Guys rejects, Hally Chester and Harris Berger, added Frankie Burke (who played young Rocky in *Angels with Dirty Faces*), Donald Haines and David Durand in a film called *East Side Kids*. When Katzman heard that the two Gorceys and Bobby Jordan were available, he cast these Dead End heavies in the next East Side Kids film *Boys of the City* (a.k.a. *The Ghost Creeps*), which was released seven months later. Introduced in this film was "Sunshine" Sammy Morrison, and with him came racist overtones. "Sunshine" is depicted in almost all the films as being scared to death of his own shadow. It is not uncommon to hear him say things like, "I wish my mammy was here" and "I wish I was back on that old plantation." At times we see Gorcey using Morrison for his personal comfort, such as when Morrison fans Gorcey in hot weather or carries him when he gets tired. As a reward, he's usually given watermelon.

There's a vague attempt at continuity beginning with the first two East Side Kids films. Bobby Jordan took the role of Danny, held by Durand in the first East Side Kids flick. His brother Knuckles, still catching his breath from his near-execution in *East Side Kids*, was played by Dave O'Brien in both films.

In *Boys of the City* the kids provoke havoc in the summer streets. The father of rich kid Algie Wilkie steps in to sponsor a trip for the boys to the Adirondecks. In the third film, *That Gang of Mine*, Wilkie puts up front money so that Muggs Maloney (sometimes Muggs McGin-

The East Side Kids. Bottom to top right: Leo Gorcey, Sunshine Sammy Morrison, Bobby Jordan, Bobby Stone, David Gorcey, and Huntz Hall, in a scene from *Let's Get Tough*.

nis) can learn to be a jockey. But at the end of the film, Muggs informs Danny and the gang that he now wants to be a boxer. *Pride of the Bowery* has Danny finagling a way for Muggs to realize his new ambition. Most of the reviews shared the opinion that the camerawork exceeded expectations and the use of the CCC Camp as a vehicle for Muggs' training and coming-of-age was good promotional material for the federally funded program.

With *Flying Wild*, Gorcey was given top billing and was on the verge of assuming full leadership of the gang — a leadership position he would retain until his retirement. But continuity has fallen by the wayside. Instead of having a brother in *Bowery Blitzkrieg*, Bobby Jordan has a sister. And Dave O'Brien, no longer his brother, is the policeman who arrests him.

Bowery Blitzkrieg is Huntz Hall's first Monogram appearance and he adds a touch of comedy. Hall was making East Side Kids and Little Tough Guy films simultaneously. Dell would later follow suit.

But the addition of Hall did not change critics' opinions. Badmouthing the East Side Kids was a matter of routine. *The New York Times* said, "Why not let the kids go really bad, then convict them of murder, execute them all and call the whole thing quits? That would be deeply satisfying."

Rather than satisfy the critics, Katzman co-starred Bela Lugosi in *Spooks Run Wild*. It doesn't come close to frightening anyone, especially since it looks like the film was made in the middle of the day with the blinds down.

Katzman continued to include well-known actors and in the case of Billy Gilbert in *Mr. Wise Guy*, his brand of comedy is undoubtedly an asset. His brief appearances add spice to a film that offers nothing new, except for Gabriel Dell's Monogram debut. Dell's position in the East Side Kids films, and later in the Bowery Boys, is different than the other boys in that most of the time he is not considered a regular member of the gang, and at times is Gorcey's adversary.

Muggs' real name in the East Side Kids' films, although he never uses it, and cringes every time somebody else does, is Ethelbert. It's a touchy issue with him, and Dell (as Skid or Fingers) ribs him about it every chance he gets. Occasionally Muggs retorts, "Just because my parents made a mistake doesn't mean you have to."

Three out of the next five films (*Smart Alecks*, *Kid Dynamite* and *Clancy Street Boys*) followed a formula set in *Bowery Blitzkrieg*, in that the main focus of confrontation is within the gang itself. In terms of credibility these films are well ahead of the rest in that they deal rather intelligently with human concerns such as loyalty, jealousy, egotism and love. In *Smart Alecks*, Muggs, against his better judgment, throws Danny out of the gang because he believes Danny plans to keep reward money that rightfully belongs to the gang. But Muggs' real reason for banning Danny is because Danny did not immediately hand the money over to him, thus refusing to acknowledge Muggs as the leader.

In *Kid Dynamite*, Muggs fruitlessly tries to overcome his inferiority complex by demanding from Danny all that is rightfully Danny's—even if it means starting a fistfight in the middle of a dance hall.

Clancy Street Boys has Muggs prevail upon the seven members of his gang to pose as his brothers and sister to show his uncle that his father was not a liar and did indeed have seven kids for whom he accepted Christmas gifts for the last two years.

"Sunshine" Sammy Morrison's last film, and Bobby Jordan's second-to-last East Side Kids film, was in 1943, *Ghosts on the Loose*. It stars Lugosi as a Nazi spy and is the counterpart to *Let's Get Tough* (1942) which deals with Japanese spies. Neither the films nor the spies were technically convincing.

By the end of 1943, the East Side Kids were no longer wandering aimlessly about the streets. They are more organized, have their own club house with their own set of rules, and in their

Sunshine Sammy Morrison in *Ghosts on the Loose.*

own way they care about their community. In *Mr. Muggs Steps Out* and *Million Dollar Kid* they are accepted into the household of the wealthy and are quick to come to the aid of the host.

In *Follow the Leader*, Gorcey repeats his role in *'Neath Brooklyn Bridge* by infiltrating a gang of professional saboteurs whose lieutenant is Gabe Dell. The difference between the two instances is that in *Bridge* Muggs acts on his own accord, whereas in *Leader* he has the support of the Army and police captain.

By the middle of 1944, the East Side Kids had simmered down quite a bit. The gang had gone through several turnovers. Instead of investing their energies in unruly behavior, they began devoting their attention to serious activities such as baseball, copy editing, boxing, horseback racing and training, and being good Samaritans. In *Block Busters*, Monogram experiments by placing a foreign boy in their midst, and watching how the East Side Kids relate to him. In *Bowery Champs*, Dell and Gorcey work together for a city newspaper as investigative reporter and copyboy respectively, and solve a murder mystery.

Contrary to the first eight East Side Kids films in which society worked either for or against the kids, the last three pictures, *Docks of New York*, *Come Out Fighting* and *Mr. Muggs Rides Again* show how they mature in a way that render them respected and helpful citizens. In these three films the kids recover a stolen heirloom, protect a police commissioner's son from racketeers, fulfill a dying woman's last wish, and help bring about several marriages.

Speaking of marriages, Katzman and the East Side Kids were about to divorce. Jan Grippo, agent of Gorcey and Hall, offered them each $10,000 a week, which was twice as much as Katzman was paying. Katzman not only didn't match the offer but didn't blink an eye. In 1946, Gorcey and Hall left Katzman and collaborated with Grippo on a new series of 48 Bowery Boys flicks. Gorcey and Hall broke new Hollywood ground, becoming the first actors to produce and own a percentage of the pictures. At one point, Gorcey was the highest-paid actor in Hollywood.

East Side Kids

Released February 10, 1940; 62 minutes; Monogram; Director, Bob Hill; Producer, Sam Katzman; Screenplay, William Lively; Photography, Art Reed; Film Editor, Earl Turner.

CAST

Pat O'Day	Leon Ames	Danny	David Durand
Mileaway	Dennis Moore	Dutch	Hally Chester
Molly	Joyce Bryant	Capt. Moran	James Farley
Whisper	Vince Barnett	Joe	Stephen Chase
Knuckles	Dave O'Brien	Skinny	Frankie Burke
Schmidt	Richard Adams	Mr. Wilkes	Fred Hoose
Pete	Sam Edwards	Eric	Eric Burtis
Cornwall	Robert Fiske	Mike	Eddie Brian
Algernon Wilkes	Jack Edwards	Tony	Frank Yaconelli

Also with Harris Berger, Donald Haines, Maxine Leslie

In retrospect, Monogram Pictures' East Side Kids debut is the odd man out. It does not star a single original Dead End Kid. This could be why *New York Times* reviewer Bosley Crowther (February 19, 1940), empathizing with his contemporaries, thought that the cycle, "one of the most wearing on adult nervous systems in the history of films, had approach[ed] the end of its already badly frayed rope...."

But then the reviewer had second thoughts, and put it this way: "a cinematic cycle, like the proverbial serpent, dies hard, with its remote tail flicking cynically long after the last light has expired from its minute reptilian brain." How prophetic!

What is apparent at the outset of this picture is its striking resemblance to *Angels with Dirty Faces*. In the former, a priest and a criminal are childhood friends. Here a cop, Officer Patrick O'Day, and a counterfeiter-murderer, Philip Mileaway, are childhood friends. In the former, the priest has trouble keeping the kids interested in basketball. Here the cop has trouble keeping them interested in radio broadcasting.

In addition to Mileaway and O'Day, there is a third boyhood friend, Knuckles; he's on death's row, convicted of murdering a policeman. The weakness here is that no evidence is ever presented to prove his guilt, nor does Knuckles ever protest his conviction. The audience knows it was Mileaway who killed the cop.

Publicity shot of the original East Side Kids. Left to right: Donald Haines, Jack Edwards, Leon Ames, Hally Chester, Eddie Brian, unidentified policeman, Frankie Burke, James Farley, Sam Edwards, Harris Berger.

A relatively strong scene is when Danny, Knuckles' brother, and leader of the East Side Kids, finds out that his brother is in jail. To spare Danny pain, Officer O'Day told him that Knuckles was in South America. In films of this era, the image of South America is the utopian fantasy of the downtrodden, the victimized urban dweller. The metaphor is illustrated in *Dark Passage* in which Humphrey Bogart flees to Peru to avoid trial for a murder he did not commit.

When a baseball accidentally lands in Schmidt's car, and the kids attempt to retrieve it, Schmidt shouts, "You thief, you steal from my car. You are going to the electric chair like your brother is!"

Though director Bob Hill exploits the tradition of the inept policeman, he can be forgiven. In what is otherwise a well-constructed sequence in Capt. Moran's office, the exploitation is the only unoriginal moment.

While Schmidt registers his complaint against Officer O'Day for manhandling him, a counterfeit plate is brought into the captain's office. Schmidt states his case as Dutch (Hally Chester), one of the kids brought in as a witness, manages to sneak the plate out of its container and tosses it out the window to Skinny. Capt. Moran, not knowing what had happened, orders O'Day to deliver the plate to the Treasury Department. When it is discovered that the plate is missing and Officer O'Day was the last person seen with it, any illegal activity connected with the plate is charged to Officer O'Day, Knuckles' only advocate. It is under these calculated circumstances that the plate falls into the lap of Philip Mileaway.

Mileaway is like Rocky Sullivan in that he too has been recently released from prison and returns to his old neighborhood to pick up where he left off. But the similarities stop here. Whereas Rocky rewards the kids for their assistance, Mileaway uses them selfishly. He is without morals or warm feelings for anybody, especially his boyhood buddies. He is more of a caricature than a character.

The kids finally realize that Mileaway double-crossed them. Dutch, in a glowing display of heroics, pursues Mileaway to the roof from which both topple to the ground. (Also in *Boys of the City* it is Hally Chester who grabs the gun away from the bad guy.)

The criminal chase scenes in *Dead End, Angels with Dirty Faces, Hell's Kitchen* and *East Side Kids* involve skirmishes through and around buildings. In *East Side Kids* the depth perception on the roof is only slightly augmented, given away by a fake New York skyline and a quick downward view of a horde of people. Same is true of other roof scenes in subsequent films. Thus, hardly any need for stuntmen in these pictures, though the use of them would have made for more excitement. In the Bowery Boys' *Trouble Makers,* however, Frankie Darro and Carey Loftin take the place of Gorcey and Hall in a few acrobatic stunts.

There are a great number of script flaws that force us to take several things on face value; for instance, Officer O'Day's assertion that Knuckles never carried a gun in his life.

Another example is Officer O'Day's revelation that Mileaway made a full confession on his death bed, allowing Knuckles to go free.

Unlike the Dead End Kids or the Little Tough Guys, the kids in *East Side Kids* are not a tightly knit group, and therefore their leader is less prominent. What is interesting is that in the end, it is not Danny but Dutch, one of the regular members of the gang, who becomes the hero and a gymnasium is purchased by the community in his memory. This ending catches the film before it completely loses sight of its own course. Its focus shifts from O'Day to Mileaway, using the kids as pawns in their private war. We know very little about the kids, we know only what the plot allows us to know. Perhaps it is because no star kid appears in the film, and that the producers felt that Leon Ames as O'Day and Dennis Moore as Mileaway would carry the film. They are not enough. Monogram Pictures never again ran into this problem, for nobody attracted the crowds more than Gorcey, Jordan and Hall.

Boys of the City

Released July 19, 1940; Monogram; 63 minutes; Director, Joseph H. Lewis; Producer, Sam Katzman; Story and Screenplay, William Lively; Photography, Robert Cline, Film Editor, Carl Pierson; Production Manager, Ed W. Rote; Assistant Director, Robert Ray; Sound, Glen Glenn; Also known as *The Ghost Creeps*.

CAST

Danny	Bobby Jordan	*Algie*	Jack Edwards
Muggs	Leo Gorcey	*Simp*	Vince Barnett
Knuckles	Dave O'Brien	*Giles*	Dennis Moore
Tony	George Humbert	*Harrison*	Stephen Chase
Johnny	Hally Chester	*Agnes*	Minerva Urecal
Scruno	Sunshine Sammy	*Louise*	Inna Gest
	Morrison	*Ike*	David Gorcey
Skinny	Donald Haines	*Cook*	Jerry Mandy
Peewee	Frankie Burke	*Judge Parker*	Forrest Taylor

Boys of the City is the best of three East Side Kids films with a haunted house motif, crude scare tactics notwithstanding. Dim lighting is the chief technique used to create an eerie atmosphere. Against this dark background we meet a variety of cagey people who send chills up the spines of the East Side Kids.

As the camera pans left from kid to kid, we are introduced to the new East Side Kids cast, with particular attention to Danny (Bobby Jordan), the quasi–gang leader, and Muggs (Leo Gorcey), being fanned by Scruno ("Sunshine" Sammy Morrison from "Our Gang"), the only black member of the gang. Muggs (sometimes spelled Mugs) wastes no time displaying his disagreeable disposition by complaining that Scruno's fanning is only making him hotter.

Classic images of the Lower East Side combine for a deftly photographic scene and marks the beginning of the story. When the kids open the fire hydrant, interfering with an Italian fruit vendor's business, a cop gets drenched and hauls Danny and Muggs into police headquarters.

This East Side Kids film, and two out of the next three, get quite a bit of mileage out of the Algie Wilkie character, the token rich kid and counterpart of Cyril Gerrard (Jackie Searl) in *Little Tough Guy*. Algie (conservatively played by Jack Edwards) surfaced briefly in *East Side Kids*. He takes it upon himself to relieve the pressure put upon his underprivileged pals by prevailing upon his father for help. In *That Gang of Mine*, the father invests in a racehorse that Muggs is set on racing; in *Flying Wild* the father (his name changed to Mr. Reynolds) provides jobs for the kids to keep them productively occupied.

Here he offers the kids the alternative of going to his country home in the Adirondacks or face reform school. That the police agree to his idea shows a vast difference among the law enforcement officers in the East Side Kids films, the Little Tough Guys films and the Dead End Kids films. In *Little Tough Guy* and *Crime School*, the narrow-minded judges decide that

Left to right: Hally Chester, Donald Haines, Leo Gorcey, Eugene Francis, Bobby Jordan, Sammy Morrison, Frankie Burke and Minerva Urecal in *Boys of the City.*

the kids must be punished for their crimes. Here, the cops ask themselves, what could they expect from underprivileged slum kids with nothing to do during the hot summer? Better to send them to the Adirondacks.

The appearance of Judge Parker, a stranger who accepts a lift from the kids after his car breaks down, and then invites them to spend the night in his estate because he thinks they might prevent a murder — which they do not — is fundamental to the story. Although Judge Parker does not make an appearance in *East Side Kids*, and Knuckles, Danny's big brother, heroically portrayed by Dave O'Brien, is seen only briefly at the beginning and at the end of that film, the idea here is that Judge Parker sentenced Knuckles to death for the murder of a policeman in *East Side Kids*. There seems to be no real reason for this coincidence to exist, except for an attempt to tie these two films together.

The judge confides to his niece that he is hiding from the enigmatic Morro gang, because he will be testifying against one of its members in court and is afraid that they are out to kill him. Since he cannot identify a single member of the gang if his life depended upon it, the prospect of being in close proximity to one or many of them increases with the number of people he invites to Briarcliff Manor. Instead of being alone with his niece — the only person he can truly trust — he is surrounded by nine kids, his slippery attorney Giles, his quirky bodyguard Simp, Agnes the whacko caretaker, and the dummy-like cook. He's miles away

The kids (left to right: Frankie Burke, David Gorcey, Bobby Jordan, Leo Gorcey, unidentified FBI agent with gun) capture the killer Vince Barnett carrying damsel Inna Gest in *Boys of the City*.

from the nearest police and his automobile has broken down. Would he not have been safer had he remained in New York?

Sure enough, he's killed.

Thus, *Boys of the City* becomes a whodunit and everybody is suspect. Simp, portrayed as a nebbish by Vince Barnett, provides one of the most alarming incidents in the film when he covers his head with his coat, corners Louise, and threatens to kill her. While putting a coat over one's head is hardly inventive, it's scary enough and produces the right effect.

Agnes, an intensely sinister, tight-lipped, weirdo, magnificently portrayed by Minerva Urecal, wears all black, keeps the house dark, and is insanely devoted to the spirit of Leonora Parker, Judge Parker's late wife. She admits that she blames Judge Parker for Leonora's suffering and is glad that he is dead. But she denies killing him and denies killing the cook, whose body is found in a closet. Why the cook is killed is never explained. "I didn't kill the cook," Agnes says. "I liked the cook." A hint that a trace of humanity lies somewhere beyond her stare of ice.

Secret passageways made accessible by tapping on a piano is a staple device in three East Side Kids films and numerous Bowery Boys films. The secret tunnel scene with Gorcey and Jordan is by far the best in the film, one of the best in the entire series. What makes it so is not the darkness of the tunnel, nor the sound of another voice, nor finding the ghost sheet used earlier to scare the kids out of the house, but the combined courage of Danny and Muggs and their dependency and concern for one another. Though Danny and Muggs work closely together in other films such as *Mr. Wise Guy*, the crisis in other films is not as intense. nor do they rely upon each other as they do here for safety.

Where the film is not predictable, it is disjointed. Knuckles finds a man in the tunnel, beats him in a fistfight and drags him into the living room: The kids assume it is the murderer and release Giles and Simp. This is an obvious mistake on the kids' part and clearly prepares us for the revelation that Giles and Simp are the murderers, members of the Morro gang. The man Knuckles fought is from the district attorney's office in New York, on assignment to look after Judge Parker. What a failure! His abrupt appearance, nay, his entire presence is out of context, and the film would have done better eliminating him altogether.

As far as *The New York Times* was concerned, the entire film should have been eliminated: "[T]his much we are certain — the boys are wasting their time on sort of hocus-pocus entertainment(?) that the Globe is serving this week" (Thomas M. Pryor, August 19, 1940).

Critically, the film is packed with flaws of every kind (obvious use of electric lighting in the background when Jordan lights a match). But the fact that this is a haunted house drama with the East Side Kids, and a mystery story with actors who can frighten the average moviegoing adolescent of the 1940s, makes it a fun movie.

That Gang of Mine

Released September 24, 1940; 62 minutes; Monogram; Director, Joseph H. Lewis; Producer, Sam Katzman; Screenplay, William Lively; Original Story, Alan Whitman; Photography, Bob Cline; Film Editor, Carl Pierson.

CAST

Danny	Bobby Jordan		*Skinny*	Donald Haines
Muggs	Leo Gorcey		*Knuckles*	Dave O'Brien
Peewee	David Gorcey		*Mr. Wilkie*	Milton Kibbee
Ben	Clarence Muse		*Algie*	Eugene Francis
Louise	Joyce Bryant		*Morgan*	Forrest Taylor

That Gang of Mine is the first of three consecutive pictures in which Muggs acquires a taste for ambition. But what inspires him to become a jockey is not a love of horses, or a passion for riding (at the time of his declaration, he has yet to even sit on a horse) but the wad of bills he sees in local jockey Johnny Sullivan's pockets.

"People treat them like they're somebody," Muggs says of jockeys.

Muggs, who takes great pride in being tough and fearless, learns the hard way that he is afraid of speed. During his first race, we actually hear him whispering to the horse, Blue Knight, to slow down.

That Gang of Mine is also the story of a dream come true for Ben, an unemployed black groomer, who owns Blue Knight.

The way the kids' and Ben's paths cross is photographically choppy. The kids are frolicking in the stable, where they waste too much film time. Suddenly, and for no apparent reason, they run to the opposite corner and amuse themselves by climbing over the wooden dividers. As Muggs tries to balance himself on the edge of a divider, he falls on Blue Knight.

In addition to Muggs' internal conflict, there is some crooked gambling activity going

Clarence Muse and Leo Gorcey in *That Gang of Mine.*

on. Knuckles, a bit more foolish than his previous namesakes, is engaged to marry Louise. (Here Louise is played by Joyce Bryant, a better actress than Inna Guest who played Louise in *Boys of the City*. Whether the film intends the two Louises to be one and the same is uncertain.) He bets all his money on Blue Knight in the first race and loses it. Blackie, a friend of Morgan's associate, is commissioned to assure Blue Knight's defeat. Blackie tries to fix the big race with Knuckles' help. Knuckles' answer is a clout on Blackie's jaw.

Tipped that something might happen to Blue Knight, the kids take the horse to another stable. Blackie follows them and sets fire to the stable.

As in *Dead End Kids on Dress Parade* Muggs' rescue of the occupants of the building makes everybody see things in a clearer light. As he drags Ben out of the fire, Muggs realizes that Ben may never see Blue Knight win if it does not win in the next race. Muggs now accepts the fact that his stubbornness may cause Blue Knight to lose and Ben to die an unhappy man.

Along with Muggs' willingness to step down as jockey comes his determination to get Johnny Sullivan in Blue Knight's saddle in the most important race for all concerned. But Sullivan, sulking over the fact that he was originally passed over for the job, refuses.

It is not until Muggs packs a few punches to Sullivan's paunch that the jockey agrees to ride.

Though we do not actually see Muggs tangle with Sullivan, one camera shot of Muggs gives every indication that he is about to take Sullivan apart. Muggs walks toward the door as if he is going to leave Sullivan's apartment. Instead, he locks the door, turns around and leaves the camera shot while taking off his jacket.

By successfully convincing Sullivan in this manner, Muggs changes career choices; he explores this new one in the next film, *Pride of the Bowery*.

A good deal of attention is given to racial differences. One night Ben sings "All God's Children Got Shoes," to which Scruno does a very good tap dance. Later that evening, Ben says to Scruno, although it is not clear what he is referring to—perhaps Muggs' unpolished riding technique—"You see things that white boys don't see but hush your lip." Later, when Ben suggests to Muggs that he should allow Sullivan to ride Blue Knight in the big race, Muggs slaps Ben's face, a liberty he does not take with anybody else.

That Gang of Mine is a film lacking in substance. The major conflict is Muggs' internal one which is neither crucial nor dramatic enough to sustain the film. The only external confrontation, between Knuckles and Blackie, does not even involve the kids. Fortunately, the next film, which also focuses on Muggs' emotional growing pains, has more appeal than this one. After all, nobody can take Muggs' place in the boxing ring.

Pride of the Bowery

Released January 24, 1941; 61 minutes; Monogram; Director, Joseph H. Lewis; Producer, Sam Katzman; Associate Producer: Pete Mayer; Screenplay, George Plympton; Story, Steven Clensos; Adapted by William Lively; Photography, Robert Cline; Editor, Robert Golden; Musical Directors, Johnny Lange, Lew Porter; Sound, Glen Glenn; opened at the Rialto.

CAST

Muggs Maloney	Leo Gorcey	*Scruno*	Sunshine Sammy Morrison
Danny	Bobby Jordan		
Skinny	Donald Haines	*Algy*	Eugene Francis
Norton	Carleton Young	*Elaine*	Mary Ainsley
Al	Kenneth Howell	*Captain*	Kenneth Harlan
Peewee	David Gorcey	*Willie*	Bobby Stone

Pride of the Bowery is a break from the usual crime story, a good character study filled with action and dramatic internal conflicts.

Muggs Maloney is coming to terms with growing up. He is the main character here and continues to climb into prominence until his pinnacle in *Spooks Run Wild*, where he is fully recognized by the other kids (and the producers) as *the* leader of the gang.

Full of himself, a personality trait that surfaced in *Hell's Kitchen* and came to a head in *On Dress Parade*, Gorcey requires something better than a stuffy indoor training room; he wants outdoor facilities. Danny obliges him. He inveigles him into signing papers committing him to six months at a CCC (Civilian Conservation Corps) camp.

Muggs' first disillusionment comes when he gets into a row with Al, the head camper, and finds himself on his back. "I musta slipped."

When he interferes with the doctor's examination of the new boys and is sent to the captain's office, Muggs' second disillusionment is facially expressed as he exclaims, "You mean this is a CCC camp?" Nevertheless he remains, knowing that a check for $22 a month will be sent to his mother in New York.

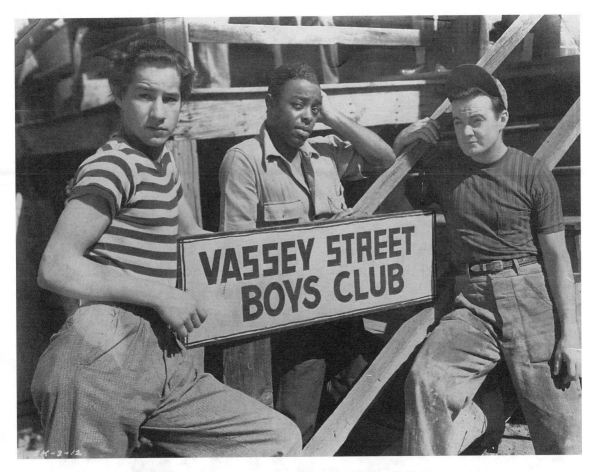

Left to right: Jordan, Morrison and Gorcey in *Pride of the Bowery*.

In *Bowery Blitzkrieg*, Muggs' capacity for human understanding, sympathy and tolerance of others is first revealed and continues to develop through the East Side Kids films and the Bowery Boys films. But it is in *Pride of the Bowery* where noble virtues such as courage and charity stand out.

Muggs, a city boy, watches a tree fall. In the distance (though the camera gives us a poor perception of space), Muggs spots Al walking through the forest, oblivious to the falling tree. There are good close-ups and good editing of the faces of Muggs and Al, as Muggs screams for Al to stop. When Al does not hear him, Muggs tackles him out of the path of the tree. The scene is an exciting exhibition of spontaneity in the face of danger. It shows that in spite of Muggs not liking Al, he is willing to risk his life to save another human being. This willingness to do good for others is shown in almost every succeeding film.

The captain is very impressed with Muggs' heroic act. "This camp may be the means to finding yourself," he says.

"Go on, I ain't even lost."

Muggs' attempt to down play the rescue is consistent with his comment in *Million Dollar Kid* after the kids save an old gentleman from a mugging. In that film he brushes off Mr. Cortland's gesture of thanks by saying, "We would do the same for any Joe."

As a reward, and with Al's consent, Muggs is given his chance to square himself with Al — his first opportunity in the boxing ring. After three rounds, the captain stops the fight

Publicity shot of Gorcey grabbing Bobby Stone.

and calls it a draw. At this announcement, Gorcey gives a convincing display of hysteria. Muggs is unable to accept the fact that he has not won and refuses to shake Al's hand. The campers show their disapproval of Muggs' poor sportsmanship by giving him the silent treatment. All except Danny avoid him.

Although Danny has been relegated to second banana, his brief moments on the screen are pivotal. He is the one responsible for the kids' stint at the camp. He is the one who unravels the truth behind Muggs' breaking and entering the captain's office to allegedly steal $100.

After chasing Willie, to the lake and engaging in a splashy fistfight, Danny drags him into the captain's office. Willie confesses that he stole $100 from the captain's petty cash box and convinced Muggs that he needed it for a sick aunt. Muggs, feeling sorry for Willie and remembering an offer by Norton's Fight Arena, after his bout with Al, asks Norton for a fight that night and $100 with a promise to fight more at a future date. Norton gives him the fight and the C-note.

The acting of Gorcey and Jordan, Joseph H. Lewis' direction, and the cinematography are above-average here, though the film does have its weaknesses. The story, trite and unimaginative, copies a good deal from *On Dress Parade* (Gorcey sent to a military camp under false pretenses). It also seems to have trouble keeping the other kids out of view while it concentrates on Muggs. They volunteer to remain on camp grounds thinking Muggs would not be

Cast of *Pride of the Bowery*. Top, left to right: Kenneth Howell, David Gorcey, Sammy Morrison, Donald Haines, Bobby Stone and Eugene Francis. Bottom, left to right: Leo Gorcey, Mary Ainsley and Bobby Jordan.

allowed out and would be lonely. Cheap techniques such as these are constantly used to remove the minor players from the action. In the case of David Gorcey, his role remained minimal for the next 18 years. It came to the point where directors no longer felt a need to make excuses for his absence and began excluding and including him indiscriminately. Why he remained so long in this capacity is a puzzle.

Bobby Stone and Kenneth Howell are dull as Willie and Al respectively. Little more is ever seen of Howell but Stone appears in several East Side Kids movies as Muggs' adversary and as one of the gang. His acting is uninspiring and it is incomprehensible why he was chosen for some of the more important roles. His membership as an East Side Kid was short and nobody missed him when he left.

There are several scenes of the camp that provide good promotional material for the government-sponsored program. Working in the forest, cutting down trees and digging canals are meant to inspire underprivileged American boys to join a CCC camp.

When *Pride of the Bowery* opened at the Rialto in New York on January 24, 1941 (and at the Capitol in Philadelphia on February 20), reviews were generally favorable. *The Philadelphia Record* gave it the nod, calling it "a pleasant yarn, full of rough humor" with "some interesting authentic shots of life and work in the C.C.C. camps which stress their value in building up growing boys" (2/20/41). The *Journal American* termed it "unpretentiously amiable" ... Less artificial than most such films" (January 24, 1941). The *New York World Telegram* noted it was "done in a sound standardized manner, has some good acting and excellent camera work.... [C]hief honors go to Leo Gorcey, with first rate work by Kenneith Howell" (January 24, 1941). The *New York Post* gave it a compliment: "For a picture which costs 'peanuts' its worth much more in entertainment value" (Irene Thirer, January 24, 1941).

Variety's comments were mixed, calling it "a hackneyed story that telegraphs its way almost from the opening scene" but then admits it's "straight-forwardly told and with more than adequate thespic and directorial skill.... Kenneth Harlan carries off the principal adult part with dignity while Robert Cline's camera work is of high order...."

The only thumbs-down holdout was *The New York Times*: "[W]e feel that somebody should turn over a new leaf — if not the Dead End kids, then certainly the script writers."

Both the *New York Post* and the *Journal American* pointed out that the associate producer, Peter Mayer, was the son of Arthur Meyer, owner of the Rialto.

═══════════════════

Flying Wild

Released March 10, 1941; 62 minutes; Monogram; Director, William West; Producer, Sam Katzman; Story and Screenplay, Al Martin; Photography, Fred Jackman, Jr.; Film Editor, Robert Cline; Music Directors, Johnny Lange and Lew Porter.

CAST

Muggs	Leo Gorcey		*Forbes*	Forrest Taylor
Danny	Bobby Jordan		*Woodward*	Bob Hill
Skinny	Donald Haines		*George*	Dennis Moore
Peewee	David Gorcey		*Tom*	Dave O'Brien
Helen	Joan Barclay		*Algie*	Eugene Francis
Louie	Bobby Stone		*Mr. Reynolds*	Herbert Rawlinson
Scruno	Sunshine Sammy Morrison		*Nagel*	George Pembroke

Flying Wild embellishes several previous motifs and broadens the scope of the kids' adventures as they constitute the most serious offensive against a group of spies.

Although Bobby Jordan gets top billing, and is technically the leader of the gang, the fact that Muggs prefers to loiter about the base tips us off that most of the action will take place outside the realm of routine maintenance work which is where Danny and the rest of them spend most of their time. (Avoiding work becomes a trademark of Gorcey's character in later East Side Kids and Bowery Boys films.)

Social intercourse with women is less of a task than it was in *Pride of the Bowery*. Helen, a nurse, explains to Muggs that the flying ambulance, owned by Dr. Nagel, is used to transport patients to the nearest hospital. Muggs, knowing Mr. Reynolds suspects sabotage on the air base, is suspicious of Dr. Nagel and his flying ambulance. But Muggs changes his opinion when Dr. Nagel agrees to use the flying ambulance for Peewee, injured by a falling airplane wing.

Paradoxically, Dr. Nagel becomes aware of Muggs' suspicion of him.

Fight scene in *Flying Wild*. Left to right on the ground: Donald Haines, Leo Gorcey, unidentified actor, Bobby Stone, Bobby Jordan, unidentified actor choking Jordan, unidentified actor looking up, Eugene Francis. Standing: unidentified actor carrying Sunshine Sammy Morrison, David O'Brien (wearing pilot hat).

This is the first of two occasions (the first of *four*, if we include the Bowery Boys films) where the David Gorcey character is bedridden. The injury scene is grossly self-conscious. Peewee is laughing at Danny and Muggs arguing over some trite issue. (While this minor skirmish between Muggs and Danny is merely a cog to move the plot, it does foreshadow major altercations between these two in *Bowery Blitzkrieg* and *Kid Dynamite*.) Out of nowhere, an airplane wing falls on Peewee. When Dr. Nagel agrees to help Peewee, Muggs remarks to Danny, loud enough for Dr. Nagel to hear, "And I thought he was a spy."

Under the auspices of Mr. Reynolds, Muggs and Danny get involved in an aggressive attempt to bait the saboteurs. Mr. Reynolds lets it be known that Danny is delivering blueprints to an office in town, hoping the saboteurs will try to steal them from Danny What the saboteurs do not know is that Danny is being monitored. But Danny has little confidence in Reynolds' agents and asks Muggs to join him on his mission. The next time we see Muggs and Danny, they are locked inside a pickle barrel. (As in, what a pickle they're in!)

Dr. Nagel arranges no air station control for the flying ambulance on the return flight for Peewee. In spite of the fog, Tom the pilot (also Helen's fiancé, but this has no bearing on

Gorcey with a black eye and Morrison with a white eye in publicity shot for *Flying Wild*. Left to right: Joan Barclay, David O'Brien, Donald Haines, Bobby Stone, Gorcey, Eugene Francis, Morrison.

the story the way the Knuckles-Louise engagement has in *That Gang of Mine*), lands the plane safely. This negligence on the part of the air station, coupled with a piece of blueprint Muggs finds on the plane, renews Muggs' suspicion of Dr. Nagel.

With the exception of the tunnel scene in *Boys of the City*, the end of *Flying Wild* is the only time in the series where Muggs and Danny conspire together to outsmart the opposition and succeed without any outside help. (In *Mr. Wise Guy* all the kids work together to prove Danny's brother's innocence, and in the end there is adult intervention.)

They find out that a bogus patient, Forbes, is being taken to Mexico with secret documents concealed in his head bandage. Muggs and Danny burst into his room, subdue him and lock him in a closet. Danny takes his place on the stretcher, while Muggs, with Helen's help, sneaks onto the flying ambulance. Now that they have foiled the smuggling, the boys and Helen must now save their own lives. (We won't dwell on the misplaced priorities.)

By the time the airplane arrives at San Cassenta, Dr. Nagel's men know about the switch and take Muggs and Danny to a hideout, leaving Helen to be picked up later.

The script is shaky here, for Dr. Nagel's men have no reason to leave Helen at the airport, only to make an additional trip back to the airport to pick her up. The reason the script calls for it is because Tom and the kids follow the flying ambulance in another airplane. Without the return of Nagel's men to the airport, they would have no way of finding Muggs and Danny. Tom and the kids force Nagel's men to take them to Muggs and Danny. It is the first time the East Side Kids engage in a fistic combat and win.

Flying Wild is frustratingly slow-moving, especially for a spy film. Instead of giving the audience an inkling of who the spies might be working for, we can only guess it is for some Axis party. The film spends too much time on sequences that remain unresolved and scenes that have little or no significance. Having Muggs and Danny go to town with counter-espionage groups on their trail is a good idea, but it is not developed fully. The scene in which Muggs coaxes Danny to take medicine is long and inconsequential.

The last scene of the film is "vintage Muggs." Rewarded for his role in the capture of the spies, Muggs accepts a job as Mr. Reynolds' chauffeur. On his first morning, with Mr. Reynolds in the back seat, he crashes into a monument. Before Mr. Reynolds can open his smashed-cigar–filled mouth, Muggs bellows, "Say no more. I quit."

Bowery Blitzkrieg

Released September 8, 1941; 62 minutes; Monogram/Banner Productions; Director, Wallace Fox; Producer, Sam Katzman; Associate Producer; Peter Mayer; Screenplay, Sam Robins; Story, Brandan Wood, Don Mullahy; Photography, Marcel LePicard; Film Editor, Robert Golden; Production Manager: Ed W. Rote; Assistant Directors, Harry Slott, Arthur Hammond; Musical Directors, Johnny Lange and Lew Porter; Set Director, Fred Preble; Sound, Glen Glenn; Title in England: *Stand and Deliver*.

CAST

Muggs McGinnis	Leo Gorcey	*Skinny*	Donald Haines
Danny Breslin	Bobby Jordan	*Mrs. Brady*	Martha Wentworth
Glimpy	Huntz Hall	*Peewee*	David Gorcey
Tom Brady	Warren Hull	*Scruno*	Sunshine Sammy
Mary Breslin	Charlotte Henry		Morrison
Clancy	Keye Luke	*Officer*	Jack Mulhall
Monk Martin	Bobby Stone		

Bowery Blitzkrieg is rich in dimension, plot, characterization and scene diversity. But is it plausible?

From the second-floor window of their tenement building Danny and his sister Mary Breslin view the makeshift parade that welcomes the celebrated East Side Kid Muggs McGinnis (not Maloney as it was in *Pride of the Bowery* and *That Gang of Mine*) after his release from jail. "Friends, Romans, countrymen, lend me your ears ... and five bucks."

Photographically, the physical distance symbolizes the discord between the two East Side Kids. It takes only a little prodding by Monk Martin, small-time local hood, to convince Danny that Muggs has been spreading vicious rumors about him.

Figures of authority as self-proclaimed guardians of the kids are commonplace in these films, from Father Connolly in *Angels with Dirty Faces*, to Mr. Reynolds or Mr. Wilkie in the later East Side Kids films. Most often, however, the guardian is a law enforcement officer (Mark Braden in *Crime School*, Patrolman Conroy in *Mug Town*, Officer Pat O'Day in *East*

A crowd celebrates Muggs' release from jail in *Bowery Blitzkreig*. Facing audience, left to right: Leo Gorcey, Huntz Hall.

Side Kids, etc.). Here it's Officer Tom Brady, who is engaged to Mary. Muggs has been taking up most of Tom's time, however. Sensing he may be the cause of Tom and Mary breaking up, Muggs moves out. We never find out where he goes, except to the street and to the gym.

The struggling small-time hood is a prevalent figure in several Little Tough Guys and East Side Kids films (Monk Bangor in *Mob Town*, Mileaway in *East Side Kids*, Gabe Dell's role in numerous East Side Kids escapades). *Bowery Blitzkrieg* is blessed with two such sleazy snakes, Slats Morrison and Monk Martin. Slats tries to impress big-city gamblers by bribing Muggs to lose his bout with Jimmy Ryan. Morrison slips $1,000 into Muggs' pants pocket, hoping this will whet Muggs' appetite.

While Muggs is able to resist the lure of bad guy's money, Danny gets a rush of adrenalin at the sight of Monk's new automobile. Danny joins Monk on his robbing binges and is soon getting his shoes shined (as opposed to *giving* shoeshines as he does in *Dead End* to "Baby Face" Martin).

But his fantasy life with Monk Martin ends abruptly. Just as Tom Barker (Billy Hallop) in *Mob Town* suddenly turns against Monk Bangor during a shoot-out with Officer Conroy, so does Danny stop Monk Martin from shooting Tom Brady; this time it is Danny who gets shot and is rushed to the hospital.

Bobby Jordan (striped shirt) and Leo Gorcey do battle in *Bowery Blitzkreig*. Watching, left to right, are David Gorcey, Donald Haines, Jordan, Sunshine Sammy Morrison, Gorcey, and Huntz Hall (standing on table). Others are unidentified.

East Side Kids films are not noted for symbolism, yet it is impossible to ignore the symbolic overtones of Muggs donating a pint of blood to save Danny's life. Muggs not only assumes the leadership position Danny once held, but infiltrates his body as well, a god-like, life-giving figure.

Danny learns that Muggs donated his blood so that he may live, realizes he was wrong about Muggs, and that it was Monk who set up the confrontation between himself and Muggs. Monk admits this before he dies of gunshot wounds inflicted by Tom Brady (just as Mile-away confesses to the murder Knuckles is convicted of before he dies in *East Side Kids*).

The events leading up to Muggs' boxing match create additional challenges for him and a dramatic climax. Word reaches the Police Athletic League that Muggs has accepted a bribe from Skip Morrison. So not only is Muggs fighting with a pint of blood missing, but under pressure to win lest he be accused of complying with racketeers. Danny is listening to the fight on the radio with his sister and Ma Brady. When the doctor is told that the boy in the ring just gave a pint of blood, he tells Ma Brady and Mary to get to the arena immediately to stop the fight.

The technical mistake here is that it is the doctor whom the promoters would be more apt to believe than a couple of tenement women.

Seeing Ma Brady at ringside telling him Danny is going to be all right inspires Muggs (as opposed to Elaine's appearance at ringside in *Pride of the Bowery*, which distracts him). Simultaneously with the count of ten, Ma Brady pulls out the letter with the $1,000 Muggs sent her earlier, and hands it to the police.

While *Bowery Blitzkrieg* is structurally sound and well-planned, execution of ideas and arrangement of events is questionable. This does not mean that all East Side Kids films, except this one, are totally believable, but the filmmakers expect too much from Muggs McGinnis and too much leeway from the audience.

The first part of the film establishes several conflicts: Tom Brady and Mary Breslin's shaky relationship; Muggs threatened by racketeers; Danny's involvement with a criminal.

That the engagement can be threatened by Tom's concern over a street kid is hardly believable in itself; that it can be patched up by Muggs moving out of the Brady home renders the story somewhat of a fairy tale.

Bobby Stone repeats his role as a sneaky, conniving crook, first established in *Pride of the Bowery*, and has not improved it any.

Bowery Blitzkrieg is Huntz Hall's East Side Kids debut as Glimpy, the comical, idiotic character that he created and expanded upon throughout his career as an East Side Kid and later as a Bowery Boy. His role is basically passive and remains so until the later East Side Kids films.

There is one outstanding comical moment that is photographically choppy. After the fight, the scene abruptly switches to the inside of an apartment where Muggs, still in his fighting trunks, is surrounded by the other East Side Kids—including Danny (which is very surprising since we just left him in the hospital in critical condition), about to be forced into a tuxedo to be best man at Tom and Mary's wedding. Prior to this, there is no indication that the wedding is to take place after the fight. Fade in-fade out. Muggs, dressed in a tuxedo, swinging his fists, and all the kids lying on the floor, giving the impression that the kids managed to get the clothing on Muggs, but got knocked out doing so. Suddenly, Glimpy appears in Muggs' trunks. "How did I get in these?"

Technical flaws and dubious credibility notwithstanding, *Bowery Blitzkrieg* compensates for its weaknesses with its variety of conflicts, a thick plot, good photography, and Leo Gorcey's charismatic appeal.

Spooks Run Wild

Released October 24, 1941; 5821 ft.; Monogram; A Banner Production; 69 minutes; Director, Phil Rosen; Producer, Sam Katzman; Associate Producer, Pete Mayer; Story and Screenplay, Carl Foreman, Charles R. Marion; Additional dialogue, Jack Henley; Photography, Marcel LePicard; Film Editor, Robert Golden.; Production Manager, Ed W. Rote; Assistant Director, Arthur Hammond; Musical Directors, Johnny Lange and Lew Porter; Sound Glen Glenn.

CAST

Nardo	Bela Lugosi		*Peewee*	David Gorcey
Muggs McGinnis	Leo Gorcey		*Scruno*	Sammy Morrison
Glimpy	Huntz Hall		*Skinny*	Donald Haines
Danny	Bobby Jordan		*Jeff Dixon*	Dave O'Brien

Linda Mason   Dorothy Short
Margie   Rosemary Portia

Von Grosch   Dennis Moore
Constable   Guy Wilkerson

Scanning the cast list, *Spooks Run Wild* would seem to be an East Side Kids–Bela Lugosi fan's delight. Unfortunately it's not nearly as impressive as its cast, nor clever as its title. Its "haunted house features" are neither original nor scary, and the story is devoid of human conflict, an essential ingredient to spice up these films. It yearns to maximize Lugosi on camera but takes little advantage of his talent. The result is a poorly constructed film, weak on originality and characterization, with no defined story line.

It begins with the same premise as *Boys of the City*: The kids are sent to the country to keep out of trouble in the city. It continues to develop the character of Muggs McGinnis and his growing independence of, and influence over, the rest of the kids.

On a stopover, the kids patronize the local soda fountain and are bedazzled by Margie, the waitress. In the middle of the night, when Muggs tries to sneak out to meet her, the rest of the gang joins him. The fact that Muggs is about to do something devious is reason enough for the other kids to want to do the same.

The kids spend most of their time roaming throughout the Billings estate trying to find

Bela Lugosi and dwarf Angelo Rossitto in *Spooks Run Wild* with the East Side Kids: left to right, Sammy Morrison, Leo Gorcey, Huntz Hall (being choked), Bobby Jordan and Donald Haines.

Peewee, who disappeared after Lugosi treated him for a buckshot wound and showed the other kids their room for the night.

"A very charming room in a repulsive sort of way," observes Glimpy.

Although he is draped in his Dracula regalia and accompanied by a dwarf, Lugosi does little more than glare at the kids. Most of his time is spent before the camera being jumped and bound and gagged by the kids ... then surprising the daylights out of them by re-emerging in another part of the house. Where you would expect to see some display of trick photography, there is none. The only comment Lugosi has to say on the matter, in his thick Hungarian accent, is, "Things are not always what they appear to be." This suggests optical illusion but there is none. Everything can be technically explained in terms of simple shot changes.

But there are two scenes where the photographer goes out on a limb to produce a few simple tricks. The first is when the mayor, the sheriff and Jeff rush into the room in search of the kids, and see a glowing Muggs head in the middle of the dark room. A second later, the lights are switched on, revealing all the kids in the room with Muggs in the middle, holding a flashlight up to his chin. In the final scene of the picture, Lugosi, who we now know is really Nardo the Magician, treats everyone to a magic act. He puts Linda, the nurse, in a box and makes her disappear. Muggs, skeptic that he is, challenges Nardo, claiming he can find her. Lugosi ushers him into the box. A few seconds later, we see Muggs holding Scruno in his arms.

Scruno's race is alluded to twice in this picture. Blatantly in one case, subtly in the other. When the bus driver looks into the exhaust pipe, black smoke gushes forth and covers his face. When Muggs sees this, he blurts out, "Hey, Scruno's uncle." When Scruno sees the bus driver, he takes the cue: "Hey, Unc!"

After putting Peewee to bed, the kids are wary about leaving him alone, but too scared to stay with him. Scruno is the favorite choice among the kids. He plays a similar role in *Let's Get Tough*, the frightened lookout.

The revelation that Lugosi is not the *Monster Killer*, that it's really Dr. Von Grosch, on his way allegedly to rescue the kids (how he knows the kids are at the estate is an unexplained mystery in itself), is a surprise only to Linda Mason. Von Grosch finds Linda on the road and offers to take her to the estate. He leads her into a dark room, slowly removes his glasses, dons gloves and puts his hands around her throat. Only then does Linda realize what's happening and screams.

There are several items that are questionable. For example, why does Dr. Von Grosch, knowing there are people at the Billings estate, take Linda there if his sole purpose is to commit senseless murder? It would be a lot simpler for him to strangle her on the road. What motivated the night watchman to shoot at the kids without establishing their identity? How does Peewee suddenly get cured?

Why is the lock on the door to the room where Von Grosch is choking Linda still not broken after several bullet shots, yet Linda can easily open it with a slight twist? And who is this Von Grosch and where did he come from anyway?

It's hard to argue with the *New York Times* reviewer's remark, "[T]he whole business is ... as authentic as a papier-mâché skeleton."

Mr. Wise Guy

Released February 22, 1942; 70 minutes, Monogram; 6303 ft.; Director, William Nigh; Producers, Sam Katzman and Jack Dietz; Associate Producer, Barney A. Sarecky; Screenplay, Sam Robins, Harvey Gates, Jack Henley; Original Story, Martin Mooney; Production Manager, Ed W. Rote; Assistant Directors, Arthur Hammond, Gerald Schnitzer; Art Director, G.C. Van Marter; Photography, Art Reed; Film Editor, Carl Pierson; Music Directors, Lange and Porter; Sound, Glen Glenn; Sound Engineer, Buddy Meyers.

CAST

Muggs	Leo Gorcey	*Scruno*	Sunshine Sammy
Danny	Bobby Jordan		Morrison
Glimpy	Huntz Hall	*Peewee*	David Gorcey
Knobby	Billy Gilbert	*Dorothy*	Ann Doran
Charlie	Gabriel Dell	*Chalky*	Bobby Stone
Manning	Guinn Williams	*Waiter*	Benny Rubin
Dratler	Warren Hymer	*Jim Barnes*	Jack Mulhall
Ann	Joan Barclay	*Police Officer*	Fred Kelsey
Bill	Douglas Fowley		

"The films told the same story every time," Leonard Maltin writes about the Dead End Kids *et al.* in his book *Our Gang*. "*Mr. Wise Guy* ... is redundant ... [T]he lads' clashes with the law, albeit for the best, are beginning to pall" says the *New York Times* review of March 5, 1942.

What these critics don't ever seem to get is that these films weren't seeking approval from adult movie critics. Watching the East Side Kids outsmart crooked adults is enough to make an audience of wannabe adolescent heroes cheer. *Mr. Wise Guy* is a perfect example because it is a mesh of the best workable elements of previous films, woven into a well-organized (albeit implausible in parts) script.

The influence of *Dead End* is apparent early in the film as the kids swim illegally in the East River. From the river, Luke Manning, a convict escaping from Blackwell's Island, is smuggled to shore in a pickle barrel by his henchmen Dratler and Knobby. The consequences of his escape are felt throughout the film, especially by Danny, whose brother is sentenced to die for the murder committed by Manning.

Like Dippy, who goes on an errand for "Baby Face" Martin, and Angel, who shines Martin's shoes in *Dead End*, the East Siders are just as eager to do odd chores for a tip. The kids offer to help lift the barrel onto a truck. When the police make their routine patrol, they see only the kids loading the truck and arrest them for truck theft. Unable to prove their innocence (as opposed to the prosecutors unable to prove them guilty, but no matter), the kids are sent to the Wilson Reformatory.

Getaway car scenes with a hostage either at the wheel, or as a passenger, are pivotal moments in two previous films, *East Side Kids* and *Mob Town* (also directed by William Nigh). In these films, Danny (Dave Durand in *East Side Kids*) and Tommy (Halop in *Mob Town*) are in a car with the friend of their older "hood" brother who's either dead or on death row because the "friend" was just a bit more elusive. While the getaway scene in *Mr. Wise Guy* bears a close resemblance to the one in *Mob Town* in that both involve the robbing and killing of a druggist, here the driver and shooter are strangers. Bill purposely swerves into a

Warren Hymer (center) and the East Side Kids (left to right) David Gorcey, Leo Gorcey, Sammy Morrison, Hymer, Huntz Hall, Bobby Jordan and unidentified actor in *Mr. Wise Guy*.

lamppost. Luke escapes unharmed but Bill is injured, treated, then accused, convicted and sentenced to die in the electric chair for the murder of the druggist.

The kids in *Mr. Wise Guy* are made of the same stuff as in *Flying Wild*, when they recognize an opportunity to change the course of events. Admittedly, though, the sequence of events leading up to the kids' capture of Luke Manning and the staying of Bill's execution relies too much on coincidence and contrivance.

At the reformatory, the kids see a newsreel of the Canadian sweepstakes. They recognize Knobby and somehow Muggs discerns the manner in which Knobby opens his cigarettes is the same as the pack that was found in Bill's car. This is confusing for two reasons. How does Muggs know anything about the found pack of cigarettes? And in any event, it was not Knobby in the getaway car but Luke Manning. Then the kids overhear Chalky Jones and Rice Pudding Charlie, their reform school adversaries, laughing at their old acquaintance Knobby. Charlie tells them that Knobby formerly worked for his uncle, Luke Manning, until his uncle drowned trying to escape from Blackwell's Island. Muggs suddenly comes up with a hunch that perhaps it was not pickles they were helping Knobby load onto the truck, but Luke Manning. With Dorothy's address obtained from Charlie, the kids break out of the reformatory and arrive at Dorothy's apartment in the city at five in the morning, minutes before Dorothy and Knobby arrive.

Hall in drag in *Mr. Wise Guy.* He would don female clothes again in *Clancy Street Boys.* Left to right: Fred Kelsey, Leo Gorcey, David Gorcey, Hall, Bobby Jordan, unidentified cop.

The presence of a newsreel at the reformatory is perplexing. How does a newsreel about an event that takes place almost simultaneously find its way to the Wilson Reformatory? And how do the kids manage to get into Dorothy's apartment without a key?

Manning arrives at Dorothy's apartment. But before he has a chance to vent his anger, Mr. Barnes, the head of the reformatory, arrives with several policemen, placing Manning, Knobby, Dratler and Dorothy under arrest. Mr. Barnes calls the governor to stay Bill Wollins' execution.

Comedy for its own sake is not much a factor in the East Side Kids' films. However, the restaurant scene with Billy Gilbert and Benny Rubin is worth discussion. Gilbert starts by ordering the maitre d' and is told he cannot have him. Next he would like some sort of lemon pastry, but because he cannot pronounce it properly and Rubin cannot understand what he is saying, Gilbert does not get that either. Gilbert and Rubin then argue over who is going to have coffee with no cream and sugar, and who is having no cream, no sugar and no cup, etc. Gilbert's comedy gives this film an extra boost.

The nature of Gabriel Dell's first appearance in an East Side Kids film establishes the trend for his later roles as either Muggs' rival or in some capacity outside the fold of the gang. Only in *Block Busters*, *Come Out Fighting* and the Bowery Boys' *Hard Boiled Mahoney* does

Dell play one of the kids. Here, Charley (Dell) refers to Muggs as Ethelbert — his given name, which he understandably abhors. Muggs tricks Charlie and Chalky into believing that he is going to help them break out of the reformatory as well. Instead, he leaves them both on the floor licking their wounds.

Gorcey's performance is above par here and he obviously enjoys his popularity. *Mr. Wise Guy* is Muggs McGinnis. (It is the second of six East Side Kids films where the title refers to his character, the others being *That Gang of Mine, Kid Dynamite, Mr. Muggs Steps Out, Follow the Leader* and *Mr. Muggs Rides Again.*) He is the one with the ideas, the muscle, the leadership skills.

Jordan is in a trance for most of the picture, dwelling on the possible execution of his brother.

But as a whole the East Side Kids are in top form in *Mr. Wise Guy.*

Let's Get Tough

Released May 22, 1942; 62 minutes; 5599 ft.; Monogram; Director, Wallace Fox; Producers, Sam Katzman, Jack Dietz; Associate Producer, Barney A. Sarecky; Story ("I Am an American" and Screenplay), Harvey Gates; Photography, Art Reed; Film Editor, Robert Golden; Production Manager, E W. Rote; Assistant Director, Arthur Hammond, Gerald Schnitzer; Art Director, David Milton; Musical Directors, Johnny Lange and Lew Porter; Sound, Glen Glenn; Working title, *Little MacArthurs.*

CAST

Muggs	Leo Gorcey		*Heinrich*	Sam Bernard
Danny	Bobby Jordan		*Matsui*	Phil Ahn
Glimpy	Huntz Hall		*Phil*	Tom Brown
Scruno	Sunshine Sammy		*Nora Stevens*	Florence Rice
	Morrison		*Marine Recruiter*	George Eldredge
German Spy	Gabriel Dell		*Music Professor*	Jerry Bergen
Pop Stevens	Robert Armstrong			

Let's Get Tough, the title and the picture, is the East Side Kids' answer to the Japanese bombing of Pearl Harbor. Its intent is to portray the Japanese in the poorest light possible, and the kids as American heroes, acutely resourceful, quick to take the initiative. Unlike films such as *Mr. Wise Guy* in which the focal point is Danny's convicted brother, or *That Gang of Mine* in which Muggs' horse-racing ability is the main issue, no single kid in *Let's Get Tough* has anything particularly personal to gain by flushing out the spies that lurk in some East Side basement. The progression of events, triggered by their uninhibited display of force and curiosity, leads them to the discovery and the dismantling of an Axis spy ring.

Glimpy's sharp eye for detail and quick, ghostlike hands, gather enough evidence for the kids to focus their suspicions on Joe Matsui, a Japanese gift shop proprietor. Glimpy not only recognizes him as the man he saw hiding in Heinrich's back room, but notices him swipe a pen from Mrs. Keno's desk and put it in his pocket.

Glimpy shows us that not only is he good at taking food from unsuspecting vendors (as in *'Neath the Brooklyn Bridge*) but pickpocketing as well. As Matsui is about to leave, Glimpy

Pulling up Scruno (Sammy Morrison) in the spy film *Let's Get Tough*. Left to right: Bobby Jordan, Bobby Stone, Leo Gorcey (about to fly), David Gorcey, Huntz Hall.

walks up to him and says, "Allow me to shake the hand of a very honest man"—and, while doing so, discreetly pickpockets the pen. Tucked inside the pen is a piece of paper with Japanese writing. The more persistent the kids are in getting the message deciphered, the more suspicious they become of Matsui.

The kids take the Japanese writing to Matsui, Sr., who grabs the paper; Muggs grabs it back. Realizing that he has lost the paper for good, Matsui, Sr., draws a long knife and commits hari kari.

Matsui could have told Muggs it is a recipe for an exotic Japanese dish. How would Muggs know? Matsui's killing himself only puts more importance on the message. The fact that this is the last we see or hear of the suicide supports the view that it is inconsequential to the story as a whole. Its primary purpose was to demonstrate the abhorrence of the Japanese suicidal ritual.

Nora, who is engaged to Danny's brother Phil, offers to take the message to an old high school friend. This old friend happens to be Joe Matsui. As soon as Nora hands Matsui the paper, their friendship suddenly ends. Matsui's two spies grab Nora and take her behind a secret panel. Soon other Japanese enter the store and disappear behind the secret panel. Scruno witnesses all of this.

Let's Get Tough is the only non–haunted house picture in which there is a secret tunnel. But here the kids know who they are after. Perhaps this is why they are not as nervous about entering it as they are about going through the ones in *Boys of the City*, *Spooks Run Wild* and *Ghosts on the Loose*.

The kids crash a meeting of Japanese and German spies, all wearing black hoods. The significance of the hoods is never explained. In fact, it is a hindrance for discovering who among them is not a member, and a benefit only to intruders. Thus the kids are able to sit through two speeches, one by Phil, oddly enough, the other by a German spy (Gabriel Dell), before everyone is told to remove their hoods. Since the kids are the only ones who do not remove their hoods, they are easily identified. A fight ensues between the kids and the spies. Phil reveals that he is working for the U.S. Navy as an agent. Danny runs for the police. By the time he returns with them, the kids have matters well under control.

So in addition to being depicted as not very smart, the Japanese are also not well adept with their fists.

Let's Get Tough is the first East Side Kids film in which trouble doesn't find them, they go searching for trouble.

Gabriel Dell is wasted as a German spy. His character is neither important nor well-developed, and he is not convincing as a German.

The acting as a whole is poor, including veteran Robert Armstrong. What is most frustrating about the film is that we never know who these Japanese and German spies are, where they came from, how they got there and, most importantly, what exactly they were planning to do. The discovery of magnesium clues us in that they were planning a bombing, but where?

Does it really matter? The East Side Kids caught 'em!

Smart Alecks

Released August 7, 1942; 63 minutes; Monogram; Director, Wallace Fox; Producers, Sam Katzman, Jack Dietz; Story and Screenplay, Harvey Gates; Photography, Mack Stengler; Film Editor, Robert Golden; Assistant Director, Arthur Hammond; Musical Director, Edward Kay; Sound, Glen Glenn.

CAST

Muggs	Leo Gorcey	*Skinny*	Bobby Stone
Danny Stevens	Bobby Jordan	*Officer Reagan*	Roger Pryor
Glimpy	Huntz Hall	*Dr. Ornsby*	Walter Woolf King
Hank Salko	Gabriel Dell	*Capt. Bronson*	Herbert Rawlinson
Ruth Stevens	Gale Storm	*Mike*	Joe Kirk
Scruno	Sunshine Sammy Morrison	*Dr. Thomas*	Sam Bernard
		Prison Warden	Dick Ryan
Peewee	David Gorcey	*Nurse*	Marie Windsor
Stash	Stanley Clements	*Receptionist*	Betty Sinclair
Butch Broccoli	Maxie Rosenbloom		

Smart Alecks is the second of three films in which Muggs and Danny are at odds. It's a more all-encompassing picture than the other two, *Bowery Blitzkrieg* and *Kid Dynamite*,

Publicity for *Smart Alecks*.

because the entire gang is involved (as opposed to Danny and Muggs only). Additionally, familiar themes such as the "wanted criminal" and the "older sibling guardian" are well-integrated into a film that emphasizes personality rather than physical conflict for dramatic effect.

Muggs' powers of persuasion, unleashed for the first time, are the impetus for almost every action, starting with Danny's unwitting capture of the criminal, Butch Broccoli.

"Go on, it's your ball, ain't it? Well, go get it, then," Muggs goads Danny.

Danny's group loyalty is questioned, and Muggs, whose ego is as big as the Brooklyn Bridge, feels his leadership contested when Danny refuses to turn over some reward money. Muggs kicks him out of the gang. Ironically, Danny planned to surprise the kids with something that would give the kids a greater sense of unity — baseball uniforms.

In contrast to his long-range plans in the early films, Muggs is short-sighted here. He and the kids purchase a broken-down automobile, never thinking that they have no travel money, and no place to go they cannot get to by foot. They end up moping around the clubhouse, with Glimpy blurting out, "I wish Danny was here," only to get the first of many hits on the head with the Gorcey hat. Hall's goofy comedy begins to take form and will continue to evolve along the same lines through the Bowery Boys. At one point he says, "Can I help it if I look like Valentino?" Thirty-five years later he would be acclaimed for his performance as Jesse Lasky in Ken Russell's film *Valentino*.

Though Gabe Dell, as Hank, remains on the fringe of the gang, his relationship with them is closer than ever before, and the closest until *Block Busters*. A convict with a sense of loyalty, he returns to the clubhouse to tell them that Butch Broccoli has escaped and is gunning for Danny.

In prior films, the kids' interactions with adults were limited to physical violence and verbal attacks. In *Mr. Wise Guy*, the kids verbally abuse Knobby. In *Let's Get Tough*, they physically club the Japanese spy ring. In *Smart Alecks*, they must persuade an adult, an eminent physician, not to board a plane to Cleveland but instead to perform surgery on their dying buddy, Danny. In a close–up, tearful plea (the first of two; the second when he prays to God for Danny's life), Muggs generously offers what remains of their reward money, $50. The doctor smiles good-naturedly. "My minimum fee is $1,000."

The doctor, however, agrees to do the operation without any fee. Once again, Muggs' power of persuasion prevails.

Muggs (Leo Gorcey, right), supported by Hank (Gabe Dell) and Glimpy (Huntz Hall, in hat), offers Dr. Thomas (Sam Bernard) what he thinks is the most amount of money the doc has ever been paid, $50.

The image of "the older sibling guardian," as we have come to know her in these films, ends with *Smart Alecks*. Muggs has an older sister in *Follow the Leader*, but her portrayal is dissimilar to the archetypal role of Drina in *Dead End*, the self-sacrificing sister who dreams of seeing her younger brother grow up to be somebody.

Ruth (*My Little Margie*'s Gale Storm), a nurse, is so committed to this goal that she fails to recognize the moral and legitimate claim the kids have to the reward money by encouraging Danny to keep all of it for himself for his education.

Ruth is the only older sister in the films who requires the aid of the kids. When she gets back from visiting Danny at the hospital, Butch Broccoli is waiting for her. Like nurse Linda Mason in *Spooks Run Wild*, Ruth finds herself locked in a room with a man bent on causing her harm. As they do in the former film, the kids break into the locked room and rescue the woman.

An important plus factor in *Smart Alecks* is the variety of issues it takes up and resolves. Unlike in *Let's Get Tough*, where the only concern is the Japanese spies, or *Mr. Wise Guy*, where the focus is on Danny's brother's conviction, in *Smart Alecks* the problems range from the internal personality clash between Danny and Muggs, to the wanted criminal Butch Broccoli. In between there is the plight of Hank and the business of whether the gang will ever have a viable baseball team. Writer Harvey Gates and director Wallace Fox deserve praise for melding these subplots into the story.

Publicity shot for *Smart Alecks*, a scene that has nothing to do with the story. Left to right: First four unidentified, Huntz Hall, unidentified, Bobby Stone, Leo Gorcey (wearing hat and holding cane). The women are unidentified.

There are lulls in the script, especially after they throw Danny out of the gang. To pick up the pace, Broccoli is brought back into the picture, determined to take revenge on Danny. Broccoli's pursuit of Danny also serves to test the kids' real feelings for the ousted member. Thus the script idea of bringing Broccoli back into the fold is a good one on two counts. The only problem is with Broccoli himself. In practical terms, why does a veteran gangster remain in the area just to try to take vengeance on a local slum kid, knowing the police are after him?

Careful to satisfy every issue introduced, *Smart Alecks* does not end without each kid owning his own baseball uniform, purchased with the reward money received for the second group effort capture of Butch Broccoli. There is even a pair of flannels for Gabe.

"Sunshine" Sammy Morrison's actions and statements needlessly reminds us he's black ("My mammy be wondering where her black crow is"). He does two tap-dancing gigs. But he also thinks outside the box, suggesting that Danny may not want to see the kids after they had just thrown him out of the gang. And it's his suggestion that they "do what Danny does, pray."

This is the first film for Stanley "Stash" Clements, to whom Monogram devotes a full-frame credit ("Introducing Stanley 'Stash' Clements"). Fourteen years later he would take Leo Gorcey's place and make the last seven Bowery Boys films alongside Huntz Hall.

'Neath Brooklyn Bridge

Released November 20, 1942; 61 minutes; 5529 ft.; Monogram; Director, Wallace Fox; Producers, Sam Katzman, Jack Dietz; Story and Screenplay, Harvey Gates; Photography, Mack Stengler; Film Editor, Carl Pierson; Music Director, Edward Kay; Associate Producer, Barney Sarecky; Assistant Director, Arthur Hammond; Art Director, Dave Milton; Sound Engineer, Glen Glenn; Banner Productions.

CAST

Muggs	Leo Gorcey	Skinny	Bobby Stone
Danny	Bobby Jordan	Sniffy	Jack Raymond
Glimpy	Huntz Hall	Bunny	Betty Wells
Skid	Gabriel Dell	Sgt. Clancy	Jack Mulhall
Butch	Noah Beery, Jr.	Mrs. Glimpy	Patsy Moran
McGaffey	Marc Lawrence	Police Captain	Dewey Robinson
Sylvia	Anne Gills	Morley	Bud Osborne
Sgt. Lyons	Dave O'Brien	Bright Eyes	J. Arthur Young
Scruno	Sunshine Sammy Morrison	Saleswoman	Betty Sinclair
		Soup Customer	Snub Pollard
Stash	Stanley Clements		

True to the insinuation of its title, 'Neath Brooklyn Bridge, conveys in photographic detail squalor that permeates the poorer corners of the city. Not since *Dead End* had the scenes of depressed New York been so graphic. Unlike prior films such as *Smart Alecks*, where there was a hospital scene, or *Let's Get Tough*, where several scenes took place in a gift shop, 'Neath Brooklyn Bridge offers no relief from urban decay.

As much as the photography renders a gray atmosphere, the script strains to evoke a well-plotted story. Unfortunately it is overtly contrived. Events leading up to the kids' meeting the young girl Sylvia, and their incrimination in the murder of Morley, Sylvia's vicious stepfather, are consolidated in one scene.

After robbing his former crooked employer, Morley storms into his sparsely furnished flat. "Pack up, we're leaving," he bellows. Sylvia, carefully spoon-feeding her paralyzed grandfather, refuses and races out of the tenement, practically into the arms of the East Side Kids, who happen to be walking by. Morley drags her back into the flat.

Continuing their acts of chivalry (Linda Mason in *Spooks Run Wild*, Ruth in *Smart Alecks*), the kids barge into the flat and scramble with Morley. Repeating the decisive action he took in *Crime School*, Gorcey belts Morley on the head with a wooden club.

Witness to the scuffle between the kids and Morley are McGaffey and Skid, hiding in the next room, unseen by all except for Sylvia's grandfather, Bright Eyes. After the kids leave with Sylvia, McGaffey and Skid kill Morley. They take with them the wooden club smeared with Muggs' fingerprints.

There are few places in the East Side Kids films where spur-of-the-moment blackmail is implemented. Toward the end of *Clancy Street Boys* and *Mr. Muggs Steps Out*, the bad guys kidnap a rich man's daughter and hold her for ransom. In *Million Dollar Kid*, Skinny is left behind in the clutches of Lefty and Spike. 'Neath Brooklyn Bridge is the only film in which blackmail is thematic. McGaffey threatens to deliver the "murder weapon" to police unless Muggs cooperates in a warehouse robbery.

"Bright Eyes" (J. Arthur Young), with Bobby Jordan and Leo Gorcey at his side, blinks morse code in *'Neath the Brooklyn Bridge.*

Danny's arrest is the result of a contrived sequence. Meaning well, and defying their own ordinance, the Kids bring Sylvia to their clubhouse. It's delightful to see the kids fuss over her as they try to put her at ease. Danny goes to fetch some of Sylvia's own clothes. As luck would have it, Clancy the cop forces Danny back up to the flat where they find Morley dead in the next room. Danny, who cannot figure out how Morley got there, is arrested.

Although the kids meet privately with Danny at police headquarters, they are wise enough to know the room is bugged. Muggs finds a listening device affixed on the wall behind the painting. He places his hat on it, which suffices to muffle Danny's story on how he was arrested.

Muggs outsmarts McGaffey by arranging for a horde of slum youth to converge at the warehouse the moment McGaffey enters. With Skid pinned to the floor, Muggs demands to know who killed Morley.

"I know why he's not talking," Muggs tells Sgt. Lyons, Danny's brother, "because he did it."

"No!" Skid utters in his own defense. "It wasn't me, it was McGaffey. Yeah, McGaffey, he did it."

And how is Muggs so sure that it is McGaffey? An eyewitness, none other than Sylvia's mute, paralyzed grandfather, Bright Eyes, told him beforehand.

How Bright Eyes got the information across is the result of a complex piece of contrivance. Butch (Noah Beer Jr.), a former member of the gang, now a sailor with a day's liberty, came to the clubhouse and found the shy girl hiding in a corner. It was revealed that Bright Eyes was an old navy admiral, and he blinks in Morse code, M-C-G-A-F-F-E-Y-K-I-L-L-E-D-M-O-R-L-E-Y.

What further adds to the contrivance of this idea is that Butch appears only this once in the films. Yet by the end of the film he has married Sylvia and they have kids the spittin' image of Muggs and Glimpy. Makes you wonder.

In a scene of the kids talking amongst themselves, Gorcey talks about how someday he would like to live on a ranch. In fact, Gorcey did retire to a ranch in Los Molinos, California (see biographies, Leo Gorcey). Perhaps the director told the kids to "small talk" and Gorcey used the opportunity to verbalize his real-life dream.

'Neath Brooklyn Bridge is a choppy yet energetic film that could have benefited greatly from careful directing and a less floundering script.

Kid Dynamite

Released February 12, 1943; 73 minutes; Monogram; Director, Wallace Fox; Producers, Sam Katzman, Jack Dietz; Screenplay, Gerald Schnitzer; Additional Dialogue, Morey Amsterdam; Based on the *Saturday Evening Post* magazine story "The Old Gang" by Paul Ernst; Photography, Mack Stengler; Film Editor, Carl Pierson; Music Director, Edward Kay; Associate Producer, Barney Sarecky; Assistant Director, Arthur Hammond; Art Direction, David Milton; Music Director, Edward Kay; Sound, Glen Glenn.

CAST

Muggs	Leo Gorcey	*Judge*	Minerva Urecal
Danny	Bobby Jordan	*Tony*	Wheeler Oakman
Glimpy	Huntz Hall	*Stacy*	Bobby Stone
Harry Wyckoff	Gabriel Dell	*Jackson*	Dudley Dickerson
Ivy	Pamela Blake	*Grundick*	Henry Hall
Skinny	Dave Durand	*Mrs. Lyons*	Margaret Padula
Nick	Charles Judels	*Clancy*	Jack Mulhall
Bennie	Bennie Bartlett	*Kay*	Kay Marvis
Klinkhammer	Vince Barnett	*Ray*	Ray Miller

Kid Dynamite tells of the relationship between two lifetime friends, one determined to be honest and more responsible, the other intensely jealous and egotistical. The bulk of the film are poignant showcases of Muggs' hostility towards Danny, and Danny's reactions to them.

Muggs' demands primarily test Danny's loyalty. Muggs' first demand is for Danny to cheat for him during a game of pool. When the time comes for Danny to exchange chalks, Danny balks. Muggs doesn't have the five dollars he wagered. He does, however, have the best pair of fists on the East Side, and applies them to his opponent's jaw. As far as Muggs is concerned, his bill with Harry (the Dead End Kid outsider Gabe Dell) is settled. The score with Danny is not. What remains unclear is how changing the chalk will improve Muggs' game.

Kay Marvis (left), Leo Gorcey's first wife, is a ringer in the dance contest against Danny (Bobby Jordan). Muggs (Gorcey, second from left) is disqualified. Pamela Blake is Jordan's partner in *Kid Dynamite*.

In films where Muggs' pugnacity plays a part, there is always some hindrance to victory in the arena. In *Pride of the Bowery*, it is Elaine showing up at ringside; in *Bowery Blitzkrieg*, it's Muggs' blood loss; in *Come Out Fighting*, Muggs is suspended from amateur boxing even before the start of the film. In *Kid Dynamite*, Harry Wyckoff has him kidnapped before his fight the West Side champ, Hank Johnson.

The method for his kidnapping is repeated several years later in the Bowery Boys' *No Holds Barred*. "Photographers" ask Muggs to pose near a car for a picture. Suddenly two sets of strong arms pull him into the automobile. Muggs spends the evening in the back seat listening to the fight on the radio as Danny, Muggs' logical replacement, knocks out Johnson.

Groundlessly, Muggs accuses Danny of masterminding the kidnapping. In the locker room, Muggs confiscates Danny's championship belt and punches Danny, satisfying himself that he is City Champ.

At first Muggs has no intention of competing in a jitterbug contest but the fact that Danny is escorting Muggs' sister Ivy changes his mind.

The dancing sequence is surprisingly entertaining and exceptionally well choreographed. Jordan and Gorcey swing remarkably well with their partners. (Gorcey's partner is Kay Marvis, his first wife in real life.) Glimpy treats the event as a big joke, jumping, kicking and handling his partner like a wrestling opponent. At the end of the dance, Muggs and Kay are left alone on the floor, the declared winners. But when it's revealed that Kay is a professional dancer at the Silver Slipper, the nod goes to Danny and Ivy.

Muggs is unwilling to concede victory to Danny. Not wanting to cause a disturbance, Danny hands over the $50. This time he loses more than the reward; he loses Ivy's respect.

Though Muggs has the support of all the kids—one wonders why—Danny has one person in his corner, Mr. Grundick. He gives Danny a job at his garage and persuades him to join the Army.

A responsible job at the garage (the camera shows him working diligently) followed by his entry into the Army signifies maturity, and there is no way Muggs can take that away from him. But he tries.

Undeterred by the uniform he orders Danny to keep Mr. Grundick occupied while he (Muggs) steals several new tires from Grundick's garage. Muggs is furious when Danny does not lead Mr. Grundick away from the garage.

"You'd have to be crazy to think I'd pull a stunt like that—especially in this uniform." Apparently being a soldier gives him a sense of pride, the message this scene conveys to the draft-age audience.

His challenge met, Muggs starts a fight with Danny right there on the street. Muggs falls.

"I always said the guy who marries my sister has to lick me first, and you done it."

The only unifying factor that ties these otherwise scattered episodes together is Muggs' deep-rooted inferiority complex that gives rise to the rivalry between himself and Danny. There is no real reason for there to be a pool game, a boxing match or a jitterbug contest, except that they are workable vehicles through which the jealousy is conveyed.

More could have been done to broaden the film's perspective. For example, Harry Wyckoff could have provided an added dimension the way Butch Broccoli supplements the conflict between Danny and the kids in *Smart Alecks*. But Harry Wyckoff is written out before the first half of the film is over.

Kid Dynamite was based on a *Saturday Evening Post* story, "The Old Gang," by Paul Ernst, and not by one of the Monogram Pictures staff members familiar with this series. Which may be why scenes with the whole gang are de-emphasized while the personalities of Muggs and Danny are highlighted. Scenes such as Danny talking with Mr. Grundick and Muggs crying to his mother that Danny has gotten parental permission to join the Army while he has not—and will not so long as his reason for wanting to join has everything to do with Danny and nothing to do with patriotism—exemplify this point.

Both Gorcey and Jordan are great tough-guy actors, so the question is, could this film been made starring Gorcey and Jordan outside the framework of an East Side Kids film? Did the series make that impossible?

While *Kid Dynamite* is deficient in scope, it is rich in confrontation, which is what East Side Kids audiences relished.

In a 1988 documentary producers Louis Alvarez and Andrew Kilker of the Center for New American Media (http://www.cnam.com/) included an excerpt of dialogue from *Kid Dynamite* for their Peabody Award–winning documentary "American Tongues," about the differences in the way Americans speak and the attitudes people have about regional and social accents.

Clancy Street Boys

Released April 23, 1943; 66 minutes; Monogram; Director, William Beaudine; Producer, Sam Katzman, Jack Dietz; Screenplay, Harvey Gates; Photography, Mack Stengler; Film Editor, Carl Pierson; Associate Producer, Barney Sarecky; Art Director, David Milton; Music, Edward Kay; Assistant Director, Arthur Hammond; Sound, Glen Glenn.

CAST

Muggs	Leo Gorcey		*Cherry Street*	
Danny	Bobby Jordan		*Gang Leader*	Billy Benedict
Glimpy	Huntz Hall		*George "The Gyp"*	
Scruno	Sunshine Sammy		*Mooney*	Rick Vallin
	Morrison		*William*	George DeNormand
Judy	Amelita Ward		*Sgt. Flannegan*	J. Farrell MacDonald
Molly McGinnis	Molly Wentworth		*Dave*	Eddie Mills
Bennie	Bennie Bartlett		*Stash*	Dick Chandlee
Uncle Pete Monahan	Noah Beery, Sr.		*Entertainer*	Jay Rubini

with Bernard Gorcey, Jimmy Strand, Johnny Duncan, Jack Normand

Inspired perhaps by the 1926 Our Gang silent comedy, *Baby Clothes*, about a couple that collects $50 a week for two non-existent children from a rich uncle, *Clancy Street Boys* is the first of three "situation comedy" East Side Kids films (the others are *Mr. Muggs Steps Out* and *Block Busters*).

Molly McGinnis, Muggs' mother, tricked wealthy Texas Uncle Pete (not a "real" uncle, but a "friend" uncle) into believing her husband's lies about having seven children, including a daughter. Along with his next gift is a note saying he and his daughter Judy are coming to visit.

Immediately, we hear the sound of Ten-Gallon-Hat Uncle Pete and cowgirl daughter Judy, tying their horse to a parking meter, as if they rode all the way from Texas to the McGinnis house as fast as the mail.

Unlike films such as *'Neath Brooklyn Bridge*, *Let's Get Tough*, and *Mr. Wise Guy*, where the kids are not sure what course of action to take until near the end, here it is clear-cut: trick Uncle Pete and Judy into believing the East Side Kids, *and* Scruno, and Glimpy as Annabelle, are all McGinnis siblings. Muggs doesn't want to make a liar out of his father, even though his father had no qualms about being one.

Gorcey posing as his own father in *Clancy Street Boys*.

Huntz Hall in drag as Gorcey's sister in *Clancy Street Boys.* Left to right: Eddie Mills, Bobby Jordan, Sunshine Sammy Morrison, Hall, Dick Chandlee, Bennie Bartlett, and Leo Gorcey.

Huntz Hall takes a giant leap toward the comical character he becomes in the Bowery Boys. In drag, Hall's high-pitched voice is the most innovative and truly comical aspect of the film.

Once Muggs has Uncle Pete and Judy believing the East Side Kids are his family, things go very smoothly—so smoothly that what follows is dull.

The film picks up when George "The Gyp" Mooney, a local no-good-nik, reveals the truth to Uncle Pete. Uncle Pete storms into the McGinnis household, where all the parents are complaining that Uncle Pete keeps their children out too late. Where were these parents in *Mr. Wise Guy*, and *'Neath Brooklyn Bridge*, when the kids needed them most?

When the kids return their gifts, Judy tells them that her father had just gotten into an accident and that George Mooney is coming to take her to him. Muggs warns it's a hoax, but tells her to go with Mooney anyway.

Danny latches onto Mooney's car and he telephones the kids when he finds out where Uncle Pete and Judy are held. From opposite directions, two gangs converge on the kidnappers.

There are a couple of quick, visual surprises here. For the first time (the only time as

Benedict paddy-wacking Gorcey in *Clancy Street Boys.* Left to right: Jimmy Strand (standing), Benedict, unidentified actor, Johnny Duncan, Gorcey (with horn); others unidentified.

East Side Kids), Gorcey and Hall speak to the audience. As they plan their attack on the kidnappers, they turn to the audience and say, "Excuse us." Muggs then whispers something in Glimpy's ear.

Billy Benedict makes his East Side Kid debut as the leader of the Cherry Street gang. Unfortunately, much of the corniness of this film involves Benedict and his gang. A group of late adolescents so determined to bestow paddywhacks on birthday boy Muggs is corny. What's even worse is them playing with Uncle Pete's saddles like five-year-old children.

Another surprise is the picture of Muggs' father on the wall in the McGinnis home. It is Gorcey spruced up to look like a distinguished old man with long thick sideburns and a mustache. Uncle Pete, played by veteran star Noah Beery, Sr., is a spiffy, fun-loving, domineering, generous, jovial, proud old man. He looks at the picture and says, "Yup, you sure did all right fer yourself."

But the real question is, did Gorcey himself do all right for himself? Judging by the attractive Amelita Ward, who plays Judy, the answer would have to say yes. She is Gorcey's third wife and mother to his children Leo Jr., and Jan. He would have two more wives after Amelita.

Ghosts on the Loose

Released July 30, 1943; 65 minutes; Monogram; Director, William Beaudine; Producers, Sam Katzman, Jack Dietz; Original Screenplay, Kenneth Higgins; Photography, Mack Stengler; Film Editor, Carl Pierson; Music Director, Edward Kay; Associate Producer, Barney Sarecky; Set Designer, Dave Milton; Sound, Glen Glenn. Released in England as *Ghosts in the Night*.

CAST

Muggs	Leo Gorcey	*Bennie*	Billy Benedict
Danny	Bobby Jordan	*Dave*	Bill Bates
Glimpy	Huntz Hall	*Scruno*	Sunshine Sammy
Emil	Bela Lugosi		Morrison
Rocky	Bobby Stone	*Tony*	Wheeler Oakman
Jack Gibson	Ric Vallin	*Lt. Brady*	Jack Mulhall
Betty Williams	Ava Gardner	*Hilda*	Minerva Urecal
Bruno	Peter Seal	*Bridesmaid*	Kay Marvis Gorcey
Monk	Frank Moran	*Minister*	Robert F. Hill
Stash	Stanley Clements		

For a film that incorporates such surefire motifs as a haunted house and Nazi spies, and such stars as Bela Lugosi and Ava Gardner, it is disheartening that the script, by Kenneth Higgins, is so deficient in plot and character development. The haunted house is the heart of the film. The film suffers from cardiac arrest.

Ghosts on the Loose is the second of four consecutive films in which the kids immerse themselves in someone's family life. Ironically, Glimpy and his sister Betty, who gets married, do not exchange a single word. The purpose of the relationship is purely technical. It serves as an excuse for the kids to enter the newlyweds' newly acquired, allegedly haunted house.

The kids hear strange voices and creaky doors. Scruno (making his last East Side Kids appearance except for a cameo in *Follow the Leader*) dusts what he thinks is a picture of Lugosi on the wall (it actually *is* Lugosi), and Lugosi sneezes. Glimpy wipes a mirror, the words "Leave while you are still alive" appear. And in the basement they find a printing press with subversive literature.

The appearance of the printing press puts doubts in the kids' minds about Jack's loyalty. So what do they do? They carry the printing press to the house next door, which it turns out, *is* Jack and Betty's house. The kids made a mistake.

What follows is a mass of confusion. When the kids overhear Jack talking to the police and see him pointing to his house, they realize their mistake, and move the printing press back to the Nazis' house. The Nazis move the press back into Jack and Betty's house. When the police arrive, they arrest Jack. The entire repetitious affair illustrates the filmmakers' lackluster efforts.

The capture of the Nazis is one of the most abrupt endings in the series. In almost any other film, the viewer can anticipate with some degree of certainty how, and by what means, the kids will prevail. In *'Neath Brooklyn Bridge*, Muggs plans something at the warehouse; in *Clancy Street Boys*, the kids plan and execute their rescue of Uncle Pete. Here, the filmmakers concoct a slapdash ending that gets Nazis captured, sets Jack free, and makes heroes of the kids.

The East Side Kids (left to right: Bobby Jordan, Leo Gorcey, Bill Bates, Bobby Stone, Stanley Clements, Sammy Morrison, Huntz Hall and Billy Benedict) in *Ghosts on the Loose.*

Bela Lugosi is once again wasted. At least in *Spooks Run Wild* he wore his Dracula outfit. Here his role is so minor, he is infrequently in view, and unconvincing as a Nazi.

The beautiful Ava Gardner is seen but hardly heard. Her role as Betty is purely functional. The rest is staging. She offers no ideas, and has very little personality.

In what amounts to little more than a cameo appearance, Minerva Urecal gives a stunning portrayal of an old wicked woman. Her gray hair is styled to look like it is reacting to electric shock. Her movements are slow and calculated. She speaks in a foreign accent that shakes with fear. Her role is irrelevant since she interacts with nobody.

Lack of interaction is a major weakness of this film. The idea of the kids alone in a house, unaware of the immoral activities going on in hidden areas, is better handled in the Bowery Boys' *Spook Busters* because there are encounters between the boys and the mad scientist. In that film, the occupants want something from the boys; here the Nazis just want them to leave.

The most clever aspect of the film is the very end when the kids and Jack and Betty are quarantined in the young couple's house because Glimpy contracted German measles. A close-up reveals tiny swastikas dotting his face. Some honeymoon!

Top: In England, the film's title was *Ghosts in the Night.* Ava Gardner and Ric Vallin are at right. Kids, left to right: Bobby Jordan, Sunshine Sammy Morrision, Bobby Stone, Bill Bates, unidentified head, Gardner, Vallin. *Bottom, left:* Jordan, Gorcey, Lugosi and Hall doing a triple choke in publicity shot for *Ghosts on the Loose.* *Bottom, right:* Ava Gardner and Leo Gorcey share a moment with a mop for *Ghosts on the Loose.*

Mr. Muggs Steps Out

Released October 29, 1943; 63 minutes; 5893 ft.; Monogram; Director, William Beaudine; Producers, Sam Katzman, Jack Dietz; Associate Producer, Barney A. Sarecky; Story and Screenplay, William X. Crowley, Beryl Sachs; Photography, Marcel Le Picard; Film Editor, Carl Pierson; Music Director, Edward Kay; Set Designer, Ernest Hickson; Assistant Director, Arthur Hammond; Sound, Gilbert E. Meloy.

CAST

Muggs	Leo Gorcey	*Charney*	Halliwell Hobbes
Glimpy	Huntz Hall	*Grogan*	Eddie Gribbon
Nolan	Gabriel Dell	*Judge*	Noah Beery, Sr.
Pinkie	Billy Benedict	*Danny*	Dave Durand
Diamonds	Nick Stuart	*Speed*	Bobby Stone
Margaret	Betty Blythe	*Skinny*	Bud Gorman
John Morgan	Emmett Vogan	*Rocky*	Jimmy Strand
Dave	Jimmy Strand	*Mazie*	Patsy Moran
Brenda	Joan Marsh	*Dowager*	Lottie Harrison
Virgil Wellington III	Stanley Brown	*Dancer*	Kay Marvis Gorcey

Every family has its quirks and the Murrays have many. In the first of two films in which the kids involve themselves in the lives of an outside family, Monogram discovers high-spirited women.

Brenda Murray cannot resist the opportunity to break a dozen traffic rules and her mother cannot resist hiring household help from the parole list. When Mrs. Murray gets a call from Brenda at the police station, Grogan the butler asks, "Want me t' go wit ya? I'm very well-known down there."

As Margaret and her daughter are about to leave the courtroom, Muggs is called to the stand by the name he scorns.

"Ethelbert McGinnis!"

Whatever he's done (it's not clear what), it's enough for the judge to threaten him with that timeworn punishment called reform school. Mrs. Murray asks Muggs if he would work as their chauffeur.

"Ma'am, was never a car made that I couldn't take apart."

Since all the suspenseful action is saved for the end (it's actually more dizzy than suspenseful), the film relies heavily on the conflux of diverse characters. First there is the playful antagonism between Muggs and Brenda. Muggs' driving is decent, but he does not take the job as seriously as Brenda would like him to.

"How about opening the door?" Brenda teases.

"Whatsa the matter?" Muggs retorts. "You crippled?"

Muggs' exchanges with the stoic Charney, the head butler, are no less cynical. Muggs is shown his living quarters. "What's the rent?" Muggs asks.

"Rent? You don't pay rent."

"I know dat. But if t'ings get tight, I may wanna sublet it."

All the events are geared towards, and stem from, the colossal engagement party for Brenda and her fiancé, a bookish Virgil Wellington III. Glimpy, who along with the other kids is a waiter thanks to Muggs, keeps his eye on a dowager's diamond necklace. He is the one to notice it's missing.

Dance scene in *Mr. Muggs Steps Out*. Leo Gorcey and Kay Marvis Gorcey (white blouse) and Hall (hat) and unidentified partner are in the foreground.

Danceland serves as the antithesis to the engagement party. It's noisy and disorderly. Brenda gets a thrill out of wearing chic clothing, while Virgil is having a nervous breakdown because Nolan is hitting on her.

Nolan and his partner Diamonds are soon planning to kidnap Brenda.

The whole affair is unnecessarily jumbled. The kids run so many times from Danceland to Diamonds' apartment in the hope of catching up with Diamonds, that we get tired just watching them. When the kids finally do catch up with him, he has already kidnapped Brenda.

The fight scene is extremely exaggerated. Everybody piles up into a ball before the kids come out winners.

The biggest surprise of the film comes from Virgil. After Brenda is rescued and the necklace is recovered, the kids return to Danceland where Virgil stuns everybody by doing a cha-cha with the zest and grace of a butterfly.

Mr. Muggs Steps Out is a better situation comedy than *Clancy Street Boys*, but the kids are only incidentally involved; it's not Glimpy's sister getting engaged; it's not Muggs' uncle being made a fool of. Only in one other East Side Kids film, *Docks of New York*, do the kids have no personal investment. (In *Let's Get Tough*, Danny's brother provides the only connection between the kids and the spies.)

Unlike most other films, this one does not commit itself to one picture-long issue that we expect to be resolved by the end. Brenda's suspended license problem is short-lived. There is no further conflict until the diamonds are stolen. This weakness is shared by only one other East Side Kids flick, *Come Out Fighting*. Thus, *Mr. Muggs Steps Out* is an assortment of trifles without a strong underlying plot to hold them tightly together.

Million Dollar Kid

Released February 28, 1944; 65 minutes; Monogram; Director, Wallace Fox; Producers, Sam Katzman, Jack Dietz, Story and Screenplay, Frank H. Young; Photography, Marcel Le Picard; Film Editor, Carl Pierson; Music Director, Edward Kay; Associate Producer, Barney Sarecky; Assistant Director, Art Hammond; Settings, Ernest Hickson; Sound Engineer, Gilbert Meloy.

CAST

Muggs	Leo Gorcey	*Spevin*	Robert Grieg
Glimpy	Huntz Hall	*Roy Cortland*	Johnny Duncan
Lefty	Gabriel Dell	*Mrs. Clusky*	Patsy Moran
Skinny	Billy Benediet	*Mrs. McGinnis*	Mary Gordon
Mr. Cortland	Herbert Heyes	*Herbie*	Al Stone
Louise Cortland	Louise Currie	*Danny*	David Durand
Maisie	Iris Adrian	*Peskie*	Jimmy Strand
Andre Dupres	Stanley Brown	*Stinkie*	Bud Gorman
Capt. Matthews	Noah Beery, Sr.	*Spike*	Pat Costello

There is no other film in which the kids get more tangled up in a family's personal problems. While *Million Dollar Kid* strives to be an intelligent portrayal of conflict between father and son, it totals up to be an overtly sentimental story that makes social workers of the East Side Kids.

The kids do for the Cortland family what the Cortlands cannot do for themselves. They (a) save Mr. Cortland from a mugging, (b) provide the cooks for Louise Cortland's engagement party, (c) make Louise aware of the real identity of the man she plans to marry, (d) bring Cortland and his son Roy closer together, and (e) set Roy back on the straight and narrow path of life. It is hard for us to accept that the Cortlands are so helpless and naïve when they are also extremely wealthy.

Rescuing defenseless folks from the fangs of would-be muggers and murderers is all in a day's work for the kids, but in this case the mugger is Mr. Cortland's son. Through some awkward staging and selective camera angles, the father does not notice whom his muggers are, and the audience is unaware of the relationship until later.

The Oedipal symbolism is clear. Roy's rebellion against his father is similar to Cyril Gerard's in Universal's *Little Tough Guy*, manifested by joining up with a couple of two-bit thugs. We get the idea that Roy's need to rebel has something to do with jealousy of his older brother. He's in the Army—that is, he *was*. A messenger (played by Bernard Gorcey, Leo's father in his first cameo appearance) arrives with a telegram from the War Department.

The image of Muggs walking a very depressed father up the stairs while his son walks out the door to meet his pool hall friends delivers a message as effectively as one sent by West-

The East Side Kids have Gabe on a pool table in *Million Dollar Kid*. Left to right: Dave Durand, Billy Benedict, Huntz Hall, Leo Gorcey, Al Stone, Pat Costello, Bobby Stone.

ern Union. Thus Roy remains as oblivious to his brother's death as Mr. Cortland is to the identity of the thugs who mugged him.

The contrast between Muggs in *Pride of the Bowery* and this film is striking. In the earlier film, Muggs is a lost, frustrated boxer who cannot answer Elaine's probing questions, and shrugs when the camp captain suggests that the CCC might be the means for "finding himself."

Here Muggs lectures Roy, just like the captain in *Pride of the Bowery* lectured him. "[Y]ou're defeating your purpose in life...." For Muggs to be able to observe this about somebody else, shows he has come a long way.

Undoubtedly, the most unconvincing show of emotion, perhaps in the entire series, is from Louise, lifelessly played by Louise Currie. The entire sequence dealing with her engagement to First Lieutenant Andre Dupres, from the party preparations to breaking off the relationship, is not only vapid, banal and insincere, but completely disconnected from the main theme. It seems like the couple first met that morning.

There seems to be no good reason why Louise is unable to find kitchen help. Having the mothers of Muggs and Glimpy slaving over the stoves in no way adds to the film. What is most astonishing is that they are volunteers!

Muggs and Glimpy overhear Andre speaking on the telephone in an authentic Brooklyn accent about how he is about to swindle a rich dame out of a lot of money.

"Million Dollar Kid" Johnny Duncan takes one in the stomach from Gorcey. Left to right: Al Stone, Jimmy Strand, Gorcey, Bud Gorman (behind Gorcey) Duncan, Bobby Stone, Dave Durand.

"That guy speaks English as good as us," Glimpy observes.

"No one speaks English as good as us," Muggs corrects him.

When Muggs invites Maizie, Andre's other girlfriend, to the engagement party, things become clear to both women. And with as much emotional strain as it takes to stamp out a cigarette butt, Louise asks Andre to vacate the premises. The party continues with Louise not wasting a single tear.

In passing, Mr. Cortland inquires about the absent young soldier. The father's lack of concern for his daughter's future and well-being is astonishingly.

Muggs' final good deed is saving Roy from going to prison. Muggs intervenes on Roy's behalf with the heart-rending story about Roy's brother killed in the war. Just as a surgeon in *Smart Alecks* is touched by Muggs' appeal, so too is Capt. Matthews moved by Muggs' plea, and releases Roy on probation.

Parallels can be drawn between this film and its predecessor, *Mr. Muggs Steps Out*. In both, the kids meet the head of a wealthy household in a law enforcement chamber and are invited to their home. In each home, an engagement party is being planned for the daughter and fiancé. Both parties are thwarted by misadventures.

In both films, there are two young criminals (Gabe Dell is in both) who prey upon the rich, and whose capture is hastened by the rich kids' assistance. Brenda in *Mr. Muggs Steps Out*, and Roy in this picture, lead the kids to the criminals' lairs.

If *Million Dollar Kid* took itself less seriously, as do *Clancy Street Boys* and *Block Busters*, it may have been less campy and more enjoyable.

Follow the Leader

Released June 3, 1944; 64 minutes; Monogram; Director, William Beaudine; Producers, Sam Katzman, Jack Dietz; Screenplay, William X. Crowley, Beryl Sahs; Story, Ande Lamb; Photography, Marcel Le Picard; Associate Producer, Barney Sarecky; Assistant Director, Art Hammond; Music Director, Edward Kay; Film Editor, Carl Pierson; Set Designer, Ernest Hickson; Sound Engineer, Glen Glenn.

CAST

Muggs	Leo Gorcey	Speed	Bobby Stone
Glimpy	Huntz Hall	Dave	Jimmy Strand
Fingers	Gabriel Dell	Skinny	Bud Gorman
Spider	Billy Benedict	Ginsberg	Bernard Gorcey
Milly	Joan Marsh	Colonel	Bryant Washburn
Larry	Jack La Rue	Clancy	J. Farrell MacDonald
Danny	Dave Durand	Mrs. McGinnis	Mary Gordon

also with Sherill Sisters and Gene Austin

The pace, tightness and comedy of *Follow the Leader*, is first-rate and the cinematic technique deserves close attention.

There are two scenes, one a dream sequence, one a flashback, edited into the early part of the picture, that have the feel of not originally meant to be a flashback or a dream. Dave Durand, making his last East Side Kids picture (the first was *East Side Kids*) as Danny, explains to Muggs how he, the surrogate leader of the gang in Muggs' absence, wound up in jail. Spider, a timid character adequately played by Billy Benedict, is his co-worker and a new member of the gang who Muggs intuitively suspects.

The dream sequence does not relate to the rest of the film at all. The strongest evidence of this is the presence of Sunshine Sammy Morrison, who does not appear anywhere else in this film. His last picture *Ghost on the Loose*, released almost a year earlier.

Muggs is portrayed as a very moral, capable young man, an image that begins to take form in the prior film, *Million Dollar Kid*, and continues through the rest of the series. He is depressed about his discharge from the Army and is determined to prove to the Army that he is worthy of his corporal stripes. In the course of doing so, he is suspected of murder. (Gorcey was actually drafted, but ten days prior to induction, he broke both arms, four ribs and fractured his skull in a motorcycle accident. A year later he was released from the hospital with a laterally displaced heart and a 4-F classification.*)

With the aid of an interrogator's spotlight, the scene in the clubhouse is chilling. Muggs questions Spider alone. He wins Spider's confidence by telling him that he too does dishon-

---

*Gorcey, Leo, Jr., Me and the Dead End Kid, *page 168.*

The East Side Kids rumble in *Follow the Leader*. In foreground, middle left: Bobby Stone (teeshirt), unidentified actor, Leo Gorcey, unidentified actor about to be slugged by Gorcey, Huntz Hall.

est things. This, of course, is a ploy to get Spider talking and Spider does just that. The trouble is, outside the clubhouse, Fingers and Slug overhear it.

The following morning, Glimpy barges into the apartment to tell Muggs that Spider was found dead at the clubhouse and all circumstantial evidence points to him as the murderer.

Just as he persuades the police in *Million Dollar Kid* to go easy on young Roy Cortland, so does he convince the police chief and Army Major John Klein to keep the police and the Army out of this matter — to allow him to prove his own innocence and put an end to the smuggling.

What follows is a relatively complex undercover operation that requires the kids to be ready for action and Glimpy stationed at Ginsberg's Delicatessen, waiting for a phone call from Muggs' sister, Millie, a cocktail waitress at the Club Maxi.

Millie has been a target of her boss' passion. When Millie overhears Fingers talking to her boss, Larry, she quickly calls Glimpy, then knocks on Larry's door. Of course, her intention is merely to keep him busy until Glimpy arrives with help.

It is interesting to compare what Muggs expects from his sister to what Tommy expects from *his* sister in *Crime School*. Millie will keep Larry busy, flirt with him to save her brother, but the idea of Tommy's sister Sue "doing favors" for Mark Braden (Bogart), so Tommy will have an easy time in reform school, is abhorrent to Tommy. How times have changed.

While Glimpy waits for Millie's phone call at Ginsberg's Delicatessen, he stuffs his mouth with junk food.

"You're a schlemiel," Ginsberg (Bernard Gorcey) mumbles to himself, as he serves Glimpy another helping of pickles.

"I heard that," Glimpy tells him.

"You know what it means?" Ginsberg asks, surprised.

"Yeah."

"Good!"*

Like the Pied Piper, Glimpy quickly gathers a crowd of kids eager to participate in the adventure. At full force, they burst into the warehouse and release Muggs from the clutches of four other men, and Millie from Larry's passions.

William X. Crowley's second East Side Kids screenplay is more fully developed and more intricate than his *Mr. Muggs Steps Out*, particularly in its handling of the rivalry between Muggs and Fingers, and the audience's progressive understanding, through Muggs' eyes, of how the smuggling operates. At the beginning of the film, all we know is that government merchandise is being smuggled and the wrong person is in jail. By the end of the film, we not only know who is responsible for the smuggling, but how it is done. Also at the beginning of the film, there is not much animosity between Muggs and Fingers; Muggs actually allows Fingers to use the clubhouse for a moment as a refuge from the cops. But by the end of the film, Muggs delivers Fingers to the police with enough evidence against him to support the charge of murdering Spider. As a reward, Muggs is not only reinstated into the Army, but promoted to sergeant and given a pair of spectacles.

Follow the Leader is an upbeat, never dull flick that has us convinced of Muggs' confidence in himself and has the audience rooting for him against all odds.

════════════════════

Block Busters

Released July, 22, 1944; 60 minutes; Monogram; Director, Wallace Fox; Producers, Sam Katzman, Jack Dietz; Story and Screenplay, Houston Branch; Photography, Marcel Le Picard; Film Editor, Carl Pierson; Associate Producer, Barney Sarecky; Assistant Director, Art Hammond; Music Director, Edward Kay; Set Designer, David Milton; Sound, Harold McNiff.

CAST

Muggs	Leo Gorcey		*Judge*	Noah Beery, Sr.
Glimpy	Huntz Hall		*Higgins*	Harry Langdon
Skinny	Gabriel Dell		*Mrs. Treadwell*	Minerva Urecal
Butch	Billy Benedict		*Irma*	Kay Marvis
Jean	Fredrick Pressel		*Meyer*	Tom Herbert
Lippman	Bernard Gorcey		*Doctor*	Robert F. Hill
Danny	Jimmy Strand		*Umpire*	Charlie Murray, Jr.
Toby	Bill Chaney		*Batter*	Jack Gillman
Jinx	Roberta Smith			

with Jimmie Noon and His Orchestra, and The Ashburns

*In the Bowery Boys' Paris Playboys, Bernard Gorcey and Huntz Hall enter into another exchange over the word schlemiel. "I know French," Hall says in the Bowery Boys picture. "Schlemiel, right, Louie?" Bernard: "You're a schlemiel in any language."

While there is nothing memorable or outstanding about the structure, direction, characterization or plot in *Block Busters*— the story is in fact trite and unoriginal — the film recalls a social theme which has not been explored since *East Side Kids* (1940).

Unlike *Dead End* and the other early films that concerns slum kids and the hardships their environment presents, here the situation is reversed. A rich kid, Jean, at the urging of his wealthy grandmother, Mrs. Treadwell (played by Minerva Urecal with spunk), struggles for acceptance from the slum kids. Add to this the fact that Jean is French. In Muggs' silent judgment, Jean's accent is a form of snobbery, and deserving of ridicule. Both are brought before a judge.

Veteran actor Noah Beery, Sr., plays the judge in both *Mr. Muggs Steps Out* and *Block Busters*. In *Mr. Muggs Steps Out*, Muggs simply must find a job to avoid reform school. Here, the judge's decision is even more constructive. He decrees that from now on, Muggs will be punished for Jean's disorderly conduct, and Jean will be chastised for any trouble Muggs causes.

Glimpy has a great idea. "Wanna get Jean in trouble? Break a window."

But Jean is not stupid. He arrives at the clubhouse to protect his interests. What follows is what the judge hoped for. The kids introduce Jean to American boxing, wrestling and football. Jean lets the punches, the full nelsons and the tackles roll off his back. Mrs. Treadwell is overjoyed and invites the kids to her house to meet Irma, (Kay Marvis, Gorcey's wife in real life), who takes an immediate liking to Muggs.

Leo Gorcey dancing with wife number one, Kay Marvis. Seated, left, is Huntz Hall; third from left, Gabe Dell; standing at right, Minerva Urecal.

Bernard Gorcey and Leo Gorcey, father and son, share a moment and a pretzel, taking a break during the filming of *Block Buster*.

As we watch Muggs and Glimpy follow Jean from party to party, we become aware that little else is going to happen in this film. The highlight of the affair is Muggs' dancing performance, which is even better than the one he gives in *Kid Dynamite*.

In this picture, Bernard Gorcey, as Mr. Lippman, the pretzel entrepreneur and sponsor of the East Side Kids' baseball team, makes an appearance. Bernard establishes his image as a nervous, generous, meek little businessman, an image that he maintains throughout his reign as a sweet shop owner in 38 Bowery Boys flicks. Here, the announcement that he has purchased baseball uniforms for the kids changes the focus of the film. Jean is attracted by the game and surprises everybody, including himself, by catching every ball that comes in his direction, and flaunts his newfound talent. Muggs assumes the grudging disposition as we know it from *Kid Dynamite*, and throws him off the team.

Mr. Lippman is annoyed with Muggs' insistence on keeping Jean off the team. Muggs leaves it to a vote which results overwhelmingly in Jean's favor. Jean promptly hits a home-run, winning the game and a trip to the country for the East Side Kids, paid for by Mr. Lippman.

Mr. Lippman's gesture is not simply a reward for the kids, but also a life saver for Toby, a poor, sickly youth whose story is revealed through short, informative scenes throughout the picture. As a subplot, it is weakly developed. Its purpose seems only to enhance the generosity of Mr. Lippman and make his offer appear to be a heroic act.

So unlike any other East Side Kids film, where the capture of the criminal is the climax, *Block Busters* has no criminal (not even Gabe Dell who is just another East Side Kid here) and must view Jean's game-winning home run as its pinnacle. In the course of the game, however, something significant in the evolution of Huntz Hall's character does occur. As he approaches the batter's box, he takes a step closer to the nutty character he finally settles into as a Bowery Boy. At the plate, he shouts about how he is going to hit the ball out of the park and practices swinging the bat. He pays no attention to the three pitches and is called out on strikes.

Of the several veteran actors in this picture, the one who is most famous is new to the East Side Kids screen: Harry Langdon, the silent screen comedian, has a small, insignificant part alongside Bernard Gorcey. While it is a pleasant surprise to see Langdon, it is sad knowing that this once-great comedian had to settle for bit parts in low-budget films at Monogram Pictures.

Minerva Urecal seems to enjoy her role no matter who she plays or where she is. It is she who has the last laugh in this picture, in spite of the pain it takes to get it. As a final token of acceptance, Jean undergoes initiation to the club. He steps behind the curtain waiting to take baseball bat whacks administered by Muggs, Glimpy and Skinny. When it is over, emerging from behind the curtain is Mrs. Treadwell, rubbing her rear end. It is one of the most humorous and surprising endings in the series.

Bowery Champs

Released November 25, 1944; 9573 ft.; Monogram; 62 minutes; Director, William Beaudine; Producers, Sam Katzman, Jack Dietz; Story and Screenplay, Earle Snell; Photography, Ira Morgan: Film Editor, John Link; Associate Producer, Barney Sarecky; Musical Director, Edward Kay; Production Manager, Ed W. Rote; Assistant Directors, Arthur Hammond, Clark Paylow; Special Effects, Ray Mercer; Art Director, David Milton; Sound Engineer, Tom Lambert.

CAST

Muggs	Leo Gorcey	*Lieutenant*	Bill Ruhl
Glimpy	Huntz Hall	*Shorty*	Bud Gorman
Jim	Gabriel Dell	*Danny*	Jimmy Strand
Skinny	Billy Benedict	*Mr. Johnson,*	Bernard Gorcey
Bobby Jordan	Bobby Jordan	*Taxi Driver*	
Diane	Thelma White	*Sportswriter*	Francis Ford
Gypsy Carmen	Evelyn Brent	*Tom Wilson*	Wheeler Oakman
Ken Duncan	Ian Keith	*Henchman*	Kenneth MacDonald
Cartwright	Frank Jacquet	*Brother*	Eddie Cherkose
McGuire	Fred Kelsey	*Apartment Manager*	Betty Sinclair
Jane	Ann Sterling		

Distressed damsels, unsolved murders and pushover cops are the overused motifs found in *Bowery Champs*. But here's another observation that cannot be made about any other East Side Kids flick: Muggs and Glimpy are bona fide members of the Establishment, copy boys for the New York *Evening Express*.

The kids keep one step ahead of the police searching for starlet Gypsy Carmen, suspected of murdering her former husband and cafe owner, Tom Wilson.

Ira Morgan's photography makes it possible for only a sharp observer, and someone who knows a bit about guns, to doubt that Gypsy pulled the trigger. Gypsy does point a gun at Wilson. The next shot is a close-up of a gun going off. What is not apparent to the average viewer is that Gypsy's gun is a .32. The gun going off is a .38.

Clancy the cop guards the Wilson house, the scene of the crime. He's a stout, good-natured man, naive enough to believe Muggs is trying to talk him into letting him go into the house to look for clues. Meanwhile, Glimpy sneaks into the house through a window. He overhears an unusually perceptive houseboy say that Gypsy got into a cab with a bumpy fender. With this lead, Muggs and Glimpy comb the streets of New York for such a cab and, lo and behold, find it.

The cab driver, played by Bernard Gorcey, remembers taking Gypsy to the Stevens apartment. There she is.

The desperate woman breaks down and admits to everything — except killing Wilson.

Gorcey distracts the receptionist as the East Side Kids sneak their way inside in *Bowery Champs*. Left to right: Betty Sinclair, Gorcey, Huntz Hall, Billy Benedict, Jimmy Strand, Buddy Gorman.

Anne Sterling and Bobby Jordan on a film-long search for his pal Muggs in *Bowery Champs*.

Her fully loaded .32 proves she is innocent. The police are not far behind. Once again, the kids divert the police, this time dressing up Skinny in Gypsy's fur coat and hat. This is the second time in the series that one of the kids is dressed in drag (the first is Glimpy in *Clancy Street Boys*).

In terms of social stature and maturity, Gypsy is worlds apart from Sylvia, the orphan girl the kids take under their wing in *'Neath Brooklyn Bridge*. But she, too, finds refuge in the kids' clubhouse and dons male clothing so as not to appear conspicuous to unexpected guests. Her motionlessness and silence amidst the kids' crude behavior (triggered by their uneasiness in the presence of a woman) makes it obvious that she is not one of them.

A good deal of attention is given to two aspects of this film that not only have minimal effect on the outcome of the story but are hopelessly unfunny, unconvincing and annoying.

Small objects, such as a coin or a button—in this case a button—tend to be significant among accumulated evidence in a murder mystery. (In the Bowery Boys series, important small objects appear with greater frequency.) Here, just before he leaves with Muggs for the Wilson house, Glimpy finds on the office floor a button which, for some reason, fascinates him. He takes it with him to the house and loses it climbing through the window.

Gabe Dell, as Jimmy, a cub reporter—the type of role he will play through most of the Bowery Boys' series—comes to investigate the house, unaware that Muggs and Glimpy are way ahead of him. He finds the button and, on the strength of this and Clancy's seemingly logical deduction, concludes that the murderer must wear identical buttons on his person. The button is traced to Mr. Cartwright, the gravel-mouthed editor of the *Evening Express*. This linkage, coupled with the police's eyewitness account of Gypsy Carmen escaping in the *Evening Express'* automobile, is sufficient evidence to arrest Mr. Cartwright on suspicion of murder. Naturally the lunacy of this accusation is quickly recognized, and Mr. Cartwright, angry and frustrated, is set free. So much for the button.

Bobby Jordan was not expected to appear in this film. Dressed in his Army uniform, he tracks down Muggs on tips from people who have seen him, but he's oblivious to what the kids are up to. Also, he does not have a character name, another indication he was an add-on. Jordan was making his first appearance since *Ghosts on the Loose* and last as an East Side Kid, while actually on leave from the Army. For Jordan, *Bowery Champs* is the last film in which he is an "individual." In the first eight Bowery Boys films in which he appears, Jordan blends into the woodwork along with David Gorcey and Billy Benedict.

Jordan catches up with Muggs at the Pussycat Cafe in time to lend a helping punch that sends killer Ken Duncan over the railing.

As in *'Neath Brooklyn Bridge* and *Follow the Leader*, the culprit is a cafe owner. Duncan admits to killing his partner, Tom Wilson, and stealing the securities, which belong to Gypsy.

Although the picture following *Bowery Champs* regresses a bit in terms of the kids' maturity, there is no doubt that the original premise of these films—tough slum kids with soft hearts, victims of the environment, not given an even break—has been de-emphasized, opting for the charismatic appeal of Leo Gorcey and the silly comedy of Huntz Hall. *Bowery Champs* represents a turning point in the evolution of the kids' pictures.

═══════════════════════════════════

Dock of New York

Released February 24, 1945; 62 minutes; Monogram; Director, Wallace Fox; Producers, Sam Katzman, Jack Dietz; Original Story, Harvey Gates; Photography, Ira Morgan; Film Editor, William Austin; Art Director, David Milton; Music, Edward Kay; Assistant Director, Mel DeLay; Sound, Tom Lambert; Special Effects, Ray Mercer.

CAST

Muggs	Leo Gorcey	*Skinny*	Billy Benedict
Glimpy	Huntz Hall	*Danny*	Dave Durand
Mrs. Darcy	Betty Blythe	*Sam*	Mende Koenig
Sandra	Gloria Pope	*Millie*	Joy Reese
Compeau	Cy Kendall	*Capt. Jacobs*	Pierre Watkin
Marty	Carlyle Blackwell	*Mrs. McGinnis*	Patsy Moran
Igor Mallet	George Meeker	*Peter*	Leo Borden
Mr. Kessel	Bernard Gorcey	*Patriot*	Maurice St. Clair
Danny	Bud Gorman	*Woman at Pawnshop*	Betty Sinclair

Murder, with a hint of espionage, is on the agenda in this carefully crafted drama. Muggs and Glimpy become increasingly involved in the plight of refugees from the small European country, Tuskania. (Don't bother looking for it on the map.)

Glimpy's knack for finding small objects on the ground is carried over from the previ-

The East Side Kids capture the bad guys in *Docks of New York*. Left to right: unidentified, Mende Koenig, George Meeker, Bud Gorman, Joy Reese, Huntz Hall, Leo Gorcey, Caryle Blackwell, Maurice St. Clair, Billy Benedict.

ous picture, *Bowery Champs*. But instead of keeping his discovery secret, he barges into Muggs' apartment through his booby-trapped bedroom window late at night to show him the necklace, found next to Creepy Slavin's body. Their investigation paves the way for a string of events that lead us to the end of the film.

Except for *Block Busters*, foreigners are portrayed unkindly. In *Docks of New York*, however, they are represented more broadly. The boys hear crying coming from the apartment upstairs. (In Bowery Boys' *Ghost Chasers*, Slip and Sach hear the sobs of an Italian in a hallway.)

"We thought you might be in a jam," says Muggs.

"Jam? I do not know jam," Mrs. Darcy tells the kids. She is troubled by the loss of a family heirloom just stolen from her apartment. Like magic, Muggs produces the diamond necklace, which miraculously dries Mrs. Darcy's tears.

That, however, is only part of the problem. She fears that the man the kids describe as "breathing like a winded horse and carries a long dagger concealed in a cane" is Compeau, a Gestapo agent who has been harassing her and her niece Sandra since they arrived on American shores.

Reminiscent of a scene in *Let's Get Tough* where the kids witness Matsui Sr.'s suicide, the kids take one diamond stone to the pawnbroker to verify its authenticity and find Mr. Kessel dead on the floor of his shop.

As in *Million Dollar Kid* and *Mr. Wise Guy*, circumstantial evidence points to the kids. When the police arrive on the scene, the kids are the ones near the body.

What is even more mysterious to the kids than Kessel's death is their sudden release from jail. Outside, Compeau (Cy Kendall, Warden Morgan from *Crime School*, now turned Gestapo agent) awaits the kids and follows them to the clubhouse.

It's touch and go at the clubhouse when Compeau, gun in hand, demands the necklace. Muggs complies. But Glimpy distracts Compeau, giving the kids an opportunity to jump him and grab back the necklace and the gun. Skinny and Danny follow him to learn where he lives. But it is Compeau who has the last laugh. Compeau pulled a switch.

There is another aspect of the film, a subplot that is rehashed as a main plot ten years later in the Bowery Boys' *Spy Chasers*. Sandra and Mrs. Darcy are not ordinary refugees. Sandra is the princess of Tuskania, incognito in New York, while the Germans occupy her country. Igor Mallet, an accomplice of Compeau and second cousin to Sandra, anticipates an Allied victory and plans to return to Tuskania as king. To do so, he must eliminate Sandra. Just as Mallet is about to strangle the young girl, the kids, as they do so remarkably well in *Spooks Run Wild*, and *Mr. Muggs Steps Out*, rush into the apartment to rescue the girl.

"Sandra, don't do a t'ing," Muggs comforts her. "We'll do everything in our power to recuperate that pile of glass for ya."

Fortunately, Skinny and Danny are reliable enough to track Compeau to his residence. Glimpy alerts the police to the Gestapo agent's whereabouts. When the police arrive, Muggs hands them Compeau and Mallet as the murderers of Creepy Slavin and Mr. Kessel.

Romance wiggles its way in between Glimpy's brother (now Marty) and Sandra. By the film's end, Marty has asked Sandra to marry him, a rather daring move on the part of Monogram Pictures to propose an American would leave his country for a small European one.

Although the flow is not always even, each successive scene offers an explanation or partial explanation to the dilemmas that emerge from the preceding one, while at the same time presents conflicts of its own. For example, during the kids' first meeting with Mrs. Darcy, they learn who owns the necklace and who Compeau is, but they are left in the dark as to why Mrs. Darcy cannot go to the police. Compeau explains their sudden release from jail, but not how they end up with a fake necklace.

This rapid turnover of events and conflicts keeps *Docks of New York* fast-paced, surprising and intriguing.

Ira Morgan's photography, particularly the dark, eerie scene in Hogan's Alley with the kids and Compeau, makes a substantial contribution.

Docks of New York is one of the more inventive adventures of the series.

Mr. Muggs Rides Again

Released July 15, 1945; 63 minutes; Monogram; Director, Wallace Fox; Producers, Sam Katzman, Jack Dietz; Screenplay, Harvey Gates; Photography, Ira Morgan; Film Editor, William Austin; Music Director, Edward Kay; Art Director, David Milton; Assistant Director, Mel DeLay; Sound, Glen Glenn; Special Effects, Ray Mercer.

CAST

Muggs	Leo Gorcey	*Scruno*	John H. Allen
Glimpy	Huntz Hall	*Dollar Davis*	George Meeker
Skinny	Billy Benedict	*Dr. Fletcher*	Pierre Watkin
Elsie	Nancy Brinckman	*Veterinarian*	Milton Kibbee
Mrs. Brown	Minerva Urecal	*Steward Farnsworth*	Frank Jacquet
Gabey	Bernard Thomas	*Meyer*	Bernard Gorcey
Shorty	Bud Gorman	*Mike Hanlin*	I. Stanford Jolley
Squeegie Robinson	Johnny Duncan	*Joe English*	Michael Owen
Sam	Mende Koenig	*Nurse*	Betty Sinclair

Muggs is in love. Her name is Alice. She is tall, has long brown hair, big brown eyes, long eyelashes, and is fast when she wants to be. Someday Muggs hopes to be able to ride her in the thoroughbred races, if he ever gets his suspension removed.

The title of this relatively dull, slow-moving picture implies that Muggs had ridden before. Perhaps the title refers to *That Gang of Mine* where Muggs, frightened of speed, actually slows down his horse in a race. If that's the case, who cares if he rides again?

By the end of the film, Muggs does ride and wins. But more significantly is the portrayal of ambitious woman horse trainer, Mrs. Brown. Her situation bears similarities to Ben, the black horse trainer in *That Gang of Mine*, in that both are old and sickly and give their all to train a prize-winning horse. The fact that they are a minority in the business world makes their struggle for success greater. The kids, for that matter, do for Mrs. Brown what they did for Ben: help make her wish come true.

In addition to her two horses, Alice and Storm Cloud, Mrs. Brown is concerned about her niece Elsie who has been spending too much time with no-good-nik Gabey Dell. Muggs, as nervy as ever, literally steps between Elsie and Gabey and tells the latter to hit the road. Not wanting to cause a scene, Gabey leaves for the moment.

The kids' second stab at separating Gabey and Elsie, admittedly more creative and more successful than the first, presumes that Elsie is a pushover for hocus-pocus. Gabey takes Elsie to the carnival where they visit the fortune teller. Muggs and Glimpy gain access to the fortune teller booth before the young couple enters and Glimpy, posing as the seer, greets them. He tells the couple that the money Gabey has in his pocket is not earned legitimately. Elsie gets angry with Gabey, and leaves him to find her own way home. (The seer motif, used only this once in the East Side Kids films, is expanded upon in Bowery Boys films such as *Ghost Chasers* and *Master Minds* with good results.)

Actor Gabe Dell is not in this picture but his name is. *Why* is never made clear. But just as Mrs. Brown and Ben share similar circumstances in their respective films, so do Gabey Dell and Gabe Dell's character, Gabe Moreno, in *Mr. Hex*. Both are torn between the affections of a sweet female and the easy buck. Both succumb to the easy buck to impress the sweet female, and both meet with injury attempting to undo their wrongdoings.

The emphasis on horses' health over people's health is illustrated by Muggs' reaction to finding Scruno, the stable hand, and Storm Cloud lying on the stable floor, drugged. Ignoring Scruno, Muggs rushes to Storm Cloud's side. (Skinny tends to Scruno.)

Unlike in the later film *Mr. Hex*, where Slip Mahoney (Gorcey) does not know Gabe Moreno has been double-crossing them, here Muggs is convinced that drugging Storm Cloud is Gabey's doing. But when he arrives at Gabey's apartment seeking revenge, Gabey is being carried out on a stretcher. The racketeers got to the stool pigeon first.

The East Side Kids, Milton Kibbee and Minerva Urecal nurse a horse in *Mr. Muggs Rides Again*. Left to right: John H. Allen, Bud Gorman, Mende Koenig, Huntz Hall, Kibbee, Leo Gorcey, Urecal and Johnny Duncan.

Mrs. Brown agrees to race Alice but knows that, without Muggs riding her, the horse is sure to lose.

Like an answer to a prayer, Gabey recovers and tells the horse-racing commissioner the truth about Muggs so that his suspension may be lifted. The audience, however, never learns the truth behind Muggs' suspension.

Predictably, Muggs wins the race. The racketeers are apprehended and Mrs. Brown chaperones Gabey and Elsie's honeymoon.

The repetition in plot and characters shows a lack of originality on the part of the filmmakers. Of the last four East Side Kids films, the seeds for two of them (this one and the next one, *Come Out Fighting*) can be found in the earlier East Side Kids films *That Gang of Mine* and *Million Dollar Kid*, while aspects of *Docks of New York* and *Bowery Champs* are borrowed for the Bowery Boys' *Spy Chasers*, *News Hounds* and *Hard Boiled Mahoney*. This late practice in the East Side Kids pictures spilled over to the Bowery Boys films. The switch to the newer series is timely, for the kids' last five films do not have flair, nor were the kids as free-spirited as in the earlier ones. For that, the reshaping into the Bowery Boys was an excellent move.

Come Out Fighting

Released September 29, 1945; 62 minutes; Monogram; Director, William Beaudine; Producers, Sam Katzman, Jack Dietz; Story and Screenplay, Earle Snell; Photography, Ira Morgan; Film Editor, William Austin; Music, Edward Kay; Art Director, David Milton; Production Manager, Mel DeLay; Sound, Tom Lambert.

Cast

Muggs	Leo Gorcey	*Fingers*	Robert Homans
Glimpy	Huntz Hall	*Mrs. McGinnis*	Patsy Moran
Skinny	Billy Benedict	*Jakey*	Meyer Grace
Blinky	Gabriel Dell	*Pete Vargas*	Pat Gleason
Rita Joyce	Amelita Ward	*Sammy*	Bud Gorman
Jane	June Carlson	*Mayor*	Douglas Wood
Danny	Mende Koenig	*Whitey*	Alan Foster
Henley	George Meeker	*Officer McGowan*	Davison Clark
Gilbert Mitchell	Johnny Duncan	*Stenographer*	Betty Sinclair
Mr. McGinnis	Fred Kelsey		
Commissioner Mitchell	Addison Richards		

Except for a few modifications in setting and circumstance, *Come Out Fighting* is an aggrandizement of *Million Dollar Kid*.

In *Million Dollar Kid*, the father is wealthy, dispassionate, and hardly takes notice of his son who falls in with the wrong crowd. He offers use of his gym to the kids.

Police Commissioner Mitchell, however, is outspoken and robust (an ex-ringer himself), and he exerts his influence to acquire gym privileges for the kids. His son (played by the same Johnny Duncan of *Million Dollar Kid*) also gets involved with the wrong crowd.

But unlike the lazy, disgusted-with-life attitude of Roy, whose only pleasure is to be out of his house, Gilbert practices ballet in his spare hours. Sexy Rita Joyce (played by Gorcey's third wife Amelita Ward) arranges for Gilbert to be found at a raided casino. (The role of the woman as a conniving seductress was used in Universal's *Keep 'Em Slugging* and became a standard role for women in numerous Bowery Boys films.)

Muggs' father, who appears for the first and only time (except for his picture on the wall in *Clancy Street Boys*), insists that Muggs help him with a plumbing job. Whether or not Gorcey's occupation before being recruited for the play *Dead End* has anything to do with this sequence is uncertain. That Glimpy does most of the work is additional testimony to Muggs' running character trait of disdain for ordinary work.

Conveniently, the plumbing job is at Fingers' new casino. Jake, Fingers' chauffeur and bodyguard, comes in demanding that Muggs move his truck so that he can park Fingers' car.

The sting of the closed fist, or the threat of one, has always commanded a great deal of respect in these films. In *Dead End*, under Tommy's raised dukes, Spit returns some coins to Tommy's sister; in *That Gang of Mine*, Muggs beats up Johnny Sullivan before the latter agrees to ride Blue Knight in the horse race; in *Million Dollar Kid*, Muggs knocks some sense into Roy Cortland. Here, Jake lifts Muggs by his shirt to his feet, and Muggs knocks Jake onto the floor. Fingers is so amazed at this that he hires Muggs and Glimpy as his new bodyguards.

As in *'Neath Brooklyn Bridge* and *Follow the Leader*, Muggs has the racketeers believing

Muggs gets himself in trouble trying to do good in *Come Out Fighting*. Left to right: Huntz Hall (hat), Bud Gorman, Mende Koenig, Gorcey, Johnny Duncan, Pat Gleason; others are unidentified.

he is on their side. But unlike in the two earlier films where Muggs knows what the criminals are up to, and works with them only to set them up for the fall, here Muggs has no idea what Fingers' racket is. He learns quickly, however, when Fingers has the kids drive him to Bill Henley's office, where he warns Henley to lay off his interests. Muggs spots Rita Joyce before she ducks into an adjoining room. When Muggs fits all the pieces together in his mind, it spells trouble for Gilbert Mitchell.

Muggs and Glimpy spot Rita and Gilbert entering the casino. Muggs picks up the other kids and prepares to storm the casino. "Remember, our main objective is to get Gilbert out. Mow anybody down who gets in your way."

Muggs is caught by the police and accused by all the newspapers of having gambling interests. Similar to Muggs' punishment for his alleged theft in *Pride of the Bowery*, he is banned from the Interboro Boxing Commission. Unwilling to damage the East Side Kids' chances of participating in the boxing tournament, and not wanting the club to be disbanded by the community, Muggs quits the East Side Kids.

Muggs is in his apartment, in self-imposed exile, when Gilbert and Jane come to thank him profusely for his selfless act. Not only does he confess his part in the scandal (as Roy does in *Million Dollar Kid*), but seeks indemnity by boxing in the Interboro Tournament, substituting for Danny, who injures his hand in the fracas at the casino.

Seeing Gilbert in the ring gives Police Commissioner Mitchell a thrill and brings father and son closer together in a more believable fashion than the forced, unconvincing way Roy and Mr. Cortland are brought together in *Million Dollar Kid*. Gilbert finishes off the fighter from the Bronx in three rounds.

The commissioner calls a news conference in which he absolves Muggs from all guilt. Muggs is not only reinstated as a good member of the community and the club, but given a medal. He is all choked up.

Come Out Fighting is well-paced with plenty of lively characters, several surprises and not one but *two* action-packed culminations. The uproar in the casino and the fight in the arena are the climaxes to the two co-plots of the film. This cross-plotting is partially responsible for the steady progression of various dilemmas which the kids so adeptly overcome.

The Bowery Boys

When they made their first Bowery Boys film in 1946, Leo Gorcey was 29 and Huntz Hall, 26. They were 39 and 38 respectively when each quit the series. Neither this conspicuity nor the obvious low budgets put a dent in the enjoyment viewers derived from the Bowery Boys. Most of the plots were repetitious, predictable, silly, even idiotic, but audiences loved it. Mainly, they loved Slip, Sach and Louie.

Technical effects were minimal. About 95 percent of the shots in the 48 flicks were medium shots. In the entire 12-year history, there are maybe ten close-ups. And the only long shot is repeated at the beginning of almost every films: an overview of New York City that gradually zooms in on the Lower East Side, a single street, and finally Louie's Sweet Shop.

Though their roles on screen changed little in 20 years, Gorcey and Hall's involvement behind-the-scenes altered considerably. They now had a hand in producing the films and were the first actors in Hollywood to own a percentage of the gross. In this regard, they were ten years ahead of their time. Their production rate was about four films per year and, according to a columnist of the 1950s, made them Hollywood's highest-paid actors.

Unlike the Dead End Kids, East Side Kids or Little Tough Guys, the Bowery Boys neither got their name, nor followed a formula established by a pilot movie. Producer Jan Grippo, Leo Gorcey and Huntz Hall hashed out the concept. Their pivotal point was usually Louie's Sweet Shop where the boys loitered until adventure came their way. A love-hate relationship developed between Louie, a middle-aged, Jewish candy store owner, and the boys. Louie threw temper tantrums and his little body shook violently when the boys took advantage of his good nature by helping themselves to ice cream, the use of his back room and his telephone, and borrowing money they never paid back. Yet, when the boys were elsewhere, Louie's belly ached of loneliness.

The leader of this unlikely group of heroes was Terence Aloysius "Slip" Mahoney (Gorcey). Regardless of whether he wore his suit and bowtie, or his sweatshirt and corduroy pants, his hat, with the upturned brim, adorned his head. Gorcey borrowed his character-defining hat from a stagehand and never returned it.

The hat came in handy when his loyal but dimwitted companion, Horace Debussy "Sach" Jones (Hall), did or said something so stupid that the quick-tempered Slip had no recourse but to hit him over the head. Slip was by no means brainy (exemplified by his choice of Sach to handle all the important matters he couldn't take care of personally) but his arrogant personality, his fearlessness in the face of danger, and his knack for confusing people with malapropisms earned him the uncontested leadership of the Bowery Boys.

Other members of the group, Chuck (David Gorcey), Whitey, (Billy Benedict) and Butch (Bennie Bartlett), had very little to say or do in any picture, and their presence was usually inconsequential. Bobby Jordan, who was also relegated to this position, quit the series after the first eight pictures. After Benedict and Bartlett dropped out, Buddy Gorman, Eddie LeRoy and Jimmy Murphy joined the boys. Gabriel Dell appeared in the first 20 Bowery Boys films as Gabe Moreno. He played opposite Gorcey either as the boys' enemy, or whatever outside character was needed to work closely with the boys. He could play a policeman, a newspaperman, a detective, a lawyer, a poker player and, once, a piano player. Only in *Hard Boiled Mahoney* was Dell one of the Bowery Boys.

In the films that kept them close to Louie's Sweet Shop, the boys were entrepreneurs. In *Spook Busters* they own an exterminating company; in *Hold That Baby!* they run a Laundromat; and in *Angels in Disguise* the boys work for a newspaper. (It was from a line in the latter film that rock star Alice Cooper got the idea for his song, "School's Out.")

Blues Busters seems to be a take-off on the joke about a doctor assuring the patient that he will be able to sing after the operation, even though the patient never sung in his life. After his doctor takes out his tonsils, Sach becomes a crooner and the boys and Louie become owners of a nightclub.

Sach often acquires peculiar powers enabling him to perform supernatural acts such as predicting the future (*Master Minds*), picking correct numbers at a roulette table (*Crashing Las Vegas*) or sniffing out diamonds (*Jungle Gents*). Usually these superhuman abilities are the result of Sach receiving a blow on the head or electric shock. But by the end of every film, whatever power was bestowed upon him disappears.

Crashing Las Vegas and *Jungle Gents* take them out of Louie's Sweet Shop and into travel mode. Besides *Las Vegas*, the Bowery Boys services are needed in the west (*Dig That Uranium*), in the "Old West" (*Bowery Buckaroos*) and in the Deep South (*Feudin' Fools*). *Jungle Gents* takes them to the heart of Africa, while *Paris Playboys* and *Loose in London* take them to those European cities. The reason they are called to Europe is similar in both films: Sach is a victim of mistaken identity.

But it isn't always necessary for the boys to travel long distances for their identities to get tangled with others. In *High Society* the boys find themselves among the wealthy with Sach Jones a possible heir to a fortune. And in *Smugglers' Cove* Slip is accidentally handed a letter addressed to his namesake, giving him legal possession of the Mahoney Mansion.

Similar to the way letters in *Smugglers' Cove* fall into Slip's hands, so does a pile of money in *Jinx Money*. A magic lamp in *Bowery to Baghdad* falls into Sach's lap.

Things happen to the boys intentionally as well as accidentally, as in *Triple Trouble* and *Jail Busters* where they put themselves in prison in order to foil illegal operations occurring behind prison walls.

And of course each division of the armed forces has their bout with the Bowery Boys: *Clipped Wings*, *Here Come the Marines*, *Let's Go Navy!* and *Bowery Battalion*.

It would be unfair not to mention the many times the Bowery Boys devote their full energies helping others. In *Mr. Hex*, Slip, with the aid of hypnotic suggestion, enters Sach in a boxing contest hoping to win enough money to help their friend Gloria launch her singing career. In *Fast Company*, Slip keeps Cassidy's taxi cabs moving to help Cassidy defray the medical costs due to an injury; and in *Fighting Fools*, Slip re-trains a depressed boxer, Johnny Higgins, to regain the lightweight title.

After the forty-first Bowery Boys picture, Leo Gorcey quit the series. His father, Bernard Gorcey (Louie), had been killed in an automobile accident and his death affected Leo. He became impossible to work with. He imagined seeing his father on the set looking up at the producer and demanding bigger and better parts. On top of this, Gorcey was going through his third and worst divorce. He began to drink more, causing him to behave like a Dead End Kid, tearing up sets.

For his last 68 hours of work, Gorcey received $12,500 salary plus $10,000 percentage. From all of his pictures since *Dead End*, Gorcey figured that he earned close to a million dollars. "And they put bank robbers in jail," he once said.

The Bowery Boys made seven more films with Stanley Clements taking Leo Gorcey's place, and Percy Helton or Dick Elliott taking Bernard Gorcey's place. Huntz Hall received top billing. But without the Gorcey-Hall team, these films had little to offer, and in 1958 Allied Artists (the new name for Monogram Pictures) ceased their production.

Films that focus on a young gang did not end with the Bowery Boys. The musical *West Side Story*, the television shows *Welcome Back Kotter*, *Happy Days* and *Flatbush* (which drew direct parallels in plot and characters) may not have been possible without the Dead End Kids and the Bowery Boys. During the 1970s and '80s there wasn't a major city in America, Europe or Japan that either did not or never had the Bowery Boys on television. In New York and Philadelphia, the East Side Kids and Bowery Boys were shown regularly.

With all the changes that took place throughout the years, most people who know about the Dead End Kids or Bowery Boys and enjoy their films can't tell which group is which. A goal of this book is to clarify these distinctions.

Live Wires

Released January 12, 1946; 64 minutes; Monogram; Director, Phil Karlson; Producer, Jan Grippo; Screenplay, Tim Ryan, Josef Mischel; Story, Dore Jeb Schary; Photography, William A. Sickner; Film Editor, Fred McGuire; Music Director, Dave Milton.

CAST

Slip	Leo Gorcey	*Herbert Sayers*	John Eldredge
Sach	Huntz Hall	*Stevens*	Pat Gleason
Bobby	Bobby Jordan	*Construction Foreman*	William Ruhl
Whitey	Billy Benedict	*George*	Rodney Bell
Eddie	William Frambes	*Boy Friend*	Bill Christy
Jeanette	Claudia Drake	*Girlfriend*	Nancy Brinckman
Mary	Pamela Blake	*Barton*	Robert E. Keane
Mabel	Patta Brill	*Jack*	Bernard Gorcey
Patsy Clark	Mike Mazurki		

Slip, the bum, is not able to hold a job. Even his simple pal Sach has a job. Urged to work by his sister Mary, Slip takes to peddling ink remover.

His rabble-rousing on a street corner is well orated, but the outcome is devastating. With his sister Mary watching, Slip pours ink over a man's lapel. The ink remover is applied and does nothing. Slip is promptly punched out. Sach, however, benefits from Slip's loss: He recognized the ink victim as a former welterweight champion and bet on him. While Slip is laying on the ground, Sach collects his winnings.

Brooding over this misfortune, Slip saunters to a job interview with H. L. Sayers, Mary's boss. Thinking the job is in a managerial capacity, Slip hurries to the address. The job is in construction; his office, a shovel. After five minutes he gets into a fight with the foreman, is fired, and given a summons.

Next, Slip accepts a position with Sach as a process server. At the same time he is pursued by Mabel, the waitress at the sweet shop (to be owned and operated two movies later by Louie Dumbrowski, played by Bernard Gorcey) Slip agrees to take Mabel to the Hi Hat Club. But his ulterior motive is to serve nightclub singer Jeanette with a summons and repossess her automobile.

The scene at the nightclub is very well-done, honors going to Gorcey. His superior air and unabashed attention-begging antics are performed with gusto. He warns the waiter not to bring the "stale" 1928 wine, as the subservient waiter suggests, but something with a current year vintage.

The waiter is also perplexed by Slip's order of two steak sandwiches. The eager debutante demonstrates a sandwich by putting his hat between two menus.

After serving the summons on Jeanette, Slip is cornered by two bouncers. He escapes unharmed, which is more than could be said for Mabel, who gets a black eye.

Ready for a more challenging assignment, Slip and Sach are given the task of delivering a summons to underworld figures Patsy Clark and Pigeon.

Searching for Patsy and Pigeon, Slip stumbles upon Jack (played by Bernard Gorcey, who had only spot appearances in East Side Kids), a cagey fellow who knows his way around the crooked city. He tells Slip that Patsy Clark can be found at Patsy's boutique shop.

Slip's resourcefulness is his chief asset. In *Live Wires*, it is apparent the writers, Tim Ryan and Josef Mische, are first learning how to convey it. Though they have a good idea of the kind of personality Slip Mahoney is, how to communicate this idea into cinematic reality is at first slippery. The way Slip learns the pass phrase to Patsy's office in the boutique shop is a good example. As soon as Jack informs Slip where Patsy Clark can be found, Slip immediately telephones the place, telling the woman who answers the telephone that he is delivering liquor. She reprimands him for not remembering to say, "So red is the rose." But how Slip knows that Patsy is expecting liquor is beyond the context of the script.

Expecting a woman, Slip is stunned to see that Patsy Clark is a seven-foot, trigger-happy hit man who gets great pleasure taking potshots at liquor bottles and bouncing people off all corners of the room. He boasts about how the last guy who tried serving him a summons was found in the river. "And I liked the guy."

It is a purely contrived coincidence that Patsy's friend, Red, arrives while Patsy is under the impression that Slip is working for Red. A phone call stops Patsy from throwing Slip against the wall yet again. It is Pigeon, telling him that he is on his way to Mexico.

With the help of Whitey, Chuck, Bobby and the police, Slip and Sach are rescued from the grip of Patsy Clark and catch Pigeon a.k.a. Mary's boss, Sayers, seconds before the crook is about to board the plane with Mary.

Besides the semi-constant storyline of Slip seeking a job, *Live Wires* is an action-packed patchwork of disassociated events. Characters come and go suddenly. Sayers' illegal activities are not made explicit nor is the connection between Pigeon and Patsy Clark definable.

The first two Bowery Boys films, *Live Wires* and *In Fast Company*, can easily be mistaken for the tail end of the East Side Kids' pictures, because the Gorcey and Hall characters have gone through no significant change. It is not until the next film that Sach dons his baseball cap, and not until *Jinx Money* that Sach morphs into the ultimate silly Sach, and remains that way through the end of the series.

In Fast Company

Released June 22, 1946; 61 minutes; Monogram; Director, Del Lord; Producers, Jan Grippo, Lindsley Parsons; Screenplay, Edmond Seward, Tim Ryan, Victor Hammond; Original Story, Martin Mooney; Photography, William Sickner; Film Editor, William Austin; Music Director, Edward Kay; Editorial Supervisor, Richard Currier; Assistant Director, Theodore "Doc" Joos; Sound, Tom Lambert; Working Title, *In High Gear*.

CAST

Slip	Leo Gorcey	*Tony*	Luis Alberni
Sach	Huntz Hall	*Mrs. Cassidy*	Mary Gordan
Bobby	Bobby Jordan	*Nora Cassidy*	Judy Schenz
Whitey	Billy Benedict	*Meredith*	Charles Coleman
Mabel Dumbrowski	Judy Clark	*Louie*	Bernard Gorcey
Marian McCormick	Jane Randolph	*Blind Man*	Stanley Price
Chuck	David Gorcey	*Officer*	George Eldredge
Father Donovan	Charles D. Brown	*Chauffeur*	Marcel de la Brosse
Steve Trent	Douglas Fowley	*Old Gentleman*	Walter Soderling
Patrick McCormick	Paul Harvey	*O'Hara*	Lee Phelps
Sally Turner	Marjorie Wood-worth	*Cop*	Jack Cheatham
		Customer	Fred Aldrich
Mr. Cassidy	Frank Marlowe	*Cop*	Mike Pat Donovan
Pete	Dick Wessel	*Bit*	John Indrisano
Gus	William Ruhl		

A more coherent film than its predecessor, *In Fast Company* uses the same formula as *Live Wires*. Slip is reluctant to do a good deed as he is lethargic about work in *Live Wires*. In lieu of an older sister looking over his shoulder, we have a priest. And as in *Live Wires*, Slip becomes more involved than he planned, putting behind bars the crooks of the Red Circle Cab Company.

Common to all the priests in the Dead End Kids–Bowery Boys films is their unorthodox methods in dealing with the boys. With Father Connolly (*Angels with Dirty Faces*) it's his white lie. With Father Donovan, it's a bit of blackmail. Father Donovan conspires with an Italian vegetable vendor and the cop on the beat to instigate a vegetable battle between the vendor and the boys. Father Donovan intervenes, "convincing" the policeman to let Slip go if he promises to drive Mr. Cassidy's cab that night.

Father Donovan offers to pay for the damage, but the vendor refuses to take the money. The priest's quick acquiescence seems hypocritical, rendering one working man's loss another one's gain.

The scene with Slip and Steve Trent, manager of the Red Circle Cab Company, displays the determination of both men. Trent offers Slip a job. Slip barks a counter-offer and storms out of the office much the way Humphrey Bogart does in *The Maltese Falcon* when he threatens Sydney Greenstreet. "Don't have your goons looking for trouble around Cassidy's cabs or they're going to find it."

Sally Turner, Trent's girlfriend, sets the precedent as a shrew, and is the most decadent of the series. She hops into the back of Slip's cab and directs him straight to an ambush. As Slip opens her door, we see a hand grab Slip by the neck and pull him away. The camera stays on Sally in the back seat, casually applying makeup, as we hear Slip being beaten up. It is one of the Bowery Boys' best cinemagraphic portrayals of a seductive and heartless female.

Slip's only good malapropism is at the hospital where Chuck is treated for cuts and bruises and the Boys cheer him up with gifts. Bobby is a bit embarrassed to give his gift. It's flowers.

"That's probably the most obnoxious present he got," says Slip, trying to reassure Bobby. "All day Chuck is breathing air, pure H_2O. Then he exhales carbon monoxide."

His hat slipped over his forehead as he's being chased off the road by a Red Circle cab cockily displays Slip's composure in the face of danger. What makes the scene significant is that Red Circle cab owner Mr. McCormick and his daughter are in the back seat. Slip no longer has to explain anything to McCormick, for the old man is now a firsthand witness.

Typical of most Bowery Boys and East Side Kids films are the rowdy winner-takes-all fistfights, and Hall staying clear of them. *In Fast Company* is the first Bowery Boys film to include such a scene.

In Fast Company is a tight-knit, fast-paced story. Its best moments are with Paul Harvey and Gorcey. Harvey is wonderful as a fitful middle-aged rich man, constantly overconcerned with the mundane. He repeats this role in *Smugglers' Cove*.

Judy Clark gets tough with Leo Gorcey in *In Fast Company*.

Besides the interaction between these two, there is very little interplay. Slip's scene with Steve Trent is powerful, and more like this would have enhanced the conflict. Otherwise, the scenes are well-constructed, marked by touches of comedy (Slip spraying seltzer at McCormick's butler) or elements of surprise (McCormick jumping into the fistfight with Trent).

This is Mabel's last appearance of any consequence and her absence is no great loss. Nagging Slip is not only annoying to him but to the audience as well. Though she is supposed to be funny, she is not, and any romantic element that is supposed to be salvaged between Slip and Mabel is sorrowful.

Bowery Bombshell

Released July 20, 1946; 65 minutes; Monogram; Director, Phil Karlson; Producers, Lindsey Parsons, Jan Grippo; Screenplay, Edmond Seward; Story, Victor Hammond; Photography, William Sickner; Film Editor, William Austin; Music Director, Edward Kay; Assistant Director, Theodore "Doc" Joos; Makeup, Harry Ross; Sound, Tom Lambert.

CAST

Slip	Leo Gorcey	*Dugan*	William Newell
Sach	Huntz Hall	*Prof. Schnackenberger*	Milton Parsons
Bobby	Bobby Jordan	*Louie*	Bernard Gorcey
Whitey	Billy Benedict	*Moose*	William "Wee
Chuck	David Gorcey		Willie" Davis
Cathy Smith	Teala Loring	*Featherfinger*	Lester Dorr
O'Malley	James Burke	*Mug #1*	William Ruhl
Ace Deuce	Sheldon Leonard	*O'Hara*	Eddie Dunn
Street Cleaner	Vince Barnett		

Bowery Bombshell has many innovations including the debut of lovable Louie Dumbrowski and his sweet shop. The story is about Sach framed for an armed robbery and Slip's daring escapade proving that the robbery was committed by nightclub owner Ace Deuce's mob.

When Louie confides that he needs $300 to solve his business woes, Slip "dehydrates his thoughts" and takes to the street to sell their dilapidated jalopy to the street cleaner. When that does not work, they try the bank.

In the first of several attempts in the series to get a bank loan, the boys don't even get through the door. (In subsequent tries, neither Gabe Moreno's position at the bank in *Blonde Dynamite*, nor their credit at Louie's Sweet Shop in *Feudin' Fools* can get them a loan.) Here, as they are about to enter the bank, bandits flee and drop a money bag at Sach's feet. The moment Sach picks it up, Cathy Smith, their photographer friend, snaps a picture.

Slip's fear that the picture might be publicized is technically groundless, since nobody but the boys and Cathy know it exists. Yet they themselves call attention to it by breaking into Prof. Schnackenberger's laboratory to develop the film. The negatives, like a bad dream come true, slip out of Slip's pants and onto the front pages of tomorrow's newspaper.

Prof. Schnackenberger is the first and best of three absent-minded professors to appear in the Bowery Boys series. The professor in *Hold That Line* has a bit role, and the one in *Jalopy* is forced to share a small piece of the spotlight with *Sach*. Though Schnackenberger's appearance seems perfunctory at first, as does the street cleaner's, they mark the exploratory use of foreshadowing as a cinemagraphic technique used sporadically and successfully.

Undoubtedly the best scene of the film is at Ace Deuce's nightclub. Ace can rest easy since the police investigation is focused on Sach as a member of the Midge Casalotti gang. But since nobody has ever seen Midge Casalotti, Slip and the boys decide to pose as the mobster and his gang, visit Ace and demand the money; also, to have Cathy use her cigarette lighter–camera to get a picture of Ace holding the money. (This device was also used in a much later film, *Fighting Trouble*.)

Leo Gorcey is remarkably convincing as gangster Casalotti. Whenever he feels threatened, he goes into an epileptic fit and frightens Ace and his gang to the point where the gang refrains from pointing their guns at him. We never do find out the consequences of these "shakes" or why Casalotti gets them.

On his way out of the nightclub, Slip produces from his pocket a pebble-sized explosive and tosses it at Ace. A keen close-up of the object reveals a tiny parachute aiding its slow descent. The little bomb, unlike the liquid explosive that the film prepares us for, takes us by surprise. It's unintelligible but cute.

Bowery Bombshell is the first film in which the "good girl" has a prominent role in the

Leo Gorcey as the notorious Midge Casalotti with Teala Loring at his side as Wee Willie Davis (Moose) offers his hand. The woman beside Moose is unidentified.

boys' success. Cathy does a good job as Slip's "dame" at the nightclub, indecorously complaining about the lack of regalement. It is not until *Blues Busters*, the eighteenth film, that the "good girl" actively assists the boys again.

The liquid experiment that Dr. Schnackenberger is working on clues us in on what will save the boys from Moose's powerful fist. Like Patsy Clark in *Live Wires*, who explains how he bounces people off walls, Moose explains to Sach how he is going to tear him apart. Before doing so, he takes a swig of what he thinks is booze only to find out it's the professor's formula. He fears he's become a human bomb; when he expectorates, his spittle explodes. Slip, who tells Moose he can "get ten years for assault without a battery," forces him to sign a confession to the robbery.

Although much in *Bowery Bombshell* is praiseworthy and precedent-setting, the individual scenes overextend themselves, making for an altogether slow-moving comedy-drama. Sequences in the nightclub scene of Slip flirting with Ace's girlfriend while she is performing a raunchy musical number lead nowhere. Moose toying with Sach before the beating that never comes is frustratingly lengthy.

The film does make a sincere attempt in the end to tie in all its diverse aspects. The reward money for the recovery of the bank loot and the capture of the robbers will take care of Louie's business debt; Cathy will get a job with the newspaper and Prof. Schnackenberger reveals that his formula is safe after all — until he absent-mindedly drops it into the boys' jalopy. The explosion sends Slip, Sach and the professor onto the street with the spare tire around their necks that reads "Dead End." Slip covers the "A" and "D," which makes it "De End."

Spook Busters

Released August 24, 1946; 68 minutes; Monogram; Director, William Beaudine; Producer, Jan Grippo; Original Story, Edmond Seward, Tim Ryan; Photography, Harry Neumann; Film Editor, William Austin; Music Director, Edward Kay; Production Manager, Glenn Cook; Makeup, Harry Ross; Sound, Tom Lambert.

CAST

Slip	Leo Gorcey		*Mrs. Grimm*	Vera Lewis
Sach	Huntz Hall		*Stiles*	Charles Middleton
Dr. Coslow	Douglass Dumbrille		*Brown*	Chester Clute
Bobby	Bobby Jordan		*Ivan*	Richard Alexander
Gabe	Gabriel Dell		*Louie*	Bernard Gorcey
Whitey	Billy Bendict		*Dean Pettyboff*	Charles Millsfield
Chuck	David Gorcey		*Herman*	Arthur Miles
Mignon	Tanis Chandler		*Police Captain*	Tom Coleman
Dr. Bender	Maurice Cass			

Dressed in caps and gowns, the Bowery Boys are proud graduates of an exterminating school — except for Sach, who sits in the corner wearing a dunce cap. It's the boys' first real attempt to earn their keep and it gets them inside the Menlo estate, an allegedly haunted house.

While the roots of the science-fiction motif are planted in *Bowery Bombshell* with Prof. Schnackenberger's bizarre formula, it begins to sprout in *Spook Busters*, with Dr. Koslow's wild experiment of transplanting a human brain into a gorilla. The idea of brain transplants is explored in three Bowery Boys films, and each adds a new twist.

Dr. Koslow's assistants Ivan and Stiles are as incompetent as Emil's (Bela Lugosi) in *Ghosts on the Loose*. Lights go on and off by themselves, a rope is suspended vertically in midair, and a message, "Leave while you are still alive," emerges when Sach cleans a dirty mirror. Slips looks for the words but they disappear as suddenly as they materialize. "Your eyes are getting bad," Slip tells Sach. "You should see an optimist. The solution to the whole problem is so delirious to be defective."

Secret passageways are prevalent in these films extending back to the *Junior G-Men* serials. Sach stumbles behind a revolving wall that leads to the stairway to the basement. In the basement he finds the doctor's laboratory and a closed circuit television.

Gabe Dell, as Gabe Moreno, is introduced in this picture as a Merchant Marine on leave. (Gabe Dell *was* a Merchant Marine.) He joins ranks with Chuck, Whitey and Bobby futilely digging a hole through the floor in search of Sach. The chore keeps them occupied for most of the picture while Slip and Sach carry the film to its end.

Like Dr. Anton in *The Bowery Boys Meet the Monsters*, Dr. Koslow is in awe of Sach's brain after listening to him speak. He reveals his true intention with the same intonation a naughty weightwatcher would use asking for just one more piece of cake. "I just want to remove your brain. I just want a little piece."

The proud graduates of Extermination school in *Spook Busters* (left to right): Leo Gorcey, unidentified actor, Bobby Jordan, unidentified actor, Billy Benedict, unidentified actor, David Gorcey and Charles Millsfield.

"How much do ya think he's got?" asks the perplexed Slip.

Director "One Shot" Beaudine and photographer Harry Neumann give us an appreciation for the choreographed fight scene. After Slip tranquilizes everybody with ether, the fight scene is shown in slow motion; the fist-to-chin contact, the block of a punch and other various details are marvelously dissected.

A flaw that repeats itself in several Bowery Boys films is the forced gag. And because it is so blatantly forced it is sadly unfunny. There is Sach by himself, holding a plank of wood used to lock the gorilla's cage. Sach takes it to ward off his attackers, and inadvertently sets the gorilla free. Slip gestures silently with his hands that the gorilla is behind him, but Sach feigns incomprehension and waves him off. In shooting Slip and Sach in separate shots, the camera strives for a long-distance effect. We know they are in the same small lab so the sign language is unnecessary. The result is a graceless gag.

Cosmos, the gorilla in *The Bowery Boys Meet the Monsters*, responds to his master, as does Atlas, the ape man in *Master Minds*. But the gorilla in *Spook Busters* is unnamed and unresponsive to Dr. Koslow. It is poetic justice for the gorilla to go after Dr. Koslow, just as the Monster in *Frankenstein* goes after his creator. If not for the timely arrival of the police who shoot the gorilla to death, Dr. Koslow would be a goner.

Douglass Dumbrille, a well-known actor noted for his "bad guy" roles, is adequate as Dr. Koslow. Though his part is small, Chester Clute, as the exasperated, failing realtor, Mr. Brown, is exceptional, especially when he throws all his ringing telephones into the waste-basket. His scene with Slip is very entertaining, culminating in Slip's assurance, "We exterminate ghosts."

There are a couple of new developments: First, Slip is dressed in a suit, bow tie and felt hat with turned-up brim. This will be his regular accoutrement as a Bowery Boy.

There is a corny scene in which the boys display their usual insecurity around pretty women. Gabe brings along his French fiancée, Mignon.

"How about a formal interjection?" asks the enthralled Slip.

When introduced to Sach, Mignon says, innocently, in her French accent, "Sach, yes? Gabe told me a lot about you. He said you are a very nice mor*on*."

Spook Busters is a two-part film; first is the mystery of the house, which segues to the doctors and their experiments. Together they composite a well-apportioned, upbeat film that deliciously interweaves mystery and comedy.

Mr. Hex

Released December 7, 1946; 63 minutes; Monogram; Director, William Beaudine; Producer, Jan Grippo; Associate Producer, Cyril Endfield; Screenplay, Cyril Endfield; Original Story, Jan Grippo; Photography, James Brown; Film Editors, Richard Currier, Seth Larson; Music Director, Edward Kay; Art Director, David Milton; Set Decorator, Raymond Boltz; Assistant Director, Wesley Barry; Makeup, Milburn Morante; Sound, Tom Lambert; Songs, "A Love Song to Remember" and "One Star-Kissed Night," Louis Herscher.

CAST

Slip	Leo Gorcey		*Raymond*	Ian Keith
Sach	Huntz Hall		*Evil-Eye Fagan*	Sammy Cohen
Bobby	Bobby Jordan		*Louie*	Bernard Gorcey
Gabe	Gabriel Dell		*Mob Leader*	William Ruhl
Whitey	Billy Benedict		*Danny the Dip*	Danny Beck
Chuck	David Gorcey		*Margie*	Rita Lynn
Gloria	Gale Robbins		*Billy Butterworth*	Joe Gray
Bull Laguna	Ben Welden		*Blackie*	Eddie Gribbon

Oh, those soft-hearted boys! What Slip wouldn't have *Sach* do for their friend Gloria, who needs money to launch her career as a singer. For starters, Slip enters Sach (the one who hides when the fighting starts) in a boxing contest. After weeks of practice, Sach cannot land a single punch.

This is the first Bowery Boys film about hypnotism and the first with Gabe (Dell) Moreno as their adversary. It is also a step forward in dramatic action, plot development and confrontation of wits. It boasts the largest cast to date, another plus.

The scene in which the boys and nightclub owner Bull Laguna first meet is excellently performed, and precisely timed. Gabe, chump that he is, gets Gloria a job at Laguna's nightclub. After the show, Laguna wants to see her in his office. When she screams Slip and Sach barge in, saving Gloria from sexual assault. Laguna decks them both. Slip and Sach are on the floor surrounded by four pairs of legs, viewed symbolically as pillars. From his pocket Slip produces the coin, "the genie" as the boys call it, used to hypnotize Sach into a "fighting tiger, a roaring lion." Like Samson, Sach knocks down the "pillars" as we watch the legs fall, two by two. It is a provocative point of view.

Gabe, as in many other pictures, is detached from the boys. Thinking Gloria will like him more if he has money, and threatened with death if he reveals that Sach's next opponent, Billy Butterworth, is really the former welterweight champion Ray Teasel, Gabe tells Laguna the secret to Sach's success—a little coin. At ringside, Gloria makes him feel ashamed for what he has done. He volunteers to tell all to the police. But one of Laguna's spies shoots him in the arm. This spy is another example of the writers' efforts to make this film as intricate as possible.

Slip's determined personality shines here. Although Gloria tells him it's not necessary for Sach to fight, Slip is bent on finishing what he has started. The means has become an end in itself, as in *In Fast Company* when Slip embraced Cassidy's cab company as his own.

The boxing scene is eventful, commencing with Sach doing the Charlie Chaplin routine in the ring until the missing Genie is found. What's even more interesting are Bull Laguna's obstacles to Sach's hypnotic strength, and the methods Slip and the boys use to overcome them.

Sammy Cohen does an extraordinary portrayal of a European mesmerist ("Evil-Eye Fagan") who makes outlandish expressions with his eyes to frighten the daylights out of Sach. Bobby and Whitey, in a rare display of ingenuity, borrow a flash camera from a noted photojournalist. While Whitey distracts the photographer, Bobby takes the camera and aims the flash at Evil-Eye Fagan. He's done.

Next, Laguna hires Danny the Dip to pick Slip's pocket.

"Hey, Slip," calls Bobby. "There's a guy outside with a brown suit, says he wants to see ya."

"Tell 'im I already got a brown suit."

Danny the Dip poses as an insurance salesman sent by a mutual friend. "You can tell this mutual friend that he ain't no friend of mine. In fact, you can tell him he's my lifelong enemy."

At one point, two battles are going on in the ring—Sach and Butterworth, Slip and the Dip. The Dip extends his hand with the coin out of reach from Slip. A hot dog vendor takes the coin and replaces it with a hotdog. Slip drags the vendor to Sach's corner where he tests every two-bit piece until the Genie is found. Sach wins by a knockout.

Mr. Hex and *Lucky Losers* are the two films in which Slip procures the tutelage of strangers to learn tricks of the con trade. But unlike in *Lucky Losers* where the instructions take time, in *Mr. Hex* the hypnotist needs only a few moments to demonstrate and teach Slip how to hypnotize Sach to be as strong as ten men. The hypnotist furnishes Slip with the Genie.

There's one brief surrealistic scene where Sach is shadow-boxing. That Sach must train at all is an exercise in futility since his strength comes not from doing deep knee-bends, but from the little coin. His shadow turns on him and knocks him out. Even against his own shadow, Sach is a loser.

Ben Welden is excellent as Bull Laguna. He gives his character color in shades of arrogance, sense of humor, persuasiveness and finesse when he calmly threatens to kill someone. Welden should have been used more often.

Mr. Hex is to be applauded for its characterizations and plot. Not until *Angels in Disguise* do we see another plot as multi-faceted as this one.

Hard Boiled Mahoney

Released April 26, 1947; 63 minutes; 5689 ft.; Monogram; Director, William Beaudine; Producer, Jan Grippo; Original Story, Cyril Endfield; Photography, Jim Brown; Art Director, Dave Milton; Editor, William Austin; Music, Edward Kay; Set Decorator, George Milo; Assistant Director, Frank Fox; Production Manager, William Calihan; Production Supervisor, Glenn Cook; Sound, Eldon Ruberg; Special Effects, Augie Lohman.

CAST

Slip	Leo Gorcey		*Salina Webster*	Betty Compson
Sach	Huntz Hall		*Lennie the Meatball*	Danny Beck
Bobby	Bobby Jordan		*Dr. Carter*	Pierre Watkin
Whitey	Billy Benedict		*Hasson*	Noble Johnson
Chuck	David Gorcey		*Prof. Quizard*	Byron Foulger
Gabe	Gabriel Dell		*Thug*	Teddy Pavelec
Eleanor	Teala Loring		*Police Lieutenant*	Pat O'Malley
Armand	Dan Seymour		*Police Sergeant*	Jack Cheatham
Louie	Bernard Gorcey		*Dr. Armand's*	Carmen D'Antonio
Alice	Patti Brill		*Secretary*	

Slip proves that all you need to be a detective is a "deductible mind and the power of treason" when they go to collect Sach's "radioactive" pay from Detective Groggin. When Salina enters and hands over a $50 retainer to the boys to find her long-lost sister, Eleanor, the boys are too tongue-tied to tell her they are not detectives.

At first the only information Slip and Sach have to go on is that Eleanor Williams visits spiritualist Dr. Carter. The boys track him down in time to witness his murder, and for Slip to get knocked on the head. When he regains consciousness, Slip identifies the woman standing there as Salina's sister Eleanor. The woman denies it. Slip retorts, "She's lyin.' She's making up lubrications." When Eleanor accuses Slip of working for "Armand," thus the plot thickens.

Lenny the Meatball is the underground nosey-body counterpart of Jack (Bernard Gorcey) of *Live Wires*. He shows Slip where Armand commands a fortune teller's syndicate. With a picture of a middle-aged woman torn out of a magazine, Slip tells Armand he wishes to contact his dead aunt. Armand reveals the names of Slip Mahoney and Sach Jones, who know the whereabouts of Eleanor Williams and "certain letters."

The scene is not only eerie (and foreshadows several scenes in a later film, *Ghost Chasers*) but introduces another layer of plot. But unlike the coded comic strip in *Angels in Disguise*, there is no man behind the crystal ball to funnel information to Armand. To believe Armand really gets information from a crystal ball without a gimmick is too far-fetched.

The next surprise is when Slip is put to sleep by Armand and wakes up to find Salina patting his head with a wet cloth. With the story now at its most confusing point, writer Enfield honors Salina by allowing her to connect the dots. She admits she is not Eleanor's sister. Through "spiritual seduction," Armand obtained incriminating information on both women. Carter, who formerly worked for Armand, tried to help Eleanor by stealing a stack of documents from Armand, hoping the letters she wrote to a young man would be among them. At the time of their writing, she had reason to believe her husband was dead. After learning he is alive and on his way home, Eleanor wants the letters back. Salina hopes to find her own letters in the pile.

The boys participate in the television game show "Prof. Quizard and His Brain Trust," a scene that goes through a lot of trouble but is irrelevant to the plot in *Hard Boiled Mahoney*. Left to right: Billy Benedict, David Gorcey, Gabe Dell, Bobby Jordan, Huntz Hall, Leo Gorcey and Byron Foulger.

Spiritualism and the like is the theme of several Bowery Boys films (*Ghost Chasers, Hold That Hypnotist*), all of which are spiced with comic interludes. But only in *Hard Boiled Mahoney* does the comical moment digress from the story. The pause is similar to the Marx Brothers film *Monkey Business* when they are being chased on the boat but have time to stop and play some musical instruments. In this case, Armand and his men chase the boys from rooftop to rooftop until they find themselves at a radio station where "Prof. Quizard and His Brain Show" is in progress. The other boys join them and exchange clothes with six professors, garbed in graduation uniforms, who are about to appear on the show. When the emcee sees the boys, he quickly escorts them to the podium where they, as distinguished professors, must answer such questions as, "For what general was the Washington monument named after?" The boys create such pandemonium on the stage that Prof. Quizard gives them prizes just to get them off. Though the show itself is weakened by such simple questions and superfluous apparel, it is visually one of the funniest scenes in the Bowery Boys series. What is also noteworthy is that the boys seem to unconsciously adopt the "wise guy" attitude of the East Side Kids.

As in the first Endfield film, Slip is given some romantic interests. He's stuck on Alice, Louie's waitress. Slip jokes with Alice about coming with him to his "dream island." It is Alice who provides Slip with the picture of a middle-aged woman from a magazine. She also gets the police to arrive a few moments after Armand shows up at Louie's Sweet Shop where Slip has arranged a meeting between Eleanor and Salina. She arranges for Eleanor's husband to come as well. In the end, all the innocent parties are freed from Armand's clutches while the spiritualist is arrested.

It is disappointing that the boys need the police to wrap up the case. More often than not, it is the police who come in at the end after the boys have quelled the opposition. Here, the boys have the opportunity to win on their own. Slip turns off all the lights and turns them back on only to find that the boys have fought each other. This is humiliating and an unearned victory for Armand. That the boys lose the fight renders the whole scene pointless.

Hard Boiled Mahoney is unpredictable. Plot developments materialize gradually and invite the viewers to participate in solving the mystery.

Dan Seymour as Armand is dull, pompous and unconvincing. Betty Compson and Tela Loring as Salina Webster and Eleanor Williams respectively are adequate.

Hard Boiled Mahoney is the only Bowery Boys film in which Gabe is one of the boys (and ridiculous as a nearsighted member) and is the second (and unfortunately last) film in a row written by Cyril Endfield, whose talent as a Bowery Boys writer is definitely distinguishable from the rest. Both *Mr. Hex* and *Hard Boiled Mahoney* are upbeat, written well and good entertainment.

News Hounds

Released August 13, 1947; 68 minutes; Monogram; Director, William Beaudine; Producer, Jan Grippo; Screenplay, Edmond Seward, Tim Ryan; Original Story, Edmond Seward, Tim Ryan, George Cappy; Photography, Marcel Le Picard; Film Editor, William Austin; Editorial Supervisor, Otho Lovering; Music Director, Edward Kay; Art Director, Dave Milton. Set Decorator, Raymond Boltz, Jr.; Production Supervisor, Glenn Cook; Assistant Director, William Calihan, Jr.; Sound, Tom Lambert.

CAST

Slip	Leo Gorcey	*"Clothes" Greco*	Anthony Caruso
Sach	Huntz Hall	*Dutch Miller*	Ralph Dunn
Bobby	Bobby Jordan	*Judge*	John Elliott
Whitey	Billy Benedict	*Red Kane*	Leo Kaye
Chuck	David Gorcey	*Dolan*	John Alexander
Gabe	Gabriel Dell	*Defense Attorney*	Emmett Vogan
Louie	Bernard Gorcey	*Mame*	Nita Bieber
John Burke	Tim Ryan	*Copy Boy*	Bud Gorman
Mark Morgan	Bill Kennedy	*Johnny Gale*	Emmett Vogan
Mack Snide	Robert Emmett Keane	*Sparring Partner*	Meyer Grace
		Dutch's Henchman	Gene Roth
Jane Ann Connelly	Christine McIntyre	*Bit*	Russ Whiteman

In *News Hounds*, the boys go after trouble like hunters after a fox. That's the problem with this film. It tries very hard to keep itself interesting. Unfortunately, it is simply a collection of contrived incidents loosely strung together by one unifying objective — to put rack-eteers Dutch Miller, "Clothes" Greco and Mr. Big, Tim Dolan, behind bars.

Attempting to stir activity in the local racketeer circles, Slip and Sach create their own hard news story for the *Chronicle*. Like in *Bowery Bombshell* where Slip passes himself off as crook Midge Casalotte, here Slip and Sach disguise themselves as Dutch Miller's henchmen when they learn that Dutch is out of town. They inform "Clothes" Greco that the Jimmy Dale-Tony Varda fight is fixed and that Dutch wishes to bet fifty grand on the outcome. The scheme is so ill-advised that even "Clothes" Greco is suspicious.

When the boys come face to face with Dutch Miller and the rest, Sach takes a few pictures of the group of racketeers. But in the scuffle that follows, the camera is thrown out the window. Its disappearance lays the groundwork for the rest of the film.

Gabe, torn between two loyalties, is castigated by Dutch Miller because of his friendship with Slip. He sets up the *Chronicle* for a four million dollar lawsuit. If the newspaper is acquitted, the racketeers are guilty.

Of all the pre-adolescents in the Bowery Boys series, none is as obnoxious as the one in *News Hounds* (Sach refers to him as "you little Dead End Kid"). He picks on Sach. These scenes are supposed to be funny but they are not. The kid is supposed to be cute, but he is a brat. But in spite of all the kid's pranks, he is not dishonest. He knows where the camera is and plays it for all its worth before showing it to Sach.

Knowing the pictures are on their way, Slip, by virtue of his gift of gab, delivers his version of the story, thereby delaying the jury's verdict. This plan is not without its obstacles, however, which Gabe, more determined than ever to take vengeance on the racketeers who beat him up, helps to overcome.

When Greco and Miller realize the photographs exist, they show up at Louie's Sweet Shop and confiscate the pictures from Sach and Bobby.

Gabe's maneuver to get the pictures back into Slip's possession while Slip is speaking to the jury is first-rate. Miller and Grego force Gabe to sit with them at the trial. While Miller's attention is diverted, Gabe pickpockets Miller's breast pocket for the pictures. He quickly excuses himself. On his way out of the courtroom, he drops the pictures on Bobby's lap.

"And this," Slip, with the pictures in his hand, tells the jury, "should conclude the conclusive conclusion."

Other films as flimsy as *News Hounds* do exist in the series, but either the boys' antics, the comedy, or Slip's malapropisms lift them from utter disappointment. Not *News Hounds*.

Another reason for its failure is that nothing of real importance is at stake. No one is in imminent danger. For the *Chronicle*, the difference between winning and losing is four million dollars. Big deal.

Bowery Buckaroos

Released November 22, 1947; 66 minutes; Monogram; Director, William Beaudine; Producer, Jan Grippo; Original Story, Tim Ryan, Edmond Seward, Jerry Warner; Photography, Marcel Le Picard; Music director, Edward Kay; Art director, Dave Milton.

Cast

Slip	Leo Gorcey		*Kate Barlow*	Minerva Urecal
Sach	Huntz Hall		*Luke Barlow*	Russell Simpson
Bobby	Bobby Jordan		*Chief High Octane*	Chief Yowlachie
Gabe	Gabriel Dell		*Indian Joe*	Iron Eyes Cody
Whitey	Billy Benedict		*Ramona*	Rosa Turich
Chuck	David Gorcey		*Rufe*	Sherman Sanders
Carolyn Briggs	Julie Gibson		*Moose*	Billy Wilkerson
Louie	Bernard Gorcey		*Jose*	Jack O'Shea
Blackjack	Jack Norman		*Spike*	Bud Osborne

Bowery Buckaroos, a Western, is the first Bowery Boys film away from Louie's Sweet Shop. It also adds to the complexity of Louie's diverse background that includes being a cowboy, an Army corporal (in *Bowery Battalion*) and the brother of a Tunisian general (in *Spy Chasers*). How can this be?

All the films that move the boys away from Louie's Sweet Shop (*Paris Playboys*, *Loose in London*) begin in Louie's Sweet Shop. The best of these opening scenes is right here in *Bow-*

The card that Slip thought he put a bullet through but was prearranged by Gabe in *Bowery Buckaroos*. Left to right: Iron Eyes Cody, Jack Norman, Gabe Dell and Leo Gorcey.

ery Buckaroos where Sheriff Luke Barlow saunters into the luncheonette on his horse as if he has finally come to the end of his 3,000-mile horseback journey. He's looking for the alleged murderer of Pete Briggs, "Louie the Lout." The boys cover for their little old friend, who takes cover in the back room. When the sheriff leaves, Louie explains to the boys that it was "Black Bart," not he, who killed his gold-mining partner Pete Briggs and framed "Louie the Lout" (as Louie was known in those days). Louie, with a map to the gold tattooed on his back, intends to give Pete's portion of the gold to Pete's daughter, Catherine, but all he has to go on is a baby picture of Catherine.

As eager as they are in *Mr. Hex* to help Gloria, the boys are just as enthusiastic to alleviate Louie's problem here. Dressed in Western regalia, they head for the Plugged Dollar Saloon in Hangman's Hollow somewhere out west.

When they arrive, Slip asks an Indian if he knows Black Bart. Chief High Octane answers in Indian English that Black Bart owns most of Hangman's Hollow.

"Oh, you mean he has a monotonous on the place?" Slip asks.

"Don't you mean a monopoly?" suggests Chief High Octane.

"I was using the past tense," Slip explains.

Sach, lecturing Indian Joe not to be a blabbermouth, ironically shows him the map to the gold reprinted on his back. Indian Joe promptly informs Black Bart of the map. That night, while the boys are asleep outdoors, Sach is lured away by Indian Joe to the Plugged Dollar Saloon.

Gabe Dell's role as a card shark (alias Klondike), sent ahead of the rest of the boys to familiarize himself with Black Bart, is ill-conceived, though he does save Slip from getting plugged when the tough Bowery Boy shoots his way into the saloon looking for his pal Sach.

Slip's bloated opinion of himself is sometimes humorous and at times bothersome. In *Spook Busters*, after a fight with Dr. Cosgrove, Slip notices a hole in the ceiling (due to the boys' busting up the floor above). In narration, Slip says, "I knew I could hit, but I didn't think I could blast a hole straight through the ceiling." In a similar vein, in *Bowery Buckaroos*, Gabe prefabricates a situation in which Slip would shoot a hole through the ace of spades, actually punctured courtesy of Catherine Briggs' marksmanship. Again, surprised at what he thinks is proof of his own precision, yet never doubting he is capable of doing anything, Slip tells Gabe, "Don't ever try that again. Next time I might miss."

But in *Clipped Wings*, where it really matters, Slip unsuccessfully tries putting a square peg in a round hole, failing the Air Force's intelligence test, but supporting the view that Slip is a virtuoso in his own mind only.

What makes *Bowery Buckaroos*, along with a much later film, *Jungle Gents*, rank above the other out-of-town films, is that is incorporates local culture into the context of the story.

To set the scene, the boys rent horses at a nearby ranch. Little do they know that the rancher is Sheriff Caroline Briggs (energetically played by Minerva Urecal) and her 20-year-old daughter, Catherine Briggs. (Slip takes note of a bull in the corral, a foreshadowing of what is to come.)

Lacking the sophistication of a cowboy, Whitey mounts his horse backwards.

"Gee," he says to Bobby, "I wish I had a horse like yours with a head on it."

"While you're at it, wish one for yourself."

It's the only funny line Bobby Jordan has in the eight Bowery Boys films he appears.

When Sach loses his map after being dragged through a puddle, a hoedown serves as the medium for Black Bart to find out which Bowery Boy has the map printed on his back. Some of Black Bart's men pull up the boys' shirts as the boys are dancing. Meanwhile, Slip pulls a gun on Black Bart and takes him to Catherine's ranch. Indian Joe observes the boys sneaking away and remarks, "This don't look kosher to me."

All the activity, from sending Gabe ahead incognito, to renting the horses, to Slip's shooting exhibition, lacks a logical progression leading to the capture of Black Bart. Slip might have pulled the gun on Black Bart any time and forced him to the ranch. And Gabe arriving ahead serves no useful purpose.

Slip ties a rope around Black Bart's torso and attaches the middle of the rope to a hook on the roof of the stable. Pulling on the other end of the rope lifts Black Bart to the stable roof; lowering the rope, Black Bart faces the bull. Thus, the boys frighten Black Bart into confessing to the murder of Pete Briggs and framing "Louie the Lout" Dumbrowski. At that moment, Sheriff Luke Barlow rides in with Louie on his horse, and just when they are about ready to follow the map leading to the gold, Sach awakens, back in Louie's Sweet Shop, unveiling the entire story as a dream.

That the writers could not resolve the ending without lapsing into the dream motif illustrates two things: They were not yet ready to expand the boys' horizons west of the Hudson River, and they were uncomfortable with the boys acquiring a great deal of money at the end of the film. Perhaps they wanted to preserve some semblance of continuity. If the boys were to be wealthy at the end of this film, they would have to be equally as wealthy at the beginning of the next film, *Angels' Alley*. Later in the series, specifically *Crazy Over Horses* and *Jalopy* (in which the boys win money by wager) and *Jungle Gents* (where they find a fortune in diamonds in a cave in Africa), the filmmakers were no longer concerned with continuity. The boys are as poor in the film succeeding the ones just mentioned as they are at the beginning of these films.

Nevertheless, *Bowery Buckaroos* is a fun film with numerous clever antics.

Angels' Alley

Released March 21, 1948; 67 minutes; Monogram; Director, William Beaudine; Producer, Jan Grippo; Original Story, Edmond Seward, Tim Ryan, Gerald Schnitzer; Photography, Marcel Le Picard; Film Editor, William Austin; Music Director, Edward J. Kay; Art Director, Dave Milton; Set Decorator, Raymond Boltz, Production Supervisor, Glenn Cook; Assistant Director, Wesley Barry; Sound, Franklin Hansen; Costumes, Lorraine MacLean, Richard Bacheler.

CAST

Slip	Leo Gorcey	*Boomer O'Neil*	Tommie Menzies
Sach	Huntz Hall	*Mrs. Mamie Mahoney*	Mary Gordon
Whitey	Billy Benedict	*Harry "Jag" Harmon*	Bennie Bartlett
Chuck	David Gorcey	*Andrew T. Miller*	Buddy Gorman
Jimmy	Frankie Darro	*Willis*	John Eldredge
Tony "Piggy" Lucarno	Nestor Paiva	*Jocky Burns*	Dick Paxton
Ricky Moreno	Gabriel Dell	*Attorney Felix Crowe*	Robert Emmett Keane
Daisy Harris	Rosemary La Planche	*Judge*	John H. Elliott
Josie O'Neill	Geneva Gray	*Mike*	Wade Crosby
Father O'Hanlon	Nelson Leigh		

Frankie Darro poses with the Bowery Boys (top to bottom: Gabe Dell, Huntz Hall, Billy Benedict, Darro and Leo Gorcey) for *Angels' Alley*.

How many of us would "adopt the code of the underworld" and risk an 18-month jail sentence for a cousin he hates? That's what Slip does until Father O'Hanlon (another Father!) bails him out. Impressed with Slip's family loyalty, no-good cousin Jimmy turns against Lucarno the crook and helps Slip break up the auto theft ring.

Angels' Alley is a plausible story with good character development and the right blend of comedy.

The film opens with Slip being driven to his date with Daisy, armed with a bouquet of flowers (stems mostly). It's obvious that the car is in front of a moving picture of the city. Equally obvious is a mannequin, not Gorcey, that's thrown from the seat. Similarly, in the later film *Dig That Uranium*, it is plain that a dummy is being lifted up from a cliff, not Huntz Hall.

Before Slip presents his bouquet, he wipes it under his armpit as if to polish it. But Daisy is the typical seductive miss who sways with the most lucrative wind. Presently it is blown in Ricky Moreno's (Gabe Dell) direction. As in the East Side Kids film *Pride of the Bowery*, Gorcey and his stems cannot compete with a man with a shiny new automobile.

Father O'Hanlon fills the same shoes as Father Connelly in *Angels with Dirty Faces*. He too sponsors a boys' club and tells Lucarno the same thing Father Connelly tells Rocky Sullivan, to stop giving the kids money. But Lucarno tells Father O'Hanlon to mind his own business. Father O'Hanlon's answer is a right uppercut to Lucarno's chin. Father O'Hanlon immediately glances upward, as if to ask Heaven's forgiveness. It is the subtlest touch in any Bowery Boys flick.

It's unclear why Slip is willing to accept full responsibility for Jimmy's robbery. Would not his mother be equally upset, if not more, if she discovers it is her son being sent to jail for 18 months?

While fixing a jalopy's engine, Slip says he would like to meet Tony Lucarno; Sach throws out a piece of engine and asks why; Slip says he wants to break up Lucarno's operation; Sach throws out another piece of engine and asks how; when Daisy comes by and beckons Slip into the jalopy, Sach tosses all the pieces back in, like potatoes in a bushel, and starts the engine. It runs smooth.

Angels' Alley is the only film in which Slip Mahoney laughs, and he does so twice. Both are results of Sach's slapstick comedy. Sach sneaks into Lucarno's office and becomes the butt of Lucarno's practical jokes. Glad that Lucarno has taken Sach's surprise entrance in good humor, Slip joins in the laughter.

Earlier, Sach's talent for doing James Cagney imitations and singing his version of "Figaro" brought Slip to laughter. Sach sings, "Figaro here, Figaro there, Figaro here, Figaro there, I can't figure this guy out."

Slip prevails with an ingenious plan. He gets permission to "steal" the mayor's car and the district attorney's car. He has Lucarno come to the garage to see what a great job he is doing. Lucarno recognizes the official automobiles and is about to "take the boys for a ride" when Sach drives in with a stolen police car pursued by a caravan of police.

From the time Lucarno realizes he is being tricked, to the moment the police arrive, the directing is faulty. Director William Beaudine leaves Lucarno holding the gun on the boys as if waiting to be caught, instead of hastening the boys' entry into the car.

Angels' Alley is only partially successful in achieving its ambitious undertaking of inter-relating all the major characters and events. Although Ricky is at first working for Lucarno, what turns him away from crime is vague. Father O'Hanlon is an important character through the middle of the picture, but never returns after punching out Lucarno.

Although their first roles as Bowery Boys are brief, Bennie Bartlett and Buddy Gorman have more to do than in any future picture.

Nestor Paiva is superb as Tony Lucarno. He gives the character a zestful personality, cool, self-assured, with a mysterious Spanish accent. He would dispassionately let one of his own men go to prison just as easily as he would squirt Sach with one of his trick flowers.

Unlike in *Fighting Fools*, where Slip gives Sach credit where credit is due, here Slip gives himself all the credit. "Well, I guess I took care of that case."

"*You* took care of it!" Sach cries. "*You* wrapped it up? This is the last picture I ever do with you."

But, of course, they had 32 to go.

Jinx Money

Released June 27, 1948; 68 minutes; Monogram; Director, William Beaudine; Producer, Jan Grippo; Screenplay, Edmond Seward, Tim Ryan, Gerald Schnitzer; Suggested by a story by Jerome T. Gollard; Photography, Marcel Le Picard; Film Editor, William Austin; Music Director, Edward J. Kay; Art Director, Dave Milton; Set Director, Raymond Boltz.

Cast

Slip	Leo Gorcey	*Louie*	Bernard Gorcey
Sach	Huntz Hall	*Butch*	Bennie Bartlett
Gabe	Gabriel Dell	*Augie*	Benny Baker
Lippy Harris	Sheldon Leonard	*Jake "Cold Deck" Shapiro*	Ralph Dunn
Lt. Broderick	Donald MacBride		
Candy	Betty Caldwell	*Virginia*	Wanda McKay
Whitey	Billy Benedict	*Officer Rooney*	Tom Kennedy
Chuck	David Gorcey	*Sgt. Ryan*	William Ruhl
Lullabye Schmoe	John Eldredge	*Bank President*	Stanley Andrews
Bennie the Meatball	Ben Welden	*Tax Man*	George Eldredge
Tipper	Lucien Littlefield	*Meek Man*	William Vedder

Jinx Money must have been the film Leo Gorcey liked best, as it is the one he recommended to writer-interviewer Richard Lamparski during their interview on WBAI–Radio in New York in 1968. It is the first film the boys are not offering to help anyone or commit themselves to anything, except for paying a five dollar debt to Louie, which, of course, never gets paid.

It's also the first not to open with the boys. It begins with Jake "Cold Deck" Shapiro, Benny the Meatball, Lullaby Schmoe, Augie Pollock, and Lippy Harris playing poker, and their servant Tipper serving them drinks. On his way home, Pollock is murdered and his $50,000 winnings, wrapped in newspaper, is left on the street. Who finds it? You guessed it!

First, to make sure it's clean, the boys give it a good scrubbing, complete with soap, scrub brush and roller dryer. While the bills hang on a clothesline, Louie enters.

"Is it real?" he asks. To calm their fears, the boys take the money to a bank. "Where is the $50,000 line?" Slip asks the teller.

"Do you know anything about money?" Slip later asks the bank president.

"Why, I'm a numismatist," the bank president answers, astounded. While this conversation is going on, the audience is privy to a mysterious figure lurking in the shadows.

"Look, I don't want to get personal. I just want your degenerated opinion. Is it real?"

Assured that the money is real, the boys return to Louie's Sweet Shop to record all the serial numbers. Suddenly Jake "Cold Deck" Shapiro barges in, gun in hand, and takes the money. He sees a cop, so he nonchalantly sits at the counter and sips a cup of coffee. What he does not know is that a moment before, someone using an umbrella handle took the cup and dropped a pill into the coffee. In minutes, Shapiro dies.

From what we know of the layout of the Sweet Shop, it is impossible to use an umbrella to sneak a pill into someone's drink and remain unnoticed.

The boys' clubhouse makes its last appearance in the series, and it is here that "The Umbrella" strikes again. Whitey displays his electronic know-how (developed further in *Triple Trouble*): He has created a hideaway for the money, protected by an electric current. Too late. Enter Benny the Meatball, gun in hand. Immediately a poison-tipped umbrella is injected into Meatball. The money remains.

Of all the dream scenes in the Bowery Boys films, the one in *Jinx Money* is the shortest, yet the best. It is purely symbolic. Black umbrellas in a sea of clouds surround Sach. He feels trapped and is trying to escape. The dream emphasizes the psychological pressure on Sach, as Sach is the only one who knows something about the murderer, yet not enough for anyone to take him seriously. He cannot get anybody to see the umbrella when he does, just like he cannot get anybody to look out the window in time to see the bearded hicks in *Feudin' Fools.*

But Sach is not such a fool and proves it by out-smarting "The Umbrella" when the last two poker players take a stab at getting the money.

Candy, whose morals are similar to those of Daisy Harris of *Angels' Alley*, is the girl-friend of Lullaby Schmoe and utilizes her sexuality to lure Slip to Lullaby's apartment.

When they arrive, both Slip and Candy are surprised. Candy, expecting to find Lullaby, finds Lippy Harris instead. Slip is surprised to find *anybody.* Lippy forces Slip to telephone Sach to have him bring the money to the apartment. Happy-go-lucky Sach arrives, swinging the bundle on a string. Lippy takes the bundle, but on his way out is stabbed, and this time Slip gets a glimpse of "The Umbrella."

Gabe, a reporter in this movie, convinces Slip that giving some of the money to charity will be good public relations—and will give Gabe the opportunity to get photographs of the new Bowery philanthropist. Sach, Whitey, Chuck and Butch cringe every time Slip pledges a thousand or two to a charity. "The Umbrella" returns.

"Dirty laundry isn't funny," he tells them, for that is what Sach stuffed into the bundle he was swinging on a string. While "The Umbrella" tries to decide who to kill first—a problem he never had to face before—Lt. Broderick shows up and saves them all. The murderer is Tipper, the servant. "They treated me like dirt. Now they're under the dirt."

What makes *Jinx Money* a good film, in spite of its predictability, is that we are never sure who the murderer is, what side each player is on, and who in the end will get the money. Usually the boys have one definable opponent. Here the poker players are all out for themselves.

Acting honors go to Donald MacBride and Sheldon Leonard. The leg shots and umbrella shots of the murderer, the body of Lullaby Schmoe falling against the clothes, the closet door, and the dream scene, all contribute to an exceptionally tight, visual production.

Smugglers' Cove

Released October 10, 1948; 66 minutes; Monogram; Director, William Beaudine; Producer, Jan Grippo; Screenplay, Edmond Seward, Tim Ryan; From a *Bluebook* magazine Story by Talbert Joselyln; Photography, Marcel Le Picard; Film Editor, William Austin; Music Director, Edward J. Kay; Art Director, David Milton; Sound, Earl Sitar.

CAST

Slip	Leo Gorcey	Digger	Eddie Gribbon
Sach	Huntz Hall	Capt. Drum	Gene Roth
Gabe	Gabriel Dell	Dr. Latka	Leonid Snegoff
Whitey	Billy Benedict	Franz Leiber	John Bleifer
Chuck	David Gorcey	Karl	Andre Pola
Butch	Bennie Bartlett	Ryan	William Ruhl
Count Petrov Bonds	Martin Kosleck	Attorney Williams	Emmett Vogan
Terence Mahoney, Esq.	Paul Harvey	Messenger	Buddy Gorman
Teresa Mahoney	Amelita Ward	Building Manager	George Meader
Sandra	Jacqueline Dalya		

"The landscape, the scrubbery, all mine. And lay off dose mosquitoes," Slip warns Sach, "'cause they happen to belong to me too."

With these words, Slip a.k.a Terence Aloysius Mahoney, takes possession of the Mahoney Manor — or at least he thinks he does, until his namesake, Terence Mahoney, Esq., appears and sets him straight. They then join forces to uncover and stamp out a group of smugglers that has been using the mansion as their base of operations.

While doing custodial work in a large New York City office building, Slip accepts a telegram for Terence Mahoney, Esq. ("Esk, what's dat?"), that says he has been willed his Uncle Pat's estate. (The namesake motif repeats in several episodes, usually involving the name Jones.)

He thoroughly enjoys the service bestowed upon him and revels when the boys bow to him and call him, "Your Majesty."

What mansion would be without a secret passageway. "There's more room behind the fireplace than there is in front of it," Slip remarks.

Unlike the previous Bowery Boys films where the conflicts are "American" in nature, here the boys uncover one of the most sophisticated international operations in the entire series. Like all foreign criminals in the Bowery Boys films, Count Petrov Bonds has an elitist, snobbish attitude. He can easily be compared to Compeo (Cy Kendall) in the East Side Kids film *Docks of New York*, an illegal German alien who harasses refugees from a smaller European country.

Gorcey saying hello to his third wife Amelita Ward, as Hall takes Paul Harvey's bag in *Smuggler's Cove.*

Count Petrov bears a closer kinship to Compeo than to the other foreign criminals in earlier East Side Kids films (Matsui the Japanese spy of *Let's Get Tough* and Emil the German spy of *Ghosts on the Loose*) in that the former are more concerned about personal gain than patriotism.

Another aspect of this film similar to the above East Side Kids films is the complex underground equipment used for diabolical purposes. *Spook Busters* is the first Bowery Boys film to employ such gimmicks. They are improved upon in *Smugglers' Cove*, and are even more intricate in *Master Minds* and *The Bowery Boys Meet the Monsters*.

Gabe Moreno, a detective, is a character of consequence when he pays the boys a surprise visit. It is he who is surprised when planting a swift whack on the butt of Mahoney, Esq. Digger throws him out.

Paul Harvey plays Mahoney, Esq., like he plays Mr. McCormick in *In Fast Company*: a conservative, hyperenergetic, successful old businessman courted by a quiet, unassuming, doting daughter, Theresa, adequately played by Amelita Ward, Leo Gorcey's third wife. Mahoney, Esq.'s, "Irish" gets the better of him, as it does in Harvey's first Bowery Boys film, and despite his high blood pressure, he floors Digger and Capt. Drumm with a couple of barroom blows.

One loose spot in the film is when Slip escapes Digger's grasp, then does nothing. These fleeting moments could have been used to alter the consequences of their situation. Since they don't, it's a pointless sequence, obviously just to fill time.

Sach's idea on how to break out of the locked room is funny because it ignores the reality of their situation. He suggests to Whitey that he should go to Louie's Sweet Shop and bake a chocolate cake with a saw inside. For that, Slip whacks him on the head with his hat — as he brainlessly deserves.

At the beginning of the film, Slip is in the classic position of the poor worker dreaming of a brighter future. But unlike the typical endings where the anti-hero rejects the rich man's life for the familiar, Slip eagerly accepts the deed to the mansion, offered to him by Mahoney, Esq. His pals desert him, opting for Louie's Sweet Shop, except for Sach who surprises him by appearing in a picture frame.

One of the strong points in the Bowery Boys' films that involve creepy houses (*Smugglers' Cove* being the second of five) are the plot twists. In other films the plots are straightforward; in *Angels' Alley*, the object is to topple Lucarno's stolen car racket; in *No Holds Barred*, it is to make Sach the world wrestling champion; in *In Fast Company*, the boys commit themselves to cripple the Red Circle Cab Company; in *Smugglers' Cove*, the boys are looking for relaxation and end up smashing a smuggling operation; in *Spook Busters*, they're supposed to exterminate insects and end up capturing a pair of nutty doctors; in *The Bowery Boys Meet the Monsters*, they negotiate for land and end up putting an end to monster experiments by two creepy doctors. In these last films the boys are less pretentious, less campy, and more entertaining, for each obstacle they face, and how they deal with it, is a surprise.

In the Bowery Boys films in which more than one conflict exists, such as *Blonde Dynamite*, the conflicts relate only marginally to one another. In *Blonde Dynamite*, converting the Sweet Shop into an escort bureau has little to do with Gabe's problem with bank thieves. But a strong feature in *Smugglers' Cove* is that the two conflicts overlap; Mahoney versus Mahoney (the weaker of the two conflicts) and the boys versus the smugglers.

Smugglers' Cove is a well-organized package of plot twists, diverse effects and interesting characters.

Trouble Makers

Released December 26, 1948; 69 minutes; Monogram; Director, Reginald LeBorg; Producer, Jan Grippo; Screenplay, Edmond Seward, Tim Ryan, Gerald Schnitzer; Original Story, Gerald Schnitzer; Photography, Marcel Le Picard; Film Editor, William Austin; Music Director, Edward J. Kay; Set Decorator, Raymond Boltz.

CAST

Slip	Leo Gorcey	*"Hatchet" Moran*	Lionel Stander
Sach	Huntz Hall	*Butch*	Bennie Bartlett
Gabe	Gabriel Dell	*Louie*	Bernard Gorcey
Whitey	Billy Benedict	*Capt. Madison*	Cliff Clark
Chuck	David Gorcey	*Jones*	William Ruhl
Feathers	Frankie Darro	*Stunt Double*	Carey Loftin
Hennessey	Fritz Feld	*for Huntz Hall*	
Butch	Bennie Bartlett	*Stunt Double*	Frankie Darro
Ann Prescott	Helen Parrish	*for Leo Gorcey*	
"Silky" Thomas	John Ridgely		

While the boys pursue their most unambitious money-making enterprise, selling peeks at the moon through a telescope, they eyewitness a murder several blocks away in the El Royale Hotel.

Characteristically, the enthusiastic heroes dash to the hotel and converge with their pal, police officer Gabe Moreno, and the hotel clerk (amusingly played by Fritz Feld). Slip confirms that he saw the murder committed at this location.

"This is the window all right. I recognize the architectural destruction."

"A murder and no body?" room occupant and immediate suspect Silky Thomas points out (yawningly played by John Ridgely).

The best scene of the film is at the city morgue.

"Is Dr. Prescott in?" asks Sach.

"Strangulation victim?"

"No. This guy was choked."

Photographer Marcel Le Picard masters a lighting technique that evokes an eerie atmosphere and the morgue keeper is gruesome but reflective as he exhibits the cadaver of Dr. Prescott.

"They did all they could to save him, even gave him artificial respiration."

"Artificial respiration!" exclaims Slip in a whisper. "Dey cudda at least given 'im da real ting."

Also arriving to identify the body is Ann Prescott, the deceased's daughter, delicately played by Helen Parrish. With the passing of her father, Ann becomes an influential stockholder in the El Royale Hotel and secures jobs for Slip and Sach as bellhops so that they may solve the murder undercover.

Sach has his moment of glory in this film by getting tough with Slip. The opportunity is provided by the dimwitted, laughable old gangster Hatchet Moran, who thinks Sach is his old prison mate, Chopper Magee. As Hatchet heartily reminisces about Chopper bumping off Midge Casalotte (a character Slip impersonated in *Bowery Bombshell*), Sach goes along with him, telling how he copped a Ferris wheel.

"Since when do you take anything from a crumb like that?" Hatchet asks Sach of Slip.

"Him? I just have him around for laughs." Hatchet and Sach share a good laugh about how ugly Slip is, then Sach, reverting into his tough character of Pig in *Little Tough Guy*, escorts Slip out the door. He needs a slap from Slip to bring him back to reality. The quick switch in character displays what an excellent command Hall has of his characters.

Slip has his "moment" too, toward the end of the film, but it is the script rather than Gorcey's acting that is responsible for his revealing monologue: "Did ya a couple of favors 'cause he's a nice guy. But it wasn't enough, ya wanted more. So ya tried to get him to sign the hotel over t' ya but he refused. So ya bumped him off."

Remarkable, considering there isn't a clue in the picture that any such deal was ever going on.

Butch, Chuck and Whitey perform well, with Whitey relaying a pantomime message to Hatchet Moran. The end result of the pantomime is Hatchet falling flat on his back, a well executed "routine five."

What is memorable and awesome about these numbered routines, used throughout the Bowery Boys series until Gorcey's retirement, is that they never fail to accomplish the task.

What puts the boys on the right track to find the murderer is a coin Sach discovers in Silky Thomas' suite. The coin somehow finds its way into Slip's possession. At the hotel, and in his bellhop uniform, Slip tosses the coin in the air several times when Thomas approaches and recognizes the coin as his own. Slip notices Thomas' worried expression when Thomas sees the coin. Slip's suspicion of Thomas is confirmed when Thomas offers to purchase the piece.

The final chase scene has the boys running through hallways, crawling on high exterior ledges, and sliding down the hotel laundry chute. When it's all over, the crooks are put behind bars and the boys continue with their business: "Step right up, this is the most terrifying view for five cents ever cremated."

Although it is good to see such fine actors as Fritz Feld, Frankie Darro and Lionel Stander, their roles are brief and relatively unimportant. In the case of Lionel Stander (later to star with Sophia Loren in *The Cassandra Crossing*, with Liza Minnelli and Robert DeNiro in *New York, New York* and with Robert Wagner and Stefanie Powers in the popular TV show *Hart to Hart* in the 1970s and 1990s), his character adds little to the plot but his scenes are some of the funniest in the Bowery Boys series. Hatchet Moran is the Patsy Clark of *Live Wires* and the Moose of *Bowery Bombshell,* all brawn and no brains.

"You mean no more Emily?" Hatchet asks, referring to his machine-gun by its pet name.

You can't help feel sorry for this rough and lovable con whose skill has become obsolete while he did time in prison.

Trouble Makers is a fun picture.

Fighting Fools

Released April 17, 1949; 69 minutes; Monogram; Director, Reginald LeBorg; Producer, Jan Grippo; Original Story, Edmond Seward; Gerald Schnitzer, Bert Lawrence; Photography, William A. Sickner; Film Editor, William Austin; Music Director, Edward Kay; Art Director, Dave Milton.

CAST

Slip	Leo Gorcey	*Blinky Harris*	Lyle Talbot
Sach	Huntz Hall	*Louie*	Bernard Gorcey
Gabe Moreno	Gabriel Dell	*Boomer*	Teddy Infuhr
Whitey	Billy Benedict	*Guard*	Tom Kennedy
Chuck	David Gorcey	*Mrs. Higgins*	Dorothy Vaughan
Butch	Bennie Bartlett	*Bunny Talbot*	Evelyn Eaton
Johnny Higgins	Frankie Darro	*Goon*	Frank Moran

Corruption, physical abuse and sentimentality are elements that make up a good boxing story. *City for Conquest* (1941), *The Harder They Fall* (1956) and *Requiem for a Heavyweight* (1963) are examples of how these elements combine for excellent exposés on the corrupt world of boxing. *Fighting Fools* has these ingredients and does its best within the context of a Bowery Boys movie.

Like *Mr. Hex* where the boys help Gloria launch her singing career, here they assist the "financially decapitated" Higgins family when the middle son, Jimmy, is killed in the ring. Slip and Sach find the oldest brother, Johnny, drunk in a local bar in the company of a woman

Slip (Leo Gorcey, center) calms down hothead Jimmy Higgins (Frankie Darrow) in *Fighting Fools* with Ben Weldon (left) and Stanley Andrews (right). The others in the photo are unidentified.

Slip (Leo Gorcey, right) doesn't trust Blinky Harris (Lyle Talbot) in *Fighting Fools*. Why should he, with a name like that (not to mention his hat)?

who dowses Johnny's troubles with liquor. Sach is surprisingly tough with Johnny and the girl: "You wouldn't have a face, sister, if you didn't put it on in the morning."

The impact of his intonation is as puissant as the musical notes that follow the telling of Jimmy's death. The gravity of the situation, together with the musical notes, are preciously corny and campy. The lively music on the jukebox is an interesting contrast with the solemnity of the affair. Not since *Dead End* when party music accompanies the knifing of Dave by "Baby Face" Martin do we have such an acute counterbalance of audio and visual effect. The boys leave Johnny guilt-ridden, gurgling his gin.

The boys promote amateur boxing tournaments for the Higgins family. As Slip declares "may the best man submerge victorious," a sobered-up Johnny Higgins arrives and announces his readiness for a comeback.

Fighting Fools is the first flick in which Slip's faculty for manipulating Louie plays a prominent role, and the consequences are financially devastating for Louie. Slip tells Louie how wonderful a father he would be if only he had a son; tearfully contemplating the son he does have, Louie agrees to offer his loft. Immediately, a stampede of boys rushes upstairs. Plaster from the ceiling falls into a customer's soup. Louie pleads with them, "I have restaurant downstairs!" which the boys take as an invitation to lunch and rush downstairs.

Though it is not as tight and as well-paced, the entire sequence seems to mirror the famous Marx Brothers stateroom scene in *A Night at the Opera*: As Margaret Dumont's opening of the stateroom's door releases a flood of people onto the hallway floor, so does Louie's plea sends an avalanche of kids down the stairs.

Eventually Johnny gets a shot at the title. In exchange for his renewed license, Johnny and Slip must promise Blinky that Johnny will lose the first fight, but is free to do what he can in the rematch. Slip agrees, but Blinky's no dummy. For insurance purposes he has Boomer, Johnny's kid brother, kidnapped. He also plants a leather-coated piece of metal in the champ's glove.

This is the only film in which Sach is instrumental in alleviating all obstacles, and is duly recognized by Slip. The way Sach finds Boomer is quite ingenious. Sach has someone tell Blinky that Marty wants to see him. Marty is the name Boomer uses when the kidnappers put him on the telephone to prove to Slip that he is really kidnapped.

Sach follows one of Blinky's men to O'Reilly's Rooming House where Boomer is being held. He knocks on the door and hides, luring Marty away from the door with a metal hot dog on a string. When Marty is far enough away, Sach runs in the room and locks out Marty. Boomer escapes and Sach remains under the blankets, posing as Boomer. While hiding, he overhears the kidnappers talking about the metal hotdog gimmick.

As soon as Sach returns to the arena, he notices the gimmick wrapped in a towel. Tactfully, Sach exchanges it with a rubber hot dog.

Slip approaches the commissioner in his ringside seat and, in a rare, purely visual shot, demonstrates to the commissioner how it was used.

The finest aspect of the film is the excellent alternating between Johnny's boxing scene (with close-ups of the gimmick bruising his skin) with Sach's rescue of Boomer. Each cut keeps us abreast of what is happening at the arena and at the rooming house.

In the final analysis, *Fighting Fools* is a successful blend of a typical Bowery Boys spoof with a serious tale of how a decent human being overcomes alcoholic depression and external corruption.

Hold That Baby

Released June 26, 1949; 64 minutes; Monogram; Director, Reginald LeBorg: Producer, Jan Grippo; Story and Screenplay, Charles Marion, Gerald Schnitzer; Music Director, Edward Kay; Film Editor, William Austin; Photography, William Sickner; Art Director, David Milton; Set Director, Raymond Boltz; Sound, Tom Lambert; Makeup, Charles Huber.

CAST

Slip	Leo Gorcey	*Cherry Nose Gray*	John Kellogg
Sach	Huntz Hall	*Gypsy Moran*	Max Marx
Whitey	Billy Benedict	*Laura Andrews*	Anabel Shaw
Chuck	David Gorcey	*Burton the Cop*	Edward Gargan
Butch	Bennie Bartlett	*Joe the Crooner*	Meyer Grace
Gabe Moreno	Gabriel Dell	*Jonathan Andrews III*	Judy and Jody Dunn
Louie Dumbrowski	Bernard Gorcey	*Hope Andrews*	Florence Auer
Bananas	Frankie Darro	*Faith Andrews*	Ida Moore

Dr. Hans Heinrich	Torben Meyer		Sanitarium	Lin Mayberry
Dr. Hugo Schiller	Fred Nurney		Receptionist	
Newsboy	Buddy Gorman			

For the third film in a row, the boys bridge the gap between parent and child. Similar to *Trouble Makers,* where in the course of their business they witness a murder, here, in the course of operating a launderette, the boys discover an infant among a pile of diapers.

In his fourth and final appearance, Frankie Darro, as Bananas, does what his character usually does: frame the boys for his own devious deeds. Spinsters Faith and Hope Andrews hire him and his partner Cherry Nose to keep the baby out of sight until after the reading of their brother's will, which stipulates that the baby must be at the reading to receive the bulk of the wealth. Otherwise, the fortune goes to Faith and Hope, the senior citizen version of greedy Candy of *Jinx Money* and thieving Clarissa of a later film, *High Society.* They are former professional criminologists.

Women in unconventional professions is common in Bowery Boys films, and always an entertaining surprise. Minerva Urecal is a Western sheriff in *Bowery Buckaroos,* Laurette Luez plays a muscular jungle woman who kills a lion with her bare hands in *Jungle Gents,* and Rene Riano plays a tough WAF drill sergeant in *Clipped Wings.*

Slip is forced to sign a document implicating him and the boys as kidnappers. Cherry Nose threatens to give the letter to the police unless the boys keep the baby at Louie's until after 9:00 that night.

Meanwhile, the aunts pay off a doctor to commit the mother to Midvale Hospital, a mental institution. Slip reads in the newspaper that she is not to receive visitors but decides to visit her anyway, and takes Sach along.

Considering Sach's tendency for fouling things up, it's a wonder that Slip takes him almost every place he goes. Yet, for as many times as Sach makes things worse (in *Bowery Buckaroos* he tells Indian Joe about the gold; in *Crashing Las Vegas* he hands over his gambling winnings to the crooks), he compensates with sudden spurts of cunning. In the previous film, *Fighting Fools,* it is his ingenious manipulation of a rubber hotdog that rescues young Boomer; in *Jinx Money* he lets the murderer-robber think he is getting away with money when it is actually dirty laundry. In *Hold That Baby!* it's his clever insanity that gets him and "Dr." Slip past the receptionist in Midvale Hospital.

Sach sits himself down with a couple of the patients who are playing with a non-existent deck of cards. Sach fits into the game quite nicely.

"Pair of aces," says one of them.

"Just a minute," Sach interrupts. "Pair of deuces. Twos are higher than ones." Sach collects the non-existent chips. When Sach leaves the table with his non-existent "winnings," one of the patients says to the other, "He bluffed me. I had a pair of threes."

This is not the first time that cheating at cards is the means to reach an end. In the Dead End Kids film, *They Made Me a Criminal,* the kids engage J. Douglas Williamson in a game of strip poker in order to win his camera.

Slip frequently disguises himself as a doctor in order to reach certain patients before undesirables do. In *Spook Busters,* he dons Dr. Bender's surgical mask and frees Sach from the operating table. Here, dressed as a doctor with thick glasses, he is able to locate Laura's room and helps her escape, while Sach, treated as a psychotic kleptomaniac, keeps most of the doctors occupied.

The aunts are shrewd and keep one step ahead of the boys. They warn Cherry Nose and Bananas that their reward is in jeopardy. The two scoundrels hurry to Louie's Sweet Shop

Slip (Gorcey, left) and Sach (Hall) are unfazed by the headline in *Hold That Baby.*

and wait with Slip, Sach, Laura, Louie, the baby and the boys until Gabe, a detective in this caper, arrives. A scuffle follows. The boys leave the sweet shop with Laura and the baby to attend the reading of the will.

In this film, the boys have no vested interest in what is at stake. Outsmarting a couple of old ladies does not make for as lively entertainment as outwitting and out-whipping a few roughnecks.

The mother's behavior is odd. For a mother to secretly leave her baby in a pile of laundry in the hope some amateur laundry attendant (the boys) will not mistake it for a diaper is hard to take and leaves open the possibility that the aunts are not so wrong to have her committed.

Gabe Dell's role is perfunctory, as it is in the prior film and will be in the next three films. As a detective, he does nothing to solve the mystery of the missing mother, and blunders with his own gun to boot.

Frankie Darro overplays his part. His roles usually require talking tough and convincing the audience his character has confidence. In *Hold That Baby!* his character lacks the creativity and guts to kidnap the baby himself and demand an even higher ransom for keeping the child away.

Hold That Baby! may have been inspired by the Gloria Vanderbilt custody case. It's a passable film that could have benefited from a more intricate plot.

Angels in Disguise

Released September 11, 1949; 67 minutes; Monogram; Director, Jean Yarbrough; Producer, Jan Grippo; Screenplay, Charles R. Marion, Gerald Schnitzer, Bert Lawrence; Photography, Marcel Le Picard; Film Editor, William Austin; Music Director, Edward Kay; Art Director, Dave Milton; Editor, Otho Lovering; Sound, Ben Remington.

CAST

Slip	Leo Gorcey	*Nurse*	Jane Adams
Sach	Huntz Hall	*Hodges*	Don Harvey
Whitey	Billy Benedict	*Bookkeeper*	Tristram Coffin
Chuck	David Gorcey	*Vickie*	Jean Dean
Butch	Bennie Bartlett	*Martin Lovell*	Rory Mallinson
Gabe Moreno	Gabriel Dell	*Watchman*	Lee Phelps
Louie Dumbrowski	Bernard Gorcey	*Officer*	Jack Mower
Angles	Mickey Knox	*Morgue Attendant*	William J. O'Brien
Carver	Edward Ryan	*Whelan*	Herbert Patterson
Miami	Richard Benedict	*Newswriter*	John Morgan
Johnny Mutton	Joseph Turkel	*Nurse*	Dorothy Abbott
Jim Cobb	Ray Walker	*Malone*	Tom Monroe
Roger T. Harrison	William Forrest	*Rewrite Man*	Jack Gargan
Bertie Spangler	Pepe Hern	*First Detective*	Peter Virgo
Millie	Marie Blake	*Pretty Nurse*	Doretta Johnson
Johnson	Roy Gordon	*Male Nurse*	Wade Crosby

Angels in Disguise is not only the most melodramatic crime film the Bowery Boys produced, but the most artistic in its handling of cinematography, characterization, and script.

Instead of the usual opening scenes of New York fading to Louie's Sweet Shop, we see (behind the credits) dark, hurried figures; suspenseful music complements the action. When the credits are over, we see the bottom of someone's shoes in an alley. As the camera tilts upward, Slip sits up, his face battered, his hair disheveled. What follows is Slip's narration of the events leading up to this violent scene, the entire film in flashback.

Slip and Sach are copy boys for the *Daily Chronicle*. Slip overhears his editor receiving a news item over the telephone.

"Officer Gabe Moreno Shot."

The role of Gabe Moreno is the biggest here since *Trouble Makers*. He was wounded while unsuccessfully trying to spoil a warehouse robbery by the notorious but enigmatic Loop Gang.

The boys comb the streets for clues to lead them to the Loop Gang. Slip's narration is not without its absurdity.

"First we picked up Whitey, America's Number One Newsboy. Some day he might be president. If he worked real hard maybe even a senator."

Slip's "female intuition" guides him into a pool hall where he and Sach rub elbows with cagey members of the Loop gang. "Hey, we've got a couple of kibbitzers here," Johnny Mutton says to Angles. But when Slip emerges victorious in an intense game of pool and reveals his ties with the police, Angles and Mutton take them to meet the boss.

Up to this point, the Bowery Boys as sleuths keep the film rolling. But when we meet

Sach (Hall, right) watches Slip (Gorcey) think in *Angels in Disguise.*

Mr. Carver, we are introduced to the most bizarre, polished and idiosyncratic hood in all the films. He is an intellectual ringleader who reads Spinoza. He is intolerant of mistakes as exemplified by killing one of his own men. He also insists on proper manners and slaps Johnny Mutton's face for picking his fingernails in public.

Originally, the plan calls for the boys to accompany the Loop Gang in a payroll heist of the Gotham Steel Works. Suddenly, Carver announces to a restless group at his penthouse apartment that they have been double-crossed.

Two things make Mr. Carver seem so smart: an auditor who supplies him with targets, and a cartoonist for the *Daily Chronicle* who, by using a word formula in his daily cartoons, relays messages via the funnies.

Despite the quasi-serious nature of the film, Sach is his usual comic, inept self. When Slip lists the names of his "gang" members to Mr. Carver, sweet shop owner Louie Dumbrowski becomes "Big Louie," who, in addition to wearing a pin stripe suit and hat like the other boys, sports a violin case like Hatchet Moran in *Trouble Makers.* In the chase scene we see that he actually does carry a real violin.

Loosely fashioned after *East Side Kids* and *Bowery Champs, Angels in Disguise* is a steady-paced detective story. Its strength lies in the continuous confrontation of wits between the boys and the Loop Gang. Slip and Mr. Carver watch each other cautiously, yet never oppose each other directly, which is atypical and regrettable. When Mr. Carver sees his girlfriend,

Millie, making obvious advances towards Slip, it is she who gets slapped and warned; Slip gets away scot-free.

The circumstances of the final scene are very well thought-out. While the Loop Gang work at cracking the safe in the warehouse office, Slip risks his life by sneaking into the next room to call Mr. Cobb to let him know where they are. The message is funneled to Gabe.

But before Gabe arrives, Harrison, who overhears the conversation in the editor's office, comes to the Beacon Machine Works. After shooting Johnny Mutton who would not let him pass, Harrison barges into the warehouse office, exposes the boys, and thus the chase begins. A few Loop gang members corner the boys, and Johnny Mutton and Harrison shoot each other to death, before the siren of Gabe Moreno's police car is heard.

Edward Ryan plays a cool, calm, but nevertheless ruthless Mr. Carver, who has the appearance of an innocent law student and the self-assurance of an aristocrat. Joseph Turkel (Johnny Mutton) is the same as his Johnny Angelo in *Lucky Losers,* an eager, reckless criminal apprentice with a chip on his shoulder.

Unlike *Hold That Baby!* and *Fighting Fools"* in which Sach delivers unexpected but significant assistance, here Slip is the sole mastermind of the entire undercover operation. For this he deserves the beautiful nurse who tends to his wounds. To Sach's disappointment, his nurse is male.

Master Minds

Released November 29, 1949; 64 minutes; Monogram; Director, Jean Yarbrough; Producer, Jan Grippo; Screenplay, Charles R. Marion; Photography, Marcel Le Picard; Film Editor, William Austin; Music Director, Edward Kay; Art Director, Dave Milton; Makeup: Jack P. Pierce.

CAST

Slip	Leo Gorcey	*Nancy Marlowe*	Jane Adams
Sach	Huntz Hall	*Juggler*	Whitey Roberts
Whitey	Billy Benedict	*Hoskins, the Constable*	Harry Tyler
Butch	Bennie Bartlett	*Woman*	Anna Chandler
Chuck	David Gorcey	*Mike Barton*	Chester Clute
Gabe Moreno	Gabriel Dell	*Mrs. Hoskins*	Minerva Urecal
Louie Dumbrowski	Bernard Gorcey	*Henchman*	Stanley Blystone
Atlas	Glenn Strange	*Young Man*	Robert Coogan
Benny	Kit Guard	*Father*	Pat Goldin
Hugo	Skelton Knaggs	*Hoskins Boy*	Tom Connor
Dr. Druzik	Alan Napier	*Second Hoskins Boy*	Kent O'Dell
Otto	William Yetter		

Master Minds is an example of what happens when filmmakers are oblivious to the potential of their own material.

By virtue of his sweet tooth, Sach acquires the uncanny ability to predict the future. The film begins to smoothly build upon this idea as the boys enter Sach in a carnival and charge people an admission fee to see him predict future events.

"I see an addition to your family," Sach tells a member of the audience. "Your mother-in-law will be paying you a very long visit."

"How long?"

"I can't see that far into the future."

Perhaps a better application of his psychic power would have been to use it for preventing tragedies. Instead, the film abandons the psychic motif altogether, opting for what fundamentally is a re-run of *Spook Busters* and a forerunner of *The Bowery Boys Meet the Monsters*, both of which are superior films.

Reading about Sach in the newspaper, Dr. Druzik kidnaps him to use his brain for Atlas, his humanoid creation. Dr. Druzik proposes to create a race of superhumans—with super-strength and super-minds, and thus take over the world. Simple enough.

When Slip realizes Sach is gone, he delivers this apology to his audience: "Not only will I be glad to refund your money but will also be highly mortified."

Concerned that their source of income took the forbidden visit to the dentist, Slip sends the boys to all the dentists in New York City. "But I've never been north of 42nd Street," says Whitey.

"So take a compass wit' ya. If ya meet Indians, send me a smoke signal."

A close scrutiny of *Spook Busters* and *Master Minds* will reveal how little the film scripts differ. Like the house in *Spook Busters,* the Forsythe house in *Master Minds* is dark, winds blow, a loose shutter sways back and forth, and there's movable grave that covers an entrance to the basement (as in the East Side Kids' *Ghosts on the Loose*).

As in *Spook Busters,* the doctor's henchmen are superstitious. In *Spook Busters,* they believe Sach's ridiculous story that an invisible man is attacking them with an axe. Here, upon seeing a suit of armor slowly approaching them with a spear (Louie attempting to rescue the boys), Otto gets on his knees and cries, "Mercy, mercy, oh great knight."

The separation of Slip and Sach through most of the film paves the way for Whitey to be Slip's foil. Whitey makes the mistake of throwing a switch, which sends an electric current streaming throughout the room. Slip gets angry and hits Whitey over the head with his hat, as he usually does to Sach. A second later, Slip inadvertently throws the same switch. Whitey, for the first and only time, whacks Slip on the head with Slip's own hat.

"That time I deserved it," he admits to Whitey. "But don't get a superiority complex."

Of Huntz Hall's three characters here (Sach, a prophet, and Atlas), his performance as Atlas is outstanding, perhaps too good. He is more ferocious, more violent, more destructive than the real Atlas. The real Atlas does little more than grunt. It is the excellent makeup job done on Glenn Strange that makes him scary. Conversely, Atlas as Sach highlights his effeminate gestures. It is laughable to see a terrifying-looking man bend his elbow and wave his hand. Slip must think he does a convincing job too, for Slip feels comfortable enough to smack him with his hat.

A monotonous chase scene with Sach and Atlas reverting into each other, and the boys and Gabe mistaking one another for the bad guys, takes up a good bit of time.

It's disappointing to see the boys rendered totally helpless, relying on outside help, instead of beating the cops to the punch as in *Trouble Makers* and *Feudin' Fools.* Just when the doctor thinks he has everything under control, Sheriff Hoskins and his wife, shotgun in hand, enter the laboratory. "If ya ain't ghosts, then ya owe taxes, and ya better pay."

The structure in *Master Minds* is familiar: Sach acquires a power; the boys capitalize on it; someone else steals it; Sach loses it on his own (used two films later in *Blues Busters).*

For the most part, special effects and photography are of the highest order (by Monogram standards, that is). Marcel Le Picard takes good close-ups of Louie's expression of fright,

Nancy (Jane Adams) goes to Slip (Gorcey) for comfort as Atlas (Glenn Strange) is about to attack them in *Master Minds.*

and the electric current flowing between Sach's head and Atlas' head is well-done. Harp music is the prelude to Sach's predictions.

As a whole, with the exception of above-average camerawork, makeup work, and Hall as Atlas, *Master Minds* is little more than other films rolled into one.

Blonde Dynamite

Released February 12, 1950; 66 minutes; Monogram; Director, William Beaudine; Producer, Jan Grippo; Screenplay, Charles R. Marion; Art Director, Dave Milton; Music Director, Edward Kay; Photography, Marcel Le Picard; Film Editor; William Austin; Set Director, Raymond Boltz; Sound, Dean Spencer.

Cast

Slip	Leo Gorcey	*Gabe Moreno*	Gabriel Dell
Sach	Huntz Hall	*Champ*	Harry Lewis
Joan Marshall	Adele Jergens	*Dynamite*	Murray Alper

Louie	Bernard Gorcey		*Tracy*	Karen Randle
Sarah	Jody Gilbert		*Mr. Jennings*	Stanley Andrews
Whitey	Billy Benedict		*Dowagers*	Constance Purdy,
Chuck	David Gorcey			Florence Auer
Professor	John Harmon		*Butch*	Buddy Gorman
Samson	Michael Ross		*Tom, the Cop*	Tom Kennedy
Verna	Lynn Davies		*Solicitor*	Robert Emmett
Bunny	Beverlee Crane			Keane

When Louie rings up the register to deposit bottle caps, talks about plucking eggs from eggplants, and scraping butter off buttercups, Slip suggests it's time to go on vacation with his "wife and his other bag." While Louie is gone, Slip converts the sweet shop into the Park Avenue Escort Bureau.

This isn't even the main plot. Sach blunders when Champ tricks him into thinking there's uranium underneath the sweet shop and digs a hole in the middle of the floor.

"Your friend has been very resourceful," Champ tells Slip upon his return.

"If by resourceful you mean imbecilic, you're absolutely right. If my ex-friend would have his brains enmeshed, he would know there ain't any uranium east of the Harlem River."

In order to understand what Champ is doing digging a tunnel under Louie's store, we must turn our attention to bank teller Gabe. When he realizes he's missing $5,000, he retraces his footsteps back to Joan's apartment, where the Champ, Dynamite, the Professor and Sampson are counting the money. And if he doesn't produce the combination to the bank vault, Joan will tell the police all about the "expensive" places Gabe took her to, spending the bank's money.

The thugs' plan, masterminded by the professor, is flawed at the outset. No matter how precisely he measures off the room in the escort bureau to the spot where digging should begin, and how careful he is to veer away from the Chinese laundry situated between Louie's Sweet Shop and the bank, the thugs drill straight up into police headquarters, where they find Gabe Moreno is spilling his guts out to the police and bank president about his embezzlement.

The two stories never really come together. Converting the Sweet Shop into an escort bureau has little impact upon the professor's plans to dig a hole in the floor.

The detailed scenes of the boys' first jobs as male escorts are amusing. Sach and Whitey attend the opera with a couple of obese dowagers. The women fidget as much with their monocles as the boys do with their candy and popcorn. Butch and Chuck attend a session of the upstanding American Womanhood League and get bounced around by a couple of women wrestlers. The scene in which they decide they're quitting after these devastating experiences is novel, for the boys must gather enough guts to tell Slip. But when Joan, Bonnie, Verna and Tracy enter, professing to be rich but lonely, the boys hastily re-don the regalia of their profession.

"We would like you to come to our warm, cozy little apartment," Joan teases.

"Madam," Slip says, "your offer is more than condescending."

The scene at Joan's apartment is wonderfully corny. Whitey gets drunk on "cherry pop"; Slip acts suave and debonair while Joan sings to him, "You're the One;" the whole group does a line dance.

Finally, Joan gives the boys mickeys. But because of Whitey's fascination with the lazy susan, the drinks get switched, and it's the women who pass out. Insulted, the boys return to the escort bureau to find the tunnel well underway.

Sach (Hall, at left) and Slip (Gorcey, right) are seduced by Adele Jergens (on sofa, facing Hall), Lynn Davies (back row, left), Beverlee Crane and Karen Randle (on sofa, at right) in *Blonde Dynamite.*

The character of Louie Dumbrowski is especially intricate here because he goes through three distinct emotions. First he's in a stupor and a state of depression. Later he's in perfect bliss on the Coney Island Beach strumming his guitar and girl-watching. Last, and perhaps the strongest emotion is when he returns to the city, and is shocked by the changes his sweet shop.

Bernard Gorcey's acting is superb as he approaches what used to be his sweet shop. After he gets his bearings, he screams, "Park Avenue Escort Bureau! Oy vey! Oy vey!" But the impact of the elegantly remodeled escort bureau is brief, and loses its potency when the little owner notices the hole in the floor. This is an error on the part of the filmmakers for we would rather see more of Louie's reaction to the boys' creation rather than to the thugs' destruction. The fact that Louie never confronts the boys about the escort bureau is a lost point of confrontation. The shock and excitement, though excellently performed by Bernard Gorcey, subsides after he descends into the hole ("At my age I should be a groundhog!").

The camera's eye calls attention to Louie's diminutive size in several ways: against the backdrop of his large wife on the beach, the furniture in the escort bureau, and the large ditch. Credit belongs to photographer Marcel Le Picard.

Another good shot, a close-up, is of the drill, boring upward, cracking the plaster of the police station floor above.

The sudden discovery of uranium ore, recognized by bank president Mr. Jennings, sends everyone into a dither. There is no hint in the film that we should expect the discovery of uranium, though it may seem like a clever way to tie in all aspects of the film. Like the IRS in *Jinx Money*, two real estate investigators arrive on the scene.

"You see, you own the property, but you do not own the minerals found on your property. It's in your deed in small print."

And even if it wasn't, remember, the thugs used a faulty map; who's to say whether or not the uranium wasn't found under the Chinese laundry?

Lucky Losers

Released May 14, 1950; 69 minutes; Monogram; Director, William Beaudine; Producer, Jan Grippo; Screenplay, Charles R. Marion, Bert Lawrence; Photography, Marcel Le Picard; Film Editor, William Austin; Music Director, Edward J. Kay; Art Director, Dave Milton; Set Decorator, Raymond Boltz.

CAST

Slip Mahoney	Leo Gorcey	Butch	Buddy Gorman
Sach Jones	Huntz Hall	Chuck	David Gorcey
Countess	Hillary Brooke	Chick	Harry Cheshire
Gabe Moreno	Gabriel Dell	Bartender	Frank Jenks
Bruce McDermott	Lyle Talbot	Tom Whiney	Douglas Evans
Louie Dumbrowski	Bernard Gorcey	Carol Thurston	Wendy Waldron
Whitey	Billy Benedict	Andrew Stone III	Glen Vernon
Johnny Angelo	Joseph Turkel	Second Conventioneer	Chester Clute
Buffer McGee	Harry Tyler	David Thurston	Selmer Jackson

The alleged suicide of David J. Thurston, Slip and Sach's Wall Street employer (they're "gophers"), stuns the boys and everyone who knew him. Slip finds a book of matches with the "Hi Hat Club" insignia on Thurston's desk. When news commentator and friend Gabe Moreno tells them club owner Bruce McDermott operates a gambling casino in the rear of the club, Slip remembers that Thurston had him mail a letter to McDermott. Slip draws the conclusion that McDermott and the Hi Hat Club, just like Silky Thomas and Hotel Royale in *Trouble Makers*, have something to do with the rich man's death.

The boys get jobs at the Hi Hat Club after expert instruction from gambler Wellington Buffer Jefferson McGee. McGee is an amusing pseudo-cosmopolitan and charlatan par excellence. His course in gambling is skillfully photographed in a five-minute block of lively music and quick, superimposed shots of dice throwing, card tricks and spinning roulette wheels, mixed with astonished expressions on the faces of Sach, Butch and Chuck.

There's a shift in the Bowery Boys' treatment of women here which sets a precedent for several films to come. The countess, unlike most other sheep-like blondes, is not relegated to playing seductress at the whim of her boss. The scene in which she catches Slip in McDermott's office — the turning point of the film — reveals her impartiality. She doesn't ask Slip what he's doing there.

McDermott enters, as does a drunken $14,000 gambling loser.

Louie (Bernard Gorcey) doesn't know when to call it quits (notice the chips on his forehead) in *Lucky Losers*.

"I can buy and sell you, you cheap chisler," he tells McDermott. "And what's more, I know Thurston didn't commit suicide, you killed him."

McDermott clips the young playboy and, to everybody's amazement, he dies.

The problem with *Lucky Losers*, which the makers apparently recognized, is that the boys find out too soon who killed Thurston. To expand the film, they have Slip declare that more information is necessary before the apprehension of McDermott & Co. can be made. The boys never do find anything else of value. Instead, the stage is handed over to Louie Dumbrowski, posing as a rich cattleman whom Slip promises McDermott will make up for the dip in business. Slip had had Buffer McGee in mind for the part and is surprised when Louie enters the casino sporting a ten-gallon hat, cowboy vest, and spurs. It was a wise choice to avoid placing Buffer McGee in the casinos. The focus of attention would have been off the boys and on Buffer. Writing him out of the scene preserves the heroics for the boys and offers Bernard Gorcey a more challenging assignment.

Bernard is a lovable, cigar-smoking, nervous cattleman who speaks with a Yiddish accent and is clueless about gambling. When Slip tells him to throw the dice, Louie hurls the dice against the wall.

Leo Gorcey's limited acting ability is demonstrated through the variety of roles he plays in this film. As a copy boy he scampers through the Wall Street offices like a squirrel gathering acorns. As a hustler, he is too boisterous at the roulette wheel; as a ladies man, he is unsophisticated in his exchange with the countess. He also plays a drunk with Dick Elliott (Elliott eventually took Louie's place behind the counter in the Stanley Clements films). Elliott carries the scene as the two conventioneers reminisce about old times. Gorcey is thoroughly unconvincing as a drunk, which is surprising since he spent most of his time off-camera drunk, according to his son Leo Gorcey, Jr.'s, book.

Joseph Turkel as Johnny Angelo holds fast to the character he created in *Angels in Disguise*, a young, tough-talking, unsmiling, nervous apprentice, hungry to get ahead in the crime world. Quick, short movements of his head and hand accent his character.

The grand finale is a riot scene, with a storm of chips, roulette wheels, playing cards and dice, hurled from all corners of the room, while Louie, oblivious to all the commotion, continues to lose at craps.

Lucky Losers draws too much from previous pictures, and relies heavily on comic padding to fill time. There are not enough interesting things happening to keep the audience satisfied. Infiltrating the casino produces only one new clue, the name Chick. He is revealed as one of the politicians who vowed, on Gabe Moreno's TV news program, to combat gambling.

Triple Trouble

Released August 13, 1950; 66 minutes; Monogram; Director, Jean Yarbrough; Producer, Jan Grippo; Screenplay, Charles R. Marion, Bert Lawrence; Photography, Marcel Le Picard; Film Editor, William Austin, Otho Lovering; Music Director, Edward Kay; Art Director, Dave Milton; Set Decorator, Raymond Boltz.

CAST

Slip Mahoney	Leo Gorcey	*Benny the Blood*	Joseph Turkel
Sach	Huntz Hall	*Chuck*	David Gorcey
Gabe Moreno	Gabriel Dell	*Butch*	Buddy Gorman
Skeets O'Neil	Richard Benedict	*Hobo Barton*	Eddie Gribbon
Shirley O'Brien	Lyn Thomas	*Judge*	Jonathan Hale
Bat Armstrong	Pat Collins	*Warden*	Joseph Crehan
Whitey	Billy Benedict	*Ma Armstrong*	Effie Laird
Louie Dumbrowski	Bernard Gorcey	*Murphy*	Edward Gargan
Squirrely Davis	George Chandler	*Convict*	Tom Kennedy
Pretty Boy Gleason	Paul Dubov	*Guard*	Lyle Talbot

What is *Triple Trouble* about? The quick answer is, it's about the boys going to jail to find the crooks responsible for robberies the boys are accused of committing. On another level it's about a battle of wits between the daring and dynamic Slip and the practical and pragmatic Whitey.

In an eerie, but rather confusing scene that begins simultaneously with the film's credits, the boys, wearing masks, hear noises and decide to "instigate" the warehouse. Instead of capturing the robbers, the boys are found by the police hovering over the bound-and-gagged warehouse guard. They're charged with assault and attempted robbery. The film doesn't explain why the boys wear masks, but wearing them certainly does not help their case.

Slip (Gorcey) looks up to Lyn Thomas in *Triple Trouble.*

"We ain't goin' no place till we get a pulmonary hearing," Slip demands.

Whitey is ridiculed for his hobby of ham radio operating. "Ham! I love ham, especially with schmaltz," cries Sach, intertwining diametrically opposed cuisines.

Slip refuses to believe Whitey about hearing instructions to rob certain warehouses on the ham radio. Nevertheless, he and Whitey listen to a message on the ham radio about robbing the Bowling Green Company. The next day, it's robbed.

Slip declares, "If we go to the cops with a story as illegible as this, they'd put us in straitjackets. Let me vegetate this matter over in my mind."

The result of Slip's "vegetation" is his guilty plea and insisting that he and Sach be locked up immediately. Slip tells Gabe Moreno, his lawyer, he has a hunch that will "not only restore our good name but will do the community a great service." To which Sach replies, "Yeah, they'll put us in jail for the rest of our lives."

In prison, Sach plants the idea in bad guy Bat Armstrong's head to rob Louie's vault. Whitey hears about it on the ham radio.

This presents a perfect vehicle for Bernard Gorcey to play a hysterical Louie Dumbrowski. Louie runs into the street screaming for Officer Murphy, jabbering that he heard over the radio that his store is going to be robbed. When it is, the police interrogate him for planning the robbery for insurance money.

The interrogation scene is authentic-looking. Louie, perspiring, his hair messy, sits in a dark room beneath one light bulb, shouted at by big men in rolled-up shirt sleeves. Lighting is used effectively in the interrogation scene, the robbery scene and in the prison escape.

There's one scene that is reminiscent of *Angels with Dirty Faces* when Rocky Sullivan saunters through the prison halls. When the boys are led to their cells, they are mistaken for two notorious criminals, Pretty Boy Gleason and Benny the Blood.

Slip takes his popularity in stride. "I guess we are figures of national promiscuity."

There is an intense night-time scene with Sach and his cellmate, psychopath Squirrely Davis, who intimidates Sach by sharpening his knife on a leather belt tied around Sach's neck. George Chandler gives a sharp performance of a very dangerous Squirrely Davis.

In the end, Whitey is the hero for he not only picks up and deciphers the message about the prison break, but is instrumental in thwarting the escape. While it may not be rocket science to decipher the code ("six pigs breaking out of pigpen need transportation for six pigs, three times three o'clock, black as night..."), taking possession of the getaway car and taking off the clothes of the other Armstrong gang members, including Bat's mother, is impressive.

Whitey's successful campaign renders Slip's efforts irrelevant and burdensome, since they cause more problems than they solve. Whitey would have found out about the prison break regardless of the boys' incarceration. In *Jail Busters*, the boys are at least led to believe that they could be released from jail as soon as they accomplish their mission. In *Triple Trouble*, they have no guarantee that they will find the radio, and if they do, that this will lead to their freedom.

The idea of pleading guilty is just as technically misguided as their decision to enlist in the navy in *Let's Go, Navy!* The chance of locating the thugs they are after in such a large institution is small, and furthermore, how is Slip sure he and Sach will be sent to the state penitentiary and not someplace else?

As discussed in the review of *Lucky Losers*, the image of women changes in the 1950–51 films. In *Triple Trouble*, the role of Ma Armstrong is small but effective, only because she is a woman in a man's role. The Bowery Boys create their own Ma Barker, a famous gangland matriarch. Effie Laird plays the gray-haired mother as firm and headstrong, with a sharp tongue and a knack for instilling fear, especially in a petrified Louie Dumbrowski.

Triple Trouble is a well-organized film, conscious of its rough edges, and does its best to smooth them over.

Blues Busters

Released October 29, 1950; 67 minutes; Monogram; Director, William Beaudine; Producer, Jan Grippo; Screenplay, Charles Marion, Bert Lawrence; Art Director, Dave Milton; Music Director, Edward Kay; Photography, Marcel Le Picard; Film Editor: William Austin; Sound, Tom Lambert; Set Decorator, Raymond Boltz, Jr.

CAST

Slip Mahoney	Leo Gorcey	*Sally Dolan*	Phyllis Coates
Sach	Huntz Hall	*Teddy Davis*	William Vincent
Lola Stanton	Adele Jergens	*Louie Dumbrowski*	Bernard Gorcey
Gabe Moreno	Gabriel Dell	*Whitey*	Billy Benedict
Rick Martin	Craig Stevens	*Butch*	Buddy Gorman

Chuck	David Gorcey		*Singing Voices*	John Lorenz, Gloria
Bimbo	Paul Bryar			Wood
Joe Ricco	Matty King			

Though *Blues Busters* closely follows the pattern of *Master Minds,* here Sach's newfound ability to sing like "Crosby, Jolson and the Andrews Sisters all wrapped into one" lacks the jolt of the supernatural. Its simplistic plot, stereotyped characters, and disappointing climax are salt in the wound after the many monotonous moments Sach spends at the microphone.

Common to the extraordinary abilities Sach unexpectedly procures in four films is that they are all discovered in the course of loitering at Louie's Sweet Shop. The difference between the anomaly in this film and the ones in *No Holds Barred, Jungle Gents* and *Master Minds* is that vocal talent, unlike physical strength and the power to sniff diamonds or read minds, must be nurtured. So it's ironic that this film includes no rehearsal scenes, yet in *No Holds Barred,* he trains continually.

Blues Busters is also as much a film about business ethics, as *Fighting Fools* is about boxing corruption. Slip first approaches Rick Martin, owner of the Rio Cabana.

"Joe takes care of all my personal matters," Rick tells the boys in all earnesty. "Joe, throw them out."

Slip turns to his usual reliable source of funds, Louie Dumbrowski. Slip uses reverse psychology. He knows Louie recognizes that a large profit can be made from Sach's talent and feigns reluctance to accept Louie's offer.

"Boys, if we're together when times are bad, why should we not stay together when things are good?" And so, Louie's Sweet Shop becomes the booming Bowery Palace nightclub.

Rick Martin feels the pinch and uses two dirty tricks to cause the downfall of the Bowery Palace. Louie is the first to notice in the audience a flock of undesirables who are determined to cause havoc.

"I don't like the complexion of things," he comments.

His second attempt is more successful. Lola, like most blondes in the series, can't be trusted. Just as Sach is lured away from the campus in *Hold That Line* and misses a football game, here he's taken to Lola's apartment where he not only misses a performance but unwittingly signs himself over to Rick Martin in the course of autographing everything Lola puts before him. There's a nice scene of the entire apartment spotted with Sach's signature like the coat of a leopard.

Meeting Slip in the street, Sach stares guiltily at the billboard at the now defunct Bowery Palace. Slip tries to uplift him: "You're at the pineapple of your career. Getting your tonsils out was just a jerk of fate."

Sach hands Slip $900 which by now Sach considers pocket money. "That's a lot of money," Slip exclaims.

"It is?"

Sally Dolan, the Bowery Palace's former feature attraction, is also sought after by Rick Martin, not only to grace his stage, but his bedroom as well. Sally remains adamantly opposed, then realizes that yielding would cause friction between Lola and Rick. Sally leaves a note for Lola at the hotel desk. "If you like surprises, come to Rick Martin's room at 7 p.m." Lola arrives in time to see Sally and Martin embrace.

Lola visits the boys, their heads in their hands, at the empty Bowery Palace, and for a cup of coffee promises to testify that Sach's signature merely represents one autograph to one Lola Stanton, not an agreement between Sach and Martin.

As in *Master Minds,* Sach's power dissipates in the middle of a performance. The scene

Crooner Sach (Hall) with the voice of John Lorenz in *Blues Busters*. Gabe Dell is seated at the piano. Others are unidentified.

is well-done. Sach is singing a familiar song when suddenly his singing voice cracks, never to return. (Gabe looks hopelessly in his piano for a defect.) Sach had had an irritation in his throat and went to the doctor to cure it. With the cure went his talent, and a fortune.

In addition to the slow pace, little action and insufficient direct confrontation between Slip and Rick Martin, *Blues Busters* is the only film where in the end the boys are the losers. There are numerous films in which the boys, if they do not succeed in reaching their goals, at least foil the opposition. Here, not only does Rick Martin profit before relinquishing claim to Sach, but the boys cannot even credit themselves for getting Sach back. The "ownership" of Sach depends on the shrewd manipulations of the two women, Lola Stanton and Sally Dolan.

Blues Busters offers us some good music and nice singing, a slapdash dance routine by Butch, Chuck and Whitey — and Slip singing "Dixieland."

Blues Busters is Gabe Dell's farewell film. He'd been a lawyer, cop, reporter, card shark, bank teller and two-bit crook. Here he's a piano player. Dell decided, and rightly so, that if he was to become a better actor, he needed to move on. He did and his career blossomed.

Bowery Battalion

Released January 24, 1951; 69 minutes; 6173 ft.; Monogram; Director, William Beaudine; Producer, Jan Grippo; Screenplay, Charles R. Marion, Bert Lawrence; Photography, Marcel Le Picard; Film Editor, William Austin; Music Director, Edward Kay; Art Director, Dave Milton; Sound, Tom Lambert; Set Decorator, Raymond Boltz.

CAST

Slip	Leo Gorcey	*Hatfield*	Russell Hicks
Sach	Huntz Hall	*Decker*	John Bleifer
Frisbie	Donald MacBride	*Conroy*	Al Eben
Marsha	Virginia Hewitt	*Recruiters*	Frank Jenks, Michael
Whitey	Billy Benedict		Ross
Louie Dumbrowski	Bernard Gorcey	*Col. Masters*	Selmer Jackson
Butch	Buddy Gorman	*Waiter in Mess*	Emil Sitka
Chuck	David Gorcey	*Branson*	Harry Lauter

After the boys are duped into joining the Army because they think New York is being attacked, Louie too enters the local recruiter's office and tells them how he, single-handedly, captured a whole platoon of Germans. He is so taken by his own story that he lies on the recruiter's table to demonstrate how he shot down the enemy. He's brought to Washington, D.C., where Col. Masters waters down Louie's dramatic tale. Louie is surprised to see his old commanding officer and is shocked when the Col. addresses him by his new rank, "Major Dumbrowski! Oy vey."

Any film that involves Louie Dumbrowski to the extent *Bowery Battalion* does should enhance its quality. It does this only a little. Slapstick takes up most of the film. In addition, much of what is original in *Bowery Battalion* is rehashed in the Bowery Boys' final, and more substantial armed forces picture, *Clipped Wings*. The plots are the same—flushing out foreign spies. Louie is recruited as bait, for he is the inventor of the highly impressive, but quite obsolete, hydrogen ray. Who knew?

"Hey, chief, what's a hydrogen ray?" asks Chuck.

"You don't know what a hydrogen ray is? Why it's a ray invented by this guy named Hydrogen," answers Slip, unaware that their little pal is the inventor.

Here, as in *Blonde Dynamite*, the boys are oblivious to the plot until the very end. In fact, the plot is not even apparent to the audience until well into the film. By that time the boys have fared so poorly as soldiers that their Army uniforms are taken away from them and waiters' outfits are substituted.

Still they manage to get into trouble. The dinner guest that evening happens to be Major Dumbrowski. The boys are in such disbelief that they spill the food on the other attending officers. In jail they go, for the third time.

Earlier, the boys disliked the uniforms they were given and donned the ones hung nearby. Dressed in officers' uniforms, they were admitted to the officers' lounge. There they had to hold their own during a high-level Army conversation.

Sach was asked, "How would you remove an enemy from entrenchment?"

"That's easy. Serve them a dispossess notice."

A film with the Bowery Boys in the Army would be incomplete without a training scene. The opportunity for some slapstick is not missed, but it is not well-executed. The colonel

Louie (Bernard Gorcey, seated) looks suspiciously at his secretary (Virginia Hewitt), and with good reason — she's a spy in *Bowery Battalion*. Others, left to right: Billy Benedict, Bud Gorman, Leo Gorcey, Huntz Hall and David Gorcey.

notices Sgt. Frisbey having trouble "trying to make soldiers out of these men," and takes a shot at it. He goes through the drill with Butch's rifle, tosses the rifle back to Butch and tells the boys to do exactly as he did. They do—to the letter. Five rifles are simultaneously tossed at the colonel, and the boys are tossed back in jail. The problem with this gag, besides its overuse in other comedies (such as in the Three Stooges), is that the time between the colonel tossing the gun back to Butch and the boys tossing their guns at the colonel is too lengthy and we could forget why the boys all throw their guns back at the colonel.

There is also a silly scene where Major Dumbrowski commands the boys to stand at attention and tries to direct them out of his office. Guided by Louie's unpolished drill, the boys climb the walls and fall over the desk before Louie, exasperated, tells them to "fall out" on the other side of the door.

As in *Clipped Wings*, the woman spy discovers the "bait." She's Louie's secretary. As soon as she overhears Louie tell the boys he "keeps a formula to the hydrogen ray in his head," the spies make plans to kidnap Major Dumbrowski.

One of the reasons Louie first agrees to take this assignment is that he feels secure knowing thousands of GIs are on his side. But when it really matters, it's his pals from the sweet shop who come through for him. Speaking the language only the boys understand, Louie whispers, "Routine 11," before the kidnappers, posing as Army officers, whisk him away.

Risking another jail sentence, the boys leave their post, take an Army Jeep and rescue Louie.

Relegating Slip and Sach to the periphery of the plot is a mistake. Substituting disjointed, slapstick padding for substantive confrontation between them and the bad guys is another.

Ghost Chasers

Released April 29, 1951; 69 minutes; Monogram; Director, William Beaudine; Producer, Jan Grippo; Screenplay, Charles R. Marion, Bert Lawrence; Photography, Marcel Le Picard; Film Editor, William Austin; Music, Edward Kay; Set Director, Raymond Boltz; Sound, Tom Lambert; Art Director, Dave Milton.

CAST

Slip Mahoney	Leo Gorcey		*Reporters*	Paul Bryar, Pat
Sach Jones	Huntz Hall			Gleason
Whitey	Billy Benedict		*Photographer*	Bob Peoples
Chuck	David Gorcey		*Mrs. Parelli*	Argentina Brunetti
Butch	Buddy Gorman		*Mrs. Mahoney*	Doris Kemper
Louie Dumbrowski	Bernard Gorcey		*Madame Zola*	Belle Mitchell
Cynthia	Jan Kayne		*Margo the Medium*	Lela Bliss
Dr. Granville	Philip Van Zandt		*Dr. Seigfried*	Hal Gerard
Jack Eagan	Robert Coogan		*Prof. Krantz*	Marshall Bradford
Gus	Michael Ross		*Girl*	Margorie Eaton
Edgar	Lloyd Corrigan		*Lady at Séance*	Bess Flowers
Leonardi	Donald Lawton			

The subject is a séance and it begins with Whitey. (Apparently his interest in ham radio operating in *Triple Trouble* has waned.) At first, Whitey can get only Sach to join him at Madam Margo's séance to "recall" the great Leonardi. The séance is open to members and the press only.

"What are you afraid of?" Whitey asks Sach at the séance.

"Leonardi might tell them I'm not a member."

Early in the picture we are invited to Slip's home, an event that has not happened since *Angels' Alley*. Slip finds his neighbor, the vulnerable Italian immigrant Mrs. Perelli, head in hands at her kitchen table, weeping because she does not have $100 Madame Zola demands to communicate with her deceased son. Slip tells her, "I think it can be deranged."

When it comes to money, Slip has only one resource — gullible Louie Dumbrowski. In most cases, Slip must pitch him hard. In *Fighting Fools,* Slip prevails upon Louie's paternal instincts; in *Blues Busters,* Slip uses reverse psychology. In *Ghost Chasers,* the method is the most creative of all. The boys stage a séance of their own to contact Louie's Uncle Jake, reputed to have stashed away a large sum of money and accumulated a large debt to Louie before he died.

David Gorcey does an excellent job as Uncle Jake. The scene culminates when Louie asks where the money is hidden. Uncle Jake balks.

"I'll think about it," says Chuck as Uncle Jake. "But first you must give me $100."

"What for?" cries Louie.

"Traveling expenses," the ghost says.

The boys barge into Mrs. Perelli's séance and exposes Madame Zola as a fraud. They also recover Louie's money and learn that Madam Margo is Madame Zola's boss.

Enter Edgar the Ghost, a "real" ghost, sent from above to smash the phony spiritualist ring giving ghosts a bad rep. Sach, whose congeniality earns him the affections of the horse My Girl in *Crazy Over Horses* and the parrot in *Let's Go Navy!*, grants him the privilege accorded no one else, the ability to see and talk with Edgar the Ghost.

"I like your outfit, Sach tells Edgar.

"These are the clothes they buried me in 300 years ago."

The spiritualists discover the boys in the house, lock them in the cellar and pipe water in to drown them. Edgar comes to their aid by magically boring a hole in the wall, releasing all the water.

Stepping out of their wet clothes, the boys put on costumes that just happen to be there. Usually when the boys wear costumes there's a reason, as in the hospital scene in *Private Eyes* or the witch doctor's regalia in *Jungle Gents*. Here, there seems to be none. They look silly in the costumes and, when they're hypnotized in their tracks, look even more ridiculous.

"Only an idiot or a moron is not affected by hypnotism," states the doctor. Sach shows that he's not hypnotized, yet he pretends to be so as not to arouse the doctor's suspicions.

Once again, Edgar intervenes by snapping the boys out of their trance—all except Slip.

"Thy friend has a strong brain. Mind, not a good one but a strong one. Ye must strike him."

Oddly enough, the only other time Sach strikes Slip is with the help of another independent spirit, the Genie in *Bowery to Bagdad*.

With all their senses and reflexes in working order, the boys engage the spiritualists in a final fist battle before Detective Eagan and police break up the fight and arrest the spiritualists.

Lloyd Corrigan's performance as Edgar the Ghost enhances what is already a well-endowed film that includes a variety of people and fanfare. Having Sach the only one who sees the ghost is a splendid idea since nobody is ever sure of his sanity anyway and it is good for a few laughs. Detective Eagan is a silly, unneeded character. Robert Coogan tries to be funny but is just annoying. The only possible reason for his inclusion is to perhaps revitalize the "outside" character Gabe Dell once filled. Coogan does not come close.

In the other films that deal with spiritualism, *Hard Boiled Mahoney* and *Hold That Hypnotist*, the film's view on the subject is definitely anti-spiritualist. Although the boys are successful in exposing Madam Margo as a fraud, Edgar the Ghost is never proven to be otherwise. As he fades away from the screen for the last time, addressing the audience, Edgar is the only unexplainable character in this series.

Let's Go Navy!

Released July 29, 1951; 68 minutes; 6149 ft.; Monogram; Director, William Beaudine; Producer, Jan Grippo; Screenplay, Max Adams; Photography, Marcel Le Picard; Film editor, William Austin; Set Director, Otto Siegel; Technical Adviser, Lt. Robert M. Garick, USNR; Art Director, Dave Milton. Music Director, Edward Kay.

CAST

Slip Mahoney	Leo Gorcey	*Horatio Hobenocker*	Dave Willock
Sach	Huntz Hall	*Nuramo*	Peter Mamakos
Whitey	William Benedict	*Lt. Bradly*	Ray Walker
Chuck	David Gorcey	*Captain*	Jonathan Hale
Louie Dumbrowski	Bernard Gorcey	*Policeman*	Paul Bryar
Butch	Buddy Gorman	*Merriweather*	Richard Monahan
Longnecker	Allen Jenkins	*Stevenson*	William Lechner
Joe	Tom Neal	*Harry Schwartz*	George Offerman
Red	Richard Benedict	*Detective Snyder*	Mike Lally
Sailors	Jimmy Cross,	*Lt. Moss*	Russ Conway
	Bull Chandler,	*Petty Officer*	Harry Strang
	Don Gordon,	*Grompkin*	
	Neyle Morrow,	*Sailor*	William Vincent
	Joey Ray	*Storekeeper*	Lee Graham
Dalton	Harry Lauter	*Disbursement Officer*	Pat Gleason
Sailor	Murray Alper	*Third Officer*	George Eldredge
Princess Papoola	Charlita	*First Aide*	William Hudson
Commander Tannen	Paul Harvey	*Second Aide*	Bob Peoples
Sgt. Mulloy	Emory Parnell	*Officer*	John Close
Lt. Smith	Douglas Evans	*Postman*	Emil Sitka
Shell Game Operator	Frank Jenks	*Fat Sailor*	Ray Dawe
Donovan	Tom Kennedy	*Recruiting Officer*	Ray Walker
Kitten	Dorothy Ford		

The boys learn the hard way that muggers dressed in sailor uniforms aren't necessarily in the Navy. The police are too busy to track down the muggers who stole $1600 of charity money so off the boys go the local recruiting office hoping Uncle Sam will be more cooperative.

When they arrive, five other men are deciding whether to go ahead with their enlistment or not. One of them, Hobenocker, is going to be a father so they decide to walk out. As they sneak out of the office, Slip, Satch, Butch, Chuck and Whitey enter. The Navy recruiter orders them to get sworn in. Instead of protesting, Slip is "infused with a brilliant idea," similar to the one he has in *Triple Trouble*.

"If you're looking for two sailors, where's the best place to look?" Thus Slip, Whitey, Butch, Chuck and Sach become Dalton, Schwartz, Merriwether, Stevenson and Hobenocker. But they are not as lucky as they are in *Triple Trouble*. Of course the difference between finding someone in the state penitentiary and finding someone by joining the Navy is that the prison is just one complex while the Navy is composed of numerous ships throughout the world. But no matter.

Their only lead is knowing that one robber has a tattoo of a broken heart with the name Marie on his chest. Between swabbing the deck and serving the captain's lunch, the boys lift the shirts off every suspected sailor. No luck.

On an island Slip suspects is "pollinated with cannibals and head hunters," they visit Neromo, the local tattoo artist who speaks only his native tongue. The pantomime and verbal gibberish is amusingly executed between Sach and Neromo. The only other time this occurs is in *Dig That Uranium* when the Indian chief tells the boys that Louie does not own

Allen Jenkins (left; he played Hunk in *Dead End*) with Hall in *Let's Go Navy!*

the uranium-filled Little Daisy Mine. The tattoo artist, however, has no recollection of the tattoo the boys describe.

Sach and First Mate Longnecker (Allen Jenkins, *Dead End*'s Hunk) seem to be engaged in a private war; the battlefield is the deck. Every time Sach picks up a mop, a vacuum cleaner or a waxer, Longnecker falls and somehow gets himself wet. The captain gets furious with both of them.

"You seem to make an effort to get into trouble."

"Oh? It's no effort at all."

Offshore, Sach purchases a parakeet with the same ability Sach has in *Crashing Las Vegas*: the foresight to win at the gambling table. With the help of the bird, he wins enough money to make up for the robbery. Satisfied with this, they abandon their search for the muggers.

On leave in New York, on their way to deliver the money to Louie, the boys pass the corner where they were mugged. And guess what? The same muggers attack them. This time the outcome is different. With the help of Longnecker, they subdue the muggers.

Let's Go Navy! is pure slapstick. There's no conflict, no drama, because the audience knows even before the boys embark on their Navy stint, that the sailors the boys seek are not sailors at all. In addition, we know the muggers' whereabouts. While Louie reads a letter from Sach, the camera pans around the sweet shop and catches a glimpse of the two big men seated at the counter. They've been boarding above Louie's Sweet Shop for the entire year the boys have been away (the longest period ever covered in a Bowery Boys picture).

The Bowery Boys. Left to right: Bud Gorman, Huntz Hall, Leo Gorcey, Bernard Gorcey, Billy Benedict, David Gorcey, in a scene from *Let's Go Navy.*

Though the film tries to end on a comic note, the ending is more frustrating than funny. When the boys arrive at the recruiting office to pick up their commendation, the real Dalton, Merriwether, Schwartz, and Hobenocker are back. Again they sneak out, and the boys, accustomed to responding to their aliases, get sworn in again.

This was Jan Grippo last film and *Variety* paid a tribute: "[A] very funny picture ... Jan Grippo leaves the series after 23 pix with a superior credit."

Crazy Over Horses

Released November 18, 1951; 65 minutes; 5819 ft.; Monogram; Director, William Beaudine; Producer, Jerry Thomas; Screenplay, Tim Ryan; Photography, Marcel Le Picard; Film Editor, William Austin; Art Director, David Milton; Musical Director, Edward Kay; Sound, Tom Lambert; Set Director, Robert Priestly; Costumes, Sidney Mintz.

CAST

Slip	Leo Gorcey		*Uniformed Guard*	Bob Peoples
Sach	Huntz Hall		*Charlie*	Perc Launders
Whitey	Billy Benedict		*Groom*	Leo "Ukie" Sherin
Louie	Bernard Gorcey		*Stable Attendant*	Robert "Smoki"
Chuck	David Gorcey			Whitfield
	(Condon)		*Announcer*	Sam Balter
Butch	Bennie Bartlett		*Evans*	Ray Page
Duke	Ted de Corsia		*Elderly Woman*	Gertrude Astor
Weepin' Willie	Allen Jenkins		*Jockeys*	Bill Cartledge,
Swifty	Mike Ross			Whitey Hughes,
J.T. Randall	Russell Hicks			Delmar Thomas,
Flynn	Tim Ryan			Bernard Pludow
Terry	Gloria Saunders		*Silent Man*	Ben Frommer
Mazie	Peggy Wynne			

When Slip and Sach offer to collect a debt for Louie, mild-manneredly Flynn (played by Tim Ryan, the screenwriter) offers the boys My Girl as settlement. Through his window the boys see a horse doing handkerchief tricks for Flynn's daughter, Terry. The boys think Flynn is referring to his pretty daughter.

"You like My Girl?"

"Do we!" exclaim the boys, eyeing Flynn's daughter.

"Well, if you like her, take her."

"Take her?"

"You see, she's become too expensive to feed and she eats an awful lot."

Breaking the news to Louie that the debt has been settled with a horse is not an easy task.

"What does Flynn think I am, a meshuginah?"

Moments later, three gentlemen enter the sweet shop and order a horse. They offer as high as $1,000 for it, more than three times Louie's loss, but Slip rejects it.

Louie later tells them that during the night, Weepin' Willy, one of the men who wanted to buy the horse, returned and talked to him about the horse for as long as it would take to steal My Girl out of Louie's back room and replace her with a slower horse, Tarzana. Sach doesn't believe it and tries to mount her. A second later we see him fly out of the stable and into a pile of hay. He looks up and says, "Wrong horse."

This shot of Sach flying out of the stable is shown twice; here, and after the boys try to switch her back, when Sach, once again, does not believe they possess the wrong horse. The repetition of this shot is a clever editorial decision.

In what seems to be a vehicle for writer Tim Ryan's ideas on how two horses can surreptitiously be switched, *Crazy Over Horses* becomes a slow-moving undertaking desperately trying to justify 65 minutes of film. The biggest problem is that it presents the boys, not the bad guys, as their own worst enemies, because of their own incompetence. The bad guys are seen in the beginning and at the end of the picture, and so the internal conflict between Slip and Sach must carry the film.

As Duke Coveleske (Stanley Clements) does in a much later film, *Up in Smoke*, Slip shows that he can be heartless as well as soft-hearted. Slip throws Sach out of the gang for being a bungler. It's the meanest thing Slip could do.

In an effort to square himself, Sach ventures out on his own. Unaware that My Girl is already back in Flynn's stable, Sach, in black face, takes My Girl back to the race track stable and, while conversing with the black groomer, switches reins. Sach returns with Tarzana. He bungles it again.

Not since Sunshine Sammy Morrison of the East Side Kids has a black person played a role of any consequence and it is a shame that in *Crazy Over Horses,* he is stereotyped as a pushover.

In most of the Bowery Boys films you can tell who the bad guys are from their speech, their clothes, and cigarette smoking. Here, you can tell by Weepin' Willy rushing to the bar for a drink.

Duke, Weepin' Willy and Swifty all work for a respectable man of society, Mr. Randall. He is much like the behind-the-scenes scoundrel Mr. Dolan in *News Hounds,* Mr. Sayers in *Live Wires* and Mr. Graham in *Private Eyes.*

With Tarzana's odds 60 to one to lose the next race, the bad guys plan on sneaking My Girl in for Tarzana, knowing the former horse is much swifter. But the boys deceive them by tricking Duke and Weepin' Willie into pulling the final switch, thereby placing My Girl back in Slip's capable hands.

Cinematography is adequate in the horse racing scene as Sach passes each horse one by one. It cannot be said with absolute certainty that Sach is not really riding a horse and listening to Slip's instructions through an earphone. The race ends in a photo finish with My Girl winning by a tongue.

Crazy Over Horses is Tim Ryan's first Bowery Boys film written without collaboration. He is the co-author of numerous prior Bowery Boys films and several succeeding pictures, all with better results. Interestingly enough, many of these films have something to do with the boys' possessing something someone else wants, such as *Jalopy* (Sach's formula), *Jinx Money* ($50,000), and *News Hounds* (photographs). But *Crazy Over Horses* neither has the seriousness of *News Hounds,* or the comedy of *Jalopy.*

Allen Jenkins, who starred with the Dead End Kids in *Dead End,* has the poor luck of being cast in two of the weakest Bowery Boys films, this one and *Let's Go Navy!,* also released in 1951. Jenkins is a good actor, particularly in comedy. But the Bowery Boys were in a low period and it was not until *Feudin' Fools* that things picked up.

Hold That Line

Released March 23, 1952; 64 minutes; 5749 ft.; Monogram; Director, William Beaudine; Producer, Jerry Thomas; Screenplay, Tim Ryan, Charles R. Marion; Photography, Marcel Le Picard; Film Editor, William Austin; Music Director, Edward Kay; Art Director, Martin Obzina; Production Manager, Allen K. Wood.

CAST

Slip	Leo Gorcey		*Dean Forrester*	Taylor Holmes
Sach	Huntz Hall		*Billingsley*	Francis Pierlot
Junior	Gil Stratton, Jr.		*Stanhope*	Pierre Watkin
Chuck	David Gorcey		*Biff*	John Bromfield
Butch	Bennie Bartlett		*Harold*	Bob Nichols
Louie	Bernard Gorcey		*Katie Wayne*	Mona Knox

Penny	Gloria Winters	*Professor Hovel*	Percival Vivian
Coach Rowland	Paul Bryar	*Murphy*	Tom Kennedy
Assistant Coach	Bob Peoples	*Police Sergeant*	Bert Davidson
Candy Callin	Veda Ann Borg	*Miss Whitsett*	Marjorie Eaton
Professor Grog	Byron Foulger	*Girl Student*	Jean Dean
Football Announcer	Tom Hanlon	*Boy Student*	Steve Wayne
Mike Donelli	George Lewis	*Players*	Ted Jordan,
Big Dave	Al Eben		George Sanders
Professor Wintz	Ted Stanhope	*Girl*	Marvelle Andre

Surrounded by cropped-hair college jocks and swooning co-eds, the Bowery Boys stand out as holdouts from the last generation. The contrast, the ironic alienation of the boys who supposedly belong to this generation, works well. This alienation is best shown through language when they're introduced to Biff, an All-American. Slip shrugs his shoulders and retorts, "Well, we're all Americans."

The boys find themselves at an Ivy League college by way of wager. Trustee Billingsley's opinion is that only people of a certain caliber can perform well in an Ivy League school. Trustee Stanhope believes anyone can do it. Thus they search for their subjects and find them at Louie's Sweet Shop. Slip baffles them with his malapropisms.

"How much will we get for the siesta?"

"Fifteen hundred dollars a siesta — er — I mean semester."

In *Jalopy* and *Paris Playboys,* power is contained in a liquid that provides energy for locomotive apparatuses. In *Hold That Line,* power is in a formula Sach concocts in his laboratory. It gives him temporary super-strength. One sample of his strength is combined with an imaginative gag. Dean Forrester meticulously pastes back together a vase the boys broke. Then he places it on his mantel beyond anybody's reach and declares, "Nothing can happen to it now." Just then Sach hurls a javelin that soars through Forrester's window, again destroying the vase. The sequence is excellently constructed, well-timed, and the camera keeps the viewers posted on the progression of both scenes.

Forrester further suffers at the hands of the boys when Slip tries to duplicate Sach's formula. When Forrester arrives to inquire about Ivy's star player, Slip uses this opportunity to test his mixture. Trick photography shows Forrester shrunk to about six inches high.

As if to make up for his unscientific mind, Slip plans a strategy that leads to an Ivy League victory. Assuming State will be watching Sach, Slip the quarterback fakes a handoff to his punch-drunk friend and runs for the touchdown.

Structurally, the script of *Hold That Line* is similar *Here Come the Marines,* both written by Tim Ryan and Charles Merion. Just as the boys devote the first 30 minutes of *Here Come the Marines* to basic training before the plot is introduced, so do the boys get acquainted with the school and attend classes and play football before we meet the opposition.

"The opposition" are crooked gamblers who send pretty Candy Collins to lure Sach away from the playing field. Kidnappers await behind closed doors.

Their plan to render Sach unconscious is too elaborate. While kissing him, Candy pushes Sach towards one of the closed doors so that one of the kidnappers can club him when Candy says the password, "Strong boy." Finally, one of them does and emerges from the closet. Candy comments, "Well, there's our strong boy." The other kidnapper suddenly comes out and hits kidnapper number one on the head.

Biff, a little like the character of Gabe Moreno, doesn't quite know which side he is on. He wants Ivy to win the football game with State, and he wants to be the hero of that game.

With Sach in the spotlight, Biff is no longer Ivy's football hero. Candy takes advantage of his jealousy. Biff knows that by introducing Hurricane Jones to Candy, Sach might just disappear.

In his 1968 interview with Richard Lamparski, Leo Gorcey laughingly recalled the way his pint-sized father stood up to the producers and said, "If you don't give me more to do or more to say, I'm quittin.'" Indeed, there are many cases where Louie's presence is unnecessary and it may be that these superfluous but energetic appearances are the result of this standoff. In each case, as with every script decision, there must be a reason (not always a good one) for bringing Louie into the picture. *Bowery Buckaroos* is the first time Louie joins the boys at the end and the only time he is forced, by another character, to do so. In *Master Minds, The Bowery Boys Meet the Monsters* and *Bowery to Bagdad,* his fear that something terrible may have happened to the boys propels him to go looking for them. In *Feudin' Fools, Here Come the Marines* and *Clipped Wings,* Louie visits the boys simply because he misses them. In *Hold That Line,* it's just the spirit of youth. With his brother from the old country minding the store, Louie attends Ivy and he is greeted by a mob of girls overjoyed at seeing this old youngster.

Hold That Line does a good job weaving images of 1950s college life into a Bowery Boys format. The film lends itself well to a variety of character possibilities from reckless student, to pedantic English professor, to nutty chemistry professor, to conservative college dean. Every scene is concise and comical and adds to the development of the story. Though none of the acting is exceptional, all the actors in the college scenes are convincing in their stereotyped roles.

Here Come the Marines

Released June 29, 1952; 66 minutes; 5924 ft.; Monogram; Director, William Beaudine; Producer, Jerry Thomas; Screenplay, Tim Ryan, Charles R. Marion, Jack Crutcher; Photography, Marcel Le Picard; Film Editor, William Austin; Music Director, Edward Kay; Art Director, Martin Obzina; Sound, Charles Cooper; Wardrobe, Frank Beetson; British title, *Tell It to the Marines.*

CAST

Slip	Leo Gorcey		*Croupier*	Sammy Finn
Sach	Huntz Hall		*Dealer*	Buck Russell
Chuck	David Gorcey		*Harlow*	Riley Hill
Butch	Bennie Bartlett		*Secretary*	Lisa Wilson
Junior	Gil Stratton		*Col. Evans*	James Flavin
Louie	Bernard Gorcey		*Cook*	Robert Coogan
Corp. Stacy	Murray Alper		*Marine*	Leo "Ukie" Sherin
Col. Brown	Hanley Stafford		*Doctor*	Stanley Blystone
Capt. Miller	Arthur Space		*Marine*	Chad Mallory
Lulu Mae	Myrna Dell		*Sgt. Lane*	Perc Launders
Jolly Joe Johnson	Paul Maxey		*Corp. Mitchell*	Alan Jeffory
Sheriff Benson	Tim Ryan		*Capt. Graham*	Bob Cudlip
Desmond	William Newell		*Medic*	Bob Peoples

Hoodlums	William Vincent,		*Salesman*	Dick Paxton
	Jack Wilson,		*Girl*	Barbara Grey
	Courtland Shep-		*Postman*	William Bailey
	ard		*Stickman*	Paul Bradley

The strength of *Here Come the Marines* lies in the relationship between Sach and his commanding officer, Col. Brown, who believes the Bowery Boy is the son of "Hard Hat Jones," the toughest Marine in the Corps. He promotes Sach to sergeant, and immediately Sach abuses his power over Butch, Chuck, Junior and, most particularly, Slip.

He leads them on a 20-mile hike while riding a bicycle and continually blows his whistle in Slip's ear. He blows his whistle to tell the boys to go to sleep and again to tell them goodnight. His whistle blows with every exhale while he sleeps.

Slip and the boys retaliate but it all backfires–literally. They place what appears to be a dud torpedo on Sach's bed, hoping to frighten Sach and expose his ignorance. Col. Brown reprimands Sach for inciting a panic in the barracks. But when the colonel throws the torpedo out the window (an unlikely action for an officer), it explodes. Sach is rewarded for saving everybody's life.

The boys dig a foxhole and camouflage it, hoping Sach will fall in. Instead, Col. Brown falls in and Sach is given another promotion for devising such a cleverly concealed foxhole. "I bet if you broke a couple of the colonel's ribs he'd make him a captain;" Slip exclaims, exasperated.

While on the 20-mile hike, Slip breaks ranks to assist an injured Marine, thus finally introducing the film's main plot. It also illustrates the meaninglessness of Sach's rank in situations that calls for leadership. Sgt. Sach wisely keeps his mouth shut as Slip orders Chuck to take Sach's bicycle back to camp and send for immediate medical assistance. Slip alerts Col. Brown to the similarities between the playing card found on the dead Marine and the one in Jolly Joe's Casino Club.

"I think that Marine we found by the lake was also onto something for which he was castigated and ultimately demised."

The second part of *Here Come the Marines*, is a reworking of an earlier film, *Lucky Losers.* Both involve an illegal gambling operation headed by a hard-nosed individual who would not think twice about killing someone if doing so would better his business. Jolly Joe Johnson and Bruce McDermott of *Lucky Losers* do kill someone, and that person's death attracts the attention of the media. At both crime scenes Slip finds clues that lead him to the respective establishment. While Bruce McDermott is backed by a corrupt city official, Jolly Joe Johnson has the support of the local Sheriff Benson. Both employ sexy blonde women hustlers, though Lulu May of this picture is more provocative and has a larger role.

Jolly Joe has Lulu sneak into the Marine barracks, confident her discovery will bring dire consequences for the boys. But Col. Brown's search comes up empty. Lulu re-emerges, declaring, "I did it with mirrors."

As the audience we are dissatisfied with this amateurish trick photography. In fact, there is no photographic trickery at all, only Lulu's verbal statement. She could have said, "I did it with bananas," for there is equal visual support (none) for either statement.

Lulu not only changes her mind about getting the boys into trouble, but escorts them to the casino after closing hours. As the boys inspect the crooked dice and roulette wheels, the lights go on. Jolly Joe and company are there threatening to kill the boys in the same fashion as they did the Marine. But at that moment, as in many other moments such as this, the FBI (or the police), who have been watching the boys' movements, come to their rescue.

There are two major problems with this film. One is the unoriginality of the whole casino affair, demonstrating a particular laziness on the part of the writers; two, unlike the other Armed Forces films, the plot has no bearing on the fact that the boys are in the Marines. The boys could easily have been fruit pickers or door-to-door vacuum cleaner salesmen, with the rest of the film remaining as is.

The only positive feature about this film is the humor provided by Sach. If his being sergeant could have had something to do with the boys' entanglement with Jolly Joe's casino, *Here Come the Marines* would be a tighter production, a more coherent story, and might have lived up to its title.

Feudin' Fools

Released September 21, 1952; 63 minutes; 5631 ft.; Monogram; Director, William Beaudine; Producer, Jerry Thomas; Screenplay, Bert Lawrence, Tim Ryan; Photography, Marcel Le Picard; Film Editor, William Austin; Music Director, Edward Kay; Art Director, Dave Milton; Sound, Charles Cooper, Special Effects, Ray Mercer.

CAST

Slip Mahoney	Leo Gorcey	*Ellie Mae*	Anne Kimbell
Sach Jones	Huntz Hall	*Tiny Smith*	Dorothy Ford
Butch	Bennie Bartlett	*Pinky*	Leo "Ukie" Sherin
Chuck	David Gorcey	*Corky*	Benny Baker
Louie	Bernard Gorcey	*Big Jim*	Lyle Talbot
Luke Smith	Paul Wexler	*Traps*	Fuzzy Knight
Clem Smith	Oliver Blake	*Grandpa Smith*	Russell Simpson
Caleb Smith	Bob Easton	*Mr. Thompson*	Arthur Space
Yancy Smith	O. Z. Whitehead	*Private Detectives*	Bob Bray, Bob Keyes

Feudin' Fools is the Bowery Boys' interpretation of the mythic Smith vs. Jones family feud, (as *Bowery to Bagdad* is the Bowery Boys' version of the Aladdin and His Lamp story, and *Up in Smoke* the Bowery Boys' answer to Mephistopheles).

Sach has been willed a piece of land called the Jones Estate by some unknown relative. (Usually when Sach is given title to something by virtue of his last name, it's a mistake, as in *Loose in London.* Here no other heir steps forward.) "This looks more like a home for old vampires," Slip comments upon seeing the dilapidated shack.

The boys are greeted with bullets from the shotguns of their straggle-bearded hillbilly neighbors, the Smiths. Slip's New York wit is put to the test in a dramatic game of interrogation.

"Which one a-y'all goes by the name of Jones?" asks Clem Smith in his slow Southern drawl.

"Jones? That's an idiosyncrasy of a name. Don't believe I ever heard of it," Slip stammers.

"Then whatiyer doin' on the Jones farm?" Clem continues.

"We came up for a huntin' expedition. We saw the place was empty so we came in," Slip nervously explains.

Slip (Gorcey) gets squirted and Ellie Mae Smith (Anne Kimbell) is ready to be next in *Feudin' Fools.*

"Whatiyer huntin' with?" Clem inquires, seeing no hunting equipment.

"Oh, uh — er, we do it primitive style with our bare hands."

Slip passes the test, and the boys are invited for "vittles." But Clem is under the impression that a Jones will always give himself away by eating a lot. Which is ironic because the Smiths' grandfather gorges himself more than anybody. That should make Clem wonder if he himself is not a Jones.

Hatchet Moran in *Trouble Makers* shares the Smiths' problem of properly identifying Sach. It is two sides of the same script idea. The difference between the two is that Hatchet wants to believe Sach is his old friend, while the Smiths want to believe Sach is an old enemy.

The gags around the dinner table are frequent and funny. Unlike *Paris Playboys* or *High Society* in which the dinner scenes are little more than comic padding, in *Feudin' Fools* how they eat determines whether they live or die.

The boys are as polite and as patient as can be. Sach takes one pea and cuts it in two with a knife. Slip turns around in his chair so no one will see him put a piece of food in his mouth. He also says something under his breath, which the hillbillies would never recognize as an insult: "This is like eating off a subway platform."

An adequate amount of time is given to this sequence before Sach breaks the tension with a hearty laugh.

"What's funny?"

"That you think one of us is a Jones!"

Blast!

Like the salivating of Pavlov's dog at the sound of a bell, Clem's trigger finger goes to work when he hears the name Jones. Once again the boys take cover underneath the wooden table. The long shot of the boys' heads lined up on the table is an excellent image of a shooting gallery at a penny arcade.

Having neutralized the Smiths' tempers, the film needs another boost. A bank robbery is the answer and we are introduced to the bank when Sach applies for a home improvement loan.

"Do you boys have any credit?" the bank president asks.

"Certainly," explains Slip. "Right now we owe Louie $1.83 worth of banana splits."

The unexpected arrival of Louie on the scene is seldom relevant to the plot. And when greeted with a barrel of four shotguns, Louie's fear is magnificently expressed in his own marvelous Jewish style.

"First I was wondering if I could take a two-week vacation. Now I'm wondering if I'll live that long."

Similar sentiments are expressed in *Blonde Dynamite* when the thieves force Louie through an underground tunnel. Louie comments, "I was better off on the [Coney Island's] chute-the-shoot." Lines such as these are what endear Louie to the fans.

In a bank robbery, one of the robbers is shot and needs immediate medical care. Slip presents Dr. Louie Dumbrowski, who will perform the operation.

Big Jim, the wounded robber and gang leader, believes Louie is a doctor. He chews out one of his men who expresses doubt. This makes him look stupid and the whole scene suffers.

Resourceful Slip uses the Smiths' hostility towards Joneses for his own use. Ellie Mae comes to visit the boys and becomes the robbers' captive. Slip notices Clem through the window and gets a great idea.

"You better get your hands off that girl, Mr. Jones," he tells the robber loud enough for Clem to hear. "And that goes for you too, Mr. Jones." He turns to Chuck. "Well, I can't help it if their names are Jones. All three of them."

Bringing together in the end the Smiths, the robbers and the bank president neatly ties all the loose ends of the film into a coherent, interrelated piece.

───────────────

No Holds Barred

November 23, 1952; 65 minutes; Monogram; Director, William Beaudine; Producer, Jerry Thomas; Screenplay, Tim Ryan, Jack Crutcher, Bert Lawrence; Photography, Ernest Miller; Art Director, Dave Milton; Austin; Music Director, Edward Kay; Sound, Charles Cooper; Set Decorator, Robert Priestly; Wardrobe, Frank Beetson; Special Effects, Ray Mercer.

CAST

Slip	Leo Gorcey	*Chuck*	David Gorcey [Condon]
Sach	Huntz Hall		
Pete Taylor	Leonard Penn	*Butch*	Bennie Bartlett
Rhonda Nelson	Marjorie Reynolds	*Hombre Montana*	Terrible Tova
Louie	Bernard Gorcey	*Gertie*	Barbara Gray

The Mauler	Henry Kulky		*Mr. Hunter*	Tim Ryan
Stickup Man	Nick Stewart		*Mildred*	Sandra Gould
Challenger	Pat Fraley		*First Mug*	Bob Cudlip
Crusher Martin	"Brother" Frank Jares		*Second Mug*	Mort Mills
			Max Ray	Ray Walker
Barney	Murray Alper		*Pete*	Bill Page
Betty	Lisa Wilson		*Dr. Howard*	George Eldredge
Sam	Leo "Ukie" Sherin		*Arena Messenger*	Meyer Grace
Referee	Mike Ruby		*Announcer*	Jimmy Cross

No Holds Barred follows the formula whereby Sach takes on an astonishing strength, which is exploited by Slip, which is coveted by thy neighbor.

In *Hold That Line* his strength comes from a creation in the chemistry lab; in *Jungle Gents*, pills give him the ability to smell diamonds; in *Master Minds*, his tooth furnishes him the power to read the future. Here, there is nothing to account for the floating muscle in Sach's body. The doctor concludes that Sach has unusual amounts of calcium on the brain. So much for doctors' scientific explanations for Bowery Boys phenomenon.

Slip triggers Sach's career as a wrestler much the same way some parents teach their children how to swim — by pushing them in. When wrestler Hombre Montana calls for volunteers, Slip pushes in the unsuspecting Sach. From then on, the only problem Slip has is knowing when to change Sach's name from Hammerin' Head Jones, to Flicking Fingers Jones, to Iron Elbows Jones, to Terrible Toes Jones. Special effects are well-executed when he kicks his opponents clear out of the arena.

What keeps the film somewhat interesting is the mystery of Sach's moving muscles and the game of wits between Slip and his chief rival, Pete Taylor.

"Your boy needs a manager, Mahoney," says Taylor. "Suppose I manage him and deal you in."

"Suppose I manage him and deal you out," Slip retorts.

While half the film is concerned with Sach as a wrestler, the other half is devoted to the various methods Taylor uses to achieve his aim. Slip reads in the newspaper that Sach's opponent for the orphanage milk fund benefit match, Tiger Thomas, has been killed in an automobile accident. As Slip lifts his eyes from the newspaper, who should be standing there but Pete Taylor and Mr. Hunter from the wrestling commission.

"I heard about Tiger Thomas' accident," says Taylor.

"Before or after?" asks a suspicious Slip.

Signing Terrible Toes to a match with Hombre Montana is not all Taylor wants. Like Skid Wilson in *Jalopy*, determined to learn what makes Slip's jalopy run so fast, Taylor needs to know just where Sach's power will be on the night of the fight. In both films a young, pretty girl invites the boys to a party to seduce information from them. In *No Holds Barred*, the girls' introduction is more discreet than in *Jalopy*. Gertie pretends she's having car trouble. When the boys help her, she invites them to a party. At the party, Sach spots one of Taylor's men and, posing as a waiter, interrupts Gertie and Slip sitting on the terrace. Sach is wonderful as the French waiter, and it is one of the few times that he stops Slip from being seduced.

Taylor tries again. This time he kidnaps the boys, much the same way Muggs is kidnapped in the East Side Kids' *Kid Dynamite*. Posing as photographers, two of Taylor's men have Slip and Sach stand near a car for pictures. The "photographers" tell the boys to wave goodbye to the camera. As soon as they do, they are pulled inside the car.

Throughout the series, Sach takes a great deal of physical and verbal abuse from many

Shot of the *No Holds Barred* cast and crew. Second row middle, left to right: Leo Gorcey, his wife Amelita Ward, unidentified actress, Huntz Hall. Second row from the top, right center (beneath tallest man), David Gorcey. Standing, third from right, in dark jacket: Bennie Bartlett.

people. Here, the crooks search for Sach's power by beating every part of his body. It is the worst physical abuse Sach receives in the series, and all Slip can do for him is try to dissuade the kidnappers from harming Sach any more than they already have. "Gentlemen," Slip pleads. "Peruse that frail, inhuman wreck, crumbling before your very eyes. I regurgitate, the power is gone."

No Holds Barred is one of three fight pictures geared for one climactic fight. *Mr. Hex* and *Fighting Fools* have other things going for them towards the end that increases the drama. In *Mr. Hex*, there's Danny the Dip and Evil Eye Fagin, who in their own way try to hinder Sach's success; it's also about Gabe Moreno and his moral dilemma. In *Fighting Fools*, there's the kidnapping of the fighter's kid brother. In *No Holds Barred*, what is suspenseful is not the fight itself, but finding out whether Sach has any more power and if so, where is it. Once that's known, the fight, for all practical purposes, is over. And as in the previous occasions, it is Slip who finds the strength as he gives his fighter a good-luck slap on his rear end.

As in *Angels' Alley*, Gorcey and Hall talk to each other at the end of the film. In light of where Sach's strength has decided to position itself, the next name for Sach becomes problematic. Slip whispers a few suggestions in Sach's ear, to which Sach responds, "Oh, no, you don't. We use that and we're out of pictures."

On the whole, *No Holds Barred* holds few surprises and few laughs. It is too single-dimensional. It could have been embellished with more plot twists.

Jalopy

Released February 15, 1953; 62 minutes; Monogram; Director, William Beaudine; Producer, Ben Schwalb; Screenplay, Tim Ryan, Jack Crutcher, Edmond Seward; Photography, Harry Neumann; Film Editor, William Austin; Art Director, David Milton; Musical Director, Marlin Skiles; Sound, Charles Cooper; Set Decorators, Robert Priestly; Wardrobe, Frank Beetson.

CAST

Slip	Leo Gorcey	*Party Guest*	Conrad Brooks
Sach	Huntz Hall	*Jalopy Drivers*	Robert Rose, George
Chuck	David [Condon]		Dockstader,
	Gorcey		George Barrows,
Butch	Bennie Bartlett		Fred Lamont,
Louie	Bernard Gorcey		Teddy Mangean,
Skid Wilson	Bob Lowery		Bud Wolfe, Carey
Red Baker	Murray Alper		Loftin, Louis
Bobbie Lane	Jane Easton		Tomei, Dude
Tony Lango	Richard Benedict		Criswell, Dick
Prof. Bosgood Elrod	Leon Belasco		Crockett, Pete
Girl	Mona Knox		Kellet, Carl Saxe
Announcer	Tom Hanlon		

What is admirable about this film, a mixture of *Crazy Over Horses, No Holds Barred* and *Hold That Line,* is its determination to produce the maximum in comedy from previous material. This is Ben Schwalb's Bowery Boys debut and, clearly, comedy blended into the plot is on his agenda.

In films where Sach contracts or invents something unusual, Slip is not doing anything but taking up space at Louie's. This is true for *No Holds Barred, Blues Busters* and *Master Minds.* But in *Jalopy,* while Sach and Prof. Elrod use Louie's back room for a laboratory, Slip is preoccupied with his "stupidsonic" jalopy, the "Meteor."

The boys are made aware of the mixture's potency while Slip tries conniving Louie out of some money. Though it's been seven films since Slip has approached Louie, he has not forgotten how, nor has Louie forgotten how to say no, at least for a while. But Slip does his best to convince.

"You'll get a sign embezzled on the car — 'Louie's Sweet Shop.'"

Where words do not work, Sach's formula does. At first Louie is not impressed. "Why don't you invent something that'll pay your bills?"

Slip orders Sach to relieve Louie from waxing the floors so that he can continue to convince the sweet shop owner to invest in the "Meteor." Sach pours some of his formula into the waxing machine. Instantly the machine takes off like an airplane.

Jalopy is the second Bowery Boys film about racing, the first being *Crazy Over Horses.*

But here Skid Wilson does not tamper with the race itself, as does Duke in *Crazy Over Horses*. Wilson wants to get his hands on the formula.

Like Taylor in *No Holds Barred*, Wilson invites the boys to a party to divert their attention. While the boys are at the party, Wilson & Co. sneak into the laboratory. They are discovered via a simple sight gag. When the boys return to the lab, Slip notices a hand reaching out and taking each ingredient as Prof. Elrod and Sach mix a new batch of formula. Slip tricks it by putting a beaker of boiling fluid in its grasp. The man behind the curtain shrieks. A rather long fistfight follows. The formula spills to the floor. Satisfied, Wilson and his men leave.

Usually when a hand (as in *High Society*) or a face (as in *Feudin' Fools*) or an umbrella (as in *Jinx Money*) appears from behind some obstruction, someone other than Slip is the first to see it. It is frustrating and unfunny trying to get Slip to see the elusive figure. But here it's Slip who spots the figure.

In a scene worthy of note, Sach is mixing his formula while Slip looks on. Every time Sach pours an ingredient, Slip turns his head and makes a funny face. The scene has a rhythm and a beat to it. It matches one in *Clipped Wings* where Sach pulls out of his bag a multitude of gifts for their jailed friend, Dave Moreno.

The time element is rarely a consideration in most Bowery Boys pictures. In *Let's Go Navy!* it is mentioned that the boys stay in the Navy for one year, though the sequence of events seems like a month or two. In *Blonde Dynamite*, Slip converts the sweet shop into an escort bureau in the course of Louie's one-week vacation. This transformation should take a couple of months at least. In *Jalopy*, the boys are made aware the evening before the race that a new batch of formula is needed. We witness Sach mixing a batch in a few minutes. Yet the next day Sach is late in delivering a new batch to the track, using the excuse that it takes a long time to mix. Of course, he is late so they could do the scene with him running after the "Meteor" on the track during the race.

When the formula is fed into the "Meteor," it speeds in reverse. In this manner, Slip wins the race.

Speeding in reverse sets the precedent for another backwards jalopy. In *Dig That Uranium*, the boys outdrive the pursuing rustlers bent on stealing their uranium. Both sequences are upbeat and suspenseful.

The Prof. Elrod character is superfluous since he has no special function. There is one scene that is amusing, however, where he suspects Slip of being a spy and refuses to mix the formula with Slip watching. Sach, siding with his colleague, forces Slip to stand with his back to the laboratory.

Magical appearances and disappearances are not uncommon phenomena in the Bowery Boys movies, and usually fit into the context of the story. In *Ghost Chasers*, Edgar the Ghost comes to Earth to expose fake spiritualists; the Genie in *Bowery to Bagdad* can make himself appear and disappear. And Mr. Bubb in *Up in Smoke* has a tendency to suddenly turn up in the strangest places. In *Jalopy*, when Sach spills his formula, there is an explosion and, once the smoke settles, a girl is present. The boys think the formula produced her, but actually she is Bobbie Lane, sent over by Skid Wilson to invite the boys to a party.

The gag is used again in the final scene. The formula is spilled and a beautiful blonde appears. Slip takes her arm and they go out. A little more formula spills and a girl with glasses appears. Prof. Elrod takes her arm.

Jalopy has a lot of rough edges, but what Bowery Boys film does not? What makes them forgivable is its willingness to experiment. Its daring is its biggest asset.

Loose in London

Released May 24, 1953; 63 minutes; Monogram; Director, Edward Bernds; Producer, Ben Schwalb; Original Story, Elwood Ullman; Photography, Harry Neumann; Art Director, David Milton; Musical Director, Marlin Skiles; Sound, Charles Cooper; Makeup, Eddie Polo; Set Decorator, Clarence Steensen; Special Effects, Ray Mercer; Alternative Title, *Bowery Knights*.

CAST

Slip	Leo Gorcey	*Earl of Waltingham*	Walter Kingsford
Sach	Huntz Hall	*Hoskins*	James Logan
Chuck	David [Condon] Gorcey	*Higby*	Alex Fraser
Louie	Bernard Gorcey	*Tall Girl*	Joan Shawlee
Butch	Bennie Bartlett	*Steward*	James Fairfax
Sir Percy Walsingham	Walter Kingsford	*Sir Talbot*	Wilbur Mack
Sir Edgar Whipsnade	John Dodsworth	*Taxi Driver*	Clyde Cook
Aunt Agatha	Norma Varden	*Bly*	Charles Keane
Reggie	William Cottrell	*Skinny Man*	Teddy Mangean
Lady Marcia	Angela Greene	*Lady Hightower*	Gertrude Astor
Herbert	Rex Evans	*Ames*	Matthew Boulton
		Pierre	Charles Wagenheim

Sach's surname lends itself well to a variety of episodes, including two about the distribution of family wealth.

Loose in London is also the first film that takes them abroad. *Loose in London*, *Jungle Gents* and *Paris Playboys* include brief but worthwhile tours of the locality. We are treated to some shots of historic London, Paris and the African jungle, along with a barrage of funny lines: "What about this guy Trafalgar?" asks Chuck. "Was he really a square?"

The boys refuse to acquiesce to the social etiquette of their new surroundings. Instead, their unpretentious behavior wins the heart of Sir Uncle Percy of Walsingham. Uncle Percy takes his alleged nephew's suggestion to stop taking medicine and start a diet of cookies, cakes and ice cream. His condition improves.

When Uncle Percy disappears and Sach declares, "I'll find my uncle if it takes every penny of his money," it's a declaration of generosity for he is first in line to receive the bulk of the earl's wealth — as opposed to the murderous intentions of the real relatives who have been filling his medicine bottle with poison.

Lady Marcia uses incongruous language for a British lady of her stature. When she learns that Uncle Percy is about to summon his lawyer to declare Sach his principal heir, she suggests, "We'll have to rub 'im out."

On their way over to London, the boys, in a very smooth sequence, outsmart the ship captain by hiding Louie when his drinking — unrevealed until now, and expanded upon in *Bowery to Bagdad* — gets the better of him.

Slip, using the same logic as he does with the master of ceremonies in *Crashing Las Vegas*, manages to secure passage on the ship for himself and the boys. "By the simple process of illumination, I don't see why one first class ticket on the *Blanca*, couldn't be traded for maybe four tickets on a smaller boat."

Louie is the only mature influence over the boys but sometimes he's attracted to frivolous and damaging diversions. The first takes place in *Lucky Losers*, where he catches gambling fever and puts his life at risk. In *Ghost Chasers*, he is a sucker for Madame Zola's séance. In *Hold That Line*, he tries to regain his youth by attending college with the boys and joining its football team.

As the boys are about to sail in *Loose in London*, Louie, in an unprecedented move, gets drunk and locks himself in the closet of the boys' stateroom during the bon voyage party. The party is crowded. This in itself is rather odd since there is never a hint that they have any other friends outside themselves. The party, like many other events that serves one particular purpose, is the means to get Louie accidentally on board to London. His presence uplifts the film for the moment, but once they arrive it is hardly felt.

In the boys' stateroom, there's a comic scene reminiscent of the Marx Brothers in *A Night at the Opera*: Slip pulls a clever trick to divert the captain's attention from the trunk in which Louie is hiding and smoking a cigar. Slip takes the captain over to the porthole to show him what someone mistook for a safe and threw out their watch out. This sends the captain laughing out the door, not noticing that the trunk is smoking like a chimney. This is the only humorous story Slip tells in the entire series.

When it becomes apparent that Sach is not kin to Percy Jones (though Slip maintains they are related when both chase a fox through the earl's living room), Sach is presented with £1,000 as a token of the earl's appreciation.

"It's heavy, but I'll take it." Hall's expert delivery is enough to bring a smile.

Walter Kingsford does a splendid job as Uncle Percy, particularly in how he conveys delight in the boys' company and painful distrust towards his real relatives.

Despite the constant comedy of *Loose in London*, the film could have done more. Another layer of conflict could have been added had there been some dissension on the part of one of the relatives. Instead, all speak as one voice. Since they do act and speak as one, Reggie and Lady Marcia would have been sufficient, better even, for the confrontation would appear to be more personal.

In the final analysis, what the film lacks in conflict and complexity, it makes up for in comedy.

Clipped Wings

Released August 14, 1953; 65 minutes; 5781 ft.; Monogram; Director, Edward Bernds; Producer, Ben Schwalb; Screenplay, Charles R. Marion, Elwood Ullman; Photography, Harry Neumann; Film Editor, Bruce B. Pierce; Art Director, David Milton; Musical Director, Marlin Skiles; Sound, Frank McWhorter; Wardrobe, Smoke Kring; Set Dresser, Bob Priestley; Dialogue Director, Tim Ryan; Makeup, Norman Pringle; Special Effects, Ray Mercer.

CAST

Slip	Leo Gorcey		Lt. Moreno	Todd Karns
Sach	Huntz Hall		Dorene	June Vincent
Louie	Bernard Gorcey		Mildred	Mary Treen
Chuck	David Condon		Eckler	Philip Van Zandt
Butch	Bennie Bartlett		Dupre	Frank Richards
W.A.F. Sergeant	Renie Riano		Sgt. White	Elaine Riley
Anderson			Hilda	Jeanne Dean

Allison	Anne Kimbell		*Sgt. Broski*	Henry Kulky
Target Plane	Lyle Talbot		*Federal Agent*	Arthur Space
Operator			*A.P.*	Lou Nova
Col. Davenport	Fay Roope		*Rookie*	Conrad Brooks

"Well," Slip, garbed in his Air Force uniform that gives him the title of basic airman Mahoney, fumes at Sach, "you certainly got us into an ambidextrous mess this time."

Slip's malapropism is on target since instead of making a left, as Sach advises, the boys turn right, heading straight to the Air Force recruiter's office demanding to see their friend Dave Moreno (as in Gabe Moreno of Bowery Boys past), who has been arrested for treason. No matter how much they insist they're only visitors, Slip is assigned to barrack "H" and Sach to Barrack "C." The misunderstanding extends to Sach's sexual identity as "C" is a W.A.F. (women's) unit. He constantly tells Slip he must keep his tea-time appointments, for one of his barrack mates is baking a cake and he doesn't want to insult her by not showing up.

In the midst of all the shenanigans, Slip reminds Sach about their "main purpose in life," to find Dave.

Slip sneaks into Barrack "C" to get Sach.

What gives Slip away is his shoes sticking out from underneath the blankets. Sgt. Anderson takes a baseball bat and whacks the soles of his feet. Sach, expecting trouble, switches off the light, and has the presence of mind to remember to take a ladder as he and Slip flee the barrack. (Director Edward Bernds misses an opportunity to show us how Sach manages to lug a huge ladder in the dark through a crowd of screaming women.)

Shoes under a blanket, and hitting someone with a baseball bat can be traced to two earlier pictures, *Crime School* and *Block Busters*. In *Crime School*, Cooper's only evidence that the kids have just returned from a forbidden outing is Hall wearing his shoes in bed. In *Block Busters*, being hit with a baseball bat is a requirement for admission to the East Side Kids club.

Once the boys climb through Dave's cell window, Sach, in the surrealistic vein of Harpo Marx, removes from his bag an incongruous collection of gifts—from a box of candy to an electric cement drill. This never-ending stream of inane objects is a welcomed switch of comic style, unforced and smoothly paced. When they leave they meet Sgt. Anderson and an AP.

"That guy can't do nutin to us. N-u-t-i-n, nutin." But Slip's estimation is as poor as his spelling.

While in jail, Sach receives his "flying wings" from a correspondence school. This gives him the confidence to climb into the cockpit of an airplane. As it turns out, it's a remote controlled target plane, and within minutes, it takes off, as does Bowery Boys comedy at its best.

The boys spot Dave, followed by what appears to be spies. Actually, they are FBI agents. The boys jump the agents. At the same moment, the real spies kidnap Dave. The boys run to the getaway car in time to cough up dust. The only vehicle available to chase them with is the target plane.

In minutes the plane ascends all by itself and the title of every chapter in Sach's flying manual is called "How to Face Death in the Air."

"Who wrote this book, an undertaker?" Slip screams in one of the rare occasions where he must rely on Sach to get them out of trouble.

Another reference to death is Slip's response to Sach's question as they are about to storm the spies' hideout.

"Chief, how come we never carry guns?"

"Because with you around, I'd wind up in the electric chair."

Gorcey gets whacked on the head by Renie Riano as Hall snickers in this publicity shot for *Clipped Wings*.

Clipped Wings, though loosely plotted, is a satiric view of how bureaucracy is the mother of ineptitude in the U.S. Air Force. Much of the footage is of the boys' separate experiences as Air Force rookies. Sach tangles his own bed sheets like an Arab sheik. Slip is incapable of watering a lawn without dousing a superior officer, or saluting without knocking himself in the head with a brick that he forgets is in his hand.

What these separate scenes reveal more than anything else is Gorcey's dependency on Hall to be funny. Without Hall, Gorcey relies on his character's self-righteousness to captivate the audience. Sach seems to know this too and tells him so when injected with the truth serum after the crooks are shot with it and spill their guts.

"Chief, you're nothing but an egotistical, ignorant egomaniac. And that's the truth."

Hall fares without Gorcey much better than Gorcey does without Hall, especially in his scenes with Renie Riano as Sgt. Anderson. Her exasperation in the face of personnel incompetence, coupled with the problem of handling Sach, is extraordinarily well-done and a perfect vehicle for Sach. He knocks her off her pedestal of authority by getting her to reveal how nice and warm it is to wear long underwear.

It has been three years and nine films since Gabriel Dell played Gabe Moreno, the "outside" member of the gang. Returning with an unknown actor to play this part does not work. We want Gabe!

Private Eyes

Released December 6, 1953; 64 minutes; 5801 ft.; Allied Artists; Director, Edward Bernds; Producer, Ben Schwalb; Screenplay, Elwood Ullman, Edward Bernds; Photography, Carl Guthrie; Film Editor, Lester A. Sansom; Art Director, David Milton; Music Director, Marlin Skiles; Sound, Charles Cooper; Set Decorator, Clarence Steenson; Wardrobe, Smoke Kring; Makeup, Norman Pringle; Working title, *Bowery Bloodhounds*.

CAST

Slip	Leo Gorcey		*Soapy*	William Phillips
Sach	Huntz Hall		*Al*	Gil Perkins
Chuck	David [Condon] Gorcey		*Chico*	Peter Mamakos
			Karl	Lee Van Cleef
Butch	Bennie Bartlett		*Oskar*	Lou Lubin
Louie	Bernard Gorcey		*Patient*	Emil Sitka
Herbie	Rudy Lee		*Andy the Cop*	Tim Ryan
Myra Hagen	Joyce Holden		*Aggie the Nurse*	Edith Leslie
Damon	Robert Osterloh		*Eddie the Detective*	Chick Chandler
Graham	William Forrest			

Sach's mind-reading ability, a talent brought on by nine-year-old Herbie's terrific wallop to Sach's nose, inspires the boys to purchase (with Louie's money of course) Eddie's Eagle Eye Detective Agency.

As Slip idly scans the newspaper, and Sach spends his time cleaning the office, Slip remarks, "Maybe we should get into a business that's a bit more ludicrous."

As in *Hard Boiled Mahoney*, where the boys are also detectives, a pretty but untrustworthy woman barges into their office begging for help. Her opening line and Sach's response are so cherished that they're repeated by Lady Zelda and Sach five films later in *Spy Chasers*.

"Strange men are following me."

"They'd be stranger if they didn't."

And like Laura of *Hold That Baby!*, Myra leaves something significant behind, a mink coat and a sealed envelope, clues that will eventually lead the boys to an international fur smuggling ring. Not recognizing a clue when it's staring them in the face, the boy detectives hock the mink for $50.

When John Graham enters, introducing himself as a representative for the Apex Insurance Company, and offers a $10,000 reward for information leading to Myra's capture, Slip exclaims, "Ten thousand dollars! There ain't that much money in all of New York!"

Myra, like Laura, is kept at a sanitarium against her will. Since the idea of Sach posing as a patient worked so well in *Hold That Baby!*, it's used again, but more imaginatively. Seeing Slip and Sach together in costume, posing as an Austrian doctor and elderly woman patient, is a comic event. The roles are not new to them, however. Hall, as Glimpy in *Clancy Street Boys*, posed as Muggs' sister, and Slip made a brief appearance as a doctor in *Spook Busters*.

Gorcey gives his character heart, speaking with a heavy European accent and wearing thick eyeglasses that cause him to bump into things. Sach gets away with well-aimed kicks and punches to suspected fur thieves without being suspected. When Sach suddenly becomes ill and requires the immediate attention of a doctor, Slip is only too happy to provide. A few slaps on the head does the trick.

Sach (Hall) flies in *Private Eyes*.

In spite of their almost identical roles, Myra is not exactly innocent, while Laura in *Hold That Baby!* is innocent to the core; dumb, but innocent. By leaving her baby at the laundromat, she is taking a precautionary measure against her sinister aunts. Myra, however, is connected in some way (the picture never explains how) with organized crime. This becomes clear when she seduces Carl, a dimwitted muscleman who defies his boss' orders and helps Myra escape.

The envelope is locked in a safe, along with the combination, thanks to Sach. In *Crazy Over Horses* he fails to exchange the horses and Slip punishes him severely. Here Slip orders him to remain in the office while the rest search for Myra to collect the $10,000. But just as Sach is ashamed and tries to make amends in *Crazy Over Horses*, here too he tries to compensate for his thoughtlessness by blowing up the safe. Hall gives an amusing solo performance as he prepares the dynamite. But the blast takes away his ability to read minds, not that he uses it much after all.

The idea of Sach being hit and hurt by a small boy is not funny, not new, and disturbing as it was in *News Hounds*.

When Herbie shows up again at the boys' office, Chico and Al are trying to force the boys to hand over the envelope. Failing this, they kidnap Herbie. Like Boomer in *Fighting Fools*, Herbie manages to sneak a telephone call to the boys and gives them the address of the sanitarium. A grandiose chase scene takes place, resulting in victory for the young detectives.

Lee Van Cleef and Emil Sitka add color to their parts as the dimwitted Carl and a wheel-chair patient. Unfortunately, the same cannot be said about the other actors, especially Joyce Holden. As Myra, she is unappealing and her seduction of Carl is unconvincing. In fact, the whole romantic affair is mishandled, beginning on an insincere note and ending with Carl and Myra remaining together for the rest of the film. Myra's intentions throughout the entire film are unclear, which is a failure on the part of the scriptwriters.

The mystery of the stolen mink and the sealed envelope should be sufficient to inspire detective work. It goes over the boys' heads. In fact, they do very little detective work. They do more detective work in *Hard Boiled Mahoney,* where they are mistaken for detectives.

Nevertheless, *Private Eyes,* though weakly plotted, is fast and funny.

Perhaps recalling the days as Spit, Bim or Muggs, when the community tried to accommodate the kids' restlessness, Slip converts the sanitarium into a Bowery Club to keep the kids off the streets.

Paris Playboys

Released March 7, 1954 62 minutes; 5602 ft.; Allied Artists; Director, William Beaudine; Producer, Ben Schwalb; Screenplay, Elwood Ullman, Edward Bernds; Photography, Harry Neumann; Film Editors, John Fuller, Lester A. Sansom; Art Director, David Milton; Music, Marlin Skiles; Production Manager, Allen K. Wood; Set Decorator, Robert Priestly; Wardrobe, Smoke Kring; Set Continuity, John Franco.

CAST

Slip	Leo Gorcey	*Celeste*	Marianne Lynn
Sach/Le Beau	Huntz Hall	*Chuck*	David [Condon]
Louie Dumbrowski	Bernard Gorcey		Gorcey
Mimi	Veola Vonn	*Butch*	Bennie Bartlett
Gaspard	Steven Geray	*Pierre*	Alphonse Martell
Vidal	John Wengraf	*Cambon*	Gordon Clark

The spirit of adventure runs high in *Paris Playboys,* the second film in which the boys are taken abroad. It is also the third of five films where the focus is on Sach; his sense of smell (*Jungle Gents*), his brains (*The Bowery Boys Meet the Monsters*), his sixth sense (*Private Eyes*), his surname (*Loose in London*) and his looks (*Paris Playboys*). The writers seem to have transformed Sach into a cartoon character from whom we can expect and enjoy absolute lunacy. Here he is the spitting image of the famous professor Maurice Gaston Le Beau, who disappears out of fear his in-progress discovery of new rocket fuel will be sabotaged. Sach's presence is required to bait the saboteurs.

Behaving as themselves in Paris is something they can afford to do, since a report preceding their arrival warns that the professor has gone slightly mad. This situation provides for a great deal of flexibility. The result is a fun-filled caper with the saboteurs keeping the plot moving by means of an occasional stab at hastening the professor's (Sach's) recovery from amnesia.

In one instance, towards the middle of the film, while Sach is preparing for bed, the audience sees a gloved hand holding a knife, sneaking from behind the bedroom door. When the knife is thrown at Sach, he is frightened and awakens Slip, who believes his pal is having hallucinations.

"If there isn't a knife there, you better evaporate."

Louie's Yiddishisms are more prominent here than in other films. When Slip says that Sach does not know one word of French, Sach objects.

"Schlemiel, right, Louie?"

"You're a schlemiel in *any* language."

When the real Maurice Gaston Le Beau quietly returns, he is greeted not with the fanfare surrounding Sach's arrival but by Louie only.

"What's the matter, Sachela?" Louis asks Le Beau affectionately.

"Get out of my house and do not call me by that horrible name, 'Sachela.'"

After both Slip and Louie get the brunt of Le Beau's anger, they meet each other in the hall and say simultaneously, "Sach has gone nuts."

"He needs a doctor," cries Slip.

"He's gone meshugah," Louie says.

"So we'll get a meshugah doctor."

It is on the strength of the satiric encounters at the dinner table, at his easel, at Le Beau's favorite Parisian cafe, his fiddling about in the laboratory, and his affair with his fiancée, Mimi, that the success of the film rests.

Bernard Gorcey (in bed) and Leo Gorcey in *Paris Playboys*.

Since the guests do not want to embarrass the professor, they imitate Sach's every move. It is hilarious to watch the ladies discard caviar to eat instead its bed of crushed ice; season the finger bowl before drinking its water; and pop peanuts in their mouths from six feet in the air.

To help bring back Sach's memory, the French saboteurs, camouflaged among his colleagues, encourage him to enjoy his familiar leisure activities. This includes some hours at his easel and an afternoon at a Parisian cafe.

Although the audience is not given a good view of Sach's painting, it doesn't matter. The critic concedes his confusion by the cluttered canvas.

"It's called Sun Behind the Alps," Sach, as Le Beau, explains.

"Yes, but where is zee sun?"

"Behind the Alps."

"Oh, I understand. But where is zee Alps?" "You can't see it because of the fog."

Later, when the real Prof. Le Beau sees the painting, he is appalled, but after a few brush strokes of his own, he's quite satisfied with it. Apparently his taste is much like his imposter's as his understanding of art no better than the art critic's.

The scene at the Parisian cafe is worthy for its special effects. Slip, Sach and Louie are taken to the cafe by one of the saboteurs so that Le Beau may enjoy his special drink.

"Don't you know? You are the only person in France who dares to drink it."

"I am? I mean, I am, I am."

Not to be outdone, Slip and Louie order the same drink. The camera focuses on Slip, Sach and Louie individually as they drink the smokey liquid. The smoke emanates from Louie's ears, Sach's hair stands on end, and Slip's bow tie spins like a propeller.

Le Beau's return coincides with the announcement of Sach and Mimi's wedding day, which Le Beau reads about in a two-month-old newspaper while basking in the Hawaiian sun, being fanned and fed grapes by beautiful Hawaiian girls. This isn't the first time the writers ignore a timing conflict. According to the newspapers, the boys have been in Paris for at least two months. But when the scene returns to Paris, there is no indication of any lapse in time.

Hall gives the character of Le Beau a personality unlike Sach. Le Beau is arrogant, short-tempered and impulsive. The fact that Hall can play him so convincingly shows that he could expand his acting horizons beyond the Sach character.

The filmmakers have fun with the notion that nobody knows Le Beau has returned and the boys are in a frenzy about Sach, who they think is losing his mind because of his uncharacteristic behavior. He beats Slip over the head with his own hat and challenges him to a duel.

The image of the mirror as an agent of knowledge is common in literary and film history. In the Marx Brothers' *Duck Soup*, one brother plays the mirror image of the other in one of the most outstanding comedy routines. In *Paris Playboys*, Sach and Le Beau first encounter each other through a mirror. Sach straightens what he thinks is the mirror image of his own loose tie. It's funny, well-timed, and demonstrate some metaphorical kinship with the classics.

The only problem in the scenes with Sach and Le Beau together is the obvious editing job, conspicuous by an additional person who plays the other Hall character when both Sach and Le Beau are in view.

As in *Jalopy*, food is the missing ingredient for the rocket formula. It is not until the climax when the saboteurs have the boys and Le Beau in the laboratory and force Sach at gunpoint to produce the formula that Sach, at a loss of what else to do, adds sour cream to his mixture, and lights the rocket. The rocket takes off like fireworks.

As the bearded French dignitary gives Sach his reward, Sach pulls an electric razor out of his own pocket and gives it to the dignitary. The dignitary is surprised. Sach explains, "An electrical razor. Turn it on, have a ball."

And that's just what viewers of *Paris Playboys* would do.

The Bowery Boys Meet the Monsters

Released June 6, 1954: 66 minutes; Allied Artists; Director, Edward Bernds; Producer, Ben Schwalb; Screenplay, Elwood Ullman, Edward Bernds; Photography, Harry Neumann; Film Editor, William Austin; Art Director, David Milton; Musical Director, Marlin Skiles; Production Supervisor, Allen K. Wood; Sound, Ralph Butler; Special Effects, Augie Lohman; Set Decorator, Joseph Kish; Hairdressor, Mary Smith; Wardrobe, Bert Henrikson; Set Continuity, John L. Banse.

CAST

Slip	Leo Gorcey	*Amelia*	Ellen Corby
Sach	Huntz Hall	*Francine*	Laura Mason
Chuck	David Gorcey	*Gorgo*	Norman Bishop
	[Condon]	*Cosmos*	Steve Calvert
Butch	Bennie Bartlett	*Herbie*	Rudy Lee
Derek	John Dehner	*Officer Martin*	Paul Bryar
Anton	Lloyd Corrigan	*O'Meara*	Pat Flaherty
Grissom	Paul Wexler	*Skippy Biano*	Jack Diamond

The only film to include the series' name in its title is an innovated science fiction delight, never dull, wonderfully funny.

To eliminate the barrage of baseballs crashing through Louie's Sweet Shop window, the boys approach the mysterious Gravesend brothers, Derek and Anton, who own the Clark Street lot. Each is working separately to discover the man of the future; both need a human brain with a "small brain count" to complete their respective experiments. When Slip calls, it's like an answer to their prayers.

"There is a little matter I'd like to disgust with you. It refrains to the lot. I'm what you call a benefracture of humanity. The matter being highly contagious, I would like me and my accomplice to come out there and prevaricate with you in person. Are you going to coagulate with us or not?"

Anton Gravesend, a twerpy man, concocts a "beautifying potion" to improve Slip's looks and tests it on Grissom, the butler. Grissom becomes a hideous monster. Towards the end of the film, the potion spills into Sach's mouth and Sach becomes the wild man Grissom had become. Single-handedly he overpowers the doctors and Grissom.

For his anthropoid ape, Derek Gravesend chooses Sach after he hears Sach's theory on how to make pickles prettier.

"You see, before you plant the seeds, you turn them inside out. Then, instead of having warts, they'd have dimples."

As amazed as Derek and Anton are at this idea, Sach is equally amazed by the sweater Amelia Gravesend (Ellen Corby in *The Waltons*) is knitting for her nephew.

Sach (Hall), transformed into a monster, chokes Slip (Gorcey) while wearing his hat in *Bowery Boys Meet the Monsters.*

"Aren't the sleeves a little short?" No, Sach simply mistook the two necklines for the sleeves.

When Slip goes downstairs to "persecute a few calories," Sach warns him, "Chief, if ya see someone with two heads, don't speak to it, let it talk to itself."

The house itself is booby-trapped with the usual haunted house gimmicks. There's a well-paced scene in which Sach feels for a clock and comes face to face with a skull. Startled, he jumps out of bed and heads for the closet; out pops a skeleton.

"Oh I see you found our skeleton in the closet," Grissom says as he suddenly appears. He leaves Sach with these parting words of comfort: "The living of today are the skeletons of tomorrow." Paul Wexler, with his cadaver-like features, is perfect in the part of Grissom.

The most exotic artifice is Amelia's carnivorous plant. Fashioned after the anthropomorphic trees in *The Wizard of Oz,* the plant uses its branches to engulf its prey and force it into its "mouth." Although it does not talk, it does belch after devouring a can of dog food and expectorating the can. Slip, holding a tray of food, hears the belch, stops with his back to the plant and reflects on the sound he just heard. The plant gobbles up the food with one branch, and slurps the milk with a twig. Clever, but forced.

There's another forced scene with Derek and Anton pulling Sach's arms in opposite directions. The door is locked but through the window above the door. Slip shouts instructions:

"Routine six! Kick one in the shins, the other give the elbow!" The scene expects the audience to ignore the main action in the foreground, and for Anton and Derek to be taken by surprise following this loud exchange between Slip and Sach.

In an earlier scene, the boys are locked in a closet. Cutting implements fall from a shelf and the boys cut a hole through the thin wall. On the other side of the wall is Cosmos the ape. Sach goes through the hole while Slip puts away the tools. Isn't *he* the orderly one (compared to Gorcey in real life, who put a hole in his ceiling shooting at a mosquito*). Why? This allows Sach time to come back into the closet only for Slip to throw him back out without realizing there's an ape on the other side. It's a routine gag, Slip unaware of some danger with Sach too scared to utter any warning.

When Louie comes looking for Slip and Sach, he is bound and gagged and put into a closet. When he frees himself, he calls the police. While Louie is on the phone, Cosmos the ape puts his paw on his shoulder, and Louie believes it is Slip. Why? He really shouldn't; just as there is no reason for the ape to wait to be seen before attacking Louie. What makes this scene insincere is that when Slip does appear, his natural reaction is to scream in astonishment at seeing Louie.

Grissom's search for the boys borrows choice material from a Walter Huston classic: He is given a hatchet and a basket big enough for a head. Running around the house with this equipment, he is reminiscent of Humphrey Bogart in *The Treasure of the Sierra Madre* where Bogart is running in the forest holding a shovel, intending to bury his companion, who is still very much alive. Both morbidly funny.

Before leaving the mansion, Slip tactfully places a pen in Derek's hand and has him sign the lease over to the Clark Street lot. Though the film leaves the Gravesends and the ape to their fate, we are left asking ourselves how Gorog the robot, now the home run champ of the little league Bowery Tigers, got his chassis repaired and how, without the benefit of a human head, it has feelings, evident by its hostile reaction to the boys calling him a "pile of junk." The irony of it all: Gorog has only to bunt to put a hole through the Sweet Shop window.

The film succeeds because it does not pretend to be anything else but comedy, as opposed to *Fightin' Fools* and *Angels in Disguise* which mix comedy and drama. In the www.scifilm.org review (9/27/2003), Dave Sindelar called it "the best of the Bowery Boys movies I've seen ... done with a certain energy...." That's true.

Jungle Gents

Released September 5, 1954; 64 minutes; 5673 ft.; Allied Artists; Director, Edward Bernds; Producer, Ben Schwalb; Screenplay, Elwood Ullman, Edward Bernds; Photography, Harry Neumann; Art Director, David Milton; Music, Marlin Skiles; Production Supervisor, Allen K. Wood; Sound, Ralph Butler; Editor, Lester Sansom; Set Continuity, John Banse; Hairdresser, Maudlee MacDougall; Makeup, Eddie Polo; Wardrobe, Bert Henrikson; Special Effects, Augie Lohman.

CAST

Slip	Leo Gorcey	*Chuck*	David Gorcey
Sach	Huntz Hall	*Butch*	Bennie Bartlett

*Gorcey, Leo, Jr., Me and the Dead End Kid, page 282.

Louie	Bernard Gorcey	*Lomax*	Murray Alper
Grimshaw	Patrick O'Moore	*Tarzan*	Jett Norman [Clint Walker]
Dr. Goebel	Rudolph Anders		
Dan Shanks	Harry Cording	*Capt. Daly*	Emory Parnell
Malaka	Woody Strode	*Painter on Boat*	Emil Sitka
Annatia	Laurette Luez	*Omotawa*	Roy Glenn
Rangori	Joel Fluellen	*Harmes*	John Harmon
Trader Holmes	Eric Snowden	*Officer Cady*	Pat Flaherty

Culturally, geographically and demographically, the farthest place on Earth from the Bowery is Africa. The boys confront wild animals, untracked terrain and warlike tribesmen who shrink strangers' heads for sport.

The reason for the trip is Sach's unique ability to smell diamonds, a side effect of the pills he takes for his "sinus infatuation." Stretching the wonders of medicine to fantastic extremes, the doctor confirms that the size of the pill, coupled with the size of Sach's nose, make such a phenomenon highly probable. What medical school did he go to?

Like the opening scenes in *Loose in London*, we are given a glimpse of the locale. The boys are in awe as they observe a "striped horse" (zebra) and a giraffe; "I wouldn't want to be the vegetarian that has to swab that neck."

Physical strength among people of the wild is an important trait. In *Dig That Uranium*, Mountainman McKenzie nearly breaks Sach's fingers when he shakes his hand in greeting. But nowhere is physical power more apparent than in Annatia the Jungle Woman. With only a knife, she kills a charging lion. She doesn't even claim credit when the natives hail Sach as a god for killing the lion bare-handed. The only thing she wants, and says in the entire film, is "kiss, kiss, kiss."

Sach is entrusted with the map leading them to the cave where an old sea captain's fortune in diamonds is hidden. In a frantic search for paper to start a fire, Sach inadvertently burns the map. When Grimshaw, their guide and sponsor, asks Sach to look at the map to see how they might get out of the thick brush, Sach, too embarrassed to tell the truth, tears an ad for women's girdles out of a mail order catalogue (why such a thing is at hand in the jungle is beyond logic), and pretends it's the map.

"Out of it? I have no idea how one gets into it."

Of course the boys are followed by bad guys, Goebel and Shanks, who plan to steal the diamonds once the boys find them. Goebel concludes that Sach must know he's being followed. This naiveté on the part of the bad guys is similar to the bad guy in *Dig That Uranium*, who thinks Sach as the "brains of the outfit." Goebel and Shanks commission a warlike tribe to capture the boys and Grimshaw, promising their heads (except Sach's) for shrinkage.

Resourceful Slip can outsmart anybody no matter whose turf he's on. He gets the idea for Sach to catch a cold, rendering his sense of smell useless. But Goebel gets a witch doctor to cure Sach's cold. Sach has fun with the witch doctor, and consequently so do we. While the witch doctor dances, Sach remarks, "Even if you don't cure me, I dig the floor show. Where did you get your degree? I know doctors in New York who can't dance a step."

Who saves him? Annatia! She whacks the witch doctor on the head, then puckers her lips: "Kiss, kiss, kiss."

For those who doubt the consistency of the "routines," Routine Eleven is visually and verbally defined in *Jungle Gents* as it is in *Bowery Battalion*. Slip says, "Let's capture the witch doctor and hold him as a hostess. Routine Eleven." In *Bowery Battalion*, Louie utters, "Routine Eleven" as he's being kidnapped.

Top: A shell-shocked Sach (Hall) in *Jungle Gents*. *Bottom:* All jungle girl Laurette Luez wants to do is kiss, kiss, kiss Huntz Hall (notice the fly swatter around his neck) in *Jungle Gents*.

Dressed as the witch doctor, Sach makes the tribesmen "bow their heads like a flock of Austrians." As they run through the jungle, chased by the natives, Slip cries, "We gotta out-manure them."

Hunting for jewelry in a cave is the climactic scene as it will be again three years later in *Hold That Hypnotist*. The scene in *Jungle Gents* is more imaginative. A stick, imbedded in the rocks like a one-arm bandit, hits Sach on the head. Sach gets angry and tries to rip it out of its socket. Lo and behold, a spout appears in the rocks and releases a flow of diamonds. At that moment Goebel and Shanks arrive. But a ghost, alleged to be the spirit of the old sea captain, floats by. Using Routine Nine, the boys subdue Goebel and Shanks and wrestle the ghost to the ground. The ghost is really Trader Holmes, friend of Grimshaw.

Gorcey, narrating most of the film, helps fill the passages of time and keeps the picture moving smoothly. Artistically it is better than most, with close-ups of the lion and long shots of jungle animals obviously clips from another feature. The set design of the African camp and the tribe seem based on the Hollywood B-movie perception of Africa which closely resembles its perception of American Indians. The natives dwell in huts, put on war paint and howl like American Indians.

Jungle Gents puts to good use all the ingredients for a wild jungle safari and maintains a balanced measure of comedy and difficult conflicts.

Bowery to Bagdad

Released January 2, 1955 [in England, October 1954]; 64 minutes; Allied Artists; Director, Edward Bernds; Producer, Ben Schwalb; Screenplay, Elwood Ullman, Edward Bernds; Photography, Harry Neumann; Film Editor, John C. Fuller; Music Director, Marlin Skiles; Art Director, David Milton: Production Manager, Allen K. Wood; Assistant Director, Edward Morey; Sound, Ralph Butler; Set Decorator, Joseph Kish; Special Effects, Augie Lohman; Wardrobe, Bert Henrikson; Makeup, Eddie Polo; Hairdresser, Mary Smith.

CAST

Slip	Leo Gorcey		*Canarsie*	Rayford Barnes
Sach	Huntz Hall		*Tiny*	Michael Ross
Chuck	David Gorcey		*Genie*	Eric Blore
	[Condon]		*Selim*	Rick Vallin
Butch	Bennie Bartlett		*Abdul*	Paul Barnes
Louie	Bernard Gorcey		*Claire*	Jean Willes
Velma	Joan Shawlee		*Caliph*	Charlie Lung
Dolan	Robert Bice		*Man*	Leon Burbank
Gus	Dick Wessel			

If Aladdin's Lamp is somewhere in the world, it can certainly turn up in the Bowery.

The title should actually read *Bagdad to Bowery*, for this film begins in sixth-century Iraq, with the Caliph of Bagdad ordering his two retainers to search for the missing magical lamp. Following this are decent superimposed scenes of the two Arabs traveling the world over, conveying changes in time, distance and apparel, from ancient to western, save their turbans. The impression is that these men have wandered since the 6th century, and now Abdul

Slip (Gorcey) picking on somebody his own size (Michael Ross) in *Bowery to Bagdad*.

and Selim, the final descendants of the two Arabs must continue the interminable search. When they do get their hands on the lamp, Rick Vallin (from *Ghosts on the Loose*) and Paul Marion, as the Arabs, fight like children, marking the end to the collective cause of their ancestors. These characters are magically whisked back to Bagdad by the Genie himself.

Then there's Slip and Sach. Slip is annoyed that Sach spent good money for "that putrid piece of pewter."

"Now if you can get your two bits back for it, that would be real magic."

The Genie is delightfully played by Eric Blore, a stout, likable fellow with an English accent, draped in a Persian garb and headdress. He announces he is slave to whomever holds the lamp. It happens to be Sach.

"Buddy, didn't I always give you what was mine?" Slip pouts.

"No!" Sach answers defiantly.

"Well, buddy, didn't you always give me what was yours?"

"Yes!"

And through this distorted logic, Sach shares ownership of the lamp with his pal, Slip.

"Henceforth and forever, you take orders from both of us only, jointly and together."

Sach asks for six malteds. The malteds consumed, Sach wants muscles so he can protect Louie from the thugs trying to take over Louie's Sweet Shop.

Slip, on the other hand, says, "I want one million dollars and I want it on that table."

One million dollars in gold bars appears. Slip demands folding money. The Genie whisks away the gold and himself.

Why? By disappearing with the million dollars, it is a warning that the Genie cannot be trusted.

When the thugs get the lamp, it's useless without Slip and Sach. Velma, posing as a Southern belle, is sent to lure the boys to the thugs' penthouse apartment.

The second half of the film is one big chase scene with either Slip or Sach escaping whenever the other is caught. But the scenes are well-staged and the chase is fast-paced, funny and diversified, with the Arabs engaging in a fistfight with the thugs, Slip being kept in a storage closet, and Sach hiding in a closet and coming out with a coat bag over his head.

Louie arrives and meets the Genie in the winery. There the two elders share a few bubbly hours. It is the second time we witness Louie's weakness to drink, though here it's not as consequential as in *Loose in London*.

Sach, with the coat bag over his head, blindly walks onto the building ledge. Slip goes out to save him. Hanging on for dear life, they still notice below a car going through a red light. The drama increases when the bad guys shoot at them. Sach suddenly remembers he has the lamp.

To be sure, the Genie performs only one real magic act for the boys and even that isn't quite right. The boys demand to be taken home. The Genie takes them to *his* home, Bagdad. The boys find themselves dressed just like the Genie, with beautiful girls feeding them grapes. One of them grabs the lamp and throws it to the Caliph. In the world of the Bowery Boys' you can't trust women no matter *what* century they live in.

With their lives threatened, the boys ask to be sent back to New York. Suddenly they are back on the ledge.

This whole sequence shows how untrustworthy the Genie is. He puts them in a position to lose the lamp by bringing them to Bagdad, then plays a dirty trick by putting them back on the ledge. In the end it is not the Genie who saves them but the familiar men in blue.

Bowery to Bagdad loses its appeal when the emphasis shifts from the Genie in Louie's back room to the thugs at the penthouse. At that point the Genie is wastefully ignored. Nor does it seem that the filmmakers realize they make a liar out of him.

The final scene, however, is skillfully written and reveals how their shaky partnership as masters of the Genie ruins their chance to profit from the lamp.

The scene opens with them sulking, sitting around a table at Louie's.

"We could have had the whole world in all of its glory right in the palm of our hands. What have we got to show for it? Nuttin'."

Suddenly, the Genie appears. His current master has allowed him to give the boys one last wish. The atmosphere changes from dreary to cheery. Sach is about to say something but Slip cuts him off, calling him a "marendering maniac."

Insulted, angry, and frustrated by his own gutlessness, Sach mumbles to himself, "I wish I had the nerve to sock him in the chin."

Done. And the Genie disappears forever.

High Society

Released April 17, 1955; 61 minutes; 5513 ft.; Allied Artists; Director, William Beaudine; Producer, Ben Schwalb; Screenplay, Bert Lawrence, Jerome S. Gottler; Story, Elwood Ullman,

Edward Bernds; Photography, Harry Neumann; Film Editors, John C. Fuller, Lester Sansom; Music Director, Marlin Skiles; Art Director, David Milton; Sound, Ralph Butler; Production Manager, Allen K. Wood; Set Decorator, Joseph Kish; Wardrobe, Bert Henrikson; Makeup, Eddie Polo; Set Continuity, Gloria Morgan; Special Effects, Ray Mercer.

CAST

Slip	Leo Gorcey	*Stuyvesant*	Dayton Lummis
Sach	Huntz Hall	*Terwilliger*	Ronald Keith
Clarissa	Amanda Blake	*Frisbie*	Gavin Gordon
Louie	Bernard Gorcey	*Cosgrove*	Addison Richards
Chuck	David Gorcey	*Marten*	Kem Dibbs
	[Condon]	*Palumbo*	David Barry
Butch	Bennie Bartlett	*Baldwin*	Paul Harvey

"Dere's only one ting more important den da money," says Slip as he softly claps his hands three times on his next words for emphasis: "When are we going to get it?"

This line (and its delivery) is one of the many polished parts of this picture in which the spotlight is shared by Slip, Sach and 12-year-old Master Twigg. All await the distribution of deceased Pierrepont Jones' wealth. All are the intended victims of an inheritance swindle.

Throughout the series, Slip has had a few magical moments hiding from bad guys. In *Trouble Makers*, he keeps his presence in Silky Thomas' closet a secret, even while the criminal is getting dressed; in *Jail Busters*, he covers his face completely with shaving cream. In *High Society*, he outsmarts the bad guys by hiding under the desk. After Stuyvesant checks the documents and locks the drawer, Slip unlocks it before Stuyvesant pulls out the key. When Stuyvesant and Martin leave, Slip removes the birth certificate.

Louie is asked to verify the birth certificate, implying that Louie knows something about Sach's childhood.

"In the first place, his mother wasn't Gwendolyn, it was Gertie."

This knowledge is quite a surprise. How far back do the boys and Louie go? The impression has always been that the boys hang out at Louie's Sweet Shop because he tolerates them, not that Louie knew them when they were kids.

Slip's ingenuity prevails when the boys, Louie, Master Twigg, and Frisbey are locked in a guarded room upstairs, while Sach is downstairs under duress to sign papers clearing the way for him to receive the Jones fortune, and subsequently have it stolen from him by Stuyvesant & Co. Slip's objective is to induce the guard, Martin, to open the door so he can hit him on the head and escape. The plan starts with wire: Slip rips out an electric cord, ties one end around Master Twigg and lets him down through the window. The next time we see him, he's on the second floor attracting Martin's attention. Martin grabs him, opens the door and gets klonked on the head. The scene provides a good climactic counterpoint to the action downstairs.

Meanwhile, Sach is doing a splendid job stalling for time. He pretends there is no ink in the pen, but when he shakes it, ink splatters all over Cosgrove; he declares he does not sign anything without a lawyer present ("Who do you think we are, plumbers?"); and demands to read the entire document before signing. All in all there is plenty going on upstairs and downstairs.

As in *Paris Playboys*, there is a dinner scene in which Sach astonishes everyone with his bizarre behavior. At the table, Sach expresses dissatisfaction with the hot menu.

"Would you have preferred a cold plate, Cousin Horace?" asks Master Twigg.

"Sure, I'll try anything once," says Sach, who now proceeds to join the company of Charlie Chaplin (who eats a shoe in *The Gold Rush*) and Harpo Marx (who eats a telephone in *The Coconuts*) by devouring the china.

In a rather silly scene, Slip and Sach do Edward G. Robinson and James Cagney imitations, telling Master Twigg the master bedroom now belongs to Sach. Sach is particularly ridiculous doing the imitation dressed in a Little Lord Fauntleroy outfit.

Master Twigg, adequately played by Ronald Keith, has some choice scenes of his own. His well-executed practical joke is sprung on the adults while they are seated, listening and watching a piano concerto with all the polite affectation of culture. Master Twigg puts a few fleas in Sach's socks and the latter begins to scratch feverishly. The youngster accidentally drops the whole container of fleas, and soon the pianist, who does a wonderful imitation of Liberace, is playing to an audience of itchy people. The scene is excellently performed as an ensemble and perfectly timed. One by one, members of the audience are affected by the fleas. They scratch once and stop. They scratch again, pause and scratch continuously until the epidemic affects the pianist. It is the best scene in the picture, and among the best comical moments in the series.

Though *High Society* is the fourth and last film that opens with the boys owning and operating a business, it is not essential to the story as in the other three films, *Spook Busters*, *Trouble Makers* and *Hold That Baby!* Whereas Laura Andrews in *Hold That Baby!* selects the boys' Laundromat to hide her baby *because* it's a laundromat, Mr. Stuyvesant's choice of Sach is on account of his last name (as in *Loose in London*) and his limited intellectual capacity (as in *The Bowery Boys Meet the Monsters*), not because Sach works at a garage. Mr. Stuyvesant could have just as easily met Sach at Louie's and come away with the same plans after speaking to him.

"Where were you born?"

"At home. I wanted to be close to my mother."

"And when was that?"

"It was at a very young age."

Although the picture does not "go anywhere" until Master Twigg and the boys join forces, we have a lot of fun getting there. In spite of its overworked theme and plot, *High Society* is endowed with comic imagination and unusually crisp performances. It ranks among the best Bowery Boys films. So good, it was nominated for an Oscar, mistaken for another film of the same title. It was voluntarily withdrawn. Huntz Hall, in an interview with Richard Lamparski, said if it were up to him, he would *not* have withdrawn it.

Spy Chasers

Released July 31, 1955: 61 minutes; Allied Artists; Director, Edward Bernds; Producer, Ben Schwalb; Screenplay, Bert Lawrence, Jerome S. Gottler; Art Director, David Milton; Music Director, Marlin Skiles; Photography, Harry Neumann; Film Editors, John C. Fuller, Lester A. Sansom; Production Supervisor, Allen K. Wood; Assistant Director, Edward Morey; Set Decorator, Joseph Kish; Sound, Ralph Butler; Special Effects, Ray Mercer; Wardrobe, Bert Henrikson; Makeup, Bob Dawn; Hairdresser, Mary Westmoreland; Set Continuity, Mary Chaffee.

CAST

Slip	Leo Gorcey	*Lady Zelda*	Veola Vonn
Sach	Huntz Hall	*Princess Anne*	Lisa Davis
Louie	Bernard Gorcey	*Little Girl*	Linda Bennett
Chuck	David Gorcey [Condon]	*George*	Frank Richards
		Michael	Paul Burke
Butch	Bennie Bartlett	*Boris*	Richard Benedict
Col. Baxis	Leon Askin	*Nick*	Mel Welles
King Rako	Sig Ruman	*Phony Courier*	John Bleifer

This tale of espionage delves into the multifaceted background of Louie Dumbrowski. The boys are hosts to Truwania King Rako and Princess Anne, who seek asylum and assistance from Louie while their country is besieged by rebel forces. Louie happens to be the brother of the Truwanian general preparing to overthrow the rebel government. Who knew?

"You mean your father was exhaled from Truwania?" a shocked Slip asks Princess Anne.

Let's review: In *Hold That Line*, Louie sponsors his brother Morris' emigration from Russia, but here his brother is the Truwanian general; in *Bowery Buckaroos*, Louie was the notorious "Louie the Lout" of the West, but in *Bowery Battalion* Louie was the "Fighting Corporal" in World War I.

Is it possible that Louie could be from Russia *and* Truwania *and* be the notorious "Louie the Lout" *and* the "Fighting Corporal"? Absolutely! Why not?

In *Blonde Dynamite*, the seventeenth film, Louie takes his wife to Coney Island. But by the twenty-fourth film, *Crazy Over Horses*, she's apparently dumped him, as Louie sleeps alone in the back room of his sweet shop. In the latter film we get the vague notion that the boys, with the exception of Slip, room together, as they arrive as a group to wake up Louie.

In general, there is little indication in any of the films that the boys have any home life. In the first Bowery Boys film, *Live Wires*, Slip has a sister (Pamela Blake) and in the ninth film, *Angels' Alley*, we meet his mother (Mary Gordon). It is not until the twenty-third film, *Ghost Chasers*, that we meet his mother again (Doris Kemper).

The inference from all this is that there are no preconceived ideas on where or how the boys and Louie exist outside Louie's Sweet Shop, and only when it suits a purpose is a wife or a sister or a mother or a home introduced.

Coins have been objects of significance in several Bowery Boys films. Without one, Sach in *Mr. Hex* could not be hypnotized. In *Trouble Makers*, a coin provides a clue leading to the murder of Dr. Prescott. Here, the correct matching of two halves of the same coin signals the fate of the Truwanian King Rako. If the pieces fit, they will know that the king must leave for Truwania immediately.

Leo Gorcey in *Spy Chasers*.

Sach (Hall, left) and Slip (Gorcey, right) hold back adversaries Lady Zelda (Veola Vonn, in black) and Princess Ann (Lisa Davis) in *Spy Chasers*.

Bogus characters have figured prominently in Bowery Boys films and unveiling their true identities to the audience while keeping them secret from the boys always heightens the drama. The most adept fraud is Roger T. Harris, the newspaper cartoonist in *Angels in Disguise*. In *High Society* the lawyer Cosgrove keeps his real intentions hidden until near the end of the picture. Here, Col. Baxis and Lady Zelda, the king and princess' bodyguards, reveal themselves to the audience as rebel spies by plotting to replace the half-coin the boys have with one of their own. They have one of their men pose as the courier so the king will leave the U.S. prematurely, and fall into rebel hands.

Lady Zelda is more than the typical conniving, evil woman depicted in Bowery Boys films, for she commands an exotic flair and the power of hypnosis.

"Using your atomic force," Col. Baxis assures Lady Zelda before Sach arrives at her apartment, "is like using a cannon to stop a sparrow."

She lures Sach to her apartment and hypnotizes him to allow two rebel spies into Louie's Sweet Shop where the spies exchange the half-coins.

Hypnotism, like bogus characters and old coins, frequently pops up in Bowery Boys films, most notably in *Mr. Hex* and *Hold That Hypnotist*. Though it adds an element of mystery, it is also the epitome of contrivance.

Slip, always suspicious of those who do not crack a smile, follows Col. Baxis to Nick's Palace, a diner. Through the window, he sees the king's bodyguard fraternizing with no-goodniks. "Why, this is just a matter of elementary seduction."

Princess Anne is kidnapped by Lady Zelda, and a fraudulent courier arrives with the message that the king must leave for Truwania immediately.

Faithful to his countrymen, King Rako prepares to depart for home without his daughter.

Slip has a hunch that Princess Anne is being held captive in Nick's back room. As in *Hold That Baby*, in which Laura Andrews is a prisoner in a hospital, Slip and Sach do a convincing act to gain entrance.

"I'd like a hamburger with everything on it, everything, everything," Sach demands.

"That's what you got," says Nick.

"Where's the ice cream and cake?"

Sach pretends he's sick from the food and goes berserk, toppling tables and chairs before collapsing. Slip suggests to Nick that he throw Sach out. When Nick bends over to pick up Sach, Slip knocks him out with a sugar container.

The boys overpower the rebels and save the king from certain death.

Spy Chasers moves smoothly with little extraneous footage. The most interesting characters are undoubtedly Col. Baxis and Lady Zelda. Leon Askin, noted for his fierce commandant expression, is perfect for the role of Col. Baxis, as is Veola Vonn as Lady Zelda. While Sig Ruman is an appropriate choice for King Rako, unfortunately the character does not say or do anything of any importance. The funniest scene is in Nick's Palace with Sach rolling all over the floor. It is a bit overdone, however, just to hit Nick over the head with a sugar container.

Nowhere in the series are the boys on such an important mission as in *Spy Chasers*, yet Slip and Sach infuse it with loads of slapstick.

Jail Busters

Released September 18, 1955; 61 minutes; 5503 ft.; Allied Artists; Director, William Beaudine; Producer, Ben Schwalb; Screenplay, Edward Bernds, Elwood Ullman; Photography, Carl Guthrie; Film Editors, William Austin, Lester A. Sansom; Music Director, Marlin Skiles; Art Director, David Milton; Production Supervisor, Allen K. Wood; Sound effects, Charles Schelling; Wardrobe, Bert Henrikson; Makeup, Emile LaVigne; Set Continuity, Richard Chaffee; Special Effects, Ray Mercer; Working title, *Doing Time*.

CAST

Slip	Leo Gorcey	*Gus*	Murray Alper
Sach	Huntz Hall	*Big Greenie*	Michael Ross
Louie	Bernard Gorcey	*Dr. Fordyce*	Fritz Feld
Butch	Bennie Bartlett	*Bowman*	Lyle Talbot
Jenkins	Barton MacLane	*Marty*	Henry Kulky
Ed Lannigan	Anthony Caruso	*Photographer*	Emil Sitka
Warden Oswald	Percy Helton	*Tomcyk*	John Harmon
Chuck	David Gorcey	*Hank*	Harry Tyler

The temptation is to say that *Jail Busters* is a remake of *Triple Trouble*, released five years earlier. Similarities abound: the boys' determination to be sentenced to the state penitentiary for crimes they didn't commit; obstacles to getting sentenced; the mess they get into in prison; and rubbing shoulders with hardened criminals engaged in surreptitious activities the boys propose to expose.

The difference? *Triple Trouble* deals semi-seriously with the subject of underground prisoner operations; *Jail Busters* comes close to being a farce.

For the first time, Chuck is not just a footman to Slip but in a pivotal position. He is an undercover investigative reporter for the *New York Blade*, writing a story about corruption in the state penitentiary. Discovered, he is beaten up by one of the inmates.

This is the fourth time that the David Gorcey character has been in a hospital (the first was the East Side Kids' *Flying Wild*). The scene at his bedside is corny and sentimental with Slip empathizing with Chuck's difficulty to speak.

"Don't talk, just tell me one t'ing, who dun it?"

Slip strains to listen as the injured Bowery Boy struggles to say, "Big Greenie." But Slip never does go after Big Greenie.

In the series, several seemingly trustworthy characters turn out to be corrupt: Mr. Sayers in *Live Wires*; Sheriff Benson in *Here Come the Marines*; and Cosgrove in *High Society*.

Emil Sitka takes Hall's mug shot in *Jail Busters.* Bennie Bartlett and Leo Gorcey wait their turn, as Barton MacLane (in doorway) and an unidentified officer keep an eye on them.

But none is worse than Bowman, Chuck's editor, because his transgression against the boys is personal.

The boys rob Plotnik's Jewelry Store leaving loads of clues. Yet the headlines reads, as if anticipating what the boys expect, and purposely disappointing them, "Plotnik's Jewelry Store Robbed, No Clues." Instead of tipping off the police about the staged affair, Bowman uses the jewelry to pay off loan sharks and leaves the boys to their fate in the state penitentiary.

In prison, convict Ed Lanigan is given a shave by one prisoner, served Eggs Benedict with sausage and bacon by another prisoner, has the boys clean up his cell, and is kept abreast of his outside affairs (though, unlike in *Triple Trouble*, we have no idea how he communicates with the outside world and what his illegal activities *are*).

The emphasis is on the interplay between the boys and Warden Oswald, spunkily played by surefire attraction Percy Helton. The misunderstanding between the boys and Oswald is good for one comic moment when the warden is laying down the ground rules. The boys wink during his discourse, indicating that they realize he is giving a speech as a matter of procedure. The expressions on the boys' faces when they wink are so weird that Oswald says, "I'll have you boys fitted for glasses later."

Just as *Triple Trouble* has criminally insane Squirrely Davis, *Jail Busters* has old Hank.

"The parole board would have turned me loose any time I want. But not me, I'm stickin' right here. For twenty-two years I've been digging a hole to take me out of this place. Why leave? When I got it almost finished. I'm no fool."

Old Hank must have been taking map lessons from the professor in *Blonde Dynamite*. The tunnel does not lead the boys to McDougall's garage, as old Hank says it will, but to Warden Oswald's office. A minute after the boys pop up from beneath the floor in the warden's office, Lanigan and his men burst into the room, swinging. When the fight is over, Lanigan is beaten to a pulp by Slip and his parole account book is confiscated.

When Warden Oswald tells the boys to wait in their cells until "the proper authorities" arrive, it is a hint that something is amiss. In the last shot of the film, the boys turn towards the camera. They have long beards. The effect is supposed to be comic, but misses. We don't like seeing the boys neglected.

The scene in the psychiatrist's office is one of the most nonsensical exchanges of the series.

"Throw yours away," Slip tells Sach, who is accused of stealing Slip's straw for his basket.

"Don't you holler at me, you schizophrenic," Sach retorts.

"Look, I don't know what those two words mean, but I'm going to look them up."

"Where are you going to look them up? In the telephone book?"

"Certainly, under classified."

Barton MacLane is another well-known veteran film star who repeats his tough-talking role of a prison guard in San Quentin. Here he is the guard on Lanigan's payroll. This is MacLane's second appearance in a Kids picture; the first was the Little Tough Guys' *Hit the Road* where he played James T. Ryan, the sole surviving gang member who takes his gang's orphans under his guardianship. Much of what is good about *Jail Busters* is the inclusion of Percy Helton (who has an even bigger part in *Spook Chasers*) and MacLane.

What would have bolstered this picture is the boys' discovery and quelching of Lanigan plotting something specific, say a prison takeover. *Triple Trouble* benefits from the robbery of Louie's Sweet Shop by Ma Armstrong, photographed in eerie darkness. More confrontation between the boys and Lanigan would have made a far better film.

Dig That Uranium

Released January 8, 1956; 61 minutes; Allied Artists; Director, Edward Bernds; Producer, Ben Schwalb; Screenplay, Elwood Ullman, Bert Lawrence; Photography, Ellsworth Fredericks, Harry Neumann; Editors, William Austin, Lester A. Sansom; Art Director, David Milton; Music, Marlin Skiles.

CAST

Slip	Leo Gorcey	*Frank Loomis*	Richard Powers
Sach	Huntz Hall	*Ron Haskell*	Harry Lauter
Louie	Bernard Gorcey	*Indian*	Paul Fierro
Chuck	David Gorcey	*Chief*	Francis McDonald
Butch	Bennie Bartlett	*Olaf*	Frank Jenks
Jeanette	Mary Beth Hughes	*Tex*	Don C. Harvey
Mac (Slim McKenzie)	Raymond Hatton	*Shifty Robertson*	Carl Switzer
Joe Hody	Myron Healey		

Gullibility prevails in the minds and hearts of Slip, Sach and Louie, when Shifty Robertson (Our Gang's Carl "Alfalfa" Switzer) nurtures their hope for instant wealth. He cons them into buying (with Louie's money, which he keeps under stale spongecake and in milkshake glasses) special uranium excavating equipment and the deed to Little Daisy Mine in Panther Pass, Nevada. (The film was shot in the Santa Susanna Mountains near Los Angeles).

The locals try to frighten the boys with a barrage of bullets. Bad guy Ron Haskell thinks along the same lines as his *Feudin' Fools* counterpart, Clem: Treat them as guests, rob them when the time is right.

Slip's remark, on target as usual: "I presume you serve stomach pumps with your meals."

What Western would be complete without a poker game? But when Louie, feeling like a "herring without the sour cream" away from home, sits down with Haskell and hustlers, the boys get nervous. Louie finds himself intercepting cards the hustlers think they are passing to themselves under the table. He squeaks out a mixture of incredible delight as he reaches for four straight aces. After seeing Louie end up with the short end of the stick for so long, it is a pleasure to see him walk away with a wad of bills, especially on the home team's turf.

The next day, the bad guys think the boys found uranium but instead they are bickering over who's going to carry the Geiger counter. Sach grabs it because Shifty is his friend; Slip grabs it, declaring Sach's ears are too dirty; Louie demands it, remembering it's his money that's financing the whole operation. Childish games such as these typify Bowery Boys comedy at its best, vital to the boys' appeal.

Just like *Jungle Gents* has Annatia the jungle woman, *Dig That Uranium* has Mountain Man Slim "Mack" McKenzie and his donkey Josephine (Leo's mother's first name).

Slip tries to cover up. "We were just taking the pulse of this ore around here. Heard it had very-close [varicose] veins."

"Oh, fer a minute I thought yer were wastin' yer time lookin' fer uranium."

Trying to lift the boys' spirits, and motivated by the spirit of the pioneer, Mack relates the story of Pecos Pete when "he held the county in an iron grip of terror." As he tells it, Sach dreams that he and Slip are rangers charged with protecting the town from gunslingers. In the dream, they saunter into the saloon dressed in white and order milk. They tell Pecos Pete and his partner (played by Frank and Joe in black) to meet them at dusk for a fair gun duel.

The Bowery Boys in *Dig That Uranium*, Bernard Gorcey's last film before he was killed in an auto accident. Left to right: Bernard Gorcey, Bennie Bartlett, Huntz Hall, Leo Gorcey and David Gorcey.

Pecos Pete, however, brings five of his friends. A gun battle ensues until only Pecos Pete remains. Sach starts to go after him, but Slip stops him, pointing his gun at his partner, and says, "I'll go get 'em, partner." Even in the dream, Sach plays second fiddle to Slip.

Pecos Pete makes a run for it. Slip aims his gun about ten feet in front of Peco's running path and hits him. "Got 'im with one of my slow bullets."

The next day, Sach is missing. All they find is his hat. "It's his hat. His initials are in it. D.W. Dim Wit."

Slip is caught in a moment of deep emotion, regretting all the times he hit Sach with his hat, when suddenly the boys hear, "Oh, Chie-e-e-f-f-f-y-y!"

"A voice from beyond," Slip declares.

"Yeah," says Chuck, bringing Slip to reality. "From beyond that rock."

Again, as in *Jungle Gents*, when Slip realizes Sach is not dead, his temper flares.

"What're you doin' down there, you idiot?"

Knowing early in this film that the jalopy is "as fast backwards as she is forwards" foreshadows an important function. The jalopy is not only used to lift Sach from the cliff (it's noticeably a mannequin they pull up) but dazzles the boys' adversaries in a thrilling chase scene that ends fatally for Haskell and his men as their car races over the mountain and explodes.

The impression is that the cars are racing all over the mountains, but it's obvious that the chase scenes are repeated. Still, it is one of the most elaborate, well-paced and well-planned scenes in this series.

For some reason, the explosion activates Louie's Geiger counter. But the joy is short-lived. Indians approach. One, apparently a lawyer, explains to the boys that Little Daisy Mine is on their reservation and therefore the uranium belongs to them. (In *Blonde Dynamite*, uranium is found on Louie's land, but the poor sweet shop owner is painfully reminded by two conventional lawyers that legally the minerals do not belong to him.)

Dig That Uranium is based on the same idea as *Jungle Gents*, and in many respects parallels *Feudin' Fools*. In *Dig That Uranium* and *Jungle Gents*, the boys are talked into going on a long trip to search for a valuable mineral. In both films, crooks follow them and plan to steal the precious stones when the boys find them. But unlike in *Jungle Gents*, the boys in *Dig That Uranium* not only receive nothing for their troubles, but the film leaves them in Bear Claw Canyon with no way to go home. In *Jungle Gents*, the boys board a boat bound for New York.

There is the usual bad blonde beauty, but no embarrassing seduction scene. The most interesting non-regular character is Raymond Hatton as Mack, but we see too little of him.

Edward Bernds' directing is in top form, including the set-up between Slip, Frank and Joe in the hotel. The two westerners face Slip holding their beer mugs in front of them — an open invitation for Slip to knock the full mugs in their faces.

Bernard Gorcey's farewell performance is first-rate in a film packed with humorous, diversified sequences. Before *Dig That Uranium*'s release, he crashed head-on into an airport bus at 4th and La Brea in Hollywood and for two weeks struggled for life in the intensive care at Leland Hospital. He died on September 11, 1955, at age 67.*

Crashing Las Vegas

Released April 22, 1956; 62 minutes; 5593 ft.; Allied Artists; Director, Jean Yarbrough; Producer, Ben Schwalb; Screenplay, Jack Townley; Photography, Harry Neumann; Film Editor, George White; Art Director, David Milton; Music Director, Marlin Skiles; Production Manager, Allen K. Wood; Assistant Director, Edward Morey; Special Effects, Ray Mercer; Sound, Joe Donaldson; Set Decorator, Joseph Kish; Wardrobe, Bert Henrikson; Makeup, Emile LaVigne.

CAST

Slip	Leo Gorcey		*Mrs. Kelly*	Doris Kemper
Sach	Huntz Hall		*Wiley*	Jack Grinnage
Butch	Jimmy Murphy		*Police Sergeant*	Terry Frost
Chuck	David Gorcey		*Host*	Bob Hopkins
Carol	Mary Castle		*Joe Crumb*	John Bleifer
Sam	Nicky Blair		*Man in Seat 87*	Emil Sitka
Oggy	Mort Mills		*Woman*	Minerva Urecal
Tony	Don Haggerty		*Croupier*	Frank Scannell
First Policeman	Dick Foote		*Floor Manager*	Joey Ray
Second Policeman	Don Marlowe		*Waiter*	Jack Chefe

*Gorcey, Leo, Jr., Me and the Dead End Kid, *page 205.*

Guard	Frank Hagney	*Waiter*	Cosmo Sardo
Elevator Operator	Speer Martin	*Bit*	Alfred Tonkel
Usher	Jimmy Brandt		

The interesting combination of luck, need and electricity brings the boys to Las Vegas where Sach correctly predicts roulette wheel numbers after getting a shock from an electric mixer. Leo Gorcey's final entry is a potpourri of overused ideas, premises, and routines, all frustratingly familiar to us, and display the sluggishness of the scriptwriters.

The only new development is Mrs. Kelly's Rooming House, a necessity since Bernard Gorcey was killed in an automobile accident. It could have been a barber shop or a bakery or even another sweet shop, which it is in the last three Bowery Boys films.

Mrs. Kelly's problem, similar to Louie's in *Bowery Bombshell*, is that she needs money for the mortgage on her rooming house.

The difference between this Slip and the Slip of *Bowery Bombshell* or *Hold That Baby!* is that here he lacks that particular quality of seriousness we have grown to enjoy. Slip would never merely shake his fist at Sach for doing something stupid, he would spontaneously hit him with his hat.

Game shows are satirized twice in the Bowery Boys series; the first time in *Hard Boiled Mahoney* with *Prof. Quizard* and *His Brain Show*, and here with *Live Like a King*. The former serves as a vehicle for pure slapstick; *Live Like a King*, sponsored by Grim Toothpaste, is the catalyst for the boys' trip to Las Vegas. When the award turns out to be "four glorious weeks in Las Vegas for one fellow," Slip asks "how about four glorious fellows in Las Vegas for one week? Do you think that can be deranged?"

Women have always been able to command control over the boys, especially Sach. Carol takes Sach to her apartment. Tony, wanted for murder in New York, feigns falling out of the window. Sach thinks he killed him. In return for Carol and Sam's silence, Sach gives them all the money he has won.

Paranoia is a theme first explored in *Bowery Bombshell*. In that film, Sach's paranoia has him hearing a vibrating echo of Officer O'Malley telling him that he's going to jail. In *Crashing Las Vegas*, Sach's dream is well-executed and quite funny.

Standing before the judge, the boys are sentenced to die for committing murder. In spite of Slip's insistence that Sach is the murderer, the judge, played by the hotel clerk, decides to execute all of them. This decision lies in Sach's perception of the hotel clerk's disdain for all of them.

But if Sach can predict the correct number on the big wheel, they will all go free. At that moment, Carol appears and renders Sach powerless.

In the execution chamber there's a sign, "Three Chairs No Waiting." Since there are four of them, a game of musical chairs determines the lucky "odd man out." Even in Sach's dream, Slip wins. As Slip is about to pull the lever Sach wakes up.

This is not the first film where Sach acquires odd powers and loses them via the same method. In *Private Eyes* Herbie's punch gives Sach the power to read minds and a second wallop takes it away. In *Master Minds* his sore tooth gives him the power of predicting the future, and extracting the tooth takes it away. Here another electric shock takes away his power to predict numbers.

Among the films that take the boys away from home, only *Crashing Las Vegas* does not give its viewers a tour of the locality. In *Paris Playboys* and *Loose in London* we are shown the famous landmarks of those splendid cities. A walk through the lighted city at night would have been more appropriate than the wasted scene on the airplane.

Sach (Hall, with sunglasses) predicts numbers in *Crashing Las Vegas* with Mary Castle, as Leo (Gorcey) looks on. Gorcey was noticeably drunk in his last film.

Another major flaw is the distance between Slip and the crooks. Slip's personal contact with the "bad guys" in *Mr. Hex* and *Angels' Alley* lends itself well to exciting games of wit. Here, Slip's contact with the bad guys at the end of the film is purely physical. Slip is at his best when verbally confronting the antagonist, or doing a scene with Sach. But he cannot carry a scene with someone not central to the plot.

It's different with Sach. His interactions with other characters are usually the highlight of the picture. Scenes with Renie Riano in *Clipped Wings* and with Allen Jenkins in *Let's Go Navy!* are prime examples.

At the end, Mrs. Kelly suddenly appears at the Hotel Pelican, wearing a Grin Toothpaste badge. Whether or not she got the money for the down payment is never clear. How she got the money to come to Las Vegas is also left unexplained.

It's a pity Leo's last film did not have him at his best.

Far from it.

"Leo slammed the chair into some casino props.... [He] swung the chair like a sling-blade at Huntz, grazing the side of his head. 'Papa! Please come back.' Huntz and David [Gorcey] drove him home. Though Leo was visibly drunk in the film, *Crashing Las Vegas* was a moneymaker."*

Fighting Trouble

Released September 16, 1956; 61 minutes; Director, George Blair: Producer, Ben Schwalb; Screenplay, Elwood Ullman; Photography, Harry Neumann; Film Editor, William Austin; Music Directors, Buddy Bregman, Jill Campbell; Art Director, David Milton; Production Manager, Allen K. Wood; Sound, Ralph Butler, Charles Schelling; Assistant Director, Don Torpin; Set Decorators, Joseph Kish, Richard Chaffee; Wardrobe, Bert Henrikson; Makeup, Emile LaVigne; Construction, Jimmy West, Ted Mossman; Working title, *Chasing Trouble*.

CAST

Sach	Huntz Hall		*Danny*	Danny Welton
Duke	Stanley Clements		*Smith*	Charles Williams
Mae	Adele Jergens		*McBride*	Clegg Hoyt
Handsome Hal	Joseph Downing		*Conroy*	William Boyett
Mrs. Kelly	Queenie Smith		*Vance*	Tim Ryan
Bates	John Bleifer		*Evans*	Michael Ross
Arbo	Thomas B. Henry		*Max Kling*	Benny Burt
Chuck	David Gorcey		*Hawaiian Girl*	Ann Griffith
Dolly	Laurie Mitchell		*Vic*	Rick Vallin

In addition to paving the way for Huntz Hall to be awarded top billing for the first time in his career, Leo Gorcey's absence opened a part for a young, tough talking actor, Stanley Clements. A child star of the 1930s, and an East Side Kid in the 1940s, Clements fits the shoes (but not the hat) and does an adequate job as Stanislaus "Duke" Coveleske. He lacks the appeal, the wit, and the natural ability to spin off malapropisms at the tip of his tongue, but then again, Clements does not have the benefit of ten years experience to polish his character.

In this picture, Sach is disguised as both a French interior decorator and a hoodlum from Chicago. The fact that Duke is Sach's apprentice and partner emphasizes the centrality of Hall's characters, a position never quite attained alongside Gorcey.

The bulk of the film is the same idea as *Crazy Over Horses*. Each attempt to photograph Frankie Arbo is more elaborate than the last, just as each scheme to exchange horses in *Crazy Over Horses* is exceedingly more clever. With each attempt, the boys get deeper and deeper involved in the life of Arbo and the breaking-up of his counterfeiting ring.

First, Duke and Sach rent a hotel room near Arbo's. There are no obstacles keeping them from taking the picture except the ones they create themselves. Sach handles the camera like

---

*Gorcey, Leo, Jr., *Me and the Dead End Kid*, *page 203.*

Sach (Hall) shows his best side to pretty Adele Jergens in *Fighting Trouble*.

a hot potato and Duke provides no assistance. The sequence is chock full of contrived imped-
iments.

The next attempt is a good deal more innovative and amusing. The boys impersonate
Parisian interior decorators who tell Arbo's girlfriend May how her apartment should be dec-
orated. Sach goes overboard and rips out the insides of a pillow.

"What are you doing?" May cries.

"When I say interior, I mean in-ter-ri-or!"

May calls Arbo to stop by and Sach snaps a picture of him.

Just as in *Crazy Over Horses*, where Sach's aimin'-to-please attitude muffs up the boys'
careful exchange of horses, here in his haste to show the editor at the *New York Morning Blade*
the pictures, he destroys his own successful mission by thoughtlessly exposing all the film.

Their most elaborate plan is glaringly influenced by a sequence in *Bowery Bombshell*,
produced ten years earlier. In that film, Slip poses as Midge Casalotte and meets Ace Deuce.
While Slip plays tough with Ace Deuce, Kathy, using a hidden camera, takes Ace's picture.
In *Fighting Trouble*, Handsome Hal Lomax never met Frankie Arbo. Sach and Duke meet
Handsome Hal at the airport and take him to Mrs. Kelly's rooming house. Chuck has prepared a closed circuit radio device and announces that New York police are aware of Handsome Hal's presence in the city. Not since Whitey's ham radio in *Triple Trouble* has the boys'
electronic know-how been so productively applied.

With Handsome Hal tucked away, Sach and Duke arrive at the meeting, sharply dressed
as Handsome Hal Lomax and his partner, Tiger Wilson. Sach has brought with him his

camera-lighter, and offers to light everybody's cigar, including the man from Los Angeles with the cough.

"I'd like to do something for that cough, but I don't have my gun with me."

Just as the saboteurs in *Paris Playboys* are faced with the problem of discerning the real Prof. Le Beau from the Sach lookalike, here the counterfeiters are befuddled when the real Handsome Hal arrives. Dolly, for some unexplained reason, has a bone to pick with her boyfriend Handsome Hal. When asked to point out the real Handsome Hal, she approaches Sach and engages him in a lingering kiss. As Frankie Arbo's henchmen lead Handsome Hal away, Sach, who could never hide the truth from pretty women (as we shall see again in *Spook Chasers*), shows Dolly how his hidden camera works.

The boys lock themselves within an enclosed passage and slide open the door long enough to launch coconuts from the counterfeiting machine. Where the coconuts come from and why and how this machine can perform such a function remains an engima.

Fighting Trouble is spiced with a proportionate miscellany of gags, melodrama, action and stunts, accented by the refreshing and zestful performances of the accomplished actors Queenie Smith (Mrs. Kelly) and Joseph Downing (Handsome Hal Lomax).

Fighting Trouble is the second production Huntz Hall, David Gorcey and Joseph Downing did together. The first was the Broadway production of *Dead End* in 1935, where Downing played "Baby Face" Martin.

Hot Shots

Released December 23, 1956; 61 minutes; 5527 ft.; Allied Artists; Director, Jean Yarbrough; Producer, Ben Schwalb; Screenplay, Jack Townley, Elwood Ullman; Story, Jack Townley; Art Director, David Milton; Music Director, Marlin Skiles; Photography, Harry Neumann; Film Editor, Neil Brunnenkant; Production Manager, Allen K. Wood; Assistant Director, Dan Torpin; Sound, Ralph Butler, Charles Schelling; Set Director, Joseph Kish.

CAST

Sach	Huntz Hall	*George Slater*	Mark Dana
Duke	Stanley Clements	*Karl*	Henry Rowland
Connie Forbes	Joi Lansing	*Tony*	Dennis Moore
Myron	Jimmy Murphy	*Mrs. Taylor*	Isabel Randolph
Chuck	David Gorcey	*Henry the Bartender*	Frank Marlowe
Mrs. Kelly	Queenie Smith	*Bit Man*	Joe Kirk
Joey Munroe	Philip Phillips	*Capt. W.K. Wells*	Ray Walker
P.M. Morley	Robert Shayne		

Flash! TV child star Joey Munroe kidnaps himself into the clutches of Sach Jones and Duke Coveleske.

The pangs of childhood stardom are poignantly and comically dramatized in *Hot Shots* (a misleading title for this episode), along with the themes of greed, parasitism, and affection.

Seemingly destitute, Joey touches a soft spot in the boys' hearts, until he starts saying things like:

"You don't expect me to wear this, do you?"

"This pork is not lean enough for my diet."

At the police station, Joey delivers an expressive monologue, portraying the boys as vicious kidnappers. Studio boss P. M. Morley intercedes. He recognizes the story as an excerpt from the next Joey Monroe show.

"There's nothing wrong with that kid," Sach tells Morley and George Slater, Joey's uncle. "Why don't you let him go to school like the other kids and play hooky?"

Joey also senses the parasitic relationship between himself and Uncle George, who is making money at the expense of Joey's happiness.

As a settlement for the damage done to their dignity, the boys are given jobs: thirty-fourth and thirty-fifth vice-presidents in charge of coordination of interrelational activities. Translation: keep Joey amused during his breaks from rehearsal.

George Slater views the boys as obstacles and is determined to get them fired.

Just as Mr. Stuyvesant in *High Society* exploits the imbecilic nature of Sach, so does Slater use Sach's gullibility and erratic behavior to infuriate Mr. Taylor, the show's sponsor. At a party for Mr. and Mrs. Taylor, Connie, Slater's mistress, shows Sach a trick using hard-boiled eggs. She urges him to try the trick on Taylor, but provides him with a raw egg. When the trick backfires, Taylor is left with egg dripping down his forehead.

Though this incident is somewhat predictable, the party scene as a whole is a good one, for it synthesizes comedy into the context of the plot. It also ends with Sach's egg trick leaving the audience with the most significant image of this sequence.

Because of this, and because of Joey's lack of productivity, Morley fires Duke and Sach. He explains to the boys that the youngster emulates them far too much. This explanation leads to self-criticism.

"He's right," Duke tells Sach after leaving Morley's office. "We can't have that kid grow up to be like us."

"Guess you're right, Dukey," Sach agrees.

"We gotta think about the future of civilization."

Paradoxically, Sach is correct when considering the impact the Dead End Kids had on American youth when they first burst on the scene.

An undeclared game of wits ensues between Joey and his Uncle George. Joey, realizing his indispensability to the show and to the studio, refuses to work. Slater, concerned about his income and an $80,000 debt (spent mostly on precious ornaments worn on Connie's wrists and neck), and remembering how acquiescent Morley was when it was thought Joey was kidnapped, arranges with his partner Carl to have Joey kidnapped. But Joey beats him to it, leaving his house via a fire escape.

When Joey shows up at Mrs. Kelly's rooming house at three in the morning, Duke, for the first time, exercises his power as leader of the group by deciding that the youngster must be sent back home. He reveals that they, too, have been parasitic at Joey's expense.

"Act your age. We needed a job and we used you to get it."

The serious intonation in Sach's voice when he finally does telephone Slater is a phenomenon that has not occurred since his persuasive barroom scene in *Fighting Fools*.

"Hello, Slater? Joe is over here. Come and get him."

There are a few uneven moments and some technical problems with this film. For example, when Carl comes to Mrs. Kelly's rooming house to pick up Joey, Sach sees through the window two mugs forcing Joey into a car. Sach and Duke go to Joey's home to make sure he arrives safely. They too enter the house through the fire escape. The fire escape is three stories high and the boys have a great deal of trouble bringing down the ladder. How did nine-year-old Joey do it?

Although her part is not large, Connie Forbes, slickly played by Joi Lansing, is the catalyst behind George Slater. She plants the idea in Slater's head of making a mad dash to Mexico once they collect the ransom money. Slater agrees but Duke and Sach storm the warehouse and in a cat-and-mouse chase scene knock out all the kidnappers and rescue Joey.

What is disturbing about every film that includes a youngster is some display of physical aggression towards the boys. Annie, the little cowgirl who will replace Joey while the lad is away on a fishing trip with Duke and Sach, is that child. When Sach and Duke squat to face her and Sach asks if her guns are loaded, she pummels them with "wet bullets."

On the whole, action and abundance of confrontation, combined with the appealing stage presence of the Joey Monroe character, makes *Hot Shots* an enjoyable film.

Hold That Hypnotist

Released February 24, 1957; 61 minutes; Allied Artists; Director, Austin Jewell; Producer, Ben Schwalb; Screenplay, Dan Pepper; Photography, Harry Neumann; Film Editor, George White; Art Director, David Milton; Music Director, Marlin Skiles; Production Manager, Allen K. Wood; Sound, Ralph Butler, Charles Schelling; Assistant Director, Edward Morey, Jr.; Set Director, Joseph Kish; Wardrobe, Bert Henrikson; Set Continuity, Richard M. Chaffee; Makeup, Emile LaVigne; Construction, James West.

CAST

Sach/Algy Winkle	Huntz Hall		Myron	Jimmy Murphy
Duke/Bartender	Stanley Clements		Gale	Murray Alper
Cleo/Wench	Jane Nigh		Clerk	Dick Elliott
Dr. Simon Noble	Robert Foulk		Blackbeard	Mel Welles
Morgan	James Flavin		Maid	Mary Treen
Mrs. Kelly	Queenie Smith			
Chuck	David Gorcey			
	[Condon]			

The third Bowery Boys' film about hypnotism and the tenth that deals with unwonted occurrences views reincarnation with a jaundiced eye. Mrs. Kelly, swayed by Dr. Simon Nobel's book, *The Former Lives of Sally Pringle*, wants the doctor to "regress" her. At first the boys think she's calling the doctor because she's sick and so they try to help by cleaning the house.

The cleaning scene is good for a few laughs as Duke trips over Chuck's vacuum cleaner cord, then slips on the floor. Interestingly, *Fighting Trouble*, *Spook Chasers* and *In the Money*, all Stanley Clements films, have the boys pushing brooms.

When the boys realize her appointment is with the alleged hypnotist, they try talking her out of it. But Mrs. Kelly hopes to find out she was Cleopatra. Sach's response captures the humor of Mrs. Kelly's impossible hope.

"Oh, you're too late for Cleopatra. My aunt Hortense who lives in Brooklyn found out that she was Cleopatra and now she has my Uncle George in the backyard building a pyramid."

The boys pose as reporters at Dr. Noble's press conference hoping to expose him as a fraud. Duke challenges the doctor to hypnotize him. Duke is unaffected by the spell but Sach,

5612-7-D

Sach (Hall) with Blackbeard (Mel Welles) and Wench (Jane Nigh) in the flashback scene in *Hold That Hypnotist*.

like Louie in *Mr. Hex* who watches from a distance, is hypnotized. He recalls being colonial tax collector Algy Winkle, who won a treasure map from Blackbeard the pirate in a game of Slaviash in South Carolina in the seventh century.

The flashback scene in the seventeenth century pub is clever, artistic and wonderfully campy. The costumes are well-designed and characteristic of the period. Blackbeard is dressed in a buccaneer hat and sports a black eye patch.

The humor of the game Slaviash lies in its absurd rules. What is *said* while making a move on the game board is more significant than the move itself.

"Yalif," says Algie Winkle as Blackbeard concedes the first plateau. Angry, Blackbeard shoots the pirate helping Algie.

"I can't stand kibbitzers," the pirate bellows.

"Zetz," roars Blackbeard as Algie begins to worry. The tax collector was not expecting a "zetz."

"Yikes."

By uttering "yikes," Algie Winkle becomes the first man ever to "triple oot" Blackbeard and wins the treasure map.

The boys' research reveals that Algie Winkle drowned off the coast of New York, never finding the treasure.

Meanwhile, Morgan, Dr. Noble's manager, dismisses their secretary Cleo because she's an embarrassment. What Morgan doesn't realize is that Cleo's earrings are needed to hypnotize Sach to delve into the sub-sub of his mind to find out where the treasure is hidden. Once again, as in several previous films, a tiny object is indispensable.

Consistent with the Bowery Boys' view of young, beautiful women (most of whom are blonde), Cleo possesses a passion for money and kisses that send an electric current through Sach's spine. It's a good thing she does. After Dr. Noble hypnotizes Sach to find out the treasure is buried in Hopkins' cave, he hands a gun to the hypnotized Sach and orders him to keep Duke, Chuck and Myron covered while he and Morgan seek the treasure for themselves. Cleo's kiss awakens Sach.

There is a subtle difference between the first and second times Dr. Noble hypnotizes Sach. In the first, Algie Winkle talks about the episode with Blackbeard during his life. The second time, Dr. Noble does not speak to Algie Winkle during his life but after he is dead. So what Dr. Noble has done, in a sense, is conjure up the spirit of Algie Winkle, who says he destroyed the treasure map after memorizing it. There is no mention of this difference by Dr. Noble, nor by anybody else. It is possible that the writers themselves did not perceive the difference.

Similar to the bottomless bag in *Clipped Wings,* Sach removes from the trunk of the car an assortment of digging implements before coming across Black Beard comic books. Sach admits to his pals that he subconsciously retold the story that he read in the comic book and identified with Algie Winkle.

Minutes later, a treasure is found in the cave and we are left wondering for the moment whether *Hold That Hypnotist* is an anti- or pro-reincarnation film. Our doubts are quelled when at the celebration at Mrs. Kelly's rooming house, adorned with the jewelry, Mrs. Kelly opens the door for two uniformed policemen and one plainclothesman. The plainclothesman announces that the jewelry was stolen six months ago from Humphrey's Jewelry Store and must be returned. An earlier hint about where the film stood on the idea of reincarnation is when Dr. Noble confides to his business manager that he believes his hypnosis "can" regress people to their previous lives as described in his book. Morgan reminds Dr. Noble at that time that they told Sally Pringle what to say and paid her plenty to do so.

Without a doubt the scene in the seventeenth century pub is one of the Bowery Boys' best, but it's featured in what is otherwise a slow-moving, predictable story. Robert Foulk, as the pompous pseudo-mystic doctor, is unappealing, while Jane Nigh as the sexy but empty-headed blonde is tiring. The filmmakers would have done better devoting more time to the flashback as is done in *Looking for Danger.*

Spook Chasers

Released June 2, 1957; 62 minutes; 5502 ft.; Allied Artists; Director, George Blair; Producer, Ben Schwalb; Screenplay, Elwood Ullman; Photography, Harry Neumann; Editor, Neil Brunnenkant; Art Director, David Milton; Musical Director, Marlin Skiles; Production Manager, Allen K. Wood; Sound, Charles Schelling; Set Decorator, Robert J. Mills; Construction, Jimmy West; Special Effects, Augie Lohman; Wardrobe, Bert Henrikson, Irene Caine; Makeup, Emile LaVigne; Hairdresser, Alice Monte.

CAST

Sach	Huntz Hall	*Snap*	Peter Mamakos
Duke	Stanley Clements	*Ziggie*	Ben Welden
Chuck	David Gorcey	*Lt. Harris*	Robert Shayne
Myron	Jimmy Murphy	*Ernie*	Robert Christopher
Mike Clancy	Percy Helton	*Dr. Moss*	Pierre Watkin
Dolly Owens	Darlene Fields	*First Doll*	Audrey Conti
Blinky	Eddie LeRoy	*Second Doll*	Anne Fleming
Harry Shelby	Bill Henry	*Photographer*	Bill Cassidy

The first film to re-introduce the sweet shop after Bernard Gorcey's demise borrows ideas from prior films. The result is a rather predictable, haphazard, but energetic picture, with its energy misguided.

Percy Helton's Mike Clancy does not know how to be anything but a nervous fellow, and it shows through every line, every movement, every nuance. So instead of giving vitality to his character, Helton hammers away at only one characteristic, and this is too much to bear.

Like Louie in *Blonde Dynamite*, Clancy is overworked and needs a rest in the country. But unlike Louie, Clancy doesn't make the mistake of leaving the boys in charge; he takes them with him to his new home.

The condition of the house, and the manner in which it is sold to him by realtors Harry Shelby and Dolly Owens, bears similarity to the Little Daisy Mine and con artist Shifty Robertson in *Dig That Uranium*.

"Looks like a spook's do-it-yourself kit," Sach says of the house, which belonged to Wee Willie Dolan, the notorious bank robber.

But the house does contain a valuable secret and Sach's discovery of it is similar to his discovery of the diamonds in *Jungle Gents*. In the course of cleaning the house, a draggy sequence spotted with a dose of mediocre slapstick, Sach falls on a coffee wagon and rolls into a wall, releasing bags of stolen money. In *Jungle Gents*, Sach finds the diamonds when he bumps his head against the tunnel wall.

Clancy pays off the balance on the house in cash. Immediately afterwards, Snaps Cicero, Dolan's former partner in crime, wants Shelby to buy back the house and sell it to him. His curiosity sparked, Shelby has Dolly invite Sach to her apartment to see if she can persuade the susceptible Bowery Boy to spill the secret.

Dolly assumes the seductive woman role, which has not surfaced since *Spy Chasers*. While most women in the series obtain information through sexual suggestion, Dolly also relies on alcohol. This film and *Blonde Dynamite* are the only ones where alcohol is used and it's interesting to compare the two. In *Blonde Dynamite*, Whitey spins the lazy susan, unintentionally switching the drinks. The girls pass out. Here, Sach and Dolly engage in a typical sight gag used numerous times in Abbott and Costello. They are seated on the couch, their glasses on the coffee table in front of them. Sach directs Dolly's attention to a spot on the wall and switches glasses. Dolly does the same thing to Sach. This is repeated several times until Dolly only clinks the glasses to make it sound like she switched them. Sach switches them one last time, giving himself the mickey.

So in *Spook Chasers*, Sach tries to outsmart Dolly and fails, while in *Blonde Dynamite*, the boys unintentionally beat the girls at their own game.

By the time Duke finds out, it is too late. The stewed Sach has divulged the house's secret.

A big chunk of *Spook Chasers* is devoted to haunted house antics. This seems to be the whole idea behind the making of this film and it is endowed with only minimal spook effects. It consists of two ghostly figures in white roaming the house, trying to scare the boys away. It is hardly surprising when they're revealed to be Shelby and Dolly.

The scariest scene is when Duke pulls aside a curtain to reveal a skull, seemingly suspended against a black background. It is a chilling and artistic detail.

Another scary scene implies there's a real ghost in the house. The real ghost appears after a three-way brawl among the boys, Shelby and Snaps. The police suddenly appear as if they were hiding on a shelf in the corner, waiting to swoop down on the bandits. Suddenly, a ghost, in the same white attire as Shelby and Dolly, floats by and disappears through a wall. Frightened, the boys scurry out and, in their haste, close the door with Sach still inside.

The film's epilogue, a party in the newly renovated house, focuses on Sach's heroism for being left alone in the house with the real ghost. Girls surround him and call him the "bravest man in the world," but Duke quells that notion as he leaves the party and returns in a ghost costume and scares everybody — including the "bravest man in the world."

The major weakness of *Spook Chasers* is the lack of conflict. Snaps Cicero, who snaps his fingers when he wants something, and is the key and most colorful character in spite of his small role, is an excellent counterpart to Duke. Unfortunately the film does not exploit the dichotomy as it should. In fact, the boys are not aware of Snaps' existence until the end of the film when they exchange punches.

Snaps' objective is by far more dramatically sustaining that Mike Clancy's quest for a quiet rest. Elwood Ullman, who wrote many Bowery Boys scripts, missed the opportunity to improve this script by not involving the boys in more direct conflict with the criminal character. *Spook Chasers* could use more polish.

Looking for Danger

Released October 6, 1957; 62 minutes; Allied Artists; Director, Austen Jewell; Producer, Ben Schwalb; Screenplay, Elwood Ullman, Edward Bernds; Photography, Harry Neumann; Art Director, David Milton; Editor, Neil Brunnenkant; Music, Marlin Skiles; Production Manager, Allen K. Wood; Sound, Ralph Butler; Wardrobe, Bert Henrikson; Makeup, Emile LaVigne.

CAST

Sach	Huntz Hall		Shareen	Lili Kardell
Duke	Stanley Clements		Zarida	Joan Bradshaw
Blinky	Eddie LeRoy		Mustapha	George Khoury
Chuck	David Condon [Gorcey]		Wetzel	Henry Rowland
			Mike Clancy	Dick Elliott
Myron	Jimmy Murphy		Watson	Harry Strang
Ahmed	Richard Avonde		Harper	Paul Bryar
Wolff	Otto Reichow		Sari	Jane Burgess
Sidi-Omar	Michael Granger		Bradfield	John Harmon
Hassan	Peter Mamakos		Waiter	Michael Vallon

In telling the incredible tale of how Duke and Sach are the unsung heroes of the Second World War, *Looking for Danger,* through exceptional visual images and corny dialogue, takes

The boys (Hall, center, and Stanley Clements, right) don't have to look far to find "The Hawk" (Lili Kardell) in *Looking for Danger*.

a paradoxical view of the United States Army, a quasi-realistic approach to government bureaucracy and spoofs the business of spying.

Our patriotic boys would be the last people to say the U.S. Army is not the best in the world, but even they must admit that the Army's recruiting methods for a suicide mission in Casablanca are less than selective. Precisely, it is unintentionally voluntary. When the general stands before a line of soldiers and calls for volunteers to step forward, the boys are the only ones who do not step backwards. Thus we have the film's first example of the Army's decision-making process.

"If you are caught," the general tells Duke and Sach, "they'll put you against the wall and offer you your last cigarette."

"You better get somebody else for the job," Sach tells him. "I don't smoke."

When the scene shifts to Casablanca, David Milton's scenery, costumes and props are to be applauded. The design and setting of the outdoor market is influenced by the outdoor market scene in *Casablanca* with its merchants haggling over their wares, German soldiers in the streets, and beggars underfoot.

Spying is a major motif in this picture and almost every character is one. The boys are disguised as German soldiers, and Sach's ring, symbolizing the owl in flight, catches the attention of a beggar who is really an Ally spy. He directs them to Sultan Sidi, who turns out to be a German spy. Not to worry, one of the sultan's dancing girls, Hawk, is an American spy.

Sach is surprised to learn that the sultan has three wives.

"In this country they have polygamy," Duke explains. "In our country we have monotony."

What *Looking for Danger* has in common with *Jail Busters* and *Triple Trouble* is that all three disregard the technical problems that massive and intricate institutions such as the U.S. Army and the state penitentiary present. This is particularly the case with regard to locating the specific people they are after, and accomplishing their mission.

Of all the American soldiers available to assist Duke and Sach, the Army decides to send Chuck and Myron, disguised as German soldiers, to rescue the boys, Hawk and her colonel from jail. Since the Hawk and her colonel are members of the underground, they must escape quickly, leaving the boys alone to warn the American Army about a German ambush. With elements of intriguing espionage, the boys evade the sultan and German soldiers long enough to send a message to the Americans via radio about the German ambush and save the U.S. Army from destruction. They then engage the Axis spies in an old-fashioned fistfight which the boys, of course, win.

Although *Looking for Danger* leads into the spy story of Duke and Sach in a roundabout way, the opening scene seems to be poking fun at government pettiness. Government agent Lester Bradfield arrives, not to bestow belated medals on the boys, or even give them an untimely thank you, but in search of a government pot missing since the war and last known to be in the possession of Duke Coveleske. The government wants its pot.

Duke and Sach proceed to tell Bradfield the story of their suicide mission, which has absolutely nothing to do with the pot. Once the story is finished, which is the bulk of the film in flashback, the pot falls on Bradfield's head. This is how the film ends.

When comparing Duke's role in all seven pictures, *Looking for Danger* is the only film in which his usefulness is not dependent on any one other character. In *Fighting Trouble,* Sach is the photographer and Duke is the assistant; in *Hot Shots,* Joey Munroe is the pivotal character; in *Spy Chasers,* Duke and the boys follow Mike Clancy; in *Up In Smoke,* Duke's character is of little consequence; in *In the Money,* he and the boys blindly follow Sach on a boat to England. Duke's more independent role here is one of the reasons *Looking for Danger* is the best of the last seven Bowery Boys films.

Looking for Danger is experimental in that the boys represent a group other than themselves, namely the U.S. Army. While the film itself makes good use of its material, in retrospect, the films that score the highest are the ones in which they have a personal stake, such as *Feudin' Fools, The Bowery Boys Meet the Monsters,* etc.

In the final analysis, *Looking for Danger* is a well-planned, inventive flick, enhanced by the unusual artistry, the satiric handling of the spies, thickened plot and general shift in time and location.

Up in Smoke

Released December 22, 1957; 61 minutes; Allied Artists; Director, William Beaudine; Producer, Richard Heermance; Screenplay, Jack Townley; Story, Elwood Ullman, Bert Lawrence; Photography, Harry Neumann; Art Director, David Milton, Music Director, Marlin Skiles; Editor, William Austin; Production Manager, Allen K. Wood; Sound, Frank McKenzie, Del Harris; Set Decorator, Joseph Kish.

CAST

Sach	Huntz Hall		*Al*	Joe Devlin
Duke	Stanley Clements		*Policeman*	James Flavin
Mabel	Judy Bamber		*Friendly Frank*	Earle Hodgins
Blinky	Eddie LeRoy		*Desk Sergeant*	John Mitchum
Chuck	David Gorcey		*Police Clerk*	Jack Mulhall
Tony	Ric Roman		*Dr. Bluzak*	Fritz Feld
Satan	Byron Foulger		*Druggist*	Wilbur Mack
Mike	Dick Elliott		*Bernie*	Benny Rubin
Sam	Ralph Sanford			

Sach's slip of the tongue just about twists his fate. Angry with himself for losing money earmarked for young Ozzie's hospital expenses, Sach mutters he'll give "his very soul" to know the winning horses before the race for a week. Thus we have another Bowery Boys interpretation of a classic. The first was Aladdin's Lamp (*Bowery to Bagdad*), now Faust. In both, Sach's mutterings gets him what he wants— or thinks he wants.

Usually, conflict among people and how it's developed is an essential ingredient to the success of every Bowery Boys film. It is one of the major reasons *Angels in Disguise* and *The Bowery Boys Meet the Monsters,* two very different films, are among the best and *Let's Go Navy!* and *Bowery Battalion* are among the worst. What is unique about *Up in Smoke* is that though Sach does confront several parties on several occasions (the boys, the Devil, and the bookmakers), the main conflict is within Sach himself. Hall carries the film with his acting craft and knowledge of his character, and does a superb job comically and dramatically describing one man's self-inflicted polarity.

The relationship between Duke and Sach in *Up in Smoke* deteriorates much the same way it does between Sach and Slip in *Crazy Over Horses*, and for the same reasons. When Duke learns that Sach wagered away the money, he kicks Sach out of the group. Slip does the same thing to Sach in *Crazy Over Horses* when Sach foils the boys' maneuver to exchange two race horses. Sach tries to make amends in both films.

Before Sach can bet on Mr. Bubb's first horse, Lazy Luke, he needs to sell the boys' car to Friendly Frank, the used car dealer. The haggling scene with Friendly Frank (smoothly handled by Earle Hodgins) and Sach is first-rate. It begins with Frank giving the car a great sales pitch because he thinks it is one of *his* cars he's selling to Sach. When Frank realizes it's Sach's car, without a flinch, he does a complete turnabout and wrecks it as he describes its imperfections.

To make matters worse, the boys have already sold the car to another party for $50. Sach is arrested. In jail, Mr. Bubb tells him to bet next on Mustard Plaster. (The many horse names are reminiscent of the numerous wrestling names the boys must think up when Sach's muscles shift to a different spot on his body in *No Holds Barred*.) Since he's in jail, Sach misses his second chance.

Sach attempts to contact Mr. Bubb by letter, telling him he wants to back out of the deal. He mails it by striking a match.

"Mailing it?" Duke yells. "You imbecile, you're burning it."

"That's the only way this guy can get a letter," Sach explains. "If it burns fast, that's special delivery."

Doctors have been given a tainted image in the Bowery Boys series since *Hold That Baby!*, largely due to their outrageous judgment. For instance, in *Hold That Baby!* Sach is declared a psychotic kleptomaniac. In *No Holds Barred*, the doctor concludes that Sach is endowed with calcium deposits on the brain. Here, Dr. Bluzack is the most pragmatic: He checks the newspaper, and when the newspaper test comes up positive, curing Sach is the farthest thing from the doctor's mind. The doctor heeds Sach's next tip and soon the word leaks that Charley Horse is a sure bet. Everybody bets on Charley Horse — except Sach — and the reason is obscure. Sach intends to bet on Charley Horse (after borrowing $20 from the surrogate Louie, Mike Clancy, adequately portrayed by Dick Elliott), but someone, supposedly out of Sach's view but visible to the audience, whispers "Heel Plate." It seems the film intends for Sach to think the voice he hears is Mr. Bubb, but who the man is, and why he whispers to Sach at this point, is never explained. Heel Plate is about to win but drops dead on the track. Charley Horse comes in first.

Down to the last horse, Mr. Bubb reminds Sach he'll be coming for his soul. But Sach no longer needs the money; the Polio Fund has agreed to finance Ozzie's operation. This is a necessary script maneuver so Sach doesn't appear selfish about trying to save himself by outwitting Mr. Bubb.

In both this film and *Crazy Over Horses,* Sach is the jockey in the decisive race. Sach will try to make Rubber Check lose. Although Rubber Check crosses the finish line first, the judge disqualifies him because Sach is not a jockey. Sach's soul is safe.

Some old faces are back. Byron Fougler, who played Prof. Quizard in *Hard Boiled Mahoney*, is the sly Mr. Bubb. Jack Mulhall, the veteran actor who appeared in several East Side Kids pictures and worked in some capacity for the screen Actors Guild before he died at age 90, makes a cameo appearance. And Benny Rubin, who played the waiter in the memorable restaurant scene with Billy Gilbert in the East Side Kids' *Mr. Wise Guy,* has a bit part here.

The variety of scenes and the numerous ways Sach fails to place a bet, culminating in the scene at the track with Sach as jockey, are entertainingly tied together and keep the audience in comic suspense to the end.

In the Money

Released February 16, 1958; 61 minutes; Allied Artists; Director, William Beaudine; Producer, Richard Heermance; Screenplay, Al Martin, Elwood Ullman; Story, Al Martin; Photography, Harry Neumann; Art Director, David Milton; Music Director, Marlin Skiles; Editor, Neil Brunnenkant; Production Manager, Allen K. Wood; Assistant Director, Jesse Corallo; Set Decorator, Joseph Kish; Wardrobe, Sidney Mintz; Sound, Phil Mitchell, Makeup, Emile LaVigne; Working Title, *On the Make.*

CAST

Sach	Huntz Hall	Inspector Saunders	Paul Cavanagh
Duke	Stanley Clements	Inspector White	Leslie Denison
Chuck	David Gorcey	Bellboy	Ashley Cowan
Blinky	Eddie LeRoy	Dowager	Norma Varden
Clarke	Leonard Penn	Mike	Dick Elliott
Babs	Patricia Donahue	Dr. Smedley	Owen McGiveney
Cummings	John Dodsworth	Randall	Ralph Gamble

Reggie	Patrick O'Moore	*Scotland Yard Valet*	Snub Pollard
Girl	Pamela Light		

Unless the title of this last film is meant to sum up Monogram–Allied Artists' 12-year history of Bowery Boys movies, it doesn't work. There's little to do with money (the boys certainly don't get any) and everything to do with a dog, a ship, hotel suites, Scotland Yard and smuggling. (Okay, there's *some* money — but not enough for a title.)

It only takes a moment for Mr. Clark, Randall's client, to conclude that Sach's limited intellectual capacities and innocence would be perfect to escort Gloria, a fox terrier with diamonds concealed in a fake collar, across the Atlantic Ocean.

Sach's departing question to Randall is: "Say, Randall, you handle all types of travel, don't you?"

"That's right."

"Well, I'd like you to fix my roller skates."

The comment infuriates Randall, as much as Sach's stubbornness frustrates Duke, Chuck and Blinky, as Sach asserts his independence from them and his loyalty to his new employers. This devotion to another group is in itself startling since in the past, particularly in the

Sach (Hall) is out on a ledge but still being hit in *In the Money*. (Woman is unidentified.)

Gorcey films, Sach remains faithful to his pals. Here again is an indication that Duke does not command the same respect Slip Mahoney did.

Sach reinforces his disassociation from them when he sees Duke, Chuck and Blinky swabbing the deck.

"I say," says the ship's lieutenant. "They wouldn't have to work like this, sir, if you'd pay their passage for them, sir."

Sach looks at each friend's smiling face, then pats Duke on the back. "Keep working, fellas."

There's a hilarious exchange between the boys and Sach, reminiscent of the one between the boys and Mr. Flynn in *Crazy Over Horses,* when Duke, Chuck and Blinky think that Babs, a woman on the ship, is Gloria, who Sach is escorting on the voyage.

"We can't stand by and see you making a fool of yourself over Gloria," says Chuck. "What do you have to do to earn all this money?"

"Take her for walks, carry her if she gets tired."

"Isn't she a little heavy?" asks Duke sarcastically.

"Not if you hold her by the scruff of the neck."

After the boat docks in London, the boys are concerned about the dog's moving gallstones.

With the results of the x-ray in hand, Dr. Smedley steps outside to look for the boys and is met by Inspector Saunders. The doctor points out the diamonds concealed on the dog.

"Gallstones!" the doctor thunders. "I should have such gallstones."

Just before the smugglers come to pick up the dog, Gloria ventures on her own through the hotel halls, causing a frantic but visually tiring search.

Wandering through hotel halls and rooms is an excellent launching pad for numerous comic situations, but the film does not capitalize enough on them. One segment of the search worth mentioning is when Sach enters a ladies' room looking for Gloria. He is chased out but when he sees Inspector Saunders in the hall, re-enters, exits through the window and crawls onto the outside ledge. All the while, a lady is beating Sach with an umbrella, shouting, "Get out, help, murder." As Sach steps onto the ledge and glances downward, he says to her, "Please, come to the funeral."

At a reception at Scotland Yard Hall, Gloria is singled out for a special award. She is more deserving of it than anyone else for the capture of the smugglers would not have been possible had she not wandered off and torn off her fake fur, scattering the diamonds throughout the hotel.

In the last shot of the last Bowery Boys picture, Gloria is awarded a bone, but Sach, believing he is deserving of the reward as much as Gloria, breaks it in half and declares, "Half of this is mine." Hardly an appropriate ending for a film entitled *In the Money.*

Although there is nothing seriously wrong with *In the Money,* it is a relatively uneventful film with misdirected confrontations and little conflict. The thrust of the film focuses on the boys' relationships rather than the smuggling of the diamonds. There is little dramatic conflict between the smugglers and Inspector Saunders or between the boys and the smugglers. Duke, the most outspoken of the group, does not come face to face with the smugglers until the very end. There are no innovative plans on the part of the boys as in *Looking for Danger*; no jams for the boys to get out of, as in *Up in Smoke,* and no goals to reach as in *Fighting Trouble.* The boys are only incidental to the plot—and never declare any real commitment to capture the smugglers as they do in *Smugglers' Cove.*

The film does not give us a feeling for London the way *Loose in London* does. The picture takes us from the boat to the hotel, which in essence is the same set of halls and rooms.

The only indication that they are indeed in London are the policemen's accents, and when the bellboy opens the door to the boys' suite, from which London fog emanates.

Some good dialogue and Hall's expertise partially compensate for a rather thin but workable script.

Cast Biographies

In 1937, an article on the Dead End Kids in *Stage Magazine* had good foresight: "[O]ne wonders whether they will be so good when they have grown up and begin to play parts not so perfectly fitted to their own skins, one would suspect not...."

In the last sentence of the *New York Times* review of *Mob Town* (1941), the writer conveys his annoyance with the Kids by asking, "Even Shirley Temple grew up, didn't she?" Indeed

Gabe Dell, Bernard Punsly, Bobby Jordan, Huntz Hall, Leo Gorcey and Billy Halop (1939).

Huntz Hall (left) and Gabe Dell.

she did, and nobody saw her on screen again. When Mickey Rooney, Judy Garland and Jackie Cooper got older, they played roles that fit their age. The Dead End Kids were different. They neither grew up nor faded away. They remained kids on screen for twenty years.

The truth is, the acting careers of Billy Halop, Leo Gorcey, Huntz Hall, Gabe Dell, Bobby Jordan and Bernard Punsly had about as much of a chance as Tommy had in *Dead End*. By the time the East Side Kids roamed the studio streets, the only way for them to get out of making these films was to retire from acting altogether. Some did, most remained. When

Bernard Punsly, Leo Gorcey, Bobby Jordan, Ben Alexander (host of "About Faces"), Huntz Hall and Billy Halop (1960).

Huntz Hall quit the Bowery Boys in 1958, the series ended, and it was ten years before anything significant was seen from him; that was when he reappeared on TV, in dinner theater, and finally again in the movies. Halop and Jordan tried to stay in show business but eventually worked in other fields. Bernard Punsly became a doctor. And when Gorcey quit, he retired to his ranch.

Only Gabe Dell was serious enough about acting to break his image as a Dead End Kid. And as soon as he realized that the image had to be broken, it was time for him to learn acting all over again. He came back to New York, studied with Lee Strasberg at the Actor's Studio, and made his way back to Broadway.

Leo Gorcey

(June 3, 1917–June 2, 1969)

As a stripling, Leo never hankered for stardom. So it's understandable why the tight-fitting wedge he created for himself as a young tough-guy actor suited his professional aspirations.

Leo Gorcey

His father Bernard (Swiss-Russian-Jewish) abandoned his family when he realized his wife, Josephine Condon Gorcey (Irish-Catholic), was unfaithful to him with a opera singer-soap salesman. Leo was 12 years old when his parents divorced and for the next three years got kicked out of at least six schools for fighting.* Finally, at age 15, he quit school altogether and worked in his Uncle Rob's plumbing shop at $6 a week. His brother Fred was an errand boy and Dave worked in a cleaning plant. And Josephine (the "ramrod," as Leo affectionately called her) sold bootleg whiskey from the apartment.

"Uncle Rob's family turned out to be a hoot," says Brandy Jo, Leo's youngest daughter. "I never met him but his wife Sadie was a delightful, witty woman. She lived in Forest Hills, Queens, New York in the same apartment that she'd been in since like the early '60s until her death in about 1985 at the age of 90-something. For his ninetieth birthday, they took him to his favorite Chinese restaurant and hired a somewhat less than full-blown stripper.... Apparently, Uncle Rob and Aunt Sadie went to visit Barney — my grandfather Bernard Gorcey — in L.A. They said they were riding along with Barney at the wheel of a huge car in which he had to look between the top and the middle of the steering wheel to see. Apparently, they got a lot of honks and stares because it appeared to passersby that there was nobody driving the car.

"Fred and my dad had a huge falling-out over money shortly after Dad and Grandpa moved to Los Angeles. I heard from somebody, perhaps Uncle David before he died, that Fred was alive and well someplace on the East Coast. At that time he would have been in his seventies."

*Gorcey, Leo, Jr., Me and the Dead End Kid, *page 50.*

Bernard Gorcey and Leo Gorcey.

To earn a few extra bucks, Leo snatched his uncle's plumbing tools, and, before he realized how little he knew about plumbing, caused a flood in an apartment building. Uncle Rob wasted no time firing him — again.

Unlike the other boys whose parents were looking for that break into theater, Leo was looking only for a job that would pay him enough to live on. Dave already had a part in the play *Dead End*, thanks to his father, who met him one day and used his theatrical connections to secure an audition for him. The first time Leo visited his brother at the theater, one of the boy actors fainted and Leo pinch-hit. His natural Washington Heights accent and size (5'6") won him the role as one of the Second Avenue boys for $35 a week. But the next day Sidney Kingsley offered him the role of "Spit." Leo countered, demanding $50 a week. Kingsley was incensed. "Are you crazy? There are hundreds of kids in New York who could play this role."

"Yeah? Then go out and find one."

Leo got the part and the $50.

From this point on, Leo's life as an actor primarily depended upon the financial success of the Dead End Kids, East Side Kids, and Bowery Boys. Since they all proved to be financial successes, Leo never again had any real money worries and could afford to behave as rambunctious off screen as he pleased. The eldest of the six Dead End Kids, Leo had a reputation for leading the other kids to mischief, causing damage and expense for the studios. Leo also collected traffic citations on an average of one a month, mostly for speeding. Once, Leo had to spend five days in jail for speeding.

Leo was notorious for getting into accidents both on and off the set. Once, in 1945, Leo broke both his arms in a motorcycle accident. And once he was so angry, he picked up a chair and threw it against the wall. The chair bounced back and broke Leo's nose.

When the Dead End Kids were touring the cities that were showing their movies, Leo was elected treasurer of their salaries, which were paid in cash. Since the sums usually totaled as high as $10,000, Leo thought it best to buy a gun. To make sure the gun worked, he aimed it at a toilet bowl and pulled the trigger. The toilet broke into pieces. He tried gluing it back together but when actress Martha Raye used it the next day, it collapsed.

The reason studios tolerated Leo, it seems, was because he was well-received by viewers and movie critics. As one *New York Times* critic wrote in a review of *On Dress Parade*: "'Spit,' as he was known in the original production, was our baby, the littlest, the one most stunted by cigarette smoking, a venomous expectorator for whom the eye of an enemy was like flying quail to huntsman ... they didn't have to take Spit away from us ... we don't regret the others but in the case of Leo Gorcey we feel like exclaiming sadly, 'Et tu, Spit?'"

In addition to the Dead End Kids films, Leo appeared in *Out of the Fog* starring John Garfield and Ida Lupino. It was during the production of this film that Leo stormed off the set after director Anatole Litvak told him, "Gorcey, as an actor, you stink." Leo later stated that he agreed with that sentiment.

After the Dead End Kids pictures and some other minor roles with Warners and MGM, Leo joined Monogram Pictures at Bobby Jordan's urging. There he received top billing in practically all the East Side Kids films. By this time the critics were accustomed to his qualities and faults, as exemplified in a review of *Bowery Blitzkrieg*: "Gorcey hasn't grown much. He can still pass for a youngster, except for his face which is beginning to sag from having to run around with such a tough fellow as himself."

After six years with producer Sam Katzman, Leo teamed up with Huntz Hall and agent Jan Grippo in 1946 to begin ten years of Bowery Boys films. They broke Hollywood ground, with Leo becoming a 40 percent owner, producing and co-writing the scripts. It was reported that Leo was one of the highest-paid actors in Hollywood. In addition, he invested in real estate with his partner Max Marx, a pharmacist.*

In 1955, after his father was killed in an auto accident, Leo could no longer work effectively, so he retired to his ranch in Los Molinos, California. His only significant return to the screen was a cameo appearance in *It's a Mad Mad Mad Mad World* (United Artists, 1963).

Leo's personal life was about as stormy as his antics as a Dead End Kid. He met his first wife Kay Marvis on the set of *Angels with Dirty Faces*. Although her father disapproved of the

---

*Gorcey, Leo, Jr., *Me and the Dead End Kid*, page 190.

Copy of Leo's contract with American Federation Radio Artists, November 20, 1939.

marriage, they eloped to Yuma, Arizona, on May 16, 1939. To please Kay's mother, they married again on June 4 in the Blessed Sacrament Church of Hollywood. Kay was 17, Leo 21.

An actress herself, Kay appeared with Leo on tour and in a few East Side Kids films. It was while touring Army bases with Groucho Marx's *Pabst Blue Ribbon Town* radio show that Leo's drinking and going AWOL disturbed Kay to the point of seeking affection elsewhere. In 1944, Kay divorced Leo to marry Groucho Marx.

"I spoke with Kay on the phone about my master's thesis, which was a partial biogra-

phy focusing on certain aspects of my dad's film career," says Brandy Jo. "She didn't give me any tidbits at the time because she was hoping to write a book comparing my dad and Groucho as husbands. I never heard from her after that. She was living in an apartment in L.A. at that time and unmarried." (She has since passed away.)

On October 22, 1945, Leo married Evalene (Penny) Banston. But three years later he fired three gunshots at his wife and two private detectives who invaded his house in Van Nuys hoping to catch him in the act of adultery. In fact, Leo's third wife-to-be Amelita jumped out the window not a minute too soon. Leo was arrested on suspicion of assault with a deadly weapon. He countersued the detective agency for illegal entry. He won the suit and was awarded $35,000, which partially offset his $50,000 divorce settlement with Penny. On February 10, 1949, Leo divorced for the second time.

On that day, Leo drove to Ensenada, Mexico, to marry Amelita Ward. This marriage lasted seven years, during which time he fathered Leo Jr. and Jan (now deceased). He bought an eight-acre farm 30 miles from Hollywood where he spent most of his non-filming hours.

Leo and Amelita had a brutal break-up. She had affairs with her doctor, dentist and a cowboy. His third divorce in February 1956 gave her custody of the two children, $750 child support, a lump sum of $50,000 and the farm. She eventually gave Leo back custody of Leo and Jan but continued to receive the child support until she remarried.

"Amelita was certifiable," says Brandy Jo. "She hung out for years in Reno with a guy, who she may have married, named Sid. At some point, not long before she died, she moved back to her family home in Virginia ostensibly to take care of her sick mother. Her father was deceased. Her mother was quite wealthy. Some concerned friend of the family intervened when Amelita was compulsively spending her mother's money. She bought a pink Cadillac (her trademark car) for the mailman. She lost the power of attorney and then got breast cancer and died. My brother took over power of attorney for his grandmother and brought her to live with him and his family in Southern California until she died in 1994 or 1995."

Leo's fourth wife was Brandy, who had been his children's governess while he was married to Amelita. They had a daughter, Brandy Jo, and purchased a ranch in Los Molinos, California. But, again because of his alcoholic behavior, he and Brandy parted company in 1962. But according to Leo Jr. during the time she lived with them, she took care of him like he was her own. Since Leo, Sr., was not working during these last six years, the alimony settlement was nominal.

For the remaining years of his life, Leo enjoyed the outdoors, supervised real estate holdings, built a swimming pool in his backyard, raised tropical fish and chickens, and consumed a great deal of liquor. Always interested in writing (he composed a few songs and published a short story when he was 20), Leo continued to write poems, some of which were included in his autobiography, *An Original Dead End Kid Presents Dead End Yells, Wedding Bells, Cockle Shells and Dizzy Spells*, published by Vantage Press in 1967. It has been one of the most sought-after books since Gorcey's death, selling on eBay for between $500 and $1000 a copy. Recently one was selling on eBay with the inscription *To Ethel — The Greatest Topless I have ever met. Leo B Gorcey 6/30/67.*

"The only Ethel I'm familiar with was my maternal grandmother and dad wouldn't have even have joked with her, offers Brandy Jo. "Unlike his mother who had a really bawdy sense of humor, my maternal grandmother was a somewhat dour and very proper English lady who had *no* sense of humor about anything."

Helping him with the finishing touches of this book was 18-year-old Julia McConnell.

Opposite: Leo and third wife Amelita Gorcey, the mother of Leo Jr. and Jan; she died at age 49.

Leo and his liquor in his private bar with a friend (unidentified).

She had written Leo a fan letter a few years earlier, and Leo invited her to his ranch. Instead of going right to college, Julia moved in with Leo. She typed up his notes, helped revise the manuscript, and befriended his young daughter Brandy Jo.

"Two of Leo's good points were that he was fair and generous," recalls Julia McConnell (now Thibodeau). "He paid me $3 per hour, and in those days that was good money."

Shortly thereafter, Julia and Leo were engaged.

"The first thing that attracted me to Leo was his humor. He was just sides-splittingly funny in life as well as in his films."

"Then, this attraction was replaced by admiration for his sheer stubborn independence — definitely not a quality appreciated by everyone. Where others were concerned, Leo was the least judgmental individual I have ever known. He simply accepted people as they were, with faults and strengths, and personal quirks. He observed them constantly and with great curiosity and interest, but I never knew a critical or judgmental Leo Gorcey.

"Another one of his qualities was that he was never impressed with himself or his position as movie star. He appreciated a good rancher or tractor repairman or plumber (naturally) as much, possibly more, as a good actor. He was quite honest about the fact that his line of work was more highly paid than many other careers, but in the end that's what it was to him: a career. I liked his bluntness and his honesty. That made me love Leo."

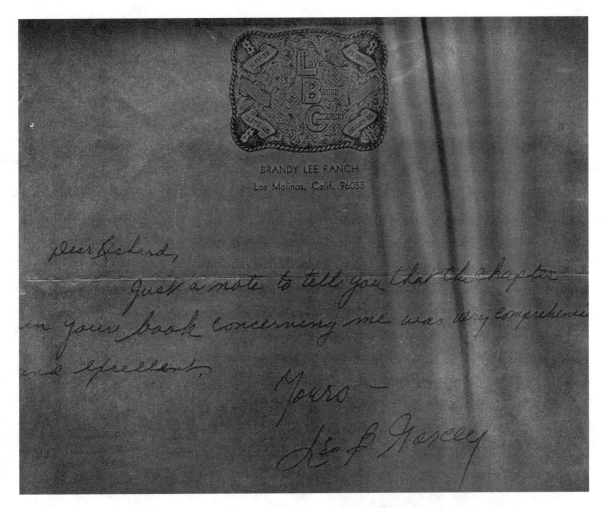

Gorcey's note to Richard Lamparski thanking him for his bio in *Whatever Became of....* Leo wrote, "the chapter in your book concerning me was very comprehensive and excellent."

But as young as she was, Julia also noticed his alcoholism. That made her take off his ring and walk away.

In spite of his many matrimonial difficulties and the amount of money the divorce settlements involved, Leo told interviewer Richard Lamparski that he didn't have any problems in life and was prepared to marry and fifth and last time to 26-year-old Mary Gannon.

"Mary Gannon remarried (secretly) in 1971 to a local Los Molinos law officer. When I was old enough, I challenged her right to live in the life homestead she successfully obtained upon my dad's death. I got nailed by statute of limitations but otherwise she would have had to buy out the other heirs (originally one-fifth each between Mary, my paternal grandmother, Leo, Jan and me). When my grandmother died in the mid-seventies, she left part of her fifth to Mary and part to her daughter Audrey. Anyway, Mary lived there all these years and then managed to sell it without challenge even though she wasn't technically the owner. None of the remaining heirs had the time, money nor really the inclination to fight her over this so we let it go. She just sold it about a year ago."

Shortly after his marriage to Mary, Leo became ill and suffered many months from cirrhosis of the liver. A day before his fifty-second birthday, on June 2, 1969, Leo passed away.

My Father, Leo B. Gorcey, Dead End Kid
A tribute by his daughter Brandy Gorcey Ziesemer

I wasn't overly aware of my father's celebrity status until long after his death. At the time he died, just before my eleventh birthday, I was cognizant of the fact that he'd been an actor but I didn't relate his former career to the actors and actresses I admired at the time. I only saw him on television one time when I was three. My mother says I went behind the console and yelled, "Get my daddy out of there!" I also read his autobiography when it was first published but as a child I didn't understand the significance of his fame before he became my daddy. Finally, I saw him in a cameo role in *It's a Mad Mad Mad Mad World* at a drive-in theater located in a cow pasture on the edge of the rural wide-spot in the road where my father had retired a couple of years before I was born.

At eighteen, I was elected to a rural school board position. A journalist from Sacramento traveled the two-hour drive to interview me for an article in the *Sacramento Bee*. The article was titled, "No Dead End Kid: Ringleader's Daughter Chalks Up a Surprise." Upon reading the article, it dawned on me that I really had no idea who my dad had been professionally. Shortly thereafter, I met the man I eventually married, Thomas Ziesemer. Tom was very familiar with my dad's movies from the feature films of the Dead End Kids through the transitional East Side Kids and finally the Bowery Boys. He rented a print of Dead End and ran it for me on my twentieth birthday. I

Leo looking for a comeback.

was amazed. Over the next year, I watched many of Dad's films and became fascinated by Dad's career. Tom helped me research my master's thesis titled, "Split Image: The Dual Life of Leo Gorcey, Dead End Kid." We spent time in New York, Washington, D.C., and Los Angeles interviewing people and digging through stacks.

Although I came to realize that my father had a dark side, I also confirmed that he brought joy and entertainment to perhaps millions of people from 1935 through the present. He also left me a legacy of happy memories of shared moments—tipping a waitress so she'd let us go to the kitchen and make our own banana splits, bedtime stories, bicycle rides, poolside chats at the local golf course, fishing, watching Red Skelton and Ed Sullivan from the comfort of his lap, nursing a pet dog back to health, listening to old LPs, and endless other moments that I cherish and that enable me to truly appreciate the man who was my father.

Above: Leo Gorcey, 1938. *Right:* In *It's a Mad Mad Mad Mad World* (1963).

Films

1937	*Portia on Trial*
1938	*Mannequin*
1939	*Too Much of Everything*
	Headin' East
1940	*Invisible Stripes*
	Gallant Sons
1941	*Angels with Broken Wings*
	Road to Zanzibar
	Out of the Fog
	Down in San Diego
1942	*Born to Sing*

	Sunday Punch
	Maisie Gets Her Man
	Hullabaloo
1943	*Destroyer*
1945	*One Exciting Night*
1947	*Midnight Manhunt*
	Pride of Broadway
1948	*So This Is New York*
1964	*It's a Mad Mad Mad Mad World*
1965	*Second Fiddle to a Steel Guitar*
1969	*The Phynx*

Huntz Hall

(August 15, 1920–January 30, 1999)

Huntz began his acting career with high expectations and became the only original Dead End Kid to complete the entire cycle of films. So the question is, did these films fulfill Huntz's expectations?

In 1959, shortly after the end of the Bowery Boys series, Huntz told a reporter, "As far as I'm concerned, we helped bring realism to the movies. We were the ones who invented the sweatshirt school of acting, not these method guys." And in an interview in "Let Me Entertain You" shortly before he died, he said, "A lot of people took from us—there's a lot of stuff out there Leo Gorcey and I invented. Take *Happy Days* or *Welcome Back Kotter*—they're rip-offs of the Bowery Boys.... I love the Bowery Boys. If I put that down, I'm putting down my whole career. I wish everybody had that success. The public loved me. I'm not about to resent the public's love."

"My dad was always proud of the pictures," Huntz's son, Reverend Gary Hall, maintains from his church office in Bryn

Huntz Hall

Mawr, Pennsylvania. "But he didn't like people mistaking him for Sach. He'd go to a bar and people would slap him. He was not at all like Sach. He was very smart, though not educated. He didn't finish high school. But he was very interested in politics. And he had a temper. He was put in the slammer for bad behavior."

"I have been slugged at least 25 times by guys who wanted to find out if I am as tough as I make out," Hall told Hedda Hopper in a 1944 interview. "I've received letters from teenage boys asking me to join them in a bank hold-up."

Huntz was pleased with *Dead End*, as he told Hopper in 1944, but disturbed by the reactions to some of the subsequent films. "Maybe I can make amends ... by making some pictures that will counteract the Dead End Kids."

Huntz' Broadway debut was *Thunder on the Left* in 1921 when he was one year old. After he attended St. Stephen's Grammar School, his parents, noticing in Huntz a keener interest for the stage than in his father's profession (air conditioning engineer), paved the way for his start by enrolling him in the Professional Children's School. During this time he was heard on radio with Billy Halop on *The Bobby Benson Show* and in two radio serials, *The Rich Kid* and *The Life of Jimmy Braddock*. He also became a member of the Madison Square Quintet that sang at the Roxy Theater in New York.

It was while Huntz was at the Professional School that Martin Gabel, already cast in the role of Hunk in Sidney Kingsley's *Dead End*, spotted him and asked him to audition for the new play during his lunch hour. By two o'clock that afternoon Huntz was cast—and

Opposite: Huntz taking a stroll in Manhattan in the 1940s.

Jerry Lewis (left) with Huntz.

Huntz performing "The Rusty Samurai Sword Blues" from the musical comedy *Goodbye Broadway, Hello Gimp!* with Gary Crosby (right) at H.D. Hover's Ciro's.

typecast. His imitation of a machine-gun got him the part. He also had to lie about knowing how to swim.

Huntz appeared in all the Universal pictures with Halop and later joined Gorcey and Bobby Jordan in the Monogram East Side Kids flicks. Later in this series, Huntz changed his image from a little tough guy to the sidekick of the gang. When the gang got into fights, Huntz (as Glimpy) was usually seen hiding under the table or atop a high shelf. He based his character Sach on a shoeshiner who worked in the theater district of New York.

"Without Slip, though, Sach wouldn't have made it. Leo and I had chemistry that was great," Huntz told *Entertainment Weekly* in June 1994. "We really loved one another."

"Leo wanted to be Huntz's friend more than Huntz wanted to be Leo's friend," explains Gary Hall. "Slip was Leo's personality. I saw him a year before he died in New York. He did a radio show with my dad and Richard Lamparski, *What Ever Became of....* Leo showed up at St. Regis Hotel with a big cowboy hat and cowboy outfit and they wouldn't let him in. My dad gravitated towards Gabe."

After the Bowery Boys, Huntz and Gabe performed together at nightclubs. They were together so much, their respective wives divorced them on the same day.

Between the East Side Kids and Little Tough Guys films, Huntz had brief roles in *The Return of Doctor X* with Humphrey Bogart, *Wonder Man* with Danny Kaye, and *A Walk in the Sun*, for which he received critical acclaim.

"Huntz Hall of 'East Side Kids' fame is particularly good in a scene wherein he argues over whether the human body or the leaf is the most complicated natural structure," said one reviewer.

But after his last Bowery Boys flick, Huntz was not in demand. He appeared on televi-

TV channel choices

SUNDAY CALL-CHRONICLE

SEPT. 12-18

The Chicago Teddy Bears

Opposite: An advertisement for *The Chicago Teddy Bears*. (Huntz Hall is at the top.) *Above:* Huntz and Colleen's wedding in 1960. Huntz and his third wife lived with Colleen's friend Augusta and her daughter Cher (of Sonny and Cher).

Huntz in drag in *College Days*. Other dancer is unidentified.

sion on *The Tonight Show* and *The Jerry Lester Show*. He also traveled the nightclub circuit with Frankie Ray.

Huntz planned to create a new Ghetto Boys, similar to the Bowery Boys, but the project never materialized. In the early 1960s very little was seen of Huntz. In the mid–'60s he again began appearing on TV and in movies such as *Gentle Ben* and *Gentle Giant*.

"He kept holding out for bigger deals, more money, top billing." explains Gary Hall. "He didn't play it right. He did commercials for Dash and Toyota."

He was in several *Flipper* shows and in 1971 was a regular on *The Chicago Teddy Bears*.

"Director Ken Russell called him one day and wanted him to play the part of Jesse Lasky," Gary says of the incident that led to Huntz landing his role in *Valentino* with Rudolph Nureyev in 1977. "He put on a tie. Russell told him he was the only person who dressed up to see him."

"Quentin Tarantino was looking for actors from my father's era and called him after *Pulp Fiction*, for *Four Rooms*. But my dad didn't like him."

Like almost all the other Dead End Kids, Huntz had his personal ups and downs, including his bouts with the law. His first arrest came on October 28, 1948, in Los Angeles when the police found him and a friend digging up four tobacco cans of marijuana valued at $200 under a tree in Huntz's backyard. In April of 1949, charges against Huntz for narcotics possession were dropped.

In 1955 and 1959, Huntz was arrested for assault and drunken driving respectively.

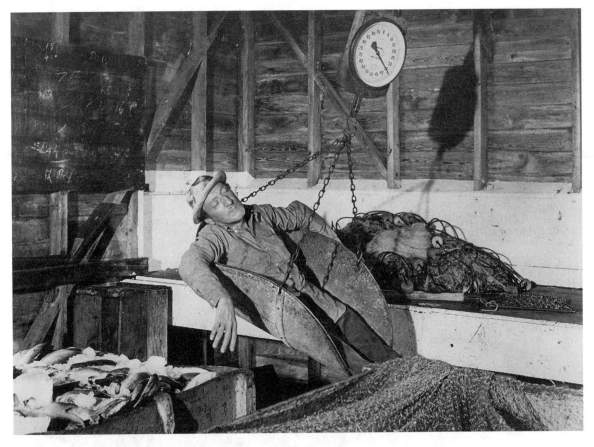

Huntz "weighing in" in *Gentle Ben* (1967).

"My dad was an alcoholic. But he turned himself around. He went to AA and was sober for the last 17 years of his life."

He participated in Princess Grace of Monaco's Council for Drug Abuse, part of the Catholic Office of Drug Education. This may explain his reaction to how he was portrayed in Terry Southern's famous novel *Candy*.

"It's a fantasy scene with my dad injecting drugs," says Gary.

Southern's son Nile explains it this way: "[Hall] is a popular culture figure mentioned within a monologue delivered by Candy Christian's nymphomaniac raconteur and trouble-maker, Aunt Livia."

"My dad was livid. He got so angry he tried to sue Terry Southern. But we convinced him otherwise. He was very sensitive and took offense, before he was pleased.

"He was not the best dad in the world. He was a loving father but not a very good one. He cared but from a distance. My parents were divorced when I was three. After that, he was in and out of my life. He remarried a few times. He married a woman named Colleen who lived in a big house with her roommate Augusta and her daughter Cher [of Sonny and Cher]. Cher was 13 and I was 10. We see each other all the time. Cher saw Huntz Hall all the time.

"Dad had a Jewish wedding with his last wife Lee in 1965 and joined the Synagogue for the Performing Arts. They went to Yom Kippur services and did Passover seder and because I was the youngest, I said the four questions. When Lee died in 1985, he sat shiva [Jewish period of mourning]. His community was the Jewish community.

"After Lee died, he just gave up. I did all his grocery shopping. He needed a heart valve replacement but wasn't up to it. I saw him the day he died. The next morning, a friend couldn't get him on the phone so he called me. I went over to his house and found him on the floor in the bathroom. When the paramedics came and checked his driver's license, they looked at him and said, "Hey, that's Sach!"

Recognized to the end.

Thoughts on My Father
A Eulogy by the Reverend Gary Hall, February 2, 1999

Huntz Hall was the tenth of 16 children. He always said he wanted to call his autobiography "I Stood in Line for Love."

Huntz Hall's son, the Reverend Gary Hall, in his office at the Church of the Redeemer, Bryn Mawr, Pennsylvania.

He left the Roman Catholic Church early in life — one too many adolescent confessions of "taking the Lord's name in vain" drove the priest on the other side of the confessional literally to come out of the booth and slap him in the face. That his only son became a priest seemed to him a combined gift of God and cosmic joke.

Although he was widely known in this country and around the world, my father probably didn't have the colossal stardom he should have. For sixty years of his life he loved to make people laugh and he did it as brilliantly and simply as anyone on stage and film has ever done it. After the Bowery Boys series ended in 1958, he never really connected with roles that worked for him. But he does leave a solid body of movies that have been both popularly successful and creatively influential. A writer friend of ours once said to me that most New York–style TV comics simply do "early Huntz Hall." One of his great joys later in life was the way younger comedians would seek him out to tell him how much his improvisational style of wild comedy had influenced them.

My father had a rather rocky personal life. He was married four times. From 1967 to 1994 he was married to his fourth wife, Lee, and as crazy and high-strung as it was, that marriage seemed to be a great blessing to both of them. When Lee died five years ago, his health deteriorated and he became quite reclusive. I was virtually the only person he saw for weeks on end. When people would ask me what he looked like these days, I would say, "Just picture Howard Hughes without the money."

As ill as he was in the last years of his life, Huntz Hall never lost the kind of hip, insane humor that made him a cult favorite of so many comics and writers. When Kathy and I went

Left to right: Jackie Coogan, Gabe Dell and Huntz Hall in the *Manchu Eagle Murder Mystery* (1975).

Huntz at a nostalgia convention in the 1990s.

Huntz Hall flanked by fans Anne Sautner (left) and Leslie Duerr at "A Premier Card, Collectable & Memorabilia Show" in Rego Park, Long Island, New York, in 1990.

to visit him at the depth of his recent five-week stay in the hospital, he looked up and asked, "Dr. Kevorkian, wherefore art thou?"

Huntz Hall never grew up. His childlike qualities were his creative qualities: He could be inventive, playful, hilariously funny, and incredibly generous. But he was often petulant, self-centered and, before he stopped drinking in 1982, belligerent and mean. He was a hard person to have for a father. When I did get his attention, he was a better playmate than he was a parent; but he loved me and Kathy and Oliver very much, and showed that love in all kinds of wonderful and infuriating ways.

So I will miss my father very much. But I know he was ready to go. He was tired, he was lonely, he was very sick. His friends Gabe and Ben, his wife Lee, his brothers and sisters had all gone before him.

Huntz at the dedication of the Dead End Kids Hollywood star.

The Bowery Boys are not as well-known these days as they should be but, like those of Buster Keaton and Stan Laurel and the Three Stooges before him, the films of Huntz Hall will one day be rediscovered and applauded for the generous and spontaneous way they celebrate community, simplicity, and the pure goofiness of being human. And when you think about it, what is a better life's work than that?

Films

1939	*The Return of Doctor X*	1970	*Gentle Giant*
1941	*Zis Boom Bah*	1974	*Herbie Rides Again*
1942	*Private Buckaroos*		*The Manchu Eagle Murder Mystery*
1945	*Wonder Man*	1977	*Valentino*
	A Walk in the Sun	1979	*Gas Pump Girls*
	Bring on the Girls	1982	*The Escape Artist*
1965	*Second Fiddle to a Steel Guitar*	1984	*The Mogul*
1967	*Gentle Ben*	1987	*Cyclone*
1969	*The Phynx*		

Television

Flipper
The Chicago Teddy Bears

Corner Bar

Bobby Jordan

(April 1, 1923–September 10, 1965)

Bobby Jordan's angelic look was instrumental in winning the role of Angel in *Dead End*. The irony is that it did not reflect the life he would lead.

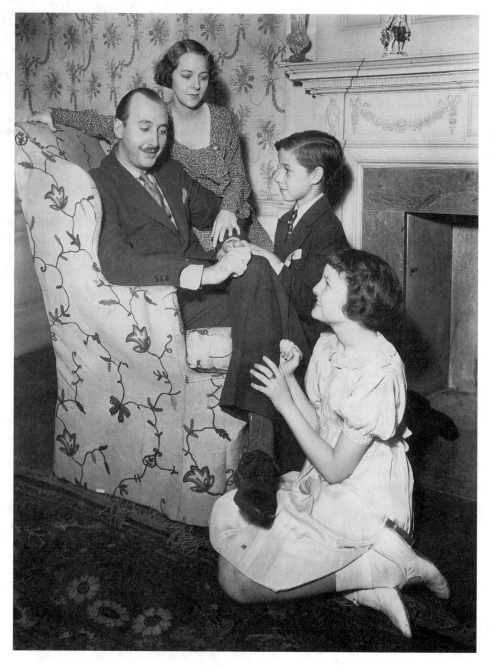

Left to right: Raymond Knight, Alice Davenport, Bobby Jordan and Emily Vass in the radio show "The Batchelors of Wheatenaville," November 26, 1934.

Son of a garage owner, Bobby, at age four, began his acting career in a Christmas Carol film. As more of his talent became apparent, which included playing the saxophone and tap dancing, his parents enrolled him in the Professional Children's School. In Harrison, New York, where his family lived most of his life, Bobby entered many amateur contests and modeled junior boys clothing. He was thirteen when chosen for *Dead End* in 1935.

After 684 performances on Broadway, and tours in Boston, Chicago, San Francisco and Los Angeles, Bobby and the boys headed to Hollywood to make Samuel Goldwyn's movie version of *Dead End*. Huntz Hall recalled in an interview with Tom Snyder that he and Bobby Jordan got into a fight on the train.

In the six Warner Brothers Dead End Kids films that followed *Dead End* personal hardships are borne most on Bobby Jordan's character, the cutest, smallest, and thus the most vulnerable. In *Crime School* it is he who is caught in a boiler room that's about to explode; In *They Made Me a Criminal* it is he who has difficulty keeping his head above water. For protection he looks up to Billy Halop or, if Halop is not around, to those in authority most sympathetic to his predicament. His solidarity with Halop, as first established in *Dead End* when he helps Tommy positively identify Spit as the one who betrays him, is reaffirmed in *Hell's Kitchen* when he opens the door to the freezer where Halop is expected to remain all night. Unfortunately, Halop cannot return the favor when Jordan is put into the freezer and freezes to death.

Following the Warner Brothers films, Jordan contracted with Universal for Little Tough Guys Films and Monogram for East Side Kids films. He made a number of other films in which he starred, including *Reformatory* and *Military Academy*. He also starred with Edward G. Robinson in *A Slight Case of Murder*. He was superb in the Little Tough Guys' *Keep 'Em Slugging*, in which he was the clearly the leader.

At first he received top billing in the East Side Kids films. Shortly afterward, however, the vibrant personality of Leo Gorcey and the comical antics of Huntz Hall overshadowed him.

In 1943, after playing in the serial *Adventures of the Flying Cadets*, he entered the Army as a foot soldier in the 97th Infantry.

When he was discharged in 1945 he was welcomed into the Bowery Boys series but rarely had more than a few lines to say. In 1947, realizing that his presence in the films made little or no difference, Bobby quit the series. He worked hard developing his own nightclub routine. After a 16-minute song-and-comedy act in Queens Terrace, New York, one reviewer noted, "[W]ith fresher material and a more vigorous attack, Jordan may develop a routine strong enough to counteract the discourtesies of the cafe crowds such as he faced.... Tightening up may take him into more lucrative vaude and nitery dates."

Bobby never did see success again, though he never lost hope.

"I've made a fortune before," he said in the early 1960s, "and I'll do it again. This is a hard town when you're not on top."

At Bobby's peak he was pulling in $1,500 a week and owned a $150,000 mansion in Beverly Hills. He was the sole support of his mother, two brothers, a sister and a niece.

After Bobby gave up nightclub acts, he took to door-to door selling, oil drilling in Coalinga, California, and bartending with Carl "Alfalfa" Switzer. Things became so bad for Bobby that in 1958 he was jailed for two days for failure to pay alimony and child support payments to his former wife, Lee, whom he had married in 1947 and divorced ten years later. They had one son, Robert Carl Christopher Jordan, Jr.

"I loved my dad," Robert said in a telephone interview. "My mom loved him too but couldn't live with him because of his drinking. She was 12 years older than him. I was seven when they divorced.

Bobby Jordan on sax and Billy Halop on drums.

"I would always look forward to him coming to see me. But sometimes he would forget to come and I wouldn't see him for six months, maybe a year. When he came, he would take me with him to the Firefly bar on weekends. He would give me popcorn and I would sleep in the car while he drank. Once he forgot about me and the bass player had to call my uncle to come get me.

"His mother spent all my dad's money on gambling. That was before the Jackie Coogan law. He had an opportunity to be in a serial but his mother nixed it, according to my Uncle Art. She screwed up his career.

"My dad did give me piano lessons and boxing lessons. He was a very good boxer. In fact, he knocked down a professional boxer when they were doing *Kid Dynamite*. He was also a very good saxophonist. And he read a lot. He read five books a week.

"But my dad had a lot of disappointment. When he was in the Army he was injured on duty. Not sure if a bullet misfired or he got a dislocated disk. He was in an elevator accident in New York. The elevator dropped five floors and he broke both kneecaps. And then he was in a car accident and was in a coma for two weeks.

"He was very frustrated with his life. Acting was everything to Bobby and he was heart-broken.

"Towards the end he was living with some friends who, I remember, had a big fish tank

Wife Lee, son Bobby Jr., and Bobby Jordan outside their home.

Bobby with a cane. He suffered an injury on duty and was also in an elevator accident in New York. The girl is unidentified.

and pit bulls. I was 16 when I got a call from the hospital. I was with him the last week of his life. His last words to me were 'I'm really sick, Rob.'"

Bobby Jordan was 42 when he died on September 10, 1965, at the Veterans Hospital in Sawtelle, California. All the Dead End Kids attended his funeral.

Bobby Jordan Was My First Beau
A Tribute by Edith Fellows* (Actress)

Bobby and I first met May 8, 1937, at a fundraiser at the El Portal Theater in North Hollywood, California. He said hello to me and my grandmother, and wanted to know if he could call me sometime. Grandma smiled and gave him our number. That was the first time she allowed anyone to call me. A few days later he called and he invited me to a movie. It was *The Citadel* with Robert Donat. He was to pick me up at 7 p.m. But he was running late. He arrived at 7:30 all upset. He had stopped at his favorite gas station where they always allowed him to pump his own gas. Something happened. It overflowed and went all over his pant leg. You could *really* smell it. When we sat down at the theater, I noticed a couple people moved away from us. Our first date!

When some of our kid friends found out we were dating, we were invited to a lot of parties. We always sat side by side, in a large chair, and of course we were teased, "Here come the Siamese twins." It was all in good fun.

We were invited to Jane Withers' sixteenth birthday party. It was held in a barn. We were to dress in Western attire. At one point Bobby and I were dancing and an announcement came over the speaker that they were dropping balloons and at the end of one balloon was a tag. Bobby and I couldn't care less, so we just kept on with our dancing. Suddenly, a balloon, with a tag, fell right between us! We couldn't ignore it. The grand prize was a very cute little baby goat. Alive! We just stood there. Then we started to discuss who was going to take the little one home. We agreed *his* mother wouldn't want it. So I agreed to take it home. Bobby was allowed visitation rights! I had him for a year and Grandma went along with the program, until he started to eat her flowers. Joel McCrea [who played Dave in the film version of *Dead End*] took him.

I noticed at each party we went to, Bobby would excuse himself. He and some of the boys wanted to just get together for a few minutes. I found out many parties later he and the guys would drop by a nearby bar. A sign of things to come?

Underneath the joy Bobby and I were sharing on our first love, there was a dark side. The moment Bobby and I left on our date, Bobby's mother would call my grandmother and they would talk about what bush Bobby and I were under tonight. Bobby and I never had sex. (Sometimes I wish we had.) Grandma admitted she didn't like Bobby and it was then I realized she was jealous of him. She said he was taking up too much of my life. I told her Bobby was the only happiness I had ever known. Next time I saw Bobby, I asked him what his mother said to him and he said it was best left unsaid. He was worried about me as I was losing weight and had trouble sleeping. He thought for our sake, not theirs, we better break up. I agreed and the rest of the evening was filled with lots of tears from both of us.

Edith's first film was Movie Night *(1929); her last film,* I Used to Be in Pictures *(2000). She was in a film called* My First Beau *(1941).*

Bobby on radio in the 1950s.

Films

1938	*A Slight Case of Murder*	1940	*Young Tom Edison*
	Reformatory		*Military Academy*
1939	*Off the Record*	1949	*Treasure of Monte Cristo*
	Dust Be My Destiny	1950	*The Man Is Armed*

Billy Halop

(February 11, 1920–November 9, 1976)

Mismanagement, the war, and a succession of bad breaks stunted the career growth of this child star and prevented him from blossoming into another Paul Muni.

Billy Halop as Bobby Benson (1932).

Billy Halop in *Blues in the Night* (1941).

If Billy was "discovered" by anyone, credit should be given to his father, a lawyer, and his mother, a dancer. When Billy was five, his mother put him on WOR radio singing on the *Children's Hour* and *Let's Pretend* shows. At 12, Billy was picked to play Puck in a production of Shakespeare's *A Midsummer Night's Dream*. Soon afterward he was promoted to play Romeo in *Romeo and Juliet* on radio.

With this classical background, NBC decided he was ready for popular entertainment such as *March of Time* and other radio plays with Maude Adams.

Billy Halop reporting for duty at Camp Upton at age 22, September 2, 1942.

What really drew audience attention to Billy, before his debut on Broadway, was his radio creation of Bobby Benson. As Bobby, Billy appeared with W.T. Johnson's Rodeo show at Madison Square Garden and later toured with him. Happy with Billy's work, Johnson gave Billy a gift of a horse which the young performer trained and eventually rode as a headliner with Barnum and Bailey's circus, touring the east. At this point he was earning about $500 a week.

He attended Children's Professional School and, later, McBurney's School for Boys. His experience, together with his education, not only convinced Sidney Kingsley to choose Billy for the role of Tommy in his play, *Dead End*, but to grant him special treatment and a salary that exceeded the other boys.'

During the years *Dead End* ran on Broadway and throughout the country, and the year the movie version was released (1937), as many times as the Dead End Kids made headlines, Billy was singled out for critical acclaim. Consequently, his salary increased to about $750 per week. This served as the main source of hostility between him and the rest of the boys, especially Leo Gorcey. Nevertheless, he let it be known that Paul Muni was the actor he emulated and he sought roles that would help nurture his capacity for character acting.

At first Billy wasn't too concerned that Warner Brothers and Universal chose him only for roles as a juvenile delinquent. He considered these roles as stepping stones to professionalism. But as early as 1940, Billy felt the mold of himself as a Dead End Kid closing in on him. Even when he got a break to play Flashman in *Tom Brown School Days*, the role was that of a youth who bullied other boys.

While he was still making Little Tough Guys films for Universal, Billy had his first character role since *Dead End* in Warner Brothers' *Blues in the Night*. Soon afterward, when the Japanese bombed Pearl Harbor, he enlisted in the Signal Corps. He felt, at this point, with his parents counseling his career and finances, and keeping himself active by performing in the European Theatre production of *Golden Boy*, that when he got out of the Signal Corps, the continuity of his career would be assured. He did not know that *Blues in the Night* would be his last major non-juvenile role of any substance.

In 1946 and 1947, while the East Side Kids films were being produced, Billy made an effort to establish his own gang, the Gas House Kids. Billy starred in one of the three pictures and that was virtually the end of his career as a motion picture actor.

"They don't see me as a mature individual, they see me as a child actor and I'm not," Billy told Richard Lamparski in a radio interview in 1968.

The sudden end of his career led to emotional and physical problems. In 1946 he married actress Helen Trupper, but they divorced seven months later, citing different views on housekeeping as the reason. The following year, he married Barbara Hoon.

In 1953 his alcoholism got so bad his wife committed him to the state mental institution at Camarillo, California. In 1956 he suffered a nervous breakdown. When Barbara left him, he called the West Los Angeles police station threatening to commit suicide. He and Barbara divorced on March 5, 1958.

Trying for a comeback, he sought the assistance of Chuck Connors, whom Billy had helped, but Connors refused. Between brief stints on radio, including weekly work for the Economic Cooperation Administration in Paris in 1950, Billy worked for Leonard Appliance Co. in Los Angeles as an electric dryer salesman. He won the National Association of Manufacturers Award for the most creative salesman in the U.S.

Billy purchased a ranch in the San Fernando Valley. He married his "first love," Suzanne Roe, on December 17, 1960. Shortly afterward, Suzanne was stricken with multiple sclerosis. His wife's ailment renewed Billy's interest in medicine and he became a male nurse at St. John's Hospital. He enjoyed nursing, and told Lamparski that it filled a tremendous void in his life. He worked mainly as a geriatric nurse and with critical alcoholics and drug addicts.

Although he was offered television commercials, he refused them, confirming his dignity as an actor. "I'm an old-fashioned actor," he told Lamparski. "I use my head, my mind, and everything else comes naturally." He did, however, make guest appearances on many TV shows, including *All in the Family* as the cab driver Munson.

While his wife's health improved, their marriage and his own health worsened. He suffered two coronaries and underwent open heart surgery in the same year. Sue and Billy divorced in 1966, got back together, and divorced again in 1971. Shortly thereafter he moved back in with his ex-wife Barbara. On November 9, 1976, at the age of 56, Billy died in his sleep.

In October 1976 a month before he died, Billy published a magazine article "Alcoholism Was Almost My Dead End" (*Screen Gems*, October 1976). In it he reviews his entire life, and his plan to write his autobiography, *There Is No Dead End*. The book was never written.

What Billy never knew is that he was much loved. Over 70 fans have paid tribute to him on the Find-A-Grave website. Billy was buried at Mount Sinai Memorial Park, Los Angeles, California (location: Garden of Sher Mot, Crypt 64181).

Who Was Billy Halop?
A Tribute by Benita G. Bowen (Billy Halop's niece)

Billy Halop was "Uncle Bill" to me, the uncle whose laugh boomed across my grandmother's huge backyard at family gatherings in Southern California. That signature laugh, his gorgeous, thick, crisp, curling gray hair, and his penchant for incomprehensible vaudevillian "double talk" conversations with unwitting relatives, made him larger-than-life in a family that had lived life largely.

His mother, my grandmother Lucille, immigrated to New York with her family from Odessa, Russia, with her parents and younger sister and brother in 1908, when she was barely eight years old. My grandfather Benjamin had emigrated earlier in 1905, and was already selling newspapers on the streets of New York that year, when he was five.

Yet within 20 years, my grandfather was putting himself through law school after graduating *summa cum laude* from night university—all the while working full time in a meatpacking plant and being a husband and father. My grandmother, who had dreamed of being in vaudeville as a dancer, was occupied with her full-time job: promoting and managing the theatrical careers of her oldest son Billy and my mother Florence.

My grandmother had recognized from the very beginning that Billy was special; his thick brown curls, large hazel eyes, and big smile made him a regular winner of "Beautiful Baby" contests in Brooklyn and New York. But when he learned to talk (a skill he practiced exuberantly throughout his life) and, more important, when he learned to read at a very early age, my grandmother knew that he could be a star in radio.

And so that life began: "schlepping" to casting calls, learning lines at night, enrolling in the Professional Children's School, juggling school, work, sports, keeping up with his growing fan club and, later, 684 nightly performances of *Dead End* on Broadway before he was 15½. During those years, he was also a great older brother to his sister Florence and brother Joel. In fact, he acted as a talent scout and agent. At the ripe old age of seven he suggested that his 4½-year-old sister would be a great replacement for a sick cast member on a radio show since "she could read." She could and she did, and my mother, Florence Halop, stayed in show business for the next 59 years until her death in 1986.

I remember both my Uncle Bill and my mom saying that being a child actor in the '30s was a great life. They loved acting, they loved working with other adult and kid performers, and they loved the feeling of being "a pro," of having a real profession and craft at such an early age. On the downside, they emphasized the self-discipline they had to practice while other kids were out playing because they were expected to be letter-perfect on their lines. They both knew that there were lots of boys and girls with fervent mothers who would be happy to replace sloppy performers.

As an adult, my Uncle Bill had a bumpy road, a fate not uncommon with former child

Left: Billy Halop, 1941. *Right:* In 1971.

stars. His career never really flourished again. He appeared in many TV shows in the '50s and '60s, tried to develop ideas into new shows, and eventually became a licensed nurse. But in the end, Uncle Bill still had the magic, proudly working as a semi-regular on *All in the Family* as Bert Munson, the cab driver.

When I was growing up in the '60s and got bored with the adult talk at my grandmother's family gatherings around the pool, I'd wander back to the house and go to the little sewing room off the kitchen. On one wall, Nana kept her "Thieves Gallery": pictures of the family from the stiff portraits of her parents to her grandchildren's school pictures. But my favorites were the professional shots of Billy and Florence growing up as actors. I loved the stills of Billy from *Tom Brown's School Days*, *Dead End* and *Angels with Dirty Faces* or the picture of Billy and Judy Garland dancing together at a party around 1939, looking so young, so happy, so carefree. I'd dig out the scrapbooks my grandmother had meticulously kept of clippings, more photos, reviews, and fan club memorabilia and spend hours reading and looking at them all. What I saw, what I knew is what every fan of Billy Halop has known: He was an exuberant, talented, handsome child star who became an instantly recognizable character actor — and that's the way I'll always remember his career.

Films

1939   *You Can't Get Away with Murder*
        Dust Be My Destiny

1940   *Tom Brown's School Days*
1941   *Blues in the Night*

1941	*Sky Raiders*	1963	*For Love of Money*
1942	*Junior Army*		*Move Over, Darling*
1946	*Gas House Kids*		*The Courtship of Eddie's Father*
1947	*Dangerous Years*	1964	*A Global Affair*
1949	*Too Late for Tears*	1966	*Mister Buddwing*
1949	*Challenge of the Range*	1967	*Fitzwilly*
1955	*Air Strike*	1974	*The Phantom of Hollywood*
1962	*Boys' Night Out*		

Television

Adam-12

All in the Family

Gomer Pyle, U.S.M.C.

Gunsmoke

Land of the Giants

Richard Diamond, Private Detective

The Andy Griffith Show

The Cisco Kid

The F.B.I.

The Jack Benny Program

The Fugitive

The New Breed

Wanted: Dead or Alive

Bracken's World

Gabriel Dell

(October 4, 1919–July 3, 1988)

Determined not to let the yoke of childhood success impede the development of his career, Gabe Dell, after years in Hollywood, re-invented himself by returning to New York to study acting with Lee Strasberg at the Actor Studio.

"Being a Dead End Kid gave them a false sense of entitlement," explains his son, Gabe Dell, Jr., in a telephone interview. "And he feared that he'd only be known as a Dead End Kid. He had to separate himself from the group — approach it like a warrior."

Gabe's Italian father, Dr. Marcello Del Vecchio (who was Rudolph Valentino's doctor), Americanized his last name when he settled in Brooklyn. Gabe attended parochial school and then DeWitt Clinton High School. He played Hamlet in a school production before his mother managed to secure a small speaking part for him in the Theatre Guild production of *The Good Earth*, with Alla Nazimova and Claude Rains (who was to co-star with him in *They Made Me a Criminal*.

Shortly afterwards, his father, with the notion that he was soon to die, returned to Italy. Gabe remained in New York with his mother. She leased the top floor of their West 50th street brownstone to actresses and clowns. Overhearing the gossip of her boarders, Mrs. Dell learned of auditions for kids at the Belasco Theatre for Sidney Kingsley's *Dead End*. Not only was Gabe chosen for the role of T.B. and was the first Dead End Kid to appear before the audience, but his mother and sister got parts in the crowd scenes as well.

"It wasn't really acting," Gabe told a reporter, referring to their roles in *Dead End*, "but that's just as well because we couldn't act. It was just a matter of being ourselves and it worked."

Gabe Dell starred in the Broadway show *The Sign in Sidney Brustein's Window*, the play that made his acting career all worthwhile (1968).

"He wanted to be a baseball player," Gabe Jr. claims. "But if he didn't get *Dead End*—he might have ended up in the Mafia. He was headed that way, running numbers."

Gabe remained with the group throughout the Warner Brothers, Universal and Monogram films, but was rarely singled out among the other boys. Perhaps this is because Gabe was more interested at that time in mischievous activity such as tossing sugar cubes into the lap of the Warner Brothers press agent.

"He and Huntz were racing their Model A on Sunset Blvd against Leo Gorcey in his Model A," Gabe Jr. says, recalling a story his father told him. "They were all drunk. Huntz was so drunk he fell asleep. My dad crushed the car into a parked car. He thought Huntz was dead. He tried to get him up but couldn't. So he left. When he sobered up, he went to the hospital. When he got there, Huntz was hiding behind the newspaper, and said to him, 'Left me for dead, huh?'

"My Aunt Ethel [Gabe's sister, who married Little Tough Guy Hally Chester] always bailed the kids out when they got arrested. And they all did. Even in the later years she bailed out Billy Halop. Uncle Billy. He came over when he was sober. He dressed me up as a clown, costumes and makeup. I loved it. His sister Florence and my aunt were best friends.

"My dad was the glue behind the scenes. When things were going wrong, they looked to Gabe to hold it all together. Gorcey knew that. Leo loved Gabe. Aunt Ethel told me, some time in 2004 before she died, that Leo came to the house to see Gabe. Leo knew he was dying and was coming to say goodbye. They kissed on the lips. Leo said, 'I love you, Gabe,' and my dad said, 'I love you too, Leo.' That was the last time they saw each other."

During the war, Gabe entered the Merchant Marines where he had time to think about three possible careers: acting, physician (a surgeon like his father, grandfather and great-grandfather) or to remain at sea. After three years in the service, then walnut-picking, then concrete-pouring, Gabe finally decided on acting. He and Norman Abbott (Bud's nephew), and later Grace Hartman, created a comedy nightclub act. While still doing Bowery Boys films, he and Huntz Hall teamed up and did a comedy nightclub act that performed to SRO audiences in Montreal and Toronto. Gabe also did industrial shows for General Motors, summer stock and was a regular on the Steve Allen TV show, where his impersonation of Bela Lugosi's Dracula appealed to many. But in the middle of doing a Western, it suddenly occurred to Gabe that he was a "primitive, an actor by accident." That's when he decided to return to New York to study acting at the Actor's Studio.

"He scrubbed floors to pay his way to learn the craft all over again at the Actor's Studio," Gabe Dell Jr. reveals.

While spending three years studying mime with Etienne Decroux (Marcel Marceau's teacher), and ballet and modern dance with Jean-Louis, he tested his performing abilities in four off-Broadway flops, *The Automobile Graveyard*, *Fortuna*, *Man Out Loud-Girl Quiet* and *Chocolates*.

"I felt like an artist for the first time," Gabe told a *New York Times* reporter. "I was by myself for the first time, working, studying, and creating."

Gabe appeared on Broadway in *Tickets Please* and *Ankles Away* in 1955. In 1962 he appeared in City Center Productions of *Can-Can*, *Wonderful Town* and *Oklahoma* before playing in the Actor's Studio presentation of *Marathon 33*. Later, in the summer of 1964, Gabe won the *Chicago Daily News* Golden Straw Award as *Best Actor* for his performance in the Sid Caesar role in *Little Me* at the Melody Top Theatre. He portrayed Comptroller Schub opposite Angela Lansbury in the musical *Anyone Can Whistle*. He played the lead role of Fiorello at the White House for President Johnson.

"The policy was that there wouldn't be any dancing because the Viet Nam War was going

Gabe played a prisoner in *Framed* (1974). Left to right: Gabe Dell, John Marley, Joe Don Baker.

on," Gabe Jr. recalls. "But my mom grabbed a general and started to dance, and soon every-one was dancing."

"My dad suffered from depression. He said to me, 'I don't think I can go much further unless I find for myself the importance of my art.'"

He found it in Lorraine Hansberry's *The Sign in Sidney Brunstein's Window*. Mort Sahl was suppose to play the role but dropped out. Twenty-eight actors auditioned for the part. Word got out that only Gabe Dell could play this part. Director Carmen Capalbo and Ms. Hansberry chose Gabe. He had only eight days before the opening. He came out on stage before the show to explain why he had to do the first show with script in hand.

"What *Sidney* meant to me was that I finally got a good part on Broadway [the Dead End Kid playing a Jewish intellectual] and I was at ease in it," Gabe said in an interview.

Gabe acted in a few motion pictures (*Who Is Harry Kellerman and Why Is He Saying Those Terrible Things About Me?* and *Earthquake*) and wrote a few scripts. He collaborated with novelist Philip Roth to write *Back-Up*, which was performed in Spoleto, Italy. He also wrote and starred in *The Manchu Eagle Murder Caper Mystery*, which also starred Huntz Hall. He and Hall bought a church in Topanga Canyon which they converted into a restaurant.

By the time Gabe replaced Alan Arkin in the role of Harry Berlin in *Luv* in 1965, he had earned the prestige of having whole newspaper articles devoted to this change. And in 1972,

Mickey Rooney (left) and Gabe playing the devil's son in *A Year at the Top* (1977).

Alan King (left) and Gabe Dell (playing a bartender) in ABC-TV's *The Corner Bar* (1972), a fore-runner to *Cheers. Below left:* Gabe playing a rabbi on ABC-TV's *Serpico. Below right:* Gabe Dell in another stage performance.

Gabe receiving an award from Lee Strasberg at the Waldorf Astoria, November 1980.

Huntz Hall and Gabe showing off his war wound.

when Gabe was to star as Harry Grant in the ABC summer comedy show *The Corner Bar*, journalists used the event as an excuse to write about Gabe himself. We learned then that Gabe had married and divorced the late ballerina Viola Essen and had a son, Beau. In 1965 he married actress Allyson Daniell, daughter of British-born actor Henry Daniell (Herr Garbage in Charlie Chaplin's *The Great Dictator*). Both were students of Zen philosophy. Their son, Gabe Jr. was born in 1967.

"The man was a present. He was everyone's father. No one was more passionate than he. Every day was an adventure. I was six years old when my dad brought me out on the Broadway stage at the end of *Prisoner of Second Avenue*.

"He never spoke about the Dead End Kids or the Bowery Boys. I'm watching them now for the first time as part of my project 'Looking for Pop Is No Dead End.' It's about how the Dead End Kids were the icons of rock 'n' roll — the first pop rebels.

"My dad was part of the movement for social change. He was very smart. Had an IQ of 180. He was a philosophic comic.

"Jack Kerouac would stay at his house in Encino when he was in town. He was best friends with Lenny Bruce and James Baldwin. He rode motorcycles with Steve McQueen. McQueen looked up to him because he was the original bad boy and acted with ironclad discipline. The only time I saw Dad cry was when McQueen went to Mexico to get treatment for his cancer.

"Herb Gardner wrote the play *I'm Not Rappaport* with Gabe Dell in mind for the part of Rappaport. But that's when my dad started getting sick and could not remember his lines. He was terrified.

"'I can't do what I love to do any more, kid,' he told me from his hospital bed.

"I was in college in Santa Cruz when I got a message to call home. I called from a pay phone. Norman Abbott got on the line. When he told me Dad died, I fell on the sidewalk. It was July 3 and there were fireworks. My father went out with a bang.

"Huntz was there for me. His son Gary Hall did Gabe's funeral; he was cremated and ashes thrown at sea. There was a wake at the Actor's Studio.

"My dad instilled in me the values of honesty, nobility, truth and compassion for others and for all things. When you feel down, do something nice for somebody else."

Theater Roles

Sadbird	*Pajama Game*
Fun Cit	*Mister Roberts*
Something Different	*Annie Get Your Gun*
The Culture Caper	*Detective Story*
The Prisoner of Second Avenue	*Brigadoon*
Lamppost Reunion	*Where Do We Go from Here?*
Adaptation	*The Sign in Sidney Brunstein's Window*
Luv	*Oklahoma*
Tickets Please	*Wonderful Town*
Ankles Away	*Can-Can*
The Automobile Graveyard	*Man Out Loud — Girl Quiet*
Anyone Can Whistle	*Chocolates*
On the Town	

Films

1960	*Escape from Terror*		1974	*Earthquake*
1962	*When the Girls Take Over*		1975	*Framed*
1971	*Who Is Harry Kellerman and Why Is*			*The Manchu Eagle Murder Caper Mystery*
	He Saying Those Terrible Things			
	About Me?		1982	*The Escape Artist*
	The 300 Year Weekend			

Television

Serpico

Barney Miller

Sanford and Son

McCloud

The Name of the Game

I Dream of Jeannie

Then Came Bronson

The Governor & J.J.

Mannix

The Fugitive

Ben Casey

Naked City

Armstrong Circle Theatre

Bernard Punsly

(July 11, 1923–January 22, 2004)

The quietest of the Dead End Kids was also the brainiest. It seems as if Bernard's career as an actor happened involuntarily. He had relatives who were agents. They took young Bernard to audition for *Dead End* and he was chosen to play the part of Milty, the new kid. He seemed to be part of the gang throughout the Warner Brother films. But in *Angels Wash Their Faces*, after Punsly dies, Halop tells Punsly's mother that they always meant to make him part of the gang. That was news to us.

In *On Dress Parade* he's the only one not in military school; rather, he's Leo Gorcey's best friend from the neighborhood. In the Little Tough Guys movies he was always one of the gang and had some funny lines.

While he always knew he would not remain in the movie business, Bernard enjoyed himself while it was happening. It also opened doors for him. He became a bat boy for the Hollywood Stars, a minor league baseball team (Pacific Coast league) in the 1940s. He became good friends with one minor leaguer who taught him deep sea fishing. That became his hobby.

"He supported his mom and dad from age 16 with the money he made for personal appearance tours. He received his checks weekly," remembers son Brian, an aerospace engineer. "I know because I saw copies of the checks. His father (my grandfather), who was either a tailor or a salesman (the family still doesn't know for sure), used my dad's money on the race track."

Unlike the other kids who reveled in disorderly conduct, Bernard let it be known while

Bernard Punsly

Bernard Punsly at the unveiling of the Dead End Kids' Hollywood Star of Fame in 1994.

rehearsing for the films that he had no intention of falling behind in his studies, especially in the science field. He scoffed at the idea of remaining an actor all his life, leaning towards bacteriology.

"The only book he could have been reading at that time was *The Microbe Hunter* by Paul de Kruif, and it changed his life" according to Bernard's son Brian. "It was about bacteriologists and the work they did and what they discovered. It's a fascinating book."

Bernard went beyond bacteriology. After making *Mug Town* in January 1943, he entered the Army and lost interest in Hollywood.

"He scored highest on the intelligence test and they told him he should be a doctor. He had an IQ of 162. He wanted to establish himself, on his own — without using the fact that he was a Dead End Kid. He never told people he was a Dead End Kid. He graduated at the top of his class in the medical school of the University of Georgia. He became Chief of Staff at South of the Bay Hospital and Chief of Medicine at Little Company of Mary Hospital.

"Many patients told him he saved their life. He was an excellent diagnostician. He was my doctor until I was in my twenties.

"He even diagnosed himself. He had diabetes and when they took out his bladder he still didn't feel right and knew it was cancer. He smoked three packs of cigarettes a day until he was 55. My brother Richard also died of cancer at age 44. My dad was never the same after that." He and his wife fought legal battles with their daughter-in-law for visitation rights for their granddaughter.

Bernard had been dating actress Marilyn Maxwell. But he married a young actress, Marilyn Kufferman, introduced to him by his Aunt Charlotte.

"I was nine or ten years old when I watched my first movie with him and was surprised to see him in the movies. It was either *Dead End* or *Angels with Dirty Faces*. I watched maybe three or four Dead End Kids films. The one where they play basketball *[Angels with Dirty Faces]*—[I remember him telling me] he had a stiff neck and was not in most of that picture."

What does his son think of his father's films?

"I can't get into it. I never saw the Little Tough Guys and couldn't tell you which Dead End Kids film is which. I saw one where they go to a date farm [*They Made Me Criminal*].

"But my dad was a very funny man. He used his intellect to be funny. One of the things I remember him saying: 'The trouble with the human psychology is that the brain is the only organ that doesn't know what it's supposed to do.' He had the energetic humor of Don Rickles. We would be laughing all through dinner.

"He was a great dad in lots of ways. I was a curious kid and he always had answers. I studied physics; he didn't but he not only understood my questions, but knew the answers."

Although he was born Jewish, he never practiced Judaism. But he did teach his son the value of never judging other people.

Bernard kept in touch with Gabe Dell and Huntz Hall, whom he had over at his house shortly before he (Hall) died.

"Before my dad died, he told me that he struggled with the fact that he wasn't around for me enough, always on call in the middle of the night for patients," Brian reveals. "I told him what a great dad he was."

Bernard Gorcey

(1888–September 11, 1955)

Bernard Gorcey in *Abie's Irish Rose* at the Boulevard Theatre, Jackson Heights, New York, in 1936.

Contrary to how we think of him (as the sweet shoppe owner Louie Dumbrowski), Bernard was not always an old man. He was born in Russia but received his early theatrical training at the Educational Children's School on East Broadway and Jefferson Street in New York. There he acted in *Little Lord Fauntleroy* and *Snow White*, and appeared in Mark Twain's production of *The Prince and the Pauper* in 1905. From there Bernard went into vaudeville, perfecting his skills as a Jewish dialect actor and playing in such shows as *Katinka*, *High Jinks*, *What Ails You*, *Wildflowers* and *Song of the Flame*. But Bernard's most important contribution to theater was his creation of the original Broadway character of Papa Cohen in *Abie's Irish Rose*. The show ran for five years (1922–27); Bernard played the role at the beginning and end of the run.

Bernard worked in other entertainment media including radio (on the *Popeye* series). His talking film debut was in Charlie Chaplin's *The Great Dictator* (1940), in which he played ghetto-dweller Mr. Mann. The following year he appeared with his son Leo and John Garfield in *Out of the Fog*. From then on, Bernard had sporadic cameos in the East Side Kids movies and then became a regular on the Bowery Boys series as the short-tempered, gullible Louie Dumbroski. This was largely due to Leo's influence.

While he did the Bowery Boys pictures, he also operated a print shop on Santa Monica Blvd. in West Los Angeles.

On August 31, 1955, shortly after finishing *Dig That Uranium*, Bernard crashed his car into an airport bus at 4th and La Brea. He died eleven days later. He was 67.

Films

1928	*Abie's Irish Rose*		*Black Dragons*
1936	*Bulldog Edition*		*Joan of Paris*
1940	*The Great Dictator*	1945	*The Picture of Dorian Gray*
1941	*Ellery Queen and the Perfect Crime*	1947	*High Wall*
	Out of the Fog	1948	*No Minor Vices*
	Footlight Fever	1949	*The Doctor and the Girl*
	So Ends Our Night		*The Set-Up*
1942	*Bowery at Midnight*	1951	*Journey Into Light*
	A Desperate Chance for Ellery Queen		*Pickup*

David Gorcey

(February 6, 1921–October 23, 1984)

David Gorcey, 1983.

Although he was the first Gorcey to be chosen for *Dead End*, and the last to leave the Bowery Boys series, David never had more than a few lines to say in any picture. He made his stage debut with his father in *Abie's Irish Rose* as a baby. When Leo left for Hollywood to do the film version of *Dead End*, David took over as *Spit* on Broadway. He appeared in the Little Tough Guys series, the East Side Kids films, and all the Bowery Boys movies. Later he used the name David Condon (his mother's maiden name).

In a way, David is responsible how Leo's life turned out, and consequently, for the entire East Side Kids and Bowery Boys series. If David had not brought his older Leo to a *Dead End* rehearsal, Leo might have spent his entire life as a plumber. As it turned out, the

Lou Costello and David Gorcey (right) in *Abbot and Costello in the Foreign Legion.*

other "small boy" who played opposite David was sick. Leo replaced him and took over the part. It wasn't long before Leo got one of the lead roles as Spit.

So when Leo worked out his arrangement with Monogram for the Bowery Boys, he made sure David would play a regular part. Regular yes, significant, no.

Outside the Bowery Boys, David had one very funny cameo as a newsboy in the Sahara Desert in *Abbott and Costello in the Foreign Legion* (1950). Gorcey says to Costello, as he sells him a paper, "Can I help it if they gave me a bad corner?"

David married his wife Dorthea during the 1940s and they divorced in 1951. They had one son, David, Jr.

When the Bowery Boys series ended, David became a reverend, helping alcoholic and drug-addicted youths. Thanks to Bowery Boys fan par excellence Richard Roat, David reunited with Bowery Boy Stanley Clements in 1971. When Stanley became very ill, David helped him with shopping and paying his bills. He extensively discussed his Dead End Kids past with his niece Brandy Gorcey. On October 13, 1984, he fell into a diabetic coma, and died on October 23, 1984, in Van Nuys, California, at age 63. Except for Huntz Hall, no one played in more Kids films than David Gorcey.

Other Films

1931 *One Good Deed*
1932 *Detective*
 His Honor
 Hot Dog
 Penrod's Bull Pen
1938 *Prairie Moon*
 Juvenile Court
1939 *Sergeant Madden*

1940 *City for Conquest*
1941 *Blues in the Night*
 Tuxedo Junction
1946 *The French Key*
1947 *Killer McCoy*
1948 *The Babe Ruth Story*
1949 *She Shoulda Said No*

Billy Benedict

(April 16, 1917–November 25, 1999)

Billy caught the acting bug in high school in Tulsa, Oklahoma. Upon graduation in 1934 he and his sister Catherine hitchhiked to California. He was picked by director George Marshall for a role in the 1935 Fox production of *Ten Dollar Raise*, starring Edward Everett Horton (with whom he would star three years later in his first Kids picture, *Little Tough Guys in*

Billy Benedict (left) and Leo Gorcey in *Ghosts on the Loose.*

Society). From then on, Billy appeared in numerous Fox movies as a "featured player" and at other studios such as Paramount, Universal, Columbia and MGM. He appeared in over 200 movies with performers such as Will Rogers, William Powell, Loretta Young, Cary Grant, Katharine Hepburn and Edward Arnold. Billy also made six serials including *Adventures of the Flying Cadets* with Bobby Jordan, *Brenda Starr, Reporter* and *Adventures of Captain Marvel* where he played *Whitey*, the name he took on in the Bowery Boys flicks.

In a 1993 interview that appeared in the book *They Fought in the Creature Features*, Billy recalls how he got started with the East Side Kids, and why he left the Bowery Boys.

"Sam Katzman latched onto the Dead End Kids and asked me to go to work in one of those pictures. I said, 'Sam, you can't pay my salary.' But I got the money I wanted.

"I got along well with Sam, but Sam and Leo Gorcey couldn't get along, so Leo and his agent Jan Grippo started producing the pictures themselves. Now we were the Bowery Boys.

"When they were away from the set, they were altogether different than when they were on. But they had to keep up appearances for publicity's sake. I got along with all of them very well."

Billy recalled making the East Side Kids films in three or four days, the Bowery Boys films in five to ten days. His last film was *Crazy Over Horses*.

"I suddenly decided I had enough, and it was getting a little rough doing 'em — emotionally. There was a lot of infighting going on and I said, 'I don't need this.'"

After the Bowery Boys, Billy appeared in 21 pictures including *Harlow, Hello Dolly, Farewell My Lovely* and *The Sting*.

He made many television appearances (*All in the Family, Quincy, I Dream of Jeannie, The Twilight Zone, The Incredible Hulk* and more) and appeared in several TV commercials, including one for *Very Fine* juice. He also made miniature sets for motion pictures.

On Thanksgiving Day 1999, Billy had heart surgery, but died shortly thereafter at Cedars-Sinai Medical Center in West Hollywood. He was 82.

Stanley Clements

(July 16, 1926–October 6, 1981)

Slated to become a baritone-tenor singing star after winning first prize on the *Major Bowes Original Amateur Hour* in 1937, Stanley Clements worked in vaudeville and was selected by Twentieth Century-Fox for the film *Tall, Dark and Handsome* with Cesar Romero and Milton Berle. Although he overshadowed the two movie stars in his debut, Stanley (better known as "Stash") was needed more as a tough-talking, tough-acting kid from Williamsburg.

"I couldn't understand why they didn't tell me to sing," a confused 14-year-old Stanley told a reporter in 1941 after he had completed two other films, "but it seemed they didn't want no singer at all; just a tough kid who acted natural with no put-on airs. So, I went to Hollywood."

Shortly afterwards, Stanley was a minor East Side Kid. But Stanley, unlike every other East Side Kid actor, "graduated" to bigger and better roles. In 1944 he appeared with Bing Crosby in *Going My Way* and the following year he played a role in *Salty O'Rourke*. For the next ten years Stanley was seen in about 25 more films. In 1956, after Leo Gorcey dropped out of the Bowery Boys series, Stanley was tapped to take his place beside Huntz Hall. After the series ended, his roles were fewer and farther between. One was a non-speaking cameo in *It's a Mad Mad Mad Mad World*.

 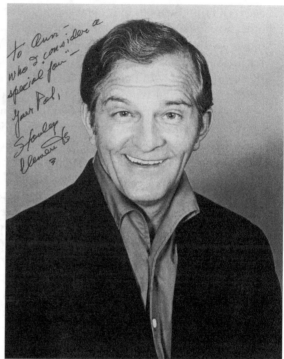

Left: Stanley Clements, 1956. *Right:* Stanley Clements, 1974.

After Stanley's three-year marriage to actress Gloria Grahame, he married Marysia in 1951.

In the 1960s, Stanley's attention was turned towards people living in Communist Poland. He wrote a scenario entitled *A Man and His Lion*, based on the life of animal trainer Klaudius Blaszak, who defected from the Polish circus when it toured the United States. But Stanley's chief victory was adopting eight-year-old Sylvester Marian Walek, Marysia's nephew, who formerly lived behind the Iron Curtain.

"Adopting this boy has been as close to me as my heart," Stanley said in 1964. "We couldn't have any children ourselves... He is the first child out of Poland under the new proxy adoption law... I want to give him the chance and education I never got."

Stanley lived in Los Angeles until he died of emphysema on October 6, 1981, at age 55. Unknown to him, his ex-wife Gloria Grahame died a few days earlier in the same hospital.

Other Films

1941	*Tall, Dark and Handsome*	1949	*Johnny Holiday*
	Down in San Diego		*Bad Boy*
1943	*The More the Merrier*	1950	*Destination Murder*
1945	*Salty O'Rourke*		*Military Academy with That Tenth*
1948	*Joe Palooka in Winner Take All*		*Avenue Gang*
	The Babe Ruth Story	1952	*Boots Malone*
	Cannon City	1953	*Off Limits*

1954 *The Rocket Man*
1955 *Mad at the World*
    Air Strike

1963 *Tammy and the Doctor*
1968 *Panic in the City*

Television

Letter to Loretta
The Lone Ranger
Death Valley Days
Navy Log
Broken Arrow
Rawhide
General Electric Theater
Leave It to Beaver
77 Sunset Strip
The Untouchables

Gunsmoke
Dr. Kildare
Gomer Pyle, U.S.M.C.
Perry Mason
The Girl from U.N.C.L.E.
Lassie
Get Smart
Baretta
Cannon

Other Little Tough Guys

Frankie Thomas (b. April 9, 1921; d. May 11, 2006). After his last flight on the TV series *Tom Corbett, Space Cadet*, Frankie began writing and producing radio's *My True Story* and TV scripts. Never married, Frankie edited *American Bridge Teacher's Association Quarterly* and wrote *The Sherlock Holmes Bridge Book*. See a January 2000 interview with Frankie at http://www.slick-net.com/space/interviews/thomas.phtml.

Jackie Searl (b. July 7, 1920). The Little Tough Guys' goody two-shoes now owns a manufacturing plant near Hollywood. His last two films were *The Paleface* (1948) and *Passport to Pimlico* (1949) but he did some TV work, usually playing a villain. He has two children.

Hally Chester (b. March 6, 1921). Also known as Hal E. Chester (Repatsky). His long-lost twin sister, who lost her memory, is said to have regained it after seeing Hally in the movies. He became a successful producer and did a series on the Joe Palooka character and *The Beast from 20,000 Fathoms*. Hal relocated to England with his wife and produced films there through the 1960s. He produced *The Secret War of Harry Frigg* with Paul Newman. He's credited with guaranteeing the finances for movies produced in Italy.

Norman Abbott. Bud Abbott's nephew, he later directed TV shows including *Get Smart*, *Welcome Back Kotter*, *The Munsters*, *Love, American Style* and *The Bad News Bears*.

Harris Berger. Before being a Little Tough Guy he was a Dead End Kid, taking Hall's place as Dippy when the original cast took off for Hollywood. He died in the 1970s from a heart attack.

Charles Duncan. After giving up his role as Spit, he returned as a Little Tough Guy. He died in the 1940s while traveling in the United States.

Other East Side Kids

Ernie "Sunshine Sammy" Morrison (1912–July 1989). After leaving the East Side Kids, the first black youngster in Our Gang comedies did some singing-and-dancing comedy routines on stage. He also served in the Army. He did very little acting after that; instead he did work involving missiles in Los Angeles. He had some cameos on *Good Times* and *The Jeffersons* but never had an urge to be back in films. Sunshine Sammy died of cancer in Lynwood at age 77.

Eugene Francis. Algie of the East Side Kids was in a television series called *Calliope* and an army training film with Ronald Reagan. He died in the late 1980s.

Bennie Bartlett (August 16, 1924–December 26, 1999). Debuted in the East Side Kids and later appeared in 24 Bowery Boys films as Butch. His early rise began as a musical prodigy in RKO's *Millions in the Air* (1935) and *Thirteen Hours By* (1936). He made several other films before he grew up. That was his mistake. His attraction as a musician petered out and became a background Bowery Boy. After that, insurance.

David Durand (b. 1921; d. 1998). Appeared in Our Gang comedies. Sang "Every Little Breeze Seems to Whisper Louise" with Maurice Chevalier. He suffered a permanent head injury and lived at the Bridge View Nursing Home from 1972 until his death. Kids' fan Richard Roat visited him regularly, took care of his affairs, and became executor of his estate.

Mende Koenig became a teacher and a principal in Los Angeles, California.

Frank Burke, Bill Bates, Bill Chany, Johnny Duncan, Donald Haines, Bobby Stone, Al Stone, Bud Gorman, Eddie Mills, Jimmy Strand, Sam Edwards, Sidney Miller.

Other Bowery Boys

Jimmy Murphy. Myron of the Bowery Boys had supporting roles in *Curse of the Undead*, *Paratroop Command* and *The Good Guys and the Bad Guys*.

Eddie LeRoy. Blinky in the last four Bowery Boys films. He appeared on *The Milton Berle Show* and *The Red Skelton Show*.

Gil Stratton, Jr. In two Bowery Boys films. Appeared with Judy Garland and Mickey Rooney in *Girl Crazy* (1943). Was a sportscaster for KNXT in Los Angeles for many years.

Frequently Seen Actors

Vince Barnett (b. 1903). Was always the bad guy opposite the East Side Kids and the Bowery Boys. Toured with actor Allan Jones and was in *The Big Show of 1936*. Seen in movies such as *The Prizefighter and the Lady*, *Zebra in the Kitchen*, *The Killers* (1946) and *Scarface* (1932).

Frankie Darro (1917–76). Always played a tough guy or a jockey. In the Bowery Boys he was almost always Gorcey's rival. His last film was 1968's *Hook Line and Sinker*. He was a regular on *The Red Skeleton Show*. Frankie's first wife committed suicide. He was married to second wife Aloha Carroll for 25 years when he died of a heart attack at the home of friends on Christmas. At the time of his death he was a welfare recipient.

Mary Gordon (1882–1963). Played Muggs' or Slip's mother in the East Side Kids and Bowery Boys movies. Played Mrs. Hudson the housekeeper in Basil Rathbone's Sherlock Holmes movies. She had a bit part in *Angels with Dirty Faces*.

Percy Helton (1894–1971). Played Mike Clancy after Bernard Gorcey died. Also appeared in *Miracle on 34th Street*, *How to Marry a Millionaire*, *A Girl in Every Port* and many more films.

Allen Jenkins (1900–1974). A comical-looking man, Allen played Hunk in Goldwyn's *Dead End* and played the hoodlum roles in *Crazy Over Horses* and *Let's Go Navy!* (Bowery Boys). He was in over 100 pictures and starred in a few of them with Edward G. Robinson.

Dennis Moore (1908–1964). Tight-lipped dramatic actor always played the bad guy in East Side Kids films. Other credits include *The Mummy's Curse* and the serial *The Purple Monster Strikes*.

Patsy Moran (1905–1968). Either played a maid or Muggs' mother.

Jack Mulhall (1887–1979). Jack could look back at the days when his movies earned him $3,000 a week and a 16-room mansion. He lost his money in 1930. Jack lived in Hollywood and worked occasionally in the office of the Screen Actors Guild. He played in several East Side Kids films and Bowery Boys' films, including *Up in Smoke*.

Wheeler Oakman (1891–1949). Enjoyed fame as the Bronco Kid in *The Spoilers* and was in many other silent films. He appeared in several East Side Kids movie.

Dave O'Brien (1912–1969). After several leading roles with the East Side Kids, he appeared in Pete Smith shorts, as the hero in *Captain Midnight* and in *Secret of Treasure Island*. He had his own TV show. *Meet the O'Brien's*, and wrote comedy for Red Skeleton.

Ronald Reagan (1911–2004). Played the lawyer in the Dead End Kids' *Hell's Kitchen* and *Angels Wash Their Faces*. He appeared in numerous films including *The Killers* with Lee Marvin. He was president of the Screen Actors Guild in the 1940s. His attention turned from drama to politics and he served as governor of the state of California, and later as president of the United States for two terms. In April of 1981 he survived an assassination attempt. During the last years of his life, he suffered from Alzheimer's disease.

Queenie Smith (1898–August 5, 1978). Played Mrs. Kelly in later Bowery Boys movies. Was a sensational comedienne in *Mississippi*, *Show Boat*, *The Killers* and *Sweet Smell of Success*.

Ronald Reagan taking a break during the filming of *Hell's Kitchen*.

Minerva Urecal (1896–1966). An excellent character actress, Minerva played a sinister care-taker, a judge, a Nazi, a youthful grandmother and a sheriff with the East Side Kids and Bowery Boys. Her real name was Holzer. Urecal was derived from Eureka, California, her birthplace. She appeared in Tony Randall' s *7 Faces of Dr. Lao* (1964).

Paul Harvey (d. 1955). Paul played a lawyer, a father or an executive in the Bowery Boys films. In the *Jones Family* comedies, he played Jed Prouty's boss.

Lyle Talbot (February 8, 1902–March 2, 1996). This soft-spoken veteran of over 100 films appeared in several Bowery Boys films and could not be trusted in any one of them. He starred on television on the Ozzie and Harriet and Bob Cummings shows and in 1975 appeared as Walter Burns in *The Front Page* at a theater in Houston. He toured the country in road companies of *The Odd Couple, Never Too Late* and *A Girl in My Soup,* and was a guest at drama classes at a variety of colleges.

Epilogue

The 1978 Revival of *Dead End*

Forty years and 92 films later, it was time to see whether the play *Dead End* was still viable. Artistic director Will Lieberson took up the challenge in the Quigh Theatre on the second floor of the Hotel Diplomat on 43rd Street in New York. The Quigh is no bigger than a good-size living room.

It didn't surprise him that his production of *Dead End* was granted several extensions. But was it *his* production or the popularity of the original Dead End Kids that brought in the crowds?

Lieberson's version of the saga of the Dead End Kids ends when Tommy is taken into custody by the police. He produced the play not as a tribute to the Bowery Boys or East Side Kids, but in response to a deep-rooted interest in social-consciousness plays of the 1930s. He does not believe, as Mel Gussow does in his *New York Times* review of the *Dead End* revival, that the play is dated: "You put black or Puerto Rican kids in there instead of Tommy and its relevancy is as strong today as it was in 1936."

Craig Alfano played Dippy as a silly but sensitive youngster whose feelings are injured when T.B. (Michael Stumm) tosses his contribution to the trash can fire into the East River, and when Spit (Peter Farrara-Jeffries) munches away at Dippy's potato, leaving Dippy with the smallest piece.

What Lieberson tried to convey in his production was not apparent in the original play, but definitely so in the movie: the romance between Drina (Priscilla Manning) and Gimpty. He claims it was Sidney Kingsley's intention that feelings stronger than friendship existed and this was expressed through Drina's subtle fits of jealousy.

Sidney Kingsley himself was on hand occasionally during rehearsal, making suggestions that were, on the whole, taken.

Of all the favorable feedback Lieberson received from his patrons, probably the most cherished were the tears of joy appearing in the eyes of the 72-year-old playwright on opening night.

The 2005 Revival of *Dead End*

Not since its opening on Broadway has there been such an expansive production of *Dead End* as the one performed by the Center Theatre Group at Los Angeles's Ahmanson Theatre to commemorate the play's 70th anniversary.

Greetings from the Dead End Kids. Left to right: Bernard Punsley, Leo Gorcey, Bobby Jordan, Billy Halop, Huntz Hall and Gabe Dell.

This endeavor was the brainchild of *Dead End* enthusiast and CTG's Artistic Director Michael Ritchie, who, like most people, was introduced to the drama on late night television. He has made it his personal calling to keep *Dead End* alive.

"I view 'Dead End' as the celebration of theatre itself and everything the medium can do," says Ritchie. "While the history of the play and the power of its message definitely impressed me, it was the theatricality of 'Dead End' that drove me to produce it."

Ahmanson's debut drama of the 2005-2006 season was not the first time Ritchie put Sidney Kingsley's play on stage. He did it at the Williamstown Theatre Festival in the Berkshires, Massachusetts, in 1997 and again at the Huntington Theatre in Boston in 2000. All three had something that Broadway's Belasco did not: real water to simulate the East River!

In Los Angeles the fire department literally trucked and hosed 11,000 gallons of water into the black pond lined orchestra pit, high enough for the those in the first few rows to literally feel the cannonball splashes of the latest Dead End Kids actors Ricky Ullman (Tommy), Sam Murphy (Spit), Trevor Peterson (T.B.), Gregg Roman (Dippy), Josh Sussman (Milty) and Adam Rose (Angel). Unlike the New York roots of the original cast, this diverse group hailed from various points across the country from Boston to Los Angeles, and appeared with 36 other actors, including 14 from the University of Southern California. Speech and dialect coaches were brought in train the actors in old New York vernacular.

The Norman Bel Geddes of this production, responsible for $397,000 worth of 48 foot high, authentic-looking tenement sets and East River water was James Noone, who designed the two New

The Dead End Kids Hollywood Star of Fame, on the corner of La Brea and Hollywood.

The set of Ahmanson Theatre's *Dead End* as the actors take a bow.

From the left: author Leonard Getz, Leo Gorcey, Jr., Gabe Dell, Jr., and Bobby Jordan, Jr., at a private home in Los Angeles, California, October 2005.

England productions as well. So high were these sets that the lights had to be mounted from a ceiling grid 58 feet in the air.

"We fly a man up to the track where there's a little seat," explained Noone to the *L.A. Times.* "He pushes himself along the track and focus the lights."

Directing this entourage was *Dead End* veteran Nicholas Martin who was with Ritchie in 1997 and 2000.

"What I like most about this play is the dynamic collision of cultures, of comedy and drama and the kids themselves who are the heart of the show, and as history shows us, as enduring as the characters of Shakespeare or Chekov.

"The original Dead End Kids defined those roles so in a sense they affected everyone who came afterwards. Yet, our actors made those parts their own."

As he did for the previous productions, Martin put together a pre-rehearsal cast-bonding ritual, engaging the kids with a Dodgers baseball game and a few rounds of poker.

"This production was much larger, the set higher and wider, and the pool deeper than the other two productions. But what it lost in intimacy it gained in magnitude."

Some of the Ahmanson actors observed the dichotomy between prestigious USC and the surrounding depressed neighborhood between the Ahmanson Theatre itself and low-income housing a block away.

"It's the same issues," Ullman (Tommy) notes. "I know it's happening in my neighborhood."

To complete another full circle, for the first time in their lives, the offsprings of the original Dead End Kids—Leo Gorcey, Jr., Bobby Jordan, Jr., Gabe Dell, Jr., and the nieces and

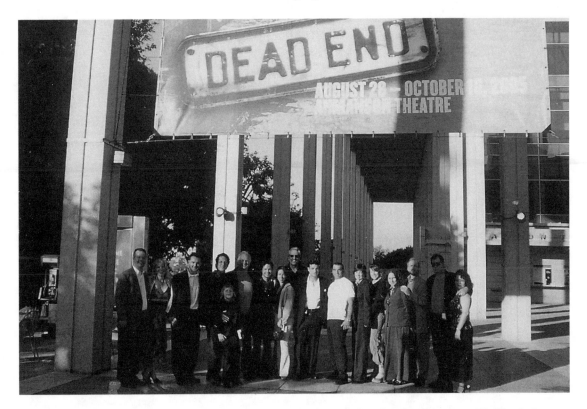

The Dead End Kids' family and friends that saw the play *Dead End* at the Ahmanson Theatre in Los Angeles, California, October 2005: fourth from left, Gabe Dell, Jr., his son Blue, Leo Gorcey, Jr.; ninth from left, tall, Bobby Jordan, Jr.; sixth and fifth from right, Melissa and Jennifer Halop (Billy Halop's grandnieces), Susan Getz, Leonard Getz (author), Zack Halop (Billy Halop's nephew), and Mrs. Zack Halop.

nephew of Billy Halop — got together and attended a Sunday matinee performance in October 2005. It was a treat for them to finally meet one another, and a treat for the new cast who, at the end of one of their last performances, came down off stage to greet the children of their counter-parts three generations past.

Now that theater has given *Dead End* another chance, what do you say, Hollywood?

Bibliography

Alvarez, Louis, and Andrew Kolker. "American Tongues." Documentary film released by The Center for New American Media, 1998.

Atkinson, Brooks. "River Realism," *New York Times*, 1935.

Balling, Fredda Dudley. "Love Story with No Dead End," TV review.

Cunningham, James. Review of *Dead End*. *Commonweal*, August 20, 1937.

Gorcey, Leo. *An Original Dead End Kid Presents Dead End Yells, Wedding Bells, Cockle Shells and Dizzy Spells*. New York: Vantage, 1967.

Gorcey, Leo, Jr. *Me and the Dead End Kind*. Leo Gorcey Foundation, 2003.

Haitman, Diane. "He's Taking the Plunge." *Los Angeles Times*, September 4, 2005.

Hall, Huntz. Interview. *Entertainment Weekly*, June 3, 1994.

Halop, Billy. "Alcoholism Was Almost My Dead End." *Screen Gems*, October 1976.

Hayes, David, and Brent Walker. *The Films of the Bowery Boys*. Secaucus, NJ: Citadel, 1982.

Isaacs, Edith J.R. "See America First." *Theater Arts*, December 1935.

Lamparski, Richard. *Whatever Became of....* Vols. 2 and 3. New York: Ace, 1968

Lee, Raymond. *Gangsters and Hoodlums: The Underworld in Cinema*. Cranbury, NJ: Barnes, 1971

"Made to Order Punks." *Colliers*, July 29, 1939.

Madsen, Axel. *William Wyler*. New York: Crowell, 1973.

Marx, Arthur. *Goldwyn: The Biography of the Man Behind the Myth*. New York: Norton, 1976

Performances. "Center Theatre Group, Ahmanson Theatre, playbill for *Dead End*.

Parish, James. *The Great Movie Series*. Cranbury, NJ: 1971.

_____. *Prison Pictures from Hollywood*. Jefferson, NC: McFarland, 1991.

Ragan, David. *Who's Who in Hollywood 1900–1976*. New Rochelle, NY: Arlington House, 1977.

Review of *Dead End*. *Literary Digest*, September 4, 1937.

Review of *Dead End*. *Nation*, November 13, 1935.

Review of *Dead End*. *Newsweek*, August 27, 1937.

Sedgwick, Ruth Woodbury. "Social Tide-Rip." *Stage*, 1935.

Sherman, Sam. "Broadway to Bowery and Back: The Story of Huntz Hall." *Screen Thrills*, July 1963.

Stumpf, Charles. "The Saga of the Dead End Kids, Little Tough Guys, East Side Kids and the Bowery Boys." *The World of Yesterday*, February 1978.

Weaver, John. *Forty Years of Screen Credits*. Metuchen, NJ: Scarecrow, 1979.

Weaver, Tom. *They Fought in the Creature Features: Interviews with 23 Classic Horror, Science Fiction and Serial Stars*. Jefferson, NC: McFarland, 1995.

Weiss, Ken, and Ed Goodgold. *To Be Continued ... a Complete Guide to over Two Hundred Twenty Motion Picture Serials With Sound Tracks*. New York: Crown, 1972.

Zinman, David. *Saturday Afternoon at the Bijou*. New Rochelle, NY: Arlington House, 1973.

Web sites

bobbyjordanfansite.com
boweryboys.bobfinnan.com
boweryboys.com
disc.server.com/Indices/206776.html (The Bowery Boys Board)
frankieburke.com
home.earthlink.net/~bcwalk/bowery.html (addendum to the Film of the Bowery Boys)
lauren.50g.com/boweryboys/pictures3.html
leogorcey.com

movies.groups.yahoo.com/group/BillyHalop
  Online/ (Billy Halop message board)
movies.groups.yahoo.com/group/thebowery/
movies.groups.yahoo.com/group/TheDeadEnd
  Docks/

TheBoweryBoys@yahoogroups.com
whyaduck.com/sounds/streaming.htm

Index